RAVEN'S
FLAG

BOOK 6

PEACEKEEPERS
OF SOL

RAVEN'S FLAG

GLYNN STEWART

FAOLAN'S PEN
PUBLISHING
faolanspen.com

This edition published in 2023 by:

Faolan's Pen Publishing Inc.

22 King St. S, Suite 300

Waterloo, Ontario

N2J 1N8 Canada

ISBN-13: 978-1-989674-41-3 (print)

A record of this book is available from Library and Archives Canada.

Printed in the United States of America

1 2 3 4 5 6 7 8 9 10

First edition

First printing: October 2023

Illustration by Sam Leung

Faolan's Pen Publishing logo is a trademark of Faolan's Pen Publishing Inc.

Read more books from Glynn Stewart at faolanspen.com

1

"ADMIRAL ON DECK!"

Rear Admiral Henry Wong of the United Planets Space Force took a full four seconds to remember that the traditional call, the pipe fanfare behind it and the honor guard of Ground Division troops flanking the route from his shuttle ramp were all meant for him.

The gaunt Chinese-American officer had, after all, been a Rear Admiral for all of three and a half hours.

Returning the salutes from the honor guard, he crossed the flight deck of the cruiser *Amethyst* and made a point of saluting the woman waiting for him before she could salute him.

The United Planets Alliance Medal of Valor, after all, was still mind-bogglingly rare in the twenty-fourth century—even after a seventeen-year conflict for the UPA's very existence and the six years of active "peace" that had followed.

Colonel Andriana O'Brin had earned hers the hard way, as he understood it, and even the best medical technology couldn't quite cover the join line along the pale-skinned woman's face, jaw, and neck marking where roughly thirty percent of the right side of her body had been reconstructed.

"Welcome aboard *Amethyst*, Admiral Wong," she greeted him,

extending her hand. "As I understand, you might have seen as much of her as I have."

Henry smiled and shook the proffered hand.

"I've seen her schematics in excruciating detail," he confirmed. "But the last time I was aboard her, she didn't even have her wings yet."

Two and a half years earlier, Henry Wong had been informed that, regardless of what *he* might think was the best use of his abilities, he needed at least a year in a desk job to qualify for his star—and the UPSF wasn't going to wait any longer to put him in that desk.

He'd spent most of those two and a half years flying a desk for the UPSF Technical Division, working on the implementation of the brand-new systems and technologies that underlay *Amethyst* and her entire class.

"We weren't sure your shuttle was going to catch up in time," O'Brin admitted. "I was expecting to bring you aboard somewhat more...conventionally."

"There was never any chance I was missing the promotion ceremonies on the Iron Ring," Henry said. "As I understand it, the Drifters moved up the schedule on us all."

O'Brin gestured for him to follow her. The new-fledged Rear Admiral had spent long enough in the cruiser's schematics to recognize the route to the bridge with his eyes closed.

"We got the drone twelve hours ago, aye," O'Brin confirmed. "They were only going to make the skip line three hours early, but it was enough to throw a wrench into everybody's plans. Most everyone is in place, though."

"Hell of a day," Henry murmured as they entered an elevator. "First alien delegation to ever enter Sol."

"The first?" O'Brin asked. "That can't be right. I know I spent a lot of time in Kenmiri space or in rehab, but I *know* I've seen aliens around Earth."

"Individuals," he explained. "Not delegations. Even with our allies, we always sent people out to them. Kind of silly, really, given that the *Kenmiri* knew where we were!"

The seventeen-year-long war with the Kenmiri Empire had started when the insectoid aliens had invaded human space. Henry's fingers touched on his pilot's wings almost absently. Unlike the vast majority of the insignia for qualified starfighter pilots, *his* had the center enameled red.

That marked him as one of the people who had flown starfighters against that invasion—and the UPSF had lost almost the entirety of its starfighter strength in that campaign. There were very few people left who wore red wings.

"So, the Drifters are the first to send diplomats to Sol?"

"Exactly. Red Stripe White Stripe Convoy is a big deal," Henry pointed out. "They're a two-stripe convoy, which means there are over five *thousand* ships under their authority and some hundred million sentients."

O'Brin whistled silently, then slid easily back into the mask of command as the lift doors opened.

"All of those ships are in Proxima Centauri," she pointed out. "But that's still a big deal. The delegation is just ten ships, though."

"Two escorts on the Kenmiri pattern and eight transports," Henry confirmed. He might have been busy at the Iron Ring—the training facility over Mars where Commodores were given a harsh and intensive bout of training before they were made Admirals—but he'd been watching *this* news with care.

O'Brin led him onto her bridge, gesturing him to an observer's seat next to the command station. Henry took a moment before sitting to survey the space, taking in the reality of the space he'd helped finalize.

The new generation of ships had, arguably, started with the *Cataphract* class of experimental destroyers—but those, in Henry's opinion, had been little more than modified *Significance*-class destroyers. They were no more a fully distinct class than the G-mod subclasses being used for the ships being refitted to use the new gravity maneuvering system.

The *Amethyst*- or Gem-class cruisers were the true firstborn of the new generation. Built from the keel out not only to incorporate the GMS, providing them with twice the maximum acceleration of their older reaction-drive siblings, but to include a thousand lessons and small technologies learned from the Kenmiri and the Vesheron rebels against the Kenmiri.

Among the more minor aspects were the holographic displays that gleamed around the horseshoe-shaped bridge. Only very recently had holodisplays become reliable enough to use in a combat situation—and they were *still* more of an augment than a key system. The key systems were still hard displays and neural feeds connected to the crews' cybernetic internal networks.

The bridge also lacked the clearly discernable hatches an older ship would have had for acceleration tanks. The GMS didn't pass inertia onto the ship at all, which rendered the protective fluid tanks unnecessary.

There were other subtle changes in both the hardware and the displays, but the design of the bridge was fundamentally Terran and Henry took his seat with a warm sense of familiarity.

Even without linking into the network shared by the bridge officers, Henry could take in much of *Amethyst*'s current status at a glance. The cruiser was running hot at her full two KPS^2 of acceleration as she pushed to make up the time they'd lost letting his shuttle from the Iron Ring catch up.

"Feels weird to see the icons for plasma cannon on a UPSF ship," he admitted to O'Brin. "Even having gone through the whole discussion around putting them on the Gems and the Phoenixes."

The *Phoenix*-class battlecruisers were still a draft, but the General Assembly had authorized funds to build six of them. They were the new generation of capital ship to go with *Amethyst* and her sisters—but every yard that could handle capital ships was either refitting the current ones or finishing the ships that had been frozen on the slips when the war had ended.

"We won't be the only people with plasma cannon around, even if the Drifters aren't bringing any," the Colonel told him. "Looks like *everybody* brought a battleship to the party. Shame none of them can skip."

"As we discovered in the Red Wings Campaign, it's wise to assume that's something they can fix faster than we would like," he reminded her.

The five Earth powers that sat on the Security Council of the United Planets Alliance had once possessed skip-capable fleets of their own. After the Unification Wars that had *created* the UPA, they'd agreed to reduce those fleets down to two ships, only one of which was supposed to have a full offensive armament.

The United Planets Space Force was the only faster-than-light-capable battle fleet in human space. But it was not, as O'Brin pointed out, the only *fleet* in human space.

More accurately referred to as *guardships* in Henry's opinion, the somewhat standardized battleship of the solar fleets had been designed for a last-ditch defense of the Solar System against the Kenmiri, which meant they were gravity-shielded reaction-drive ships with arrays of Kenmiri-style heavy plasma cannon.

The previous national fleets had been called up to aid the UPSF during the Red Wings Campaign, the initial invasion—and had proven sufficiently straightforward to refit with skip drives that it was absolutely *certain* all of them had been designed for just that modification.

"Ten battleships, two from each of the national fleets," O'Brin told him. "*Helios* from the Solar Fleet. *Crichton* and her battle group to represent the UPSF—and us, as a showpiece."

The Solar Fleet, as opposed to the *national* fleets, was a joint organization funded and crewed by basically every nation and planet in the Sol System that *didn't* get their own seat on the Security Council. *Helios* was that group's allowed skip-capable ship and was, for all intents and purposes, a modern UPSF *Corvid*-class battlecruiser. That she was the *only* non-UPSF skip-capable warship in the honor guard was likely an intentional point.

"*Amethyst* is the most modern warship in the UPSF," Henry noted. "That means she can fight above her weight class against anything in space. Kilo for kilo, she outclasses even our G-mod ships."

"Which means we're doing what the old Commonwealth Extra-solar Squadron used to do," O'Brin said with a chuckle. "Acting as a sales pitch without ever saying a word."

"There's not much on *Amethyst* that we're likely to sell the Drifters," he pointed out, glancing at the ETA for the Drifter delegation. "But then, not that long ago, I wouldn't have expected us to ever let a nonhuman power send diplomats into Sol."

Especially the Drifters, who had come very close to war with the UPA at one point—and who Henry and the UPSF High Command *knew* included actual Kenmiri among their number.

2

THE PROBLEM with assembling an honor guard with ships from over half a dozen organizations was that none of them were sufficiently well trained together to do proper "parade" formations.

"*Crichton* has transmitted our position in the formation," O'Brin's coms officer reported. "Looks like we're keeping it nice and simple."

"Put us in our slot, Lieutenant," O'Brin told her navigator. She glanced over at Henry. "Looks like Admiral Bokor decided to start giving orders to make sure we don't *completely* embarrass ourselves."

Henry kept his face straight as he gave O'Brin a level nod. Reputation, rumor, and his own experience said that Vice Admiral Izabella Bokor commanded Carrier Group *Crichton* with an iron fist.

The carrier and her two battlecruiser escorts formed the heart of a spread-wing formation imitating an old Roman aquila eagle made up of her destroyers and starfighters. *Helios*'s crew had apparently exercised enough with Carrier Group *Crichton* that Bokor trusted them to take the tip of the port wing—and as he watched, *Amethyst* delicately maneuvered into the starboard wing tip.

The national battleships had been given significantly less trust. The UPSF ships were in a gorgeously arrayed parade formation, with the Solar Fleet's battlecruiser included at one end. The ten battleships, while larger than anything except *Crichton* herself, had been formed into the "base" of the aquila, in a simple two-high and five-wide wall of warships.

And Henry knew perfectly well it was no accident that *Constellation* and *Congress*, the two USA Space Force battleships present, were at the far end of the wall from *Mikhail Gorbachev* and *Pyotr Velikiy*, the two Russian ships.

While the current United States and Russian governments got along as well as they ever had, it had been the conflict between the two states' extrasolar territories that had triggered the Unification War. The European, Chinese and African ships were positioned between them, just in case.

"What is our guests' estimated time of arrival?" Henry asked aloud. He was a passenger aboard *Amethyst* at that moment, for all of the inherent weight of his new rank. That meant his internal network didn't have as much access to the ship's systems as he normally would.

"Between eight and fifteen minutes, per the last update we received," the coms officer told him. "Everyone should be in position to be as impressive as possible."

Henry wasn't certain how impressive the collection of warships would be to the Drifters. A two-stripe convoy like Red Stripe White Stripe had a *significant* fleet of defending ships, including the Guardians, multi-megaton warships that mounted the firepower of Kenmiri dreadnoughts.

But the effort and the gesture were necessary anyway. He just wished his girlfriend were around to take part in the discussions that were going to be taking place over the next few days. Ambassador Sylvia Todorovich was one of the most capable and senior diplomats the United Planets Alliance *had*, but she was busy in the Ra Sector, building relationships and arbitrating conflicts in that former part of the Kenmiri Empire.

He mentally poked at the ship's network and was pleasantly surprised when it did allow him in. Someone had apparently taken the time since his arrival to authorize his network codes. Given how long he was supposed to be aboard the cruiser, that had been unnecessary—but it was appreciated anyway.

With that access and the displays around him on *Amethyst*'s bridge, he saw the moment the Drifter delegation arrived.

An escort vessel came first, one of the ubiquitous and utilitarian half-megaton warships the Kenmiri had mass-produced to secure their empire. Many of the successor states were still operating fleets made up entirely of ships built prior to the Kenmiri's withdrawal to their core stars—and even most of the rest were building with Kenmiri tools to Kenmiri schematics.

Henry had seen a *lot* of escorts over the last quarter-century, and this ship had one very clear difference from most of them.

"I see the Drifters have disseminated the Enteni energy-screen tech," he murmured. During the war against the Kenmiri and the years immediately after, escorts had been uniformly unshielded. Kenmiri energy screens couldn't be engineered small enough to provide useful power levels on the small ships.

The Enteni, one of the Ra Sector's native species, had solved the size issue. Even their *starfighters* now carried energy screens, and a different Drifter Convoy had purchased the tech a few years earlier.

Without it, the escort would have relied on armor and antimissile lasers to protect itself. That said, even with those energy screens, the escort was vulnerable compared to the Terran warships. Even the national battleships had the gravity shields that had allowed the UPSF to turn the tide of a war.

More contacts followed the escort, an even dozen large transports averaging almost two kilometers in length. According to the notes Henry had, those ships would be carrying roughly a hundred million tons of cargo between them.

That "small" cargo represented the products that the Drifters were hoping to sell there in Sol. Those discussions and agreements, thankfully, weren't Henry's concern.

He was there as decoration, so far as he could tell.

"Second escort has exited the skip line," O'Brin told him. "I think that's all of them. Clean jump; I'm impressed."

A "skip line" was the literal line that could be drawn between two stars. A ship equipped with a skip drive could use icosaspatial momentum to bounce along that line, using the gravity of one star to push and the other to pull them through three-dimensional space faster than light.

Since the line went from the heart of one star to the heart of another, making a specific rendezvous point took careful calculation—and the Drifters, unsurprisingly, had hit their intended emergence point within half a kilometer.

"Flag bridge on *Crichton* is sending courses to everyone," the coms officer reported. "Forwarding to Nav."

"Thank you, Lieutenant," O'Brin told the officer before turning back to Henry. "Bokor is taking no chances, I see."

"I wouldn't," Henry admitted. He doubted he'd be trying to exert *quite* so tight a control over the ships belonging to the UPA's member nations, but he could see exactly where Admiral Bokor was coming from.

This was the first time the UPA had allowed aliens into Sol. The last thing they wanted was to look incompetent or, worse, *weak* to those strangers.

"Invitations are starting to fly out for the initial meet-and-greet," the coms officer added. "Admiral Wong is to join Admiral Bokor aboard *Crichton*. From there, it looks like you'll be transiting to the Drifter ship *Rising Commerce*."

"Thank you, Lieutenant." He turned to O'Brin. "And thank you, Captain, for the ride."

Her expression didn't really change—but Henry had spent a long time among the various Ashall species throughout the Kenmiri Empire, aliens that could often pass for human in dim lighting.

Despite the different worlds and evolutionary paths of the Ashall species, they were all disturbingly similar and shared, among other things, much of their facial musculature—and the dozens of tiny ways that musculature unconsciously responded to emotions.

O'Brin's microexpressions betrayed her pleasure at his thanks.

"All we really did was slow down long enough to pick up the shuttle, ser," she pointed out.

"And if you hadn't, Captain, I'd have had to choose between

meeting the Drifters or attending my own Iron Ring graduation and promotion ceremony," he reminded her. "Both of which are equally critical in their own ways."

He didn't think he'd have been *allowed* to miss the Iron Ring completion ceremony—but the UPA's diplomatic corps had really, *really* wanted him there at the meet-and-greet, too.

And Henry Wong served as the UPA required, no matter what.

3

HENRY HAD BEEN aboard all kinds of Drifter ships now, ranging from the all-too-utilitarian Guardians to the gorgeous but multipurpose garden ships that provided mental-health relief and food to the massive Drifter Convoys.

Rising Commerce fell somewhere in between, he judged as he followed Vice Admiral Bokor off the shuttle and onto the Drifter ship. The bay they'd landed in was clearly intended for more-formal interactions, made more spacious than required for its current needs by lacking the massive cargo-handling equipment that he'd expect aboard a transport.

It was possible, of course, that the cargo equipment was just tucked away inside the bulkheads. That would fit with Drifter norms and esthetics.

The honor guard waiting for them was *definitely* aligned with Drifter norms and esthetics. Every Drifter wore bulky body-concealing robes and a mask that covered their face. The honor guards were Protectors, Drifter soldiers clad in matching black cloaks and black masks only differentiated by gold rank insignia.

The Protectors formed an aisle that Bokor led the way down, with Henry and a small party of mind-bogglingly senior diplomats following behind her. The two Admirals stopped and saluted the trio of white-robed Drifters waiting at the far end of the bay.

That trio wore individualized masks, Face Masks that were theoretically unique to them. The central Drifter towered over the other two—and, indeed, everyone else in the room. Even Henry's own towering height came in half a meter or more beneath the Drifter, who bowed deeply to the human delegation. Their mask was red for its bottom third and black for the rest, with stark perpendicular white lines dividing it into quarters.

"I am Third-Red-White-Cross," the stranger greeted them in Kem, the trade language of the Kenmiri Empire. "I am honored to act as Chosen Speaker for the Red Stripe White Stripe Convoy in the discussion with the United Planets Alliance."

A concealed but clearly massive hand gestured to Third-Red-White-Cross's companions.

"This is Red-Spirals-on-Blue and Red-Cross-on-Blue," the big Drifter introduced them.

"I am Vice Admiral Izabella Bokor of the United Planets Space Force," Bokor told the Drifters. "I am tasked with the security of your delegation while you are in the Sol System."

And, Henry knew, the security of the Sol System *from* the Drifters. Carrier Group Crichton had the firepower to *vaporize* the Convoy delegation's ships, making sure that even a suicide run at Earth would fail.

Hopefully. The theory shouldn't need to be tested.

"This is Rear Admiral Henry Wong of the United Planets Space Force," Bokor continued, gesturing toward Henry.

"The Destroyer is, of course, known to us," Third-Red-White-Cross told Henry. "The man whose hand ended the Kenmiri is no stranger among the Drifters."

"My *ship* destroyed the last of the Kenmorad," Henry corrected quietly. And even that had been a matter of timing rather than planning.

Still, it was true. His battlecruiser had been part of Golden Lancelot, the risky all-or-nothing strike the Vesheron and the United Planets Alliance had launched to wipe out every single breeding sect of Kenmorad—the *only* Kenmiri capable of reproduction.

Henry had destroyed the last evacuation ship and killed the last known Kenmorad. Without them, the Kenmiri were doomed to a slow death by entropy—and they *knew* it. There would be Kenmiri for decades yet, but unless some other answer was found, the Kenmiri would die.

Henry didn't like what he'd done. He didn't like that it had been planned or that he and the rest of the Lancelot crews had been *lied* to to make it happen. But it was done, and he'd made some semblance of peace with it over the last half-decade.

"Your actions since the fate of the Kenmorad have only increased your reputation, Admiral Wong," Third-Red-White-Cross told him. "And the Convoys are gratified to see your people recognize your value. Congratulations on the promotion, Admiral."

"Thank you."

Sensitive to the complexities of the situation, Henry stepped slightly backward and gestured the diplomats forward. The most senior of the party was the Security Councilor for the Solar System, and he was, frankly, surprised the shockingly pale spaceborn woman had allowed the Drifter leader to focus on Henry.

THE MEET-AND-GREET inevitably turned into a party, with the Drifters hosting the humans in a large open space Henry presumed could function as a dining room, a meeting room or a glorified cocktail party space.

Since Drifters didn't remove their masks among strangers, food wasn't an option. Drinks were provided—and Henry waited for the Security Councilor's bodyguards to clear them before touching any of the liquids.

It wasn't even that he didn't trust the Drifters. Even Ashall had sufficiently different metabolisms to react oddly to what should have been safe consumables. *Usually*, those strange reactions were relatively harmless—there was at least one species that found Earth-grown chocolate to be as intoxicating as alcohol for humans—but not always.

There were several planets in the Ra Sector where *coffee* was illegal due to its level of addictiveness and side effects on the main local population.

The drink Henry had chosen was a pale violet "wine" he knew from previous visits to Drifter ships. The name in Kem translated roughly as "pear-star," and while the taste was pleasant, it was also nearly indescribable in English.

The closest Henry had ever heard a human come to describing the flavor of pear-star wine was maple syrup mixed with pomegranate and burned chocolate, but not sweet. He found it an interesting flavor profile—and its more "medicinal" ingredients were chemically comparable to alcohol and caffeine.

It wasn't going to make him drunk without him consuming enough of it that he'd *slosh* getting back on the shuttle, but he still sipped carefully as he surveyed the crowd.

Between the security details—even Henry was being followed at a discreet couple of steps by a GroundDiv trooper from *Crichton*—and the aides and staff, the UPA greeting party totaled just over thirty people.

There were roughly four times that many Drifters present at the party, including the servers, but there were almost three hundred different people in the room.

The "extras" were, Henry figured, trade envoys from people the Drifters had picked up once they'd decided to head for the UPA. Red Stripe White Stripe had entered the Ra Sector from the Apophis Sector —clockwise around the sphere of the old Kenmiri Empire—and it was unsurprising to see delegations from the powers of that Sector.

Some might even come from farther away, the Geb or even the Shu Sectors. The UPSF was already making overtures into the Apophis Sector, after all, and Henry knew that APOCOM—Apophis Peacekeeper Sector Command—was already taking shape as an administrative structure prior to beginning operations.

While he wouldn't say so aloud, Henry would privately give two-to-one odds that he was going to end up in charge of the second Peacekeeper Command. That, plus the recognition that there would be people tagging along with the Drifters from that Sector, was part of why he figured he'd been sent along to this meeting.

As soon as he spotted the odd group out, his spine stiffened. The group moved as a military unit even at the party, towering over most of the Ashall and non-Ashall guests. They were eerily skinny and almost translucently pale, with a blue tinge to their skin that Henry had only seen on one race.

The manes down the back of the Londu's necks and the white robes of the dress uniforms of the Blades of the Scion only confirmed what Henry realized the moment he spotted them. There shouldn't have been *any* Londu aboard the Drifter ship—they were a long way from home.

The Blades of the Scion were the Londu space force, sworn to the Great Scion of the Londu. Their nation was an El-Vesheron power—like the UPA, a race outside the borders of the Kenmiri Empire that had joined the Vesheron rebel alliance to protect themselves from Kenmiri expansion.

They were also closest to the *Isis* Sector, putting them a third of the way around the outer perimeter of the old Empire from the United Planets Alliance, and had always been genteel…*rivals* wasn't quite the right word, but there had always been a tension to their alliance with Earth.

And where every *other* non-Drifter sentient in the room was clearly a diplomat or trade representative, the white-robed Londu with their matte-black ceremonial breastplates were unquestionably military.

POTENTIAL PROBLEM, Henry sent out to the internal networks of the senior humans present.

What kind of problem? Bokor replied instantly.

The degree to which modern humanity was networked with each other and their technology was known to alternately confuse and disturb the species they dealt with—but if most of the UPA's technology had been designed by their slave masters, Henry wouldn't have trusted it in his skull either.

Seven Londu Blades of the Scion, Henry explained, flagging the tall, pale Ashall with the message. *They're a long way from home and they're neither diplomats nor merchants.*

Do the Londu have diplomats and merchants? Bokor asked. Even through text, her mild disdain came through.

They're a centralized authoritarian state, not killing machines. Henry hadn't got along overly well with Londu in the past, but he *had* worked with them. His partner, Sylvia, had been part of the original delegation to negotiate with the Great Scion.

He had a pretty solid handle on the Londu. That didn't mean he *trusted* the maned aliens.

So, if they were sending a party with the Drifters for the same reason everyone else is, they would be diplomats, Councilor Bosch concluded. Henry had a tiny spike of panic when he realized that "the senior humans present" included a member of the UPA's multi-person executive committee.

Why do you think they sent soldiers, Admiral Wong? Bosch asked.

Swallowing a second spike of panic and realizing that, yes, as the flag officer in the room with the most experience with the Londu—and in the Kenmiri Empire, for that matter, as Bokor had mostly served in the defensive fleets—he was the logical person for the *Security Councilor for Sol* to ask for an opinion.

I'm not sure, he admitted. *If they were a scouting party to assess our defenses or something similarly hostile, they'd have brought civilians just as cover. That it's* just *soldiers suggests something relatively aboveboard, but it's odd.*

Henry realized that the Londu had spotted him and two officers had split off from the group and were heading in his direction.

I believe I may be about to get some answers, Admiral, Councilor, he reported. Then he smiled thinly as he realized he *recognized* the shorter of the two Londu. *But, if nothing else, I know one of them. Which should make this interesting.*

Lord of Ten Thousand Miles Kahlmor, after all, had been present at the Great Gathering when the attempts to build a new post-Kenmiri order had come crashing down in flames and violence. And Henry, for one, still wasn't *entirely* certain the Londu hadn't been involved in the trap his ship had fallen into.

4

"IF I AM READING your insignia correctly, it is now Rear Admiral Henry Wong, yes?" Kahlmor asked in Kem as he approached Henry and offered a small bow. "I hope I am remembered fondly from the Resta System."

"You are remembered, if nothing else," Henry said blandly. He took a moment to study Kahlmor before saying more. The man himself hadn't changed much. Short for a Londu, he was still fifteen centimeters taller than Henry and pale even for his alien kin, with a pitch-black mane of hair from the back of his skull to the nape of his neck.

Kahlmor's intentionally crudely hammered black iron collar now bore four vertical gold bands where it had once held three, marking him as a Lord of Fifty Thousand Miles—approximately the same as Henry's new rank.

"Lord of Fifty Thousand Miles Kahlmor," he finally said. "Welcome to the Sol System. You will forgive us, I hope, for holding some concern at your presence. We are a long way from the Isis Sector and the stars of the Great Scion."

Kahlmor was an experienced senior military officer, the man chosen to command the Londu flagship at the Great Gathering. He had a solid control of his features, but Henry was watching for his reaction to that.

Henry had been expecting something. Embarrassment at being called on their game. Surprise at him being quite so forthright. Something else, he wasn't sure.

He had not been expecting surprise, concern, and *fear*.

"We... We should have been expected," Kahlmor said after a few seconds. "Lord of a Million Miles Okavaz should have arrived in your systems thirty or more days ago."

The translation from Kem time units to the UPA's standard based on Earth's calendar was automatic for Henry. Even if he hadn't drilled it into his organic memory a long time before, his internal network did the conversion routinely.

A Lord of a Million Miles was the equivalent to a UPSF full Admiral, an officer who reported directly to the Great Scion. To Henry's knowledge, Lords of a Million Miles left Londu space in two circumstances: in command of full battle fleets, or as the personal spokesperson of the Great Scion when the Scion could *not* afford errors.

"We have had no contact with any Londu officers or representatives since the Great Gathering," Henry said softly. "No Londu ships have entered UPA space or even the Ra Sector, so far as we know."

Kahlmor closed his eyes for a few seconds, then turned to his companion.

"Return to the others, Lotaris," he ordered. "Inform them that it appears Lord of a Million Miles Okavaz's contingency will be necessary."

The other officer—Lotaris, Henry assumed—saluted and withdrew, leaving Henry and Kahlmor alone on one side of the party.

"We were not supposed to be a surprise," Kahlmor finally repeated. "I was Lord of a Million Miles Okavaz's Voice of the Steel. When we encountered a Drifter Convoy on our way to the United Planets Alliance and learned that Red Stripe White Stripe would be entering UPA space, Okavaz decided that she desired a contingency. In case something went wrong with her mission.

"I and a small staff were detached to meet Red Stripe White Stripe and pay for passage to your stars. Lord of a Million Miles Okavaz and her task group were to proceed to the UPA as originally planned."

"And what was the original plan?" Henry asked.

"Okavaz was to function as an ambassador to your United Planets Alliance on a matter of great import." Kahlmor tapped his iron collar nervously, then straightened and met Henry's gaze.

"And if she did not arrive, then I must serve as she was charged," he told the Terran officer. "I need to request a meeting with your leadership as quickly as possible, Admiral Wong. Can you assist me with this?"

"I can," Henry said levelly, sending a silent message to Vice Admiral Bokor and Councilor Bosch. "But if you will wait a few moments, I will introduce you to an individual who will be more able to assist."

Kahlmor looked confused for a moment, then a touch of discomfort crossed his face.

"I see," he allowed. "And who am I meeting?"

"Councilor Andrea Bosch, member of the Security Council of the United Planets Alliance for the Solar System," Bosch introduced herself crisply as she stepped up behind the Londu officer.

Vice Admiral Bokor was a handful of steps behind the Councilor, the pair trailing a stream of bodyguards and aides like a comet trailing steam.

"Lord of Fifty Thousand Miles Kahlmor, be known to Councilor Bosch and Vice Admiral Izabella Bokor," Henry said gently. "The Councilor would be the best person, I believe, to decide if the Security Council should meet with you."

"Indeed," Bosch agreed. The Councilor's Kem was surprisingly fluent—which told Henry why Bosch, of the Council's thirteen permanent members, was the one who'd been sent to greet the Drifters. "So, tell me, Lord of Fifty Thousand Miles, what brings the Londu to the United Planets Alliance?"

Kahlmor was doing a surprisingly good job of concealing his emotions and discomfort, but Henry had a lot of practice at reading Ashall. The Londu flag officer was a soldier, not a diplomat, and he clearly hadn't expected to find himself as the spokesperson for his monarch.

"We…" He paused, considering his words. "It has been over six months since I left," he noted. "But when I left, the Scion's stars were under attack by an unknown enemy. An enemy using warships equipped with powerful gravity shields that shrug aside our weapons and distort our sensors.

"Shields such as those possessed by the United Planets Space Force."

5

THE IRONY, Henry realized, was that at no point had Kahlmor explicitly accused the UPA of attacking the Londu. The implication had been enough for Councilor Bosch to want him on Earth and speaking to the Security Council immediately.

"Immediately" was, of course, impossible. The Drifter delegation had emerged roughly in the orbital radius of Jupiter, putting them thirty-six light-minutes from Earth. Any conversation would have had over an hour lag between question and answer, which Bosch didn't think was appropriate.

The Drifter ships were freighters, lacking the high-end inertial dampeners and engines of warships. The Terran warships were limited by Terran inertial-dampening technology, restricting them to about the same half-kilometer-per-second-squared of acceleration as the Drifter freighters.

Any of those ships would take twenty hours to reach Sol, and Councilor Bosch had decided *that* was too long.

The Drifter escorts had higher accelerations, but no one was going to remove them from their charges. That left exactly one ship that could make it to Earth in a time frame the Councilor found acceptable.

So Henry Wong found himself as Kahlmor's escort and honor

guard aboard *Amethyst* as the cruiser "dropped" toward Earth at her maximum acceleration, four times what any of the other Terran warships could have handled.

Henry wasn't going to bring a foreign flag officer onto the bridge of the UPSF's most advanced warship, but *Amethyst* didn't currently have a flag officer aboard. Councilor Bosch had taken over the Presence Mission Section, a chunk of the ship intended to carry civilian dignitaries like her, and Henry had installed himself and Kahlmor in the cruiser's flag decks.

"We've secured everything of concern here, ser," the systems specialist behind him reported. "The flag bridge wasn't operating, so there wasn't too much to lock down. A few things we wanted to move out of sight."

"Thank you, Chief," Henry told the man. "Can you let the young GroundDiv lady at the door know that her compatriots can send Kahlmor up whenever he wants?"

"Of course, ser."

He didn't even need to turn around to know that the Chief Petty Officer was somewhere between amused and embarrassed at Henry calling the commando at the door a "young lady." Henry had a pretty good idea of just how competent a Ground Division Petty Officer Second Class wearing the *Una Salus Victis* pin of the Commando Regiments was.

But she was also maybe twenty-five and Henry would be celebrating his sixtieth birthday all too soon. Too many of his subordinates were starting to look like children to him.

A different Petty Officer with a commando pin entered the flag bridge a few minutes later and saluted Henry.

"The Lord of Fifty Thousand Miles is on his way up, ser," the PO told him. "I'm just going to go prop up a wall over there, ser."

Henry wasn't entirely sure at what point the pair of regular troopers who'd followed him onto the Drifter ship had been replaced by a commando fire team. He wasn't even sure which *ship* they'd come from—presumably *Crichton,* but no one had actually told him anything in particular.

"PO Stevens," Henry said as the commando turned to walk away. "When did your team get assigned to me?"

Stevens paused.

"According to my orders, ser, at the exact moment that you received your star," he replied. "Catching up to you was a bit of a headache, and I believe we have two more fire teams in transit. They've been redirected to meet us at Earth, along with our CO."

"And why am I suddenly surrounded by commandos, PO?"

"Standard protocol places the security of the UPSF's flag officers in the hands of Ground Division, ser," Stevens said crisply. "All flag officers have a permanently assigned security detail."

Henry smiled thinly.

"I understand that, PO Stevens, but I was not under the impression that the *Commando Regiments* generally provided said security details."

"I can't speak to that, ser," the commando said crisply. "My orders are from Commodore Romanova at Regimental Command. You might want to ask Commander Palmerston those questions when she joins us at Earth."

"I may just do that, PO," Henry promised. "But for now, carry on. That bulkhead definitely needs a commando to keep it from falling on me."

FIVE YEARS EARLIER, Kahlmor had given Henry a detailed tour of one of the Londu's most powerful battleships. Henry was a touch guilty about not returning the favor, but *Amethyst* was the most advanced starship in the UPSF's arsenal.

He was cleared to see every part of her—but even Councilor Bosch wasn't, not without special permissions.

Fortunately, the Londu officer seemed unbothered as he entered the flag bridge, looking around him at the screens and holographic projectors —all currently locked to a basic visual display showing the Solar System.

"The last one of your ships I was aboard lacked holoprojectors," he observed in Kem. "You are upgrading."

"We are changing a lot of things," Henry agreed. "I am not convinced of the value of the holograms myself, but we do possess alternatives."

"Yes, your cybernetics would assist with that," Kahlmor murmured. He walked forward to stand in the center of the flag bridge, next to the Admiral's seat that everything orbited around.

"They work for us," Henry said. "I understand why the Vesheron are hesitant to use them, though I have wondered about the Londu."

Kahlmor shrugged.

"We had some serious issues with our early cybernetics," he said. "A number of deaths, some unfortunate rampages. As a society, we decided they were unnecessary."

"We find them extraordinarily useful, but we are adapted to them by now," Henry admitted. "I am not sure we would know what to do without them."

On every human world that he was aware of, the internal network was implanted in a series of procedures—with nanotech modification, they didn't quite qualify as surgeries—from about age seven through seventeen.

UPSF personnel received further hardware during basic training, bringing them up to the level Henry was, after four decades, entirely used to.

The value of that equipment was at least partially proven by what they could see around them. At that moment, the cruiser was still accelerating toward Earth, passing through the asteroid belt and with a commanding view of Mars.

The asteroid belt swarmed with icons. Even four centuries of extraction and refining hadn't made a noticeable dent in the mass of the belt. Several of the larger asteroids were home to heavily populated colonies built into tunnels left over from the original mines.

Mars was almost as busy. Efforts to terraform her had never quite worked out, but that had only made the Martian settlers *more* stubborn. Much of Sol's industry now operated in Mars's lighter atmosphere and gravity, and *Helios* had been built in the yards trailing Deimos—along with a quarter of her UPSF sisters.

"Your home system is surprisingly well developed," Kahlmor

observed. "I am not sure what I expected, but I will admit that some among the Londu have always believed your people to be...young."

The Kem word he used was *loratch,* which carried strong connotations of "undeveloped" and "immature" as well as explicit age.

"How so?" Henry asked. "Given that, well, we always had the gravity shields, and you did not, there is an argument that we are *more* technologically advanced than you."

At that moment, they were standing aboard a starship with a reactionless engine moving at an acceleration no Londu ship could match, protected by multiple layers of defenses the Londu couldn't duplicate. There was more than *an argument* that the UPA was more advanced than the Londu.

"Technology is only one measure of a people," Kahlmor replied, looking around the displays and seeming to assess the Solar System as one aggregate whole. "We knew you only controlled a handful of systems, inhabited by a single species. Your technology was impressive, but you remain a divided people, operating as a nation ruled by the many rather than the wise."

The Londu's right hand turned palm-upward in what Henry took for a shrug.

"These are lessons the Scion and my people learned long ago in blood and fire," he observed. "I saw the divisions among you even in the honor guard that met the Drifters. Until you grow past them as one people and learn to place your faith in the wise instead of the many, there will always be Londu who see you as young."

Henry had to chuckle at that.

"We feel similarly about the Londu, I suppose," he conceded. "To us, autocrats and expansionist empires are things of the past. We grew past such structures and desires."

Not, perhaps, as quickly or thoroughly as some would have expected or liked, but the current UPA felt stable and democratic to Henry. He could be *wrong*—he'd freely admit that he spent very little time in civilian life—but there was certainly a regular cycle of different people in the seats at the table giving him orders, one that suggested democracy was working.

"Where to us, that very statement is a sign of your youth," Kahlmor told him. "But this system is as heavily developed as Londar, our home. In many ways, I look at this and wonder why the UPA brought so little to the war against the Kenmiri."

"And how large a portion of the Scion's strength was committed against the Empire at any moment?" Henry asked. "You saw us once our worlds were safe, when we were fighting the Kenmiri in their own stars."

And while that had still seen as much as sixty or seventy percent of the UPSF actively deployed at times, the emergency mobilization that had seen the national fleets equipped with faster-than-light engines had ended.

He supposed that was part of Kahlmor's point. If the UPA didn't have the member nations with their own needs, demands and fleets, *all* of those ships would be UPSF and equipped with FTL drives. The hundred-odd sublight warships scattered across the UPSF—including about thirty battleships—were limited in power as well as number by treaties, but the same resources could have increased the UPSF's strength by fifty percent.

Though it would *also* have vastly increased the UPSF's *responsibilities*.

"We never saw the Kenmiri in our own stars," Kahlmor admitted. "Our commitment to the Vesheron was always second to protecting ourselves. That, I think, is part of our current struggle."

"Oh?"

The Londu grimaced.

"I think I would prefer to only explain the entire mess once," he said. There was a pregnant pause. "I must ask, Henry Wong. Am I likely to receive a fair hearing before your leaders? I do not know you humans well."

"I see no reason why you would not," Henry said. "With the loss of the subspace network, the Londu are no threat to us or our interests. We are a long way from each other."

"Distance creates both problems and opportunities, I suppose," Kahlmor allowed. "I fear for the fate of my commander. I fear for the fate of my people, if something happened to the Lord of a Million Miles."

"I do not know what answer you are seeking here," Henry warned. "And so, I cannot say if you will find our reception to be useful. But the Londu are not our enemies and were once our friends. You will be heard."

"The word of Henry Wong is worth something to us," Kahlmor told him. "To *me*, especially. I saw your 'word' in action in Resta. I trust you. I am not certain I trust your...*leaders*."

Like *loratch*, the Kem word Kahlmor used had additional connotations. In this case, the word was for the animal at the front of a stampede.

Not for a politician or governor.

Henry looked past the icons and lights over Mars to the distant lights of Earth. Hopefully, Kahlmor would be more politic when speaking to the Security Council. It wasn't Henry's job to warn the Londu, though.

Sylvia might have. But Henry's partner was a diplomat and an ambassador. Henry was a soldier. He'd play politics when he had to... but Kahlmor hadn't given him enough information to judge whether he wanted to play politics on the alien's behalf.

6

"THIS WAY, SER."

Henry gave the junior officer who'd met him at the shuttle pad a questioning look.

"I'm presuming you know something I don't, Lieutenant Commander, but an introduction would be helpful," he said gently.

"Apologies, ser!" The young man drew himself up straight and saluted crisply—for a second time, he *had* saluted on arrival. "Lieutenant Commander Cornell Strickland. I've been assigned as your flag secretary. I was coordinating your arrival with *Amethyst*'s crew and Commander Palmerston, your security detail CO. The plan was for myself and Commander Palmerston to meet you on the Iron Ring, but..."

"Then the Drifters reported they were coming early," Henry allowed. He had picked up the officer's name from his network but hadn't put that together with the file he'd reviewed when approving his initial staff.

"So, we ended up in a bit of a mess, ser," Strickland confirmed. "I have a vehicle waiting for you and Lord of Fifty Thousand Miles Kahlmor to take you to the Assembly Building. The driver is one of Palmerston's people, but the Commander ended up on Mars."

If Henry hadn't had a senior alien flag officer standing at his right hand, he would have laughed helplessly. If Palmerston had gone astray, that meant he had no idea where Master Chief Petty Officer Anita Sharma, his senior noncommissioned officer, had ended up.

Master Chief Sharma had at least been *on* the Iron Ring with him—there were two categories of people who trained on the Ring: Senior Chief Petty Officers making the jump to E-9, and Master Chief and Commodores making the jump to O-8 and Rear Admiral.

Henry felt a bit foolish that it had taken him almost half of the year-long course to realize that the instructors were assessing the larval flag officers and Master Chiefs to pair them off in professional partnerships that were expected to last out both careers.

"Do we have orders for after we deliver Lord Kahlmor?" Henry asked, gesturing for Strickland to take the lead toward the promised vehicle.

"You are to attend the Security Council meeting with him, ser," Strickland told him. "I'm coordinating with the rest of your staff, and I think we *should* have everyone in New York by local morning."

New York City, on the eastern coast of North America, remained the center of the United Planets Alliance as it had once been the center of the United Nations. Henry could count on his fingers the number of times he'd been in the Assembly Building—and he'd been in front of the Security Council *once*.

It seemed his new star was dragging him directly into the deep end.

✦✦✦

RED-UNIFORMED TROOPERS of the Assembly Security Force met Henry's party in the decorative plaza in front of the General Assembly Building. While the UPA mostly operated out of offices on the moon, they had taken over the UN General Assembly Building to host the UPA General Assembly.

Henry even recognized the ASF officer who came up to greet them. She'd been promoted since he'd last been there, he noted, and he gave the energy-weapon-armed woman a crisp salute.

"*Major* Cole," he greeted her. "You'll note I did not come armed, this time."

Last time he had come to meet the Security Council, he'd been in dress uniform and brought dress weapons. This time, he remembered Cole's complaint that the UPSF didn't *tell* their people to come unarmed.

"A pleasure, Rear Admiral Wong," she told him. "My people will still need to scan you all for hidden weapons and potential network malware."

An alert popped up on Henry's network, informing him that high-level authorization codes had just activated deep firmware security scans. It wasn't a particularly comfortable feeling, but he understood the need.

"No weapons, and networks are clear of intrusion worms," an ASF noncom reported. "They are clear. IDs match the appointment. Except, of course, for Lord Kahlmor."

Kahlmor's sudden tension suggested that he either understood more English than he was letting on or had a hidden translator. Either way, it was something for Henry to keep in mind while working with the Londu officer.

"Lord of Fifty Thousand Miles Kahlmor doesn't have an identification beacon," he pointed out wryly. "But I assure you that I or my security detail have accompanied him since he boarded *Amethyst*.

"I also met him previously to this, but I assume his documents have been reviewed?"

The corner of Cole's mouth quirked in what might have been the start of a smile. She turned to Kahlmor and switched to serviceable Kem.

"Lord of Fifty Thousand Miles, I need to review your credentials before I can permit you to enter the General Assembly Building. I hope this is acceptable?"

"I am an envoy of the Great Scion and your guest today," Kahlmor told her with a minimalist bow. He produced a scroll bound in dark blue ribbon and passed it to Cole.

Henry had only seen the digital version of the Londu's credentials. He hadn't realized that Kahlmor *had* a physical document.

From the way the scroll opened to Cole's review, it wasn't paper. If anything, it appeared to be thin, carefully alloyed metal.

The ASF officer clearly knew what she was looking for, too, as she skimmed it, rerolled it, and returned it to Kahlmor.

"Everything is in order. Walk with me, Admiral, Lord. Your security details and aides will be directed to a waiting room, and we will reunite you when this is over."

Henry nodded his understanding and glanced over at Kahlmor. The Londu's aides *were* his security detail and vice versa. There were only two other Londu with them, and from what Henry understood, Kahlmor only had a dozen people with him in total.

The plan had been to present a far more impressive visage, Henry suspected, but Kahlmor would have to make do with what he had.

THE FIRST TIME Henry had met the Security Council, it had been in a regular conference room. Meeting with the representative of an alien empire, though, the leaders of the United Planets Alliance had decided to impress. Cole led them *through* the General Assembly Building to the Interplanetary Spire.

The Spire was on the site where the UN Secretariat Building had once stood. *That* structure had suffered from the decline in the United Nations' power and prestige, eventually being wrecked by an internal fire, abandoned and finally demolished.

Only after the creation of the UPA had the Secretariat Park been sacrificed to the creation of a new administrative building: the Interplanetary Spire, a seven-hundred-meter tower with four elevated public parks on immense buttressed galleries wrapping around the structure at even intervals.

Cole and the Spire's elevators delivered Henry and his charge to the very peak of the Interplanetary Spire, where an armored transparent roof hung over an atrium wrapped around one of the more grandiose conference spaces Henry had ever seen.

A curved semicircular table, with seats on the outside, faced a slightly raised stone dais with a smaller table and media projection equipment. Two straight tables had been added outside of the curved table—and while those tables were still solidly built hardwood, it was clear they weren't normally part of the room.

There was enough space for nineteen people to sit at the main table, but it only had fourteen occupants. Each had a small plaque, identical per tradition to those used by the United Nations in the twentieth century, declaring who they were and who they represented.

In the central seat was Ji-Yeong Ottosen, a Norwegian politician of Korean descent and the current Secretary-President of the United Planets Alliance. Henry didn't know the dark-eyed head of state overly well—*he'd* voted for their predecessor, Vasudha Patil, to remain in the position. Patil had been the one to sign off on the Peacekeeper Initiative, after all.

Arrayed to Ottosen's left were the eight Councilors for the star systems of the UPA: Sol, Alpha Centauri, Epsilon Eridani, Tau Ceti, Procyon, Keid, Ophiuchi, and Altair. To their right were the five Councilors for the most powerful of Earth's nations and alliances: the United States, Russia, China, the European Union, and the African Union.

Those fourteen politicians represented the central executive of the United Planets Alliance and no one else had been seated at their table.

Behind the star system Councilors, however, Henry recognized the senior Admirals of the UPSF. It didn't take much of a hint, barely a suggestion of a gesture from Major Cole, for him to cross to that table and join the other flag officers.

He presumed that the collection seated behind the national Councilors were bureaucrats and diplomats, though he didn't recognize any of them.

As Henry took his seat, Cole guided Kahlmor up to the dais, where the officer turned envoy managed to look commanding, tense, ready and terrified all at the same time.

A young man in the ubiquitous five-button suit of the UPA bureaucracy was seated next to the dais and rose to quietly speak to Kahlmor —in Londu, Henry realized. He was presumably the translator.

"Lord of Fifty Thousand Miles Kahlmor, welcome to Earth,"

Ottosen declared, rising from their seat, and gesturing toward the Londu as they spoke in English.

The translator quickly repeated the comments in Londu. While Henry figured that every military officer and diplomat in the room spoke Kem, he wouldn't have expected the Security Council to. And in many ways, both they and Kahlmor would be better served translated directly from Londu to English than translating it twice.

"Thank you for your grace in welcoming me," Kahlmor said slowly, waiting for the translator to catch up with him. "I must remind you all that I am not the envoy who was intended to stand before you. While I am aware of the situation my Scion faces and I can speak for him, I am not authorized to commit the Sovereignty to treaties or payments as Lord of a Million Miles Okavaz would have been."

Henry was intrigued to hear that the translators had *finally* come up with a usable translation for the name of the Londu nation-state. The Kem word the Londu tended to use translated more closely as *property*, which he knew didn't really encompass the meaning of the Londu's name for their nation.

"But nonetheless, I am charged to speak to you for my Scion," he continued. "And I come to you in the darkest hours of the Londu. As I told Admiral Wong and Councilor Bosch, the Sovereignty is under attack. So far, our worlds and our protectorates have remained untouched, but this can only last so long.

"This enemy is unknown to us, a stranger who has endeavored to conceal their identities from us—but their ships are protected by powerful gravity shields, such as those used by the United Planets Alliance."

Kahlmor let that hang for several seconds, until Alistair Kennedy, the Councilor for the United States, cleared his throat loudly.

"Do you mean to imply, 'Lord' Kahlmor," he drawled slowly, "that the United Planets is behind these attacks on your people?"

Everyone had been thinking it, but no one else had been quite ready to demand an answer to the question.

7

KENNEDY'S QUESTION cut to the heart of the matter from the UPA's perspective, and Henry didn't quite hold his breath as he waited for Kahlmor's answer.

"I will admit that the thought has certainly been suggested in the halls of my Scion's government," Kahlmor said slowly. "And I allowed Councilor Bosch to suspect that was our belief.

"But no," he concluded sharply. "The distance between the Londu and the United Planets Alliance is too vast. In an era without the subspace networks to allow communication or the Kenmiri Empire to require our cooperation, we are of little interest to each other.

"These attackers are an enigma and appear to have gone to great effort to remain so. Their greatest advantage over us is their possession of gravity-shield technology."

Kahlmor paused to let the translator catch up—and probably to let his audience catch up. Henry had spent enough time living with a senior diplomat in his back pocket to recognize that Kahlmor definitely had some oratorical training, but the officer was definitely *not* a diplomat.

If nothing else, Henry was quite sure that Sylvia wouldn't have given up the potential lever of the Scion blaming the United Planets Alliance for the attacks that quickly.

"The UPA has possessed this technology since prior to the Londu's first encounters with them," Kahlmor observed. "During the war with the Kenmiri, we made several overtures to purchase the system from the UPA. I have no information on what the offers we made were, but I am advised they were generous."

One of the diplomats on the other side of the atrium space raised a hand, leaning forward when the Secretary-President nodded to her. Henry's network identified her as Patience Mbeki, a South African member of the Diplomatic Corps. It did *not*, he noted, give her a current role or a reason to be in this meeting.

"I was involved in those discussions, Councilors," she explained. "Lord of Fifty Thousand Miles Kahlmor's description is roughly accurate. I believe the one that we gave the most consideration to was for twelve brand-new Londu battleships in exchange for six gravity-shield-equipped destroyers and technical aid in duplicating them.

"At the time, the decision was made to protect what was regarded as our primary tactical advantage, even from allies."

Henry had to conceal a moment of surprise at the scale of the Londu offer. Even at the height of the UPSF's strength, just before Golden Lancelot, they'd had barely one hundred capital ships in commission. And while he'd back even his old wartime battlecruiser against any Londu battleship he'd ever seen, the Londu ships were easily the equal of any other energy-screened and plasma-cannon-armed battleship he'd ever seen.

Unspoken, though, was that Mbeki had not referred to the Londu as *trusted* allies—because even during the war, the UPA had looked askance at an expansionist authoritarian regime. Even one on their side.

"Thank you," Kahlmor said with a nod after the translator repeated her words in Londu. His failure to use a title or name for Mbeki was a small reminder that *he* didn't have access to the internal networks of the humans in the room.

"While my Scion hoped, I believe, that time and the new distance between us would reduce the risks such that you would be prepared to provide us with gravity-shield technology, the truth is that we could not duplicate such an offer now," he admitted. "We have extended the Blades of the Scion into the Isis Sector as promised at the Gathering, and shielding our new protectorates consumes much of our resources."

Translation: the Londu had seized five hundred star systems with sixty inhabitable planets, more than doubling the size of the Sovereignty, and were utterly overextended. Henry suspected the new attacks would have been a problem anyway, but if the Sovereignty were stretched that thin, it would be worse.

"If you do not know who is attacking you other than that it isn't us," Kennedy drawled, "what exactly are you looking for from the United Planets?"

"Friends." The word hung in the air like a ticking bomb, and Kahlmor *let* it hang. He was better at this than Henry had initially given him credit for.

"We were friends and allies with the UPA once," he finally continued. "Against the Kenmiri, we and hundreds of other nations and peoples stood as one to fight for freedom. For a world without slaves.

"We do not agree on what freedom means. We do not agree on what a perfect world should look like. But we agree that it cannot be slavery, enforced by the threat of genocide and starvation. We fought that together once, side by side, and now the Londu ask for aid.

"These enigmas have destroyed our ships and slaughtered innocents. We fear for our own and for the people we protect. Against an enemy who wields a defense we cannot breach, we turn to an old friend who had the same defense and ask for help."

He spread his hands.

"We will take whatever you are prepared to give," he admitted. "I am *asking* for technical specifications of whatever anti-gravity-shield weapons you possess." He glanced downward at the floor, losing some of his practiced certainty.

"I may also need to ask to borrow a ship to get home. Somewhere between the borders of the Sovereignty and the borders of the United Planets Alliance, eight Londu cruisers went missing. I do not ask you to learn their fate, but it complicates matters."

Henry knew that the silence following his plea was a sign of silent conversation, exchanged by text messages between the people gathered in the room. He was, at least, *aware* of that conversation though not included in it.

He wondered how it looked and felt to the Londu officer standing in front of his government.

"If I may, Lord of Fifty Thousand Miles Kahlmor," an androgynous shaven-headed officer interjected from the military table. "I am Admiral Lee Saren, the head of the United Planets Space Force Space Division."

Saren, at least, realized she needed to introduce herself to someone who didn't have an internal network. Henry found it odd that the diplomat Mbeki *hadn't*. Someone, he suspected, had spent too long on Earth.

"While I hesitate to prod what I understand to be a special relationship, we are not the only allies of the Londu in possession of gravity-shield technology," Saren told Kahlmor. "The Terzan were brought into the Vesheron *by* the Londu and command similar technology.

"If you are talking to *us*, does that mean you believe *they* are these Enigmas?"

That was something of a stretch. The Terzan had only demonstrated gravity shields on a handful of occasions during the war—but the ten-legged arachnoform aliens were better known to the Londu than anyone else.

The Londu were the people who'd made contact and somehow managed to set up translations with a species that had *no* verbal language. The Terzan communicated solely by short-range natural radio.

"The Terzan's possession of a form of gravity shielding is known to the Blades of the Scion," Kahlmor admitted. "There are…reasons we could not ask them for help. It is possible that they are the Enigmas, but the sensor data we have on the enemy ships does not match that for even Terzan gravity shields."

Kahlmor didn't elaborate on the reasons. There was more going on in the Sovereignty than he was going to admit to.

"I think," Kennedy interjected, "that we should allow our Londu friend to rest while we discuss matters. In private council."

"Agreed," Ottosen said. "Admiral Wong, please escort Lord of Fifty Thousand Miles Kahlmor to a waiting area. I ask that everyone remain in the Interplanetary Spire, but the Security Council should discuss this in private."

8

THE SECURITY COUNCIL deliberated for just over two hours before Henry was instructed to bring Kahlmor back in. This time, the Londu officer was directed to a seat with a small desk facing the curved table with the Security Council.

A second desk had also been added, and Henry realized that the directions in his network were taking him to it. Hesitantly, he accompanied Kahlmor in front of the Security Council and took the indicated seat, facing the leadership of his nation alongside a man he could barely call an ally, let alone a friend.

"Lord of Fifty Thousand Miles Kahlmor," Kennedy addressed the Londu, the title sounding odd in his soft Southern drawl—not least because the American Councilor hadn't yet *given* Kahlmor the respect of his full title. "We have considered your words and your Scion's request for aid."

Henry grimly suspected that Kennedy speaking for the Council, given his earlier casual disrespect, was a bad sign.

"The distance between our territories, as you have stated, reduces the UPA's interest in or vulnerability to the Londu—or the Londu's new enemy," Kennedy observed. "These Enigmas are no danger to the UPA."

Henry could see Kahlmor attempt to disguise his disappointment, but he could *also* see Kennedy's concealed sardonic amusement. The bastard was playing a game of some kind at Kahlmor's expense.

"But." The Councilor let the word hang in the air for a long moment. "We have learned, over the years, that friends are only friends when both sides work to keep paths open—and that assuming a friend remains so when you have made no such effort is a dangerous choice."

That was a piece of history that Kahlmor wouldn't know…and no one except an American would have referenced in a Security Council meeting. The Unification War had turned from a contained conflict between the United States Colonial Administration and the Russian Novaya Imperiya when the United States Space Force First Fleet had fallen back on Tau Ceti, a Chinese colony, and demanded resupply.

In the ensuing chaos, the Americans had ended up invading the Chinese colony. Their attempt to contain the news by locking down all shipping had ended in violence and the destruction of the Commonwealth Extrasolar Squadron—and the birth of the Terran Alliance that had broken both rogue states and become the UPA.

"We do not, as a rule, engage in the sale of technology," Kennedy continued. "And it is and remains our highest strategic doctrine to maintain the limited proliferation of gravity-shield technology.

"While arming the Londu with weapons capable of threatening our ships is a risk, the distance and time reduce that risk. More so, however, the risk is reduced by solidifying our friendship."

Kennedy was a bastard, Henry mentally repeated. He'd intentionally let Kahlmor think they were going to refuse any help, while planning on offering everything the Londu had thought they were going to get.

"Rear Admiral Wong," Kennedy continued, drawing Henry's attention. "Admiral Saren has informed us that you are currently unassigned. According to the Admiral, you are the available officer most experienced in long-range expeditions."

"I am at the disposal of the Security Council," Henry said calmly. There were definite *downsides* to what he saw coming—not least an extended time away from the UPA and Sylvia Todorovich—but it didn't sound like something he could turn down. Not that turning it down was an option, he suspected.

"You will take command of a long-range expeditionary fleet of the United Planets Space Force," Kennedy told him. "You and Admiral Saren will need to establish the exact force structure and necessary logistics for that expeditionary fleet, but your mission is straightforward enough.

"You will escort a convoy carrying weapons and technical advisors to support the Londu. Upon arrival in the Sovereignty, your next steps will be up to you and the ambassador we will send with you, but you will be authorized to engage in combat operations against the Enigmas in support of the Londu Sovereignty and the Blades of the Scion."

"I understand, Councilor," Henry said levelly, managing not to glance over to the table of senior military officers for confirmation. He suspected he was going to be walking out of the Interplanetary Spire and heading *right* for Admiral Saren's office.

"Lord of Fifty Thousand Miles Kahlmor." Secretary-President Ottosen took over from Kennedy smoothly. "I hope that this expeditionary fleet and the accompanying technical assistance are sufficient to meet the Londu's call for aid?"

"It is more than we dared to hope for," Kahlmor admitted freely. "My Scion will remember that the UPA honors their alliances—and the Londu will repay in kind once we are able again.

"In this, I am certain that I speak with the voice and will of the Great Scion of the Londu. We do not forget our friends, Councilors."

"Nor does Earth, Lord Kahlmor," Ottosen told him. "The Vesheron may have broken with the fall of our shared enemy, but friendships endure even as alliances age."

9

"BEER, ADMIRAL WONG?"

Henry shook his head as Admiral Saren's steward made the offer.

"I'm not sure what time it is locally," he admitted, "but I'm running on Iron Ring time and it's only about lunch. Too early for me."

The head of the UPSF's Space Division's Earth-side office was in the European Operations Center, a facility that had started as an intermittent base for assorted branches of the British armed forces in Cornwall. When the UPSF had been founded, the UK had given the land to the new formation as an attempt to get a foot in over their EU counterparts.

Now, three skyscrapers sprouted from Cornish hills like sore thumbs, surrounded by a secured compound. All of it was collectively unofficially known as the Coal Mines—mostly because the tunnels underneath the base, which made up most of the actual working space, had originally been just that.

"Coffee, then?" the steward asked.

"Green tea, please."

The steward withdrew for a moment, returning with a steaming tea pot and cup for Henry—and a chilled stein of a dark beer of some kind for Admiral Saren.

"Iron Ring time should be GMT," Saren told Henry as she claimed the beer glass. "And it's lunchtime here. Local tradition calls for beer at lunch, but then..." She shrugged. "...From what some of the locals around here say, I suspect some of them grew up having beer for breakfast."

The tea smelled excellent and Henry let it steep on the desk between them as he waited for Saren to get to the point of their hastily arranged meeting.

Her day office was in the southwest corner of the southernmost of the three towers of EurOps. While EurOps wasn't particularly *close* to anything, the tower was also roughly three hundred meters tall. He could see about a third of the UPSF base, an island of high-tech militarism in a sea of rough green hills dotted with sheep—and in the distance, past those hills, a hint of sharp rock and gleaming sunlight on water.

"You've guessed, I presume, that this Expeditionary Fleet came into existence during the Security Council's closed meeting earlier," Saren finally told him. "It's not the role I had in mind for you."

"As I told the Council, I serve the United Planets Alliance," Henry replied. "While that is definitely the politically apt answer to give in that circumstance, it has the virtue of being true."

Saren nodded and took a sip of her beer, considering the room around the two admirals.

Henry was actually surprised at how impersonal the space seemed. There was a painting on the wall of an Asian man he didn't know—the style and clothing suggested someone of Saren's own generation, so either family or her partner.

Other than that, the gorgeously located office was undecorated and equipped with the higher end of UPSF standard-issue furniture, the kind used by Captains and flag officers aboard ship.

"It's going to take us a few days to sort out what kind of force you'll have," she finally told him. "I have good news and bad news right now, though. More of the former, I think, but the latter is going to hurt, and I apologize for it."

"The bad news then, ser," he asked gently.

"Outside of your core staff that are already assigned to you, you aren't going to have the ability to select your officers," Saren told him bluntly. "This mission is just too…political. It's interstellar, it's diplomatic…and it was ordered by the Security Council themselves.

"Everyone with a gram of political pull is going to try to get their particular candidates onto your ships and into your staff, and I have no choice but to let them." She let that sink in. "I've spoken with Blake already and we'll filter out anybody who can't do their jobs, but she and I are going to give in to a lot of pressure over the next few days— because it will give us the ammunition to give you a proper task force."

Admiral Octavia Blake was the commander of the UPSF Personnel Division, operating out of Base Halo above Jupiter. Henry didn't know her—or Saren, for that matter—well. But he had to trust that they'd have his back.

He certainly didn't have the pull to insert his own candidates into that kind of political firestorm, though he certainly had people he'd *prefer* to have in his staff.

"I can't say I like it, ser," he admitted. "But I suppose it's buying us that good news you mentioned?"

"If it doesn't, you won't have a damn task force, Wong," she said flatly. "Since the Security Council gave us our marching orders, I can guarantee you'll at least have *that*. It's a question of how much of a task force we can put together."

"I see. You said there was more good news than bad, though?" Henry asked. The news would have to be good to make up for *that* stinker.

"Firstly, you're going to be carrying a senior diplomat with extended experience negotiating with the Londu," Saren told him. "I believe you already knew that Ambassador Sylvia Todorovich was on her way back from the Ra Sector?"

"I did." She'd been on her way back to visit him during a stint of post-promotion leave he'd been promised. "I understand she is going on vacation."

"So were you," the Admiral said drily. "I hope that the pair of you can, ah, find a chance to make that up to each other somehow."

They'd been supposed to have two weeks together. A minimum

trip to and from Londu space would be closer to eight months. Not a vacation, but Henry was sure he and his partner could find time together to make up for a missed vacation.

"I imagine we may be able to," Henry agreed. "What do we know about the task force itself—or the convoy I'm escorting?"

"Not a lot yet, but what I've established is good news, I think," she told him. "You're getting *Raven* back, Admiral Wong."

He swallowed in surprise, then smiled.

The United Planets Space Vessel *Raven* had been his last single-ship command, one of the UPSF's *Corvid*-class battlecruisers and one of the most powerful non-carrier warships in their fleet. She'd been battered into a wreck under his command—and so had become the very first of the *Corvid*-G-class, repaired and refitted with the new gravity maneuvering system.

"A large reason why the Security Council decided on this mission is to allow for a full-scale test of a GMS-equipped fleet in a region and against an enemy that does not threaten the UPA or our interests." She smiled thinly. "Operations in Ra, even our planned expansions into Apophis and Hathor, can't do that. We don't have a known threat in those regions, but anything we do encounter in those regions *will* be a threat to our interests.

"You're going to have a core striking force of GMS-equipped ships," she continued. "*Raven*, obviously, is one of exactly *two Corvid*-Gs in commission."

"*Raven* and *Renown*," Henry confirmed aloud. *Renown* had been the only *Corvid*-C command ship to survive the war. Since the G-series ships were updated to include significant command facilities, they were intended to render the *Corvid*-Cs unnecessary—so the last *Corvid*-C had been the first operational ship to go under the dockyard's knife.

The next two ships to go in, the first standard *Corvid*s, had been *Richelieu* and *Rook*—both among the oldest of the new battlecruisers and due for refit anyway.

While in TechDiv, Henry had been in the meeting where they'd seen the pattern and *knowingly* slated *Riffen* and *Ryūjō* to be the next pair.

"Outside of *Raven*, all I can really guarantee is that you're not getting another GMS battlecruiser," Saren said drily. "You know what we have for GMS ships as well as I do, I suspect."

"The two *Corvid*-Gs, four *Lexington*-Gs, four *Amethyst*s and twenty *Cataphract*s," Henry said instantly. "I wrote our conversion plan."

"I know." She snorted. "Did you really just give the Iron Ring that plan as your thesis?"

"No," he objected, but he smiled as he said it. "I gave them the conversion plan with the footnotes and explanations integrated into the text, explaining *why* we needed to do it that way."

Saren chuckled and shook her head wryly at him.

"That's probably fair," she conceded. "And now that you've finished, I suppose I can admit the Iron Ring's darkest secret."

"Oh?" he asked carefully.

"Nobody *fails* the Iron Ring, Henry. That's not the point. The point is to train you to look at things a certain way and to integrate you with a senior noncommissioned officer to be your right hand.

"More of our flag candidates have died of natural causes attending the Ring than have been dismissed. Anyone we send there has to screw up epically to get dismissed," she admitted. "And no one has ever been dismissed from the program who wasn't promptly dismissed from the service. You probably *could* have just handed the conversion plan in as your thesis."

"I suspected," Henry confessed. "But that would have felt…weak as a proposition."

"Which is why no one is surprised you didn't," Saren said. "We don't send people to the Iron Ring who take the easy way out." She paused, then smiled again. "We send the kind of people who end up having to skip a destroyer through a planet to survive saving said planet."

Henry shivered. The Stand of the *Cataphracts*, as it had rapidly been dubbed, was the only reason the planet Anderon had survived a revanchist Kenmiri faction's attack. He'd lost most of his destroyer squadron, including his flagship, in the process—and had, yes, used the crippled destroyer's skip drive to bypass the planet to avoid hitting it at a world-ending velocity.

"As I understand it, ser, I appear to have a lot of work to do," he murmured.

"You do. But I have some more additions and problems I'm going to lay on you, Admiral," Saren told him. "First. Your opinion on the B-series *Cataphract*s?"

"They're going to be a surprise to anyone who met the original ships," Henry said slowly. "From the outside, they look exactly the same. But we installed Kozun-style power plants to allow us to power an Enteni-style energy screen."

And that sentence made part of what the UPA was getting from the Ra Sector very clear. The Kozun had caused a *lot* of trouble for the UPA, but they'd eventually come around to being allies. Not necessarily *reliable* allies, but allies nonetheless.

The Kenmiri's rogue Vengeance Fleet had seen to that.

The UPA had operated for a long time on a standardized fusion core that, while smaller than the Kenmiri version used by their allies, had a higher power density. The Kozun had been quietly working on improving Kenmiri technology and had implemented an entire new generation of fusion reactors when they'd built their cruisers.

The Enteni, on the other hand, were mobile carnivorous plants that had ended up at war with the Kozun. Their trump card had been breaking the size minimum on energy-screen generators, allowing them to produce both smaller and more refined energy shields for their ships.

Between trade and debris, the UPA now had access to both of those technologies. Combined with their own tech base, they were part of the conversion plan Henry had written up.

"Anyone who has fought against or alongside us knows the gravity shield is a numbers game," Henry noted. "The chance of any given shot getting through is low, but it exists. Now, if a shot burns through, it will hit the energy screen—and an energy screen stops *every* shot until it overloads.

"Combined, the B-series *Cataphract*s and the other new ships are going to be incredibly hard to kill. So, I can say that, yes, I'm *very* pleased with the B-series ships," he concluded.

As the first Commodore to command a squadron of the gravity

maneuvering system destroyers, the specifications and design of the B-series *Cataphract*s had been one of Henry's first tasks at TechDiv.

"Good. Currently, most of them are still at Base Halo, working up. They all have places they're *supposed* to go, but I should be able to reclaim them for the Expeditionary Fleet. You're going to end up with some reaction-drive ships, though."

"Unless we have magically constructed some GMS logistics ships while I wasn't looking, those will be more useful than you think," Henry pointed out. "If the convoy for the Londu and our own logistics is limited to reaction drive and half a KPS-squared, having ships with the same limitations won't hurt us overall."

"Fair. Which brings me to the biggest weight I'm going to hang around your neck, Rear Admiral," Saren told him. "This is sufficiently classified that you are *not* authorized to brief anyone until the Expeditionary Fleet has left UPA space. Certain of your staff officers will be briefed before they arrive on *Raven*, and you will be informed *which* ones, but outside of those designated officers, you will not discuss this with anyone until you are well on your way.

"Do you understand, Admiral?"

Henry nodded slowly. He wasn't aware of anything going on that would require *that* level of secrecy from people in the UPSF—but that only proved the success of the secrecy, he supposed.

"What are we talking about, ser?" he asked.

The windows looking out over Cornwall dimmed to reduce the sunlight, and a holographic image of a ship appeared above the desk between them. Saren's silent commands adjusted the lighting for a few more seconds until the hologram was clear.

Henry recognized the style of ship immediately. She was a *Tvastar*-class fast fleet auxiliary, a reaction-drive transport designed to keep up with battlecruisers and destroyers on long-range operations.

Among other things, that made the *Tvastar*s the only gravity-shielded freighters that Henry knew of.

"I'd be delighted to get a *Tvastar* in the logistics train," he noted. "But I'm guessing there's more going on here."

"If I can manage it, Admiral, you're *only* getting *Tvastar*s in your convoy," Saren told him. "Not least to cover *Sanskrit*'s existence. As you guessed, she's not a munitions collier."

The hologram of the ship slid apart, showing that the interior of the vessel had been heavily refitted, engineering and cargo bays moved around to open up her entire five-hundred-meter length for what looked like nothing so much as a giant antenna—or a gun.

He studied *Sanskrit* for a few moments, considering the ship, her clear new primary purpose, and her name. Named for a dead language...

"That's a subspace communicator," he said softly. "They did it."

"They did it," she confirmed. "Very, very quietly, at the most-classified research facilities and suchlike we own, we have managed to break down some of the key engineering and physics behind the Kenmiri's subspace stabilizers."

The ugly shock that had broken the Great Gathering had been the discovery that what everyone had thought was a natural island of stability in subspace frequencies, a stable band that allowed for instant communication across interstellar distances, had in fact been *artificial*—built and maintained by the Kenmiri.

After turning off the main stabilizers, the Kenmiri had used a smaller system to create localized and time-limited stable zones for FTL communication, but that tech had been well beyond the UPA.

"Other than taking up an entire starship, what are the limitations?" Henry asked.

"Basically, as it was explained to me, we are nowhere near being able to create an omnidirectional stabilizing signal the way the Kenmiri do," she said. "Our system creates a tunnel between two known transceivers.

"It's a one-to-one communication and it doesn't work in FTL. Reestablishing the link after transiting between systems is the second-largest pain of operating the ansible, but it works. You will be able to communicate with Command here."

That had both its advantages and disadvantages, Henry knew. During the war, the subspace network had allowed UPSF command to manage far-reaching operations to the ends of the Kenmiri Empire.

Prior to the war, though, he had seen more than one instance of it being used to *micro*manage operations.

"What is the *largest* pain of operating the ansible?" he asked, picking up on the key point of Saren's description.

"Anyone with an old-style subspace communicator in the same star system can detect it in operation," she told him. "It is not stealthy in the slightest. So, while it is going to be valuable and critical to your operations, you are not to activate the ansible while in a system with any non-UPA vessels at all."

He nodded, grimly considering the impacts of that.

"Lord Kahlmor and his people will be aboard our ships," he noted. "That will keep them from realizing anything odd. Once we make contact with the Londu, that will grow more difficult.

"But the risk is clear. Our alliance with the Londu is valuable, but the Scion may be tempted to decide that restoring FTL communications is *more* valuable."

"Exactly." Saren grimaced. "The other end of *Sanskrit*'s tunnel is a permanent installation in orbit of Ganymede. That will make it possible for *Sanskrit*'s crew to reestablish a link regardless of how long they need to go dark."

Possible didn't mean *easy* or *straightforward*, but he could see the point.

"Any other surprises I should be aware of, ser?" he asked.

"Not yet. But trust me, Admiral, there will be more."

10

LUXEMBOURG FIRES WAS DEFINITELY among the more comfortable ships Sylvia Todorovich had ever traveled aboard. The diplomatic courier was Eridani-built, UPA through and through, but because she didn't have a gravity shield, *Luxembourg Fires'* builders had been able to install Kenmiri-style compensators instead of the UPA's usual system.

That allowed the ship to maintain a full kilometer-per-second squared of acceleration without requiring her crew and passengers to shelter in acceleration tanks. Having spent time in said tanks aboard the battlecruiser *Raven*, Sylvia was delighted to never need them again.

That acceleration easily cut a third off the sublight time needed to travel home from Base Vakarian in the La-Tar System, the main headquarters and forward operating base of RACOM, the Ra Sector Peacekeeper Command.

Officially, Sylvia Todorovich was the UPA Ambassador to the La-Tar Cluster, a five-system polity near the center of the Ra Sector. In practice, she was the senior Diplomatic Corps official in the Ra Sector and the boss of every ambassador in roughly sixty star systems.

It had been a busy two and a half years, during which she'd stolen a grand total of five weeks of time with her boyfriend. Letters and video mail had kept them caught up on each other's lives and work, but if absence made the heart grow fonder, her heart was so fond it *hurt*.

It was a week's travel to the UPA from La-Tar, and more to get to Sol. Her five weeks with Henry Wong had taken over twelve weeks away from her work, and she'd been surprised by how little grief she'd incurred over her annual vacation.

She supposed both the Diplomatic Corps and the UPSF had learned to deal with this kind of situation during the war. Her own relationships back then had almost universally been with men working on the same diplomatic teams.

Henry, on the other hand, had been married for the first ten years of the war—and Sylvia, for all that she had met Henry's ex-husband and could see how things had gone wrong, was absolutely *delighted* that Henry had caught up and now passed his ex-husband's rank.

Commodore Barrie would take his own tour at the Iron Ring soon enough, but he would be at least a year behind his former husband in seniority now.

Sylvia was diplomatic by nature. She had made efforts to reconcile the two men back toward being friends—but for all that, she was unquestionably *Henry's* partisan in any discussion there.

The sharp-featured Russian woman, a native of the Epsilon Eridani colony, chuckled at her own woolgathering as she studied the wet bar in her suite aboard *Luxembourg Fires*. The ship belonged to the Diplomatic Corps, but she was *quite* certain none of their wartime consular ships had been this well equipped.

A chime sounded in her internal network, informing her that a member of the crew was at her door.

"Enter," she ordered.

A middle-aged woman Sylvia knew to be responsible for communications aboard the courier stepped into the living room, nodding respectfully to the Ambassador.

"Em Ambassador, a drone just emerged from the skip line toward Centauri," she reported crisply.

Just, in this case, probably meant around an hour before—*Luxembourg Fires* was still a long way from the second-to-last skip of her journey, and while light was faster than the courier in normal space, it still had to cross the distance. The drone, like the courier ship, would outspeed light between stars but not within a given star system.

"And?" Sylvia prodded.

"As soon as the drone's systems detected *Fires'* diplomatic and identity codes, it sent a high-density burst transmission directly to us," the woman said. "The message is Alpha Security, your eyes only, Em Ambassador."

She held a chip out to Sylvia.

"Thank you, Em Regal," Sylvia told the woman as she took the chip. "Any further information?"

"The drone continued on its way, so I don't think we're expected to provide a response," Regal told her. "But with that security, I imagine it's important."

"So do I," Sylvia murmured. "Carry on, Em Regal. Thank you again."

SYLVIA TODOROVICH HAD VERY little false humility. She knew that she was in the top half dozen diplomatic operatives available to the United Planets Alliance at this point and that her position in the Ra Sector made her the single most important extraterritorial official the UPA had.

She was still surprised when the message from the courier drone turned out to be a holographic recording from Secretary-President Ji-Yeong Ottosen. The short and somewhat chubby Korean-Scandinavian politician looked like they had a busy day—but Sylvia knew Ottosen.

She hadn't worked with Ottosen closely, but she had met the politician and knew people who *had* worked with them. If Ottosen was allowing Sylvia to see any level of fatigue on the Secretary-President's part, it was an intentional piece of manipulation.

"Ambassador Todorovich," Ottosen greeted her. "This message is classified Top Secret Gamma and is not for further distribution. Some background should be attached to this message that is less classified, but I'll give you the high level as it becomes relevant.

"Firstly, I have to apologize. We're canceling your vacation."

Sylvia grimaced. She'd expected as much, but she'd be *damned* if she wasn't going to fight it rather than accepting—unless Ottosen had a damn good reason, at least.

"We've made contact, via some rather roundabout means that you'll find in the general package, with the Londu Sovereignty. They appear to be under attack by an unknown enemy that the UPSF has designated the Enigmas. This enemy is in possession of gravity-shield technology, and the Londu have asked for our assistance."

Sylvia could see how the Londu would come to that conclusion, but she was still surprised. The Londu had made it clear at the Great Gathering that they saw the UPA as a potential challenger to the central position they hoped to hold in the post-Kenmiri age.

On the other hand, she supposed the loss of communications did make that challenge less relevant.

"We are providing that aid. You are one of our few remaining diplomats that speak fluent Londu and are known to them. You are also more than senior enough to serve as Ambassador Plenipotentiary on behalf of the United Planets Alliance, which is what you'll be doing.

"You will be accompanying a UPSF strike fleet under the command of Rear Admiral Wong," Ottosen continued. "We have multiple objectives at play here, and I don't believe I will have the opportunity to brief you in person with sufficient security for this."

That made the cancelation of Sylvia's vacation *slightly* less annoying, she supposed. A large portion of the reason she was coming back to Sol was to spend time with Henry. If he was being deployed, she wasn't going to get that *unless* she went with him.

"First, and the main selling point from the UPSF's perspective, Admiral Wong is being provided with a forward force of gravity-drive warships. This will be the first time we've deployed an all-gravity-drive fleet, and the information from that will be valuable to our military.

"From *my* perspective, that is an ancillary benefit that would be achieved no matter what. I have other concerns and they will rest mostly in your hands, Ambassador Todorovich."

Sylvia paused the message for a moment, leaning back in her chair and grimacing again. She knew her lover. Henry would do everything in whatever power they gave him to protect the Londu; that was his nature.

Ottosen was correct in assuming that if they needed to do something more underhanded, it would fall to her. Henry was *capable* of such things, but his focus would need to be on the actual war they were joining.

She hoped that her instructions wouldn't be anything she had to keep secret from him. Putting that fear aside, she took a moment to pour a glass of wine and double-check the security on her office before unpausing Ottosen.

"Our primary concern in all of this is the Londu," Ottosen told her. "They were always uncomfortable allies, with both of us thinking poorly of each other. But they were allies nonetheless and powerful ones.

"We do not want the Londu to fall, but…" The UPA's head of state paused and considered their words. "It would be to our advantage, I believe, if the Sovereignty were in no position to consider further expansion. It might even be of value to us if they are forced to withdraw from parts of the Isis Sector.

"We also want the Londu to owe us. We need you to build a relationship that will endure, Ambassador, one we can build upon in the time frame after this war, when we hope the costs and damage will render them unable to expand. In a perfect universe, they would come out of this war and that period of necessary calm a changed people, without interest in expansion.

"All we can work toward *right now* is lengthening the period where they must be non-expansionist by necessity and strengthening our relationship with them. My understanding is that with the annexation of the Isis Sector, the Londu now claim over a hundred and twenty inhabited worlds and nearly a thousand star systems. We *must*, one way or another, minimize or remove their threat to us.

"This is not a danger that has a military solution," Ottosen concluded. "We must either weaken them sufficiently that they can never threaten us or bind them to us so strongly that they *will* never."

Sylvia chuckled grimly. She could see Ottosen's logic…but she'd also just spent the last five years doing the latter to *everyone* in the Ra Sector. They'd fought a short-but-nasty war with the Kozun Hierarchy —and even the Kozun Hierarchy was now a useful, if carefully watched, ally.

She'd assess the situation herself and make her own decisions.

"The last piece to this is in some ways the least critical and in others the most," Ottosen told her. "Prior to learning of the Enigmas, the UPA was aware of three other species with gravity-projector technology, the key system underlying the gravity shield.

"The Terzan were close neighbors and allies of the Londu. Something has happened there. We need to know what. The other two are potential sources for the Enigmas, and we need to be *certain* who the Enigmas are.

"One of those species, Ambassador Todorovich, simply has a randomly generated catalog code—X-K-Nine-Five. You will be provided with our intelligence reports on them to allow you to confirm if they are the Enigmas.

"They are the most likely candidate, as they have avoided communication or extended contact, though they are not close to the Londu."

Ottosen shook their head.

"Our greatest concern, however, is that the Enigmas are the Dar," they said flatly. "They are not a race you will know. What little information we possess on the Dar is all classified Top Secret Gamma or above, but they are located on the far side of the Kenmiri Empire from the Londu. If they are harassing the Sovereignty, they appear to have some reason to do so and some way to reach the Londu quickly."

The Secretary-President paused for a few seconds, then shook their head.

"Unfortunately, our limited contact with the Dar suggests that if anyone has developed a superior FTL drive to the Icosaspace Traversal System, it is them. The information on the Dar is attached, secured under a genecode encryption only openable by you.

"If the Enigmas are the Dar, an isolationist power that refused to engage with the Kenmiri and we presumed would stay out of the galaxy's way...they may be more of a problem than we dared consider."

THE INFORMATION on the two classified gravity-shield-equipped races made for sober reading. The UPA didn't know much about species XK95 beyond a rough area where they'd been encountered. UPSF ships and explorers had met seven ships with matching energy signatures and gravity shields in a region about a hundred light-years out from the Geb Sector.

Their Vesheron allies in Geb had also encountered them when they'd looked for allies against the Kenmiri, but they'd had no better luck at making contact with them than the humans.

The Dar, on the other hand, had only had three contacts with the UPSF, all with long-range explorer cruisers. Those ships, basically early war *National*-class battlecruisers with the spinal guns removed in favor of more supplies and fuel, had spent the war mapping the extremes of Kenmiri space and looking for allies outside the Empire's borders.

One of those ships, *Magyarország*, had been the first to encounter the Warded Zone of the Dar. Even watching Lieutenant Colonel Larissa Kaluza's recorded encounter didn't tell Sylvia whether the Warded Zone was the Dar's territory or a buffer zone outside their territory— but given the tone the alien had taken, she suspected the latter.

The Dar had made contact and ordered Kaluza to prove her nonhostile intentions by leaving the system. Given that the single vessel the woman had encountered had been more heavily shielded and accelerated more quickly than *current*-generation UPSF warships —and this had been twelve years ago—Kaluza had obeyed with alacrity.

Her obedience had apparently earned the UPSF some grace on their two later encounters with the Dar. All three followed the same pattern, suggesting that the Dar simply had no interest in dealing with anyone. Attempts to open negotiations had been firmly rebuffed.

On the other hand, the Kenmiri dreadnoughts that had been following the battlecruiser *Caracal* at the last encounter had turned tail and run the moment they would have detected the approaching Dar ship. *Caracal* had attempted to talk to the Dar and been ordered to leave.

The Kenmiri had *fled* at the very sight of the Dar ship. With three sets of data, the UPA had a rough assessment of what the ships in the Warded Zone looked like. Each time, only one vessel had approached the Terran ship, and the ships all appeared to have been of a single class.

A class that matched the mass and size of Kenmiri dreadnoughts with more powerful shields and gravity drives than the UPA could build now.

Ottosen hadn't been kidding. Even isolated and ignoring everyone, the Dar were a concerning group to know existed. If they were behind the Enigmas, things could get very bad very fast—and given that the Londu were on the far side of the Kenmiri Empire from the Warded Zone, a lot of other people would *already* be in trouble.

Sylvia judged the unknowns of XK95 to be more likely to be involved...with a decent chance that the Enigmas were someone completely new.

She also suspected that the Londu, if not necessarily Lord of Fifty Thousand Miles Kahlmor, knew more about what was going on than they'd admitted so far. Finding that out would be her job.

At least she was going to get to share a ship with Henry again. Not only was that *personally* positive, she knew he'd listen to her and vice versa. They made a good team.

The Enigmas were never going to know what hit them.

11

"YOU KNOW, ser, if you'd stopped moving for twelve bloody hours at some point, catching up would have been a *lot* easier."

Henry chuckled as Master Chief Petty Officer Anita Sharma kvetched. His *very* British Keid-born senior NCO had ended up visiting, so far as he could tell, *every* major military installation in the Solar System trying to catch up with him.

"I'm glad you kept your hands on Quaid," he admitted. Chief Steward Arthur Quaid had been his personal steward since he'd first made Commodore. "Palmerston managed to get enough commandos out ahead of herself to make tracking me easier, but even *she* only caught up with us when we got pulled into TechDiv at Ceres."

Henry felt like *he'd* revisited every military installation in Sol he'd been to before in the last few days, but their current locale should be his last stop for the moment. Or second-last stop, he supposed, watching as his personal staff corralled each other across the arrival concourse of Base Halo's main space station.

Commander Adelaide Palmerston had made it clear that *Henry* wasn't doing any such pushing through crowds, even aboard a secure station in a section of Jupiter orbit that was basically a military reservation.

Henry still wasn't entirely clear on how he'd ended up with a Commando Regiment platoon assigned to his personal security, but he wasn't going to *argue* with the extremely intense blonde woman he'd apparently acquired as head of security.

"Strickland is supposed to have quarters sorted out for us," he told Sharma as he saw that worthy get collared by a flag-secretary-seeking missile that took the form of a GroundDiv Commando Petty Officer. "On the other hand, the Lieutenant Commander was supposed to sort out the travel schedules so everyone rendezvoused well before we made it to Base Halo."

The *only* person on his staff he could confide that kind of not-quite-criticism to was Sharma. He'd mention it to *Strickland*, of course, but that would be gentle. The situation had been a mess and a surprise for everyone.

"I've got a bug into the Chiefs' network already," Sharma noted. "Should I double-check we have everything set up?"

"Quietly," Henry ordered. "I can't hold this disorganized mess against anybody except *maybe* the Londu." He chuckled. "But I'd like to be sure I have somewhere to *put* everyone."

He didn't have a single officer or rating from his full command staff yet. The officers and personnel Palmerston's commandos were rounding up were just his *personal* staff, the people he would be expected to take from post to post.

Unlike the command staff he had been warned would be *given* to him, he'd picked Strickland and the junior Ensign following in the flag secretary's trail personally. Strickland had been his third choice, but his first choice was forward-deployed somewhere in the Ra Sector, and his second choice had died in a shuttle accident six months earlier.

He had less to go on with Ophiuchi-born Ensign Alexis Giannino than he did with Strickland, if he was being honest. Strickland had a full, solid record, and he would eventually go from Henry's staff to a destroyer command of his own.

Alexis Giannino, on the other hand, was fourteen weeks out of the Academy. Her one and only recommendation was that her eldest sister, Aruna Giannino, had been the executive officer aboard *Paladin* when Henry's flagship had been beaten to crap saving Anderon.

Aruna Giannino hadn't survived the Stand of the *Cataphracts*. Taking her younger sister under his wing wasn't much of a repayment, but it was something Henry could do.

Giannino, Strickland and Palmerston were his only officers. The commandos were, so far as he could tell, at least a rank senior for their roles in other GroundDiv units, but the Commander was their only officer.

Quaid now had a junior steward under his authority to help keep Henry wrangled, and the officers split a dozen other junior enlisted between them. Sharma was in charge of all of the SpaceDiv enlisted, and even the commandos would think twice about ignoring the Master Chief.

All told, between officers, noncoms, commandos and secretaries, Henry's *personal staff* was fifty people, and he had no idea what he was going to do with them all.

But he trusted that between Strickland and Sharma, they'd have places to rest tonight while they waited for the next step in their journey to arrive.

BASE HALO HAD LOST *some* of its importance as the war had moved out of UPA territory and into Kenmiri space, but it had been the single largest shipyard and logistics facility the UPSF possessed before the war and had never given up that importance.

Base Skyrim in Procyon, the closest full-member system to the Kenmiri Empire, had become the operational center of the war, while Base Mario, on the Moon, remained the administrative center of the entire UPSF.

But while the aggregate capacity of the rest of the UPA's military shipyards had passed Base Halo's capacity, it remained the largest yard and the logical center for organizing new formations.

That meant that there were entire wings set up to handle the staff of Admirals who were assembling their commands but didn't yet have a flagship. Henry stood at the end of the corridor and just stared silently at the doors and the two large lounges he could see from there.

"Just what am I looking at, Master Chief?" he asked Sharma slowly.

"Flag Staff Interim Wing Charlie," she reeled off instantly. "I understand that Base Halo has four of these, each designed to hold an entire fleet-command staff while waiting on a flagship to arrive."

"So...how much space am I looking at here?"

"We won't fill it all, not least because we should have *Raven* to hand before we have all of your staff, but the command staff of a heavy carrier group is designed around a personnel list of eight hundred."

Henry choked and was glad that Sharma was the only one standing with him, as the rest of his staff were looking for their assigned quarters in the maze that apparently belonged to him and his people.

"That seems...a lot."

"Remember that once we're on our way, you will effectively be the head of state and sole authority over fifteen thousand or more people," she said softly. "These wings were originally built to hold seven hundred and fifty people each, but as staffs expanded in the face of a real war, they subdivided some of the junior enlisted and junior officer quarters to add space for another three hundred."

"A thousand people," Henry concluded. "They expect an Admiral to have a staff of a *thousand people*?"

"That would be for a full fleet command anchored on multiple carrier battle groups," she reminded him. "*Raven* doesn't have the space for that many people, anyway."

Henry sighed and grimly chuckled.

"I remember thinking that the flag-deck allocations on the G-mod were excessive," he told her. "Five hundred flag personnel and another two hundred diplomatic. You're telling me that might be *low*?"

Despite his shock at the numbers, he had a pretty decent idea what all of those people would be doing. A *lot* of logistics and administrative reporting, basically. Their job would be to take every scrap of information produced by however many ships he ended up with and refine it down to a level that a single human could comprehend.

The internal network meant they could throw more data at him than at an unaugmented human, but the human mind could only hold so much information.

"Admiral, Master Chief."

Henry turned to see Commander Palmerston approach, the commando officer saluting crisply.

"I've inspected the wing," she reported. "It's well set up from a security perspective, with capacity for independent atmosphere and gravity. There are three accesses, all of which now have guards on them.

"I've made arrangements for us to pick up some regular GroundDiv personnel to augment my commandos for the broader security of the staff."

"Which begs the question, Commander, of just why a commando platoon is anchoring my security," Henry asked mildly. "I've checked, over the last few days. I'm supposed to have GroundDiv security, yes, but they're usually drawn from the regular contingent assigned to the flagship unless I'm expecting to be between commands for a while."

Palmerston eyed him for a moment, as if considering what she could get away with, then shrugged.

"There are certain officers that GroundDiv judges to be extreme high-value assets," she said, frankly. "Colonel Thompson's reports from La-Tar, among other reports from officers you've served with and a general assessment of the course of affairs in the Ra Sector, moved you into that category.

"While that is an informal assessment that stays internal to Ground Division as much as possible, it does result in us making certain that those officers have the security they need to remain assets to the Alliance."

Somehow, Henry didn't think *arguing* with that assessment was going to do him any good, so he just sighed and nodded.

"I see, Commander. So long as you don't get in the way of me doing my *job*, I don't think that will be a problem," he told her.

"If my people get in the way of you doing your job, ser, we are failing to do ours," she replied. "We protect you so you can protect the United Planets Alliance.

"Which does mean, ser, that I need to know if there's any unusual security concerns we're going to have."

Henry considered the situation he was looking at and then nodded very slowly.

"I assume I have a secure office around here somewhere, Master Chief?" he asked Sharma. "If you can get Strickland to join us as well, there are some unfortunate realities of our situation that I will need to fill you all in on.

"I don't *believe* that they are likely to be true security concerns, but I do want to fill you all in."

He suspected he'd end up with a subset of his senior officers acting as an inner staff alongside his main staff as he worked out who he could trust and who would be a problem.

Henry didn't expect to get any outright incompetents, but he didn't like the fact that his staff was being decided on the basis of whose sponsors could do favors to get him ships.

It was just better than not getting those ships.

12

THE FIRST OF his new staff arrived the next day. Palmerston was waiting by the door to Henry's temporary office as he arrived to start going over paperwork.

"Commander," he greeted the commando. "Something up?"

"You have a guest, ser," she told him. "Commodore Emilia Hawthorne, your new operations officer—according to her, anyway. I can't seem to validate that anywhere, so she's waiting in the lounge until someone *does* confirm that."

That felt paranoid to Henry, but he wasn't going to argue, either. Palmerston was responsible for his security and unless she managed to actually get in the way, his plan was to give her complete free rein.

"Let me sit down and check things over," he told the GroundDiv officer. "I expect I'll have Strickland send her in a few minutes regardless, but if Commodore Hawthorne is supposed to be on my staff, I presume I have *something* in my mail."

His bodyguard chuckled and unlocked his office door with a chuckle.

"So, I should have someone fill Cornell in?" she asked innocently.

"He is my secretary and supposed to be responsible for my schedule," Henry pointed out. "Work with him, Commander. Or you start to walk close to the precipice of causing trouble; am I clear?"

"As crystal, Admiral. I'll let the Lieutenant Commander know the Commodore is waiting on your word, ser."

Henry managed not to shake his head as he entered the office put aside for him. Given that it was a temporary space in a glorified hotel, he had to feel that the secure space was *somewhat* excessive. A large chunk of the room was simply empty space, as there were only a desk and a half dozen chairs in there.

The desk and chairs looked like they'd probably belonged to a senior officer in the Unification Wars. They were high-quality pieces and the chairs had decent automatic adjustments, but they were *old*. Probably antiques, though most likely they were there because they'd been installed when Base Halo was *built*.

Hundred-year-old military bases tended to have things like that floating around, he figured.

He'd realized yesterday that the entire back wall was one massive screen that woke at his mental command as he took his seat at the desk. A view of Base Halo appeared around him, the dozen or so space stations dominating his view. The spacecraft, even the carrier *Crichton*, were barely more than lights, but there were a lot of those lights.

Past the space stations and defensive forts, he could see Ganymede —and at that moment, Base Halo was on the right side of the moon for him to be able to see Jupiter behind her, filling the background of the screen.

The view distracted him for a few seconds before he dove into his messages—which probably worked out in his and Commodore Hawthorne's favor, he realized when he saw the timestamp on her orders.

Henry's new operations officer had arrived at their temporary base at least twenty minutes before *he'd* received the confirmation she was coming. That was *probably* a good sign.

He hoped.

"Strickland, did Palmerston tell you about our guest?" he commed his secretary.

"Yes, ser," the other man replied. "Quaid is on his way to your office with breakfast, tea and coffee. Should I bring the Commodore in, or is this back to being a Palmerston problem?"

Strickland seemed to have a better sense of what the GroundDiv officer was responsible for than vice versa, Henry noted. Of course, part of that was the fact that he figured Palmerston saw Strickland as a pure paper-pusher.

Henry, on the other hand, had seen Strickland's record before he'd taken the man onto his staff. The man's last tour of duty had been in administration on Earth, yes—because he'd been undergoing treatment for PTSD incurred flying shuttles in disaster relief at one of the UPA's minor colonies.

"She's legit, Lieutenant Commander," Henry told his secretary. "Send her on in."

Leaving that in his people's capable hands, he turned his attention back to the orders and found the addendum he was half-expecting. An encrypted text file, marked with the personal code of Admiral Antonia Blake, the head of the UPSF PersDiv.

His own codes decrypted the short text message.

Hawthorne is good but greener than her rank suggests. She's never left the UPA because her father kept finding strings to pull. But if she wants her *chance at the Iron Ring, she needs combat experience, and her father appears to have decided her star was more important than keeping her safe.*

And since Admiral Hawthorne-Abatantuono was supposed to get a Lexington-G *carrier for the Keid defense fleet, tit-for-tat gets* you *a carrier.*

None of this is in the orders and you never saw it. Good luck.

The note was unsigned and Henry chuckled. There were a *lot* of things he'd tolerate to get one of the handful of GMS carriers that existed. The refitted *Lexington*s had been reclassified as "light carriers," but they'd been *built* as fleet carriers.

And their ten squadrons might not be a *Crichton*'s fifteen squadrons, but no one who collided with eighty gravity-drive- and gravity-shield-equipped starfighters was going to really notice the difference!

⁂

THE STAR SYSTEM OF KEID—KNOWN for a while as 40 Eridani—had been colonized by the African Union. A vast quantity of both British and Chinese money and expertise had been involved in the process, though, as both nations did everything to maintain influence beyond their own borders—and that meant there were significant enclaves on Keid that saw themselves as both citizens of Keid and British.

Commodore Emilia Hawthorne was, he suspected, typical of the people from those enclaves. She had the midnight-black coloring of a woman of East African descent despite her extraordinarily British name and wore her UPSF uniform like a second skin as she came to attention in front of his desk and saluted.

"Reporting for duty, Rear Admiral," she said precisely, presenting him with an envelope that contained a standard data chip. Presumably, her orders.

"Our copy of your orders arrived after you did," Henry told her softly. "Hence the confusion with Commander Palmerston. I haven't had a chance to review your record in detail, Commodore, so why don't you fill me in on your most recent posting, if nothing else?"

"Of course, ser."

She remained standing while she marshaled her thoughts and Henry concealed a somewhat-exasperated smile.

"Sit down first, Commodore," he instructed.

"Of course, ser. Thank you, ser."

He let the excess formality slide for the moment as he waited for her to give him some idea of what he'd just inherited.

"My last posting was as the liaison and training officer to the Procyon System Fleet," she told him. "It is critical to the UPSF's emergency plans that the various national and system fleets maintain shared training and operational standards with us. The PSF is more aligned with us than most, as it needed to be almost completely rebuilt after the Battle of Procyon in the Red Wings Campaign."

Henry touched his red-centered pilot's wings without even thinking. The Procyon System Fleet and the remaining carrier-cruisers of the prewar UPSF had known they had reinforcements coming. They *hadn't* known, with any certainty, that the people of Sandoval—Procyon's inhabited planet—would be safe if they left the planet to the Kenmiri.

So, they'd fought. Enough of the UPSF had survived to form a kernel of the fleet that had taken the war to the Kenmiri—not least because the PSF had intentionally prioritized the survival of the UPSF's FTL-capable ships over their guardships.

Not one mobile unit of the Procyon System Fleet had survived that battle. Being the liaison officer for that force would have been easy in some ways—and, hopefully, eye-opening in others.

"So, you're used to working with non-UPSF military personnel," he observed. "That may come in handy once we reach Londu space. Do you speak Kem, Commodore?"

"I do, ser, but I have very little practical experience using it," she said, surprising him. He'd expected that an officer who had never entered Kenmiri space wouldn't have learned the Kenmiri trade language.

"I don't know how many Kem-speaking Londu officers we'll have to interact with once we reach the Sovereignty," he warned her. "On the other hand, I believe the only *Londu*-speaking personnel we're going to have will be from the diplomatic corps."

He knew Sylvia spoke the Londu language and hoped that she'd scrounge up a few more.

"Do we expect to need to coordinate with them on an operations level, ser?" Hawthorne asked, sounding concerned. "My impression is that the units of the Expeditionary Fleet will be far superior to anything the Londu possess."

He smiled thinly.

"Quantity has a quality all its own, Commodore," he told her. "In more ways than one. The average Londu battleship masses four million tons. I am currently expecting to have *one* battlecruiser, *Raven*, which masses a touch over *two* million tons.

"We do not know the full strength of the Blades of the Scion, but my understanding is that it's on the order of fifty battleships," he concluded. "*Raven* may be able to outmaneuver, outshoot, and outfight any single battleship in their ranks, but we couldn't fight them all.

"We are best served working in conjunction with them, something you *will* be responsible for as my operations officer. Is that going to be a problem, Commodore?"

"No, ser!" she replied instantly. "Just…outside my experience, ser. I am familiar with battleships, though not the Londu version, and the *Beethoven* class left…"

"…much to be desired," Henry concluded for her. He had her record up in his network now. Hawthorne had served in the Battleship Squadron for the entire nine years of the formation's existence. She'd been a newly graduated ensign when *Beethoven*, *Mozart*, *Chopin* and *Tchaikovsky* had been commissioned to form the "steel wall" to protect the UPSF's rear.

But given that the *Beethoven* class had been *carrier* hulls with first salvaged and then reproduced Kenmiri plasma cannon attached, they had been absolutely terrible at being, well, anything. They'd commissioned four years into the war and been *decommissioned* well before it had finished.

And, like Commodore Hawthorne herself, they'd never entered Kenmiri space.

"I never served aboard the *Beethoven*s," he admitted. "Even while they existed, I was a battlecruiser officer."

"I rose to tactical officer aboard *Mozart* before they were stood down, ser. After that, I served aboard *Crichton* until taking command of the destroyer *Hadrosaur*."

He nodded and gave the woman a level look.

"You have spent your entire career in home-defense formations, Commodore," he said quietly. "First the Battleship Squadron, then the Home Fleet, then liaison with the Procyon System Fleet. The lack of forward operations experience isn't unusual, but it does make you seem an odd fit for this particular role.

"We're going a long damn way from UPA space, Hawthorne. It's a ninety-four-day journey, if everything goes *right*, for us to reach the Londu home system. You understand, I hope, why I feel the need to be certain you are up for this?"

"Permission to speak bluntly, ser?" Hawthorne said after a few moments, her eyes dark and focused somewhere well past Henry's shoulder.

"If this is to work, you will be my eyes, ears and hands through much of the Expeditionary Fleet, Commodore," Henry told her. "Free and blunt communication will be critical. Permission to speak freely granted."

She swallowed, still focused on the screen behind him.

"I *know*, ser, that I was supposed to be transferred from *Mozart* to the carrier *Saratoga* when she commissioned," Hawthorne said quietly. "Something happened. I *know* that *Hadrosaur* was supposed to be attached to a forward task force, one that was eventually in the heart of Golden Lancelot.

"While I can't bring myself to regret missing Lancelot, I *was* supposed to command a destroyer in offensive operations. That didn't happen. I volunteered for the Peacekeeper Initiative, only to find myself picked for the Procyon System Fleet liaison role.

"I am aware of the fact that I have an overprotective father who is uninterested in allowing me to escape his shadow," she concluded. "I should have called him out on it, but, well…I didn't. I *did* convince him that I needed this role to make Rear Admiral.

"I am aware of the weaknesses in my experience, ser, but I am entirely familiar with our doctrine, our informal networks, our computer systems and every other aspect of the job in front of me.

"I can do the job, ser. I *need* to do the job. If that's not enough for you, I will request a transfer to another posting."

Henry studied the woman. Her father's influence had done more than shelter her from the war. It had clearly accelerated her promotions, too. She'd joined the UPSF ten years after he had and made Commodore at the same time as him.

He had a stack of medals the height of his arm explaining his promotions. She didn't.

"I suppose your honesty deserves equal frankness from me," he finally said. "There are limited resources available to the UPSF still. To pull together the Expeditionary Fleet, we are robbing Peter to arm Paul.

"So, a lot of quiet deals are going on to reduce the complaints about that. If I *don't* take you as my operations officer, I am led to understand your father will raise complaints about us claiming the carrier he was supposed to receive."

He smiled thinly.

"I need that carrier, Commodore Hawthorne. So, I hope you can do the job. I'm going to make sure you have some of the best assistants I can scrounge up, but at the end of the day, *you* will be the Expeditionary Fleet's ops officer.

"If you think you can manage it, I'll give you the chance."

"Thank you, ser. I promise you will not be disappointed."

Henry wasn't so sure—but he would talk to Sharma about sourcing the right kind of operations staff. If he was lucky, he'd be able to find an officer to stand behind Hawthorne and fill in her weak points.

Or, in the worst case, *replace* her once they were on their way.

13

HENRY FIGURED he owed Admiral Antonia Blake something expensive but subtle. He'd talk to Sylvia about what would fit—there were limits to what could be gifted between flag officers without raising the kinds of questions he didn't want to deal with.

Apparently "ships" and "important staff postings" didn't fall outside those limits, which was a sobering experience, but considering his tentative order of battle, Henry was prepared to live with it.

Each of his senior staff officers had arrived with a short text note attached to their orders. Blake had been surprisingly frank about the deals that had been made to make the Expeditionary Fleet worthy of the name—and of the potential weaknesses of the officers Henry had received.

In the back of his mind and a very locked-down file in his internal headware, Henry was beginning to assemble plans for if and when those weaknesses bit him in the ass. Even with the ansible on *Sanskrit*, he would have basically a completely free hand once he'd passed the borders of the UPA.

He'd give his shiny collection of politically connected officers a chance to prove that they could do their jobs. Every one of them had served during the war, after all, and even formations that had never left the UPA had seen the winnowing process of war clear away the incompetent.

There was one officer, though, that he would never be able to replace and *needed* to work with. As a shuttle carried him, Sharma and Palmerston—who came with half a dozen commandos—toward *Raven,* he focused his mind on the first impression that was going to make or break the Expeditionary Fleet.

Raven herself was a familiar presence and shape, though the battle-cruiser approaching Base Halo looked far different from the one he'd commanded. The refit to the G-mod had started with rebuilding much of her existing hull and removing most of her fusion engines, but it hadn't *stopped* there.

The entire top section of armor and hull had been removed and an additional five decks installed, increasing her height and volume by fifty percent. A portion of her fusion engines had been reconfigured to serve as an immense two-gigawatt fusion reactor—and then her orig-inal four quarter-gigawatt plants had been replaced with two of the new one-gigawatt fusion cores.

Much of the four-fold increase in her power generation went into maintaining the gravity projectors that managed the increased power of her gravity shield and the gravity maneuvering system itself. Enough was left that they'd added a second pair of lasers and upgraded the grav-driver to fire its projectiles at ten percent of light-speed instead of seven.

The extra eight missile launchers, four in each wing, were almost an afterthought in the increase to the battlecruiser's firepower. The Enteni energy screen wrapped around the core hull was equally minor, in some ways, though it was also classified to the level where there were people aboard *Raven* who didn't know it was there.

Henry had seen *Raven* during her refits and helped finalize the design. He knew the newest version of his ship backward and forward.

The concern was her captain, his new flag captain.

His Lordship, Colonel Artair Campbell, Marquess of Lorne and heir to the Duchy of Argyll, *had* been captain of UPSV *Renown. Renown* was one of the ships on the UPSF's List of Honor, ships from before the

UPA's existence whose names were kept in commission and often had additional traditions.

Tradition said that *Renown*, named for the flagship of the Royal Navy Extrasolar Squadron when they'd covered the retreat of the couriers from Tau Ceti, was commanded by a British officer.

The UPSF couldn't have found anyone *more* British, Henry supposed, than an active member of one of the few remaining peerages. But when *Renown* had been stood down for her own refit into a *Corvid*-G, they'd needed a post worthy of one of their most decorated and politically influential battlecruiser captains—and once they'd moved him, he clearly wasn't *leaving*.

Campbell had earned most of his decorations *in* Operation Golden Lancelot, where the then-Commander had taken command of a badly damaged destroyer and used her gravity shield to protect an equally damaged Vesheron battleship, allowing the battleship to land the killing blow on the dreadnought coming after both of them.

Given that the dreadnought in question had been the last escort for the fleeing Kenmorad creche ship, Campbell had, like Henry, directly contributed to the slow genocide the Kenmiri now faced.

Maybe that would be enough common ground. Henry wasn't sure —but he suspected there wasn't much *else* the Chinese-American son of a Montana rancher was going to find in common with a Scottish Marquess!

It wasn't getting any less weird for Henry to hear that and realize the bosun was talking about him. At least he *knew Raven*'s shuttle bay, even if it had been cleaned up, refitted—and duplicated in the place of one of the old fusion engines, at the stern of the battlecruiser's inverted-canoe-shaped central hull.

An honor guard of GroundDiv troopers greeted him, snapping to attention as his commando escorts led the way out of the shuttle and onto his old ship. A small group of officers was waiting for him on the other side of the honor guard, but the mix of familiarity and strangeness occupied his attention for a few critical moments.

Raven looked the same, but she even smelled different now. This shuttle bay had probably seen the fewest changes and modifications, but it was clear that the life-support plant had been completely replaced. The ship *smelled* new, not refitted.

Henry pulled his attention back to the officers, focusing on what he *knew* would be the most critical first impression of this mission—and then concealing a surprised blink as a hoverchair led the three other officers toward him.

The occupant of the hoverchair had just as much of the sharp dark-haired aristocratic features as the file photo had led Henry to expect, but he had *not* expected Colonel Campbell to be missing both legs.

The Scottish officer's left leg ended just above the knee and his right ended just below the knee, and his uniform had been custom-tailored to make the sharp line across the two limbs very clear.

Henry returned Campbell's salute without missing a beat, smiling beatifically as he realized *Raven*'s Captain was *very* much judging him based on his reaction to the chair.

"Welcome back aboard *Raven*, Rear Admiral Wong," Campbell said cheerfully, his voice a pleasant deep baritone. "I know she's not what you remember, but I do believe we will live up to your expectations regardless."

"I am sure you will," Henry agreed. "*Raven* earned quite a reputation before her refit. While I understand the crew has almost entirely transferred away, I have faith in her ability to inspire her current people."

"She can do that, yes," Campbell agreed. "My senior officers, Admiral. Lieutenant Colonel Normand Vanev, my executive officer. Commander Hong Mi, my chief engineer. Commander Vazgen Bedrosian, my Commander, Air Group."

The two men, Vanev and Bedrosian, both had the darkly Slavic coloring and hawkish features of Eastern Europeans—though Vanev was from Procyon and Bedrosian was from Altair. Hong was a gawkily tall woman with the coloring and eyes of her Chinese family name but the build of someone born in Sol's asteroid colonies.

Those colonies had gravity generators *now*, but they'd spent long enough without them to shape a new ethnotype.

"I look forward to getting a chance to get to know all of you better," Henry said. "We've got a lot of work to do, and I'm going to have a lot of people coming aboard *Raven* to help do it, but *Raven* is going to be at the heart of everything we do as the Expeditionary Fleet moves out. You will be our single most powerful warship and the best demonstration of the might of the United Planets Alliance.

"I have full faith in *Raven*'s ability to meet that duty head-on and in your ability to get her and her crew to do so," he finished.

"Would you like the tour, ser, or should I have someone direct you to your quarters?" Campbell asked.

"The tour, I think," Henry said with a smile. "All of my things are on a different shuttle with my steward. Chief Quaid will manage all of that for me while I get reacquainted with the old girl."

And acquainted, he hoped, with *Raven*'s new captain.

PALMERSTON AND SHARMA stuck with Henry as Campbell showed them through the key sections of the battlecruiser. So much of his old ship had changed or was just gone, either to battle damage or replacements, that she barely felt like the same vessel at all until Campbell led him into the Captain's office.

That was the same, even down to the solidly built standard-issue desk. Only two decorations remained, but those hadn't been Henry's in the first place: the matched set of flags, one the V of eight gold stars on a blue field of the United Planets Alliance itself, the other the eight gold stars flanking a stylized rocket of the United Planets Space Force; and the golden commissioning seal of *Raven* herself, a side view of a raven in flight holding a quill pen above the simple letters *BC-061*.

The main addition Henry noted was a pair of flattened, though still three-dimensional, models of *Raven* herself in both her original and refitted configurations mounted on one wall. The ship was built to a relatively standard pattern for the UPSF, with the core hull taking the shape of an inverted canoe and her wings extending from about halfway down her length to her full width at the stern.

The obvious difference between the iterations of *Raven* was the size, with the *Corvid*-G being half again as tall as the original. The only slightly less-obvious difference was that the original *Raven* had massive fusion engines and the refitted *Raven* had only a few concealed thrusters for emergency maneuvering.

Turning away from the models, Henry saw that Campbell had done away with the chair behind the desk, simply driving his hoverchair into place and smiling evenly at his new commander.

"I am surprised your guards didn't insist on searching the room before waiting outside," Campbell observed. "The protection of our Admirals is important, after all. I would not have been offended."

"Knowing Palmerston, I suspect that my escorts have scanners concealed in their gear that allowed them to check the room without entering," Henry said with a chuckle. A silent command summoned a rolling chair from a hidden cupboard, allowing him to sit across from Campbell.

"You've been taking good care of my ship, I see," he continued with a wry smile. "She's been back on active duty for a year, right?"

"Thirteen months," Campbell confirmed. "We basically transferred *Renown*'s entire crew over, which means, uh...you know about the corgis, yes?"

Henry blinked at the non sequitur, then remembered one of the *furrier* traditions of the British named ships on the List of Honor.

"You brought the Colonels?" he asked. Tradition put four corgi dogs, theoretically trained as vermin-catchers but he had his suspicions, aboard both the battlecruiser *Renown* and the carrier *Ark Royal*. And tradition also gave all eight of those dogs the rank of Colonel, with the puppies holding the courtesy rank of Major when they were being trained.

Given that Major wasn't even a *rank* in the UPSF, the confusion was probably understandable.

"Unfortunately, Colonel Arkansas passed away six months ago," Campbell told him. "But we have Colonels Wichita, Windsor and

France; along with France's puppies, Major Tom, Major Washington and Major Colombia."

Henry shook his head, but he was smiling.

"I see. I certainly don't need to argue with such a concentration of rank into such small packages," he told *Raven*'s Captain. "Shouldn't they have transferred back to *Renown* once she completed her refit?"

"Theoretically. *Raven* isn't one of our traditional ships, after all. The Chiefs surprised me with a petition to keep them, though, so we did."

Henry chuckled and leaned back in his chair, studying his new flag captain. He hadn't expected the hoverchair, but it certainly seemed to bring the other man up to the mobility he'd need.

"You were surprised to see the chair," Campbell observed after a few moments of surprisingly comfortable silence. "The full explanation is in my files, of course."

"I make a point, Captain, of not reading the medical section of my subordinates' files," Henry said quietly. That was how his mentors had trained him and how he'd trained his people. There was a summary in any officer's file that would flag recent or critical medical information, and otherwise, he felt that people deserved their privacy.

He was a touch surprised that Colonel Campbell *not having legs* hadn't made it into the summary, but he admitted that it didn't seem to affect the man's work.

"Fair enough," Campbell conceded. "Long and short of it: *Valiant* took another round of hits after the initial mess that delivered a job lot of medals to her crew. I was in secondary control, trying to keep us together after the fire I'd intentionally flown us into to protect *Sand and Glory*."

He shrugged.

"Laser burnthrough put a four-meter-wide hole on one side of the ship and a two-meter-wide exit wound on the other side. Went clean through secondary control and took the bottom halves of my legs along the way.

"*Valiant* was a wreck and the Shoya pulled us off." He chuckled. "For some reason, the crew of *Sand and Glory*—the Shoya battleship that we saved and who put the killing blow in on the last dreadnought that day—felt like they owed us something.

"But as it turns out, aristocratic inbreeding has some...*interesting* side effects."

Henry controlled his features to avoid challenging or even openly acknowledging that description of Campbell's family history.

"How so?" he finally asked.

"My nerves don't regrow the way they're supposed to," Campbell said bluntly. "So, we can't integrate them properly with macro-scale cybernetics, and if I went through regen to grow new legs, they'd be useless lumps of flesh that couldn't talk to my brain."

He gave a one-handed shrug.

"I have a pair of prosthetic legs that lock on to the stumps and are controlled from my internal network, but, frankly, they're damn uncomfortable and I'm *more* mobile in the chair most of the time."

"You earned your Colonelship and command of *Renown* while in that chair, Colonel," Henry noted slowly. "So, if you expect me to think it's a problem, I feel that you're expecting me to be *damn* stupid."

"I would agree with you, ser, but you never know what to expect in my experience," Campbell said. "I know I'm perhaps not who you might choose as your flag captain, but I assure you that I have every intention of making sure this mission goes as well as it can."

Henry smiled evenly.

"As it turns out, Captain, I actually *have* the officer who I would have chosen as my flag captain, if not here," he murmured. "Both of the men I would have considered for the role, in fact. Commodore Tatanka Iyotake will command the Expeditionary Fleet's Task Group Two, while Colonel Okafor Ihejirika will serve as his flag captain aboard *Urraca*."

Iyotake and Ihejirika had both served as Henry's executive officer aboard *Raven* and would have been his first and second choice, respectively, to be his flag captain. He could live with Iyotake as the second-in-command of the Expeditionary Fleet and Ihejirika as the junior of his two battlecruiser captains, though.

"I've reviewed both their records aboard this ship," Campbell said. "I can't think of better men to serve alongside. *Urraca* is unrefitted, correct?"

"That's correct. She's one of the last *Corvids* completed after the end of the war, BC-Eighty-Two. The entirety of Task Group Two will be reaction-drive ships, Captain, as will the convoy they're escorting."

"Do we know what everything is going to look like at this point, ser?" Campbell asked.

"I have a pretty good idea but I'm waiting for a handful of final confirmations," Henry told him. "I plan on briefing my senior staff in the morning, once everyone is aboard. If you can attend that briefing, I can avoid going over the same information twice or giving you information that might be obsolete by tomorrow."

"Understood." Campbell paused. "Do you know how long until our diplomatic contingent arrives, ser?"

"Ambassador Todorovich should be arriving in Sol in the next hour or so," Henry said. "She'll be coming directly aboard and will be part of that briefing in the morning. My understanding is that she will have a new staff, as her usual people are all in the Ra Sector, but her staff should start coming aboard tomorrow.

"*Urraca* will be joining us in our orbit by morning as well, and both Commodore Iyotake and Colonel Ihejirika should be aboard for the briefing."

"I'll make sure the stewards are aware, in case your people aren't sufficiently settled and need assistance," Campbell promised. "Speaking of the Ambassador, do we need to arrange quarters for her or…"

Even Henry's iron control of his features faltered in surprise. Apparently, his relationships were common enough knowledge these days that no one was even *trying* to be subtle—though he supposed Campbell really did have a need to know.

"We'll want to confirm that with her," he said carefully, "but my understanding is that she will be sharing my quarters, yes."

14

SYLVIA TODOROVICH WOULD, if pressed, admit that she had no real attachment to humanity's home world. She'd been born on the Novaya Imperiya colony of Tsar in Epsilon Eridani and had grown up on the rolling fertile plains that had led her ancestors to think they could build a new, better Russian Empire.

Said ancestors had been *idiots*, but comparing the resources of Tsar and the Epsilon Eridani System to the resources of Russia on Earth, she could see where they'd been coming from. She'd visited Russia. She'd been very cold.

Her home area of Tsar more resembled the prairie breadbaskets of the modern United States than anywhere in Russia. In some ways, she'd been more comfortable on Henry's Montana family ranch than in Russia.

Still. The Solar System had a deep and enduring hold on all of humanity. There was always a sense of homecoming, even for someone like her who'd been in her twenties before she'd ever seen Sol itself.

Even from *Luxembourg Fires'* current position just outside of Jupiter's orbit, the light of the Sun felt vaguely *right* in a way no other star did. Whatever shared genetic seed had pushed the Ashall races to their similarities hadn't taken away from the fact that humanity had evolved under this sun, this light.

"We've received updated orders from Jovian Control," the courier captain, Camille Fournier, informed her. "*Fires* is to deliver you to Ganymede Orbital Facility D-Nine-Seven-F."

They shook their head, arching a perfectly groomed eyebrow at Sylvia.

"Everything *looks* legit, but I'm wondering if you want to double-check the authentication codes," they suggested. "I'm a touch uncomfortable delivering you to a station that only has a *serial number*."

"That's fair, Captain," Sylvia assured them. "Let me check."

She picked up the message that *Fires* had received and ran it through the authentication systems in her internal network. The message might have been *sent* from Jovian Control, the massive organization that handled *all* traffic in the Jupiter planetary system, but the codes attached to it were quite clear.

The message had *come* from Diplomatic Corps HQ on Earth. All the codes were correct.

On the other hand, she'd been supposed to head directly to *Raven* and had been looking forward to it.

"Everything looks correct, Captain," she told Fournier. "Please have someone advise *Raven* that I will be delayed. It appears that the station will be responsible for my transfer to the UPSF flagship."

"Yes, Ambassador," Fournier confirmed. "Forgive me, but do you have any idea what this station is?"

Sylvia smiled thinly.

"At a guess, Captain, *classified*."

GANYMEDE ORBITAL FACILITY D97F resembled nothing so much as a giant balloon. A small square station on the exterior provided docking for the courier ship, but the rest of the facility was concealed inside a massive plastic sphere, almost four kilometers across and covered in heat radiators.

That suggested three things to Sylvia: that the place was generating a *lot* of power, that the heat was being distributed to conceal where the generators were, and that D97F *really* didn't want anyone to see what was going on inside it.

Bubbles like that weren't *unusual*, per se, but they weren't all that common, either. Somewhere busier, it might have drawn attention—it might have even drawn more attention if it was in the military reservation around Base Halo.

Here, it was one of two such structures, the other belonging to a hydroponics producer, according to her quick datasearch.

She was the only person allowed off *Luxembourg Fires*, and she entered an initially empty receiving area from the courier's personnel tube. Someone, Sylvia suspected, was being highly paranoid.

Her internal network warned her that she was being scanned and that the network itself had been pinged for challenge-response codes to confirm her identity. She waited patiently for the process to finish, then strode toward the door at the far end of the receiving area.

It slid open before she reached it, allowing a white-haired gentleman in a tailored suit that matched his hair to enter.

"Ambassador Todorovich, welcome to the Call Center."

"And you are?" she asked delicately.

"Antton Feliciano, Director of Operations for D-Ninety-Seven-F," he introduced himself, bowing. "Since we've confirmed your identity, you should know that this is also the UPA Sol Interstellar Communications Facility."

"Also known as *the Call Center*," she guessed, echoing his original nomenclature. "Just what I have walked aboard, Director?"

"Most of even the high level of the SICF remains extremely classified," Feliciano told her, gesturing for her to follow him as he turned and walked deeper into the station. "Given the mission you've taken on, however, you've been fully cleared for SICF operations, and someone on Earth decided to take advantage of that."

It would take well over an hour to exchange a message back and forth with someone on Earth. To accelerate that, though, would require...

"This is a subspace communications station?" Sylvia asked.

Feliciano held a finger to his lips in a *quiet* gesture, then stepped through a door and made a grand wave encompassing the observation deck beyond.

She walked past him and studied the interior of the SICF. The station they were on was a bit more substantial than she'd expected from the outside, but it was still tiny in comparison to the four-kilometer-wide sphere it provided access to.

Inside the sphere, she could see half a dozen structures, all identical. The scale suggested that each was huge in its own right, but gantries and connectors bound all of them together.

"What am I looking at, Director?" she finally asked.

"Subspace quantum-tunnel generators," he told her, then chuckled at her annoyed—and somewhat-blank, she knew—look in response.

"We call them *ansibles*," Feliciano explained. "We're nowhere near up to creating regional stable bands of subspace. Hell, our last attempt to duplicate the communicator Rear Admiral Wong brought back from Ra *blew up*."

Sylvia grimaced. The Kenmiri Artisans, their scientist and engineering caste, had developed a new form of their subspace communicators after the war. It temporarily stabilized a section of subspace to allow for an omnidirectional communications pulse with a limited range.

Compared to the vast geographical expanse of stabilized frequencies that had underpinned communications before the Kenmiri's Fall, it was an inefficient tool—but it was a hell of a lot more than any of the Kenmiri's former slaves and enemies possessed.

"So, what did you do?" she asked.

"Prior to our discovering what we now know to be an artificial island of stable frequencies in subspace, a lot of our FTL communications research had been focused on quantum entanglement," he told her. "So far as anyone can tell, it's not faster than light in normal space, though there are enough edge cases that people keep prodding it.

"But one set of experiments conducted before Unification was on putting entangled particles into subspace. Even at the time, it was just a curiosity," he noted. "The amount of energy necessary to do *anything* with subspace is ridiculous. But it turned out that if you can transfer both halves of a quantum-entangled pair into subspace, their connection *there* is instantaneous.

"To actually get enough entangled particles into subspace to create useful bandwidth is…" He trailed off, considering his words carefully. "Impractical," he concluded. "It would require most of the power output of a mid-sized star, basically.

"But putting a few *dozen* particles into subspace is doable and maintainable. About two and a half years ago, we tested using that as a beacon to allow for a focused subspace stabilization system."

"And it worked?" she asked.

"It worked. It's not…amazing, by any stretch of the imagination." He gestured out the window. "Each of those tunnel generators has *one* counterpart. Just one. We currently have six locations that can talk to this facility. Three are mobile, one is concealed in Base Mario, one is in Alpha Centauri and one is en route to be installed at Base Fallout in the Zion System."

The Zion System was the closest UPA-occupied system to the Kenmiri Empire. That was changing, as other systems were surveyed and flagged for what Sylvia suspected would be a colonization boom now that the area was safe, but the Zion System still served as their outer frontier and tripwire watch post.

"And I take it I have a scheduled call with the one on the Moon?" Sylvia asked.

"You do, Ambassador. One of the other ansibles is being sent with the Expeditionary Fleet," he noted. "You won't be quite back to where we were before, but you'll be able to phone home."

"That's more than I expected to have, Director," she admitted. "Thank you."

"If you'll come this way, we have about ten minutes to get you situated and grab you a coffee before your meeting."

THE ROOM SYLVIA was ushered into was as basic as she'd expected. It had a chair, a holoprojection suite and a table for her to put her coffee on. That was it, and all of the furniture was the mass-produced standard issue from the UPSF.

Still, the equipment *worked* and silently came to life with a holographic image of Dr. Shouhei Matsumura, the Foreign Secretary of the United Planets Alliance and Sylvia's ultimate boss. The Japanese man eyed her calmly with black eyes and then slowly smiled.

"It is a strange feeling to be able to speak in real time at vast distances once more," he murmured. "Your journey treated you well, I hope, Em Todorovich."

"*Luxembourg Fires* is honestly excessive for my needs, Dr. Matsumura," Sylvia told him. Matsumura, at her last count, held three PhDs he'd earned the hard way and seven more honorary ones he'd been granted during his long, *long* career in diplomacy and politics.

"I understand that *Raven* should be more what you're used to, working with the military as you have," he said. "And will have other benefits, I'm told."

"My relationship with Rear Admiral Wong is no real secret," Sylvia said calmly. "I presume it is part of why we were selected for this mission."

"Truthfully, it makes for a pleasant bonus for the two of you, but there are no other choices as optimal for the roles you have been assigned," her boss told her. "You are the most senior diplomat left of the original delegation to the Scion. You have *met* him and you speak the language."

"I'm rusty, but I've been taking refreshers since I got the update," she confessed. "I understand that we have a Londu detachment we will be taking back to the Sovereignty with us."

"Yes. You have, I understand, been briefed on the complications by the Secretary-President."

"I have." Sylvia didn't overly like them, but she understood where the need to either neutralize the Londu Sovereignty or secure its allegiance came from. "We don't know enough about what we're walking into, in my opinion. Kahlmor is out of date on the events in his home stars.

"We'll have our work cut out for us."

"I have the utmost faith in your ability to manage the situation,"

Matsumura told her. "Your warrants, papers and so forth should be waiting for you aboard *Raven*. I wanted this chance to speak to you in person, or as close as we can manage, before sending you off to the great beyond.

"If you have any concerns or questions, now is the time."

"How much are we going to be able to use this ansible system?" she asked.

The old man shook his head.

"As it was explained to me, anyone with a subspace transceiver can detect its use," he warned. "Intercepting the communication is supposedly impossible, but we also cannot afford for the Londu to realize we are once again in possession of FTL communication technology.

"While the ansible ship *Sanskrit* will accompany you, Admiral Wong has strict orders that the tunnel is not to be established while there are any Londu vessels in the same star system. That will be a major limitation on your ability to call home."

"Without both ends of the tunnel, wouldn't the ansible be useless to them?" Sylvia asked.

"I have no idea," her boss said bluntly. "And neither would they until it was far too late. We do not wish to add additional complications to a relationship we already know is going to be fraught.

"You are authorized to negotiate a long-term military alliance with the Londu. Trade agreements are certainly on the table, but the sheer distance renders them less than critical."

"What about technology? They're going to ask."

"Within our standard set of export systems, you have blanket authority," he told her. "Outside of that, you are explicitly to provide samples and schematics for skip-courier drones, penetrator missile systems and resonance warheads."

"That does make us vulnerable to them," she pointed out.

"It does. We are trusting your judgment, Ambassador. If you feel that the Londu are deceiving us to acquire technologies we would not otherwise trade, you know what to do."

"And if the situation is truly desperate and the only way to preserve the Sovereignty and their Protectorates is to enable the Londu to build gravity drives and gravity shields?" Sylvia asked quietly. "We do not know the scope of this enemy's power. A single small fleet of GMS-equipped ships may not be enough to turn the tide of the war the Londu face."

"Even prior to their annexation of the Isis Sector, the Londu outweighed the UPA by a significant margin in terms of population and industrial capacity," Matsumura reminded her. "Given anything approaching technological parity, we would very quickly find ourselves a junior partner at best.

"And being a junior partner to an expansionist autocratic power is a dangerous place to be. Again, Ambassador, we trust your judgment, but in the final accounting, we must protect the United Planets Alliance first.

"Officially, those technologies are not on the table." He shrugged. "In truth, you are our Ambassador and hold full plenipotentiary powers. While the General Assembly will need to ratify any treaty you negotiate, distance renders that almost meaningless. You must do what you judge best to serve the interests of the United Planets Alliance and humanity."

"Even if that means abandoning the Londu?" she asked.

"Yes. They would be a powerful ally, but we must recognize that the same distance that makes it difficult for us to aid them will work the other way around as well. In the long run, reestablishing FTL communications may make them more valuable to us, but in the short run, maintaining containment of gravity-projector technology is absolutely critical."

That was a giant knot of contradictory desires and orders. Fortunately, as Matsumura had pointed out, she would hold full plenipotentiary authority. That meant she could disregard a large portion of her instructions as needed.

And her boss knew it.

"We will do what we must," she echoed back to him. "Is there anything else I should be aware of before I report aboard *Raven* and prepare for this mission?"

"Your highest priority, Ambassador, is to negotiate a treaty with the Londu. Only slightly lower than that, however, is to identify who these Enigmas are. Our strategic interests require that we have complete knowledge of who else has the key technologies that underlie our advantages.

"Identify these Enigmas. Speak to them, if you can. If the improbable becomes possible, negotiate a peace between them and the Londu. We don't know enough about this enemy to want to be at war with them—and I suspect that even Lord of Fifty Thousand Miles Kahlmor has not told us all that he knows.

"I have spoken with him myself," her boss admitted. "He is not *lying* to us. But I do not believe he is telling us everything. We are being manipulated. He's just not very good at it, so I believe the fundamental truth of the situation remains."

"And if it turns out that we are being deceived more than that?"

"Then my faith is in you and Rear Admiral Wong to...deal with that appropriately."

15

IT HAD BEEN over ten months since Sylvia had last seen her boyfriend. The *plan* had been for them to meet up in more private circumstances as well, not in the main shuttle bay of an active-duty battlecruiser.

Amidst shuttlecraft and starfighters and the constant stream of personnel that Sylvia took for a sign that the Expeditionary Fleet was coming together nicely, she was more reserved than she had been intending to be, simply swiftly embracing Henry.

"Welcome aboard *Raven*," he told her in a voice that said he understood *exactly* what she was feeling. "She's changed a bit since the last time we were here together, but I'm glad to have her."

"I'm glad to be here," Sylvia said. "I won't pretend I wouldn't *rather* be meeting you in a resort on the Mediterranean, but…"

"Duty calls for us both, it seems," he said with a helpless shrug. "At least we're traveling together."

A junior noncom took Sylvia's luggage and waited expectantly for her to give instructions.

"I'll be staying in the Admiral's quarters, PO," she told the young woman with a smile. "Deliver my luggage there, please."

Sylvia had, like Henry, learned to read the unconscious microexpressions shared by almost all Ashall. She also knew *him* like a favorite novel at this point, and could feel his concealed amusement at the steward's sudden spike of awkwardness.

"Quaid is putting together a dinner for us in the flag dining room," he said. "It'll just be the two of us, though I'm sure we will have plenty of people waiting to pin you down for questions."

Sylvia chuckled.

"I have a briefing with you and your senior officers scheduled in the morning," she told him. "And after that, I have back-to-back-to-back meetings with the diplomatic team that's supposed to arrive between now and then.

"Until then, Admiral Wong, I appear to be at your disposal."

"I see," he murmured with a small smile. "Then we should not keep Chief Steward Quaid waiting, should we?"

LATER—*MUCH* later—Sylvia curled up against the wall of Henry's quarters in a blanket and watched him bring two mugs of tea into the bedroom. He wasn't going to pretend he'd *made* the tea—that had either been Quaid or a junior steward—but he earned points for bringing it to her in bed.

That way, only one of them needed to get dressed, after all.

"Thank you."

"Quaid is better at sourcing good green tea than I ever was," Henry admitted. "It's dangerous for my image. As a SpaceDiv Admiral, I think I'm supposed to only drink black coffee. Possibly flavored with whisky or the tears of my enemies."

Sylvia shook her head at him and took a sip of the excellent tea.

"How many people does he have running herd on you now?" she asked.

"Once everyone has reported aboard, he's got sixteen people," Henry said. "Which is ridiculous, but they're not actually all tasked with handling me. Mostly, that's so I can hold big grand dinners with all of my captains without borrowing people from Captain Campbell."

Sylvia chuckled.

"There will be at least that many people with similar skillsets in the diplomatic contingent I'm getting sent from Earth," she told him. "It's not necessarily about taking care of us as it is about upholding the appearances and needs of the UPA itself."

Henry took a seat on the bed next to her. The bed was, in her opinion, potentially the best perk being the Admiral's partner had. She'd slept in better beds in her life, but few aboard starships and *none* aboard warships.

"Not that they aren't doing their best to spoil me," he observed, his hand resting on the mattress and suggesting he was following her thoughts. "Though, one thing I should warn you of…"

"Oh?" She prodded at his half-complete thought.

"Someone somewhere in the Ground Division—I don't know who yet—decided that I was a *high-value asset* compared to other junior Admirals," he said with a tinge of concern in his voice. "The biggest result of that so far is that my personal bodyguard is from the Commando Regiments."

"I thought all GroundDiv were commandos," she asked.

Henry chuckled and smiled wryly.

"We will often call GroundDiv troopers *commandos* or something similar," he confirmed. "Mostly to make them feel better about the fact that they are, unequivocally, *not* Marines."

The United States Marine Corps, for all of its proud history, had found itself tied up with the United States Colonial Authority. Even more than the United States Space Force, the Corps had found itself the ironclad right hand of the USCA when it had gone somewhat rogue and ended up fighting, well, *everybody*.

The United Planets Space Force had been established out of the alliance that had *defeated* the USCA. There had never been any chance the troopers of Ground Division would use the name *Marine*, even though the Royal Marines and several other organizations had made their case strenuously.

"But while we use the word *commando* as a generic for our people, Ground Division also has a number of regiments that operate as special forces units." His smile grew wryer, if that was possible. "How *many* Commando Regiments exist is intentionally opaque. But, for my sins, I've been assigned a bodyguard drawn from those regiments.

"And given that the Regiments are known for everything *except* strict adherence to protocol, I suspect that means you're going to acquire some shadows wearing *Una Salus Victis* pins."

"The last hope of the damned?" Sylvia asked.

"Una salus victis nullam sperare salute," Henry reeled off, the words flowing freely. "The commandos wear the first three words, but the motto is the full phrase. *The last hope of the damned is not to hope for safety.*"

Sylvia slowly parsed that. It…was a rather dark phrase, really.

"And the difference between them and regular GroundDiv is…"

"Most relevant for this? I might assign regular GroundDiv to you for security on an operation where you would clearly be at risk. The commandos will assign *themselves* to you. Twenty-four-seven.

"Because I sincerely doubt that anyone decided *I* was a high-value asset without realizing that you and I, working together, are greater than the sum of our parts."

16

"AT EASE, EVERYONE," Henry ordered as he walked forward to the presenter's lectern at the front of the briefing room.

Raven had been back on active duty for over twelve months, but the flag spaces hadn't been occupied until the last few days. Since the entire squadron command section was brand-new, that gave it not only the distinct new-ship smell but also the new-ship *appearance*, with no visible scuffs on the furniture and absolutely *no* unique decoration in the main conference hall.

The layout of the room reminded him more of an Academy lecture hall than anything else, with five rows of five seats, each about ten centimeters higher than the row in front. The seats themselves, on the other hand, were wonders of modern technology designed to put the entire data network of a fleet at the fingers of the people in them.

Holoprojectors and wallscreens could virtually expand the space to allow for dozens or even hundreds of more officers to attend a briefing while the Admiral explained the mission.

Today, none of those systems were active. Everyone he needed could fit in the same room, and Henry had arranged for an in-person meeting to get everything started.

Sylvia Todorovich, Colonel Campbell, Commodore Ihejirika and

Colonel Iyotake filled the first row. Those four would be critical to the success of the mission: his diplomat, his second-in-command and the two flag captains.

His staff filled the two rows behind them. He was still missing an intelligence officer—which was fine by him, given that his last intelligence officer had spoon-fed him the deceptions of Golden Lancelot—but he had operations, logistics, communications, engineering, personnel and legal officers.

Including Palmerston, Sharma and Strickland, there were thirteen people in his audience. It was a small briefing—but the person in the room with the *least* number of people reporting to them was Colonel Sheri Marszalek of the UPSF's Justice Division, his legal officer.

Marszalek had a *mere* twenty-two people in her department. On the other end of the scale was Colonel Campbell, responsible for eighteen hundred souls. The *other* seven hundred people who would be aboard *Raven* were Henry's *direct* responsibility.

"I'm glad we were able to pull together this meeting," Henry told them all. "Right now, this room contains the command staff and capital-ship-command crews of the Expeditionary Fleet. We're due to receive more capital ships along with our escorts over the next two days, while our convoy is being finalized."

"Do we know what ships we're getting?" Iyotake asked. Henry's second-in-command was a broad-shouldered Native American man—from Henry's own Montana, even!—with a neat black braid. Named for the historical Teton Dakota Chief, he had somehow managed to acquire an even stronger aura of solid calm since being promoted away from *Raven*.

"Yes," Henry replied with a nod. The holoprojectors activated and miniature ships began to float in the air between him and the front row.

"Which exact vessels we will be receiving is still in discussion," he warned, "but I am informed that our order of battle in terms of classes is now set."

Almost everyone in his audience should have been able to read the iconography and images hanging in the air in front of him, but he wasn't going to take bets on the Ambassador following it—or his legal officer, if he was being completely honest.

"The Expeditionary Fleet, people, will be composed of three separate elements," he told them. "Task Group One, AKA Task Group *Raven*, will be anchored on this ship and under my direct command.

"We will have the Gem-class cruiser *Turquoise*. That has been confirmed and she is on her way to Base Halo from the working up zone around Vesta. Accompanying her are all eight of the Flight Two *Cataphract*s, the *Cataphract*-Bs.

"The eleventh and final ship of Task Group One is still being determined," he noted, "but I *have* been promised a *Lexington*-G class carrier. There are two of them in the Solar System right now, and my understanding is that the Captains are basically playing an extended game of political rock-paper-scissors."

That got a chuckle from his people as intended. The irony, of course, was that while Blake had expended influence to get one of the carriers assigned to his fleet at all, the Commodores in command of the two light carriers were spending capital like water to be the ship that went.

The entire UPSF was expecting the Expeditionary Fleet to be a career-making mission. Henry would love for it to be a quiet voyage without the crises that called for medals and promotions...but he had no illusions.

He was taking these people to war.

"Every vessel in Task Group One will be fully modernized, possessing both the gravity maneuvering system and dual-layer shields," he told them. "The intention is that TG One will be the primary striking force of the Expeditionary Fleet, using Task Group Two as a base of support and escorts for the convoy."

The hologram shifted, moving the eleven modern ships closer to Henry and focusing on the ten ships of the second task group.

"Task Group Two, AKA Task Group *Urraca*, will consist entirely of reaction-drive vessels, commanded by Commodore Iyotake from Colonel Ihejirika's battlecruiser," he continued, nodding to both of his old Xos.

"Where TG One's destroyers don't have an official formation yet,

TG Two is receiving the complete Twentieth Destroyer Squadron under Colonel Amaka Jo. That is eight *Significance*-class destroyers.

"The last vessel in TG Two is the starfighter support ship *Archon*," he finished. "*Archon* is a heavily refitted *Foundation*-class carrier. Her command decks, organic weaponry and a portion of her active flight bays have been replaced with workshops and storage.

"Her primary role is to provide replacement fighters and repairs for TG One and the battlecruisers' fighter wings, but *Archon* remains capable of deploying six squadrons of Lancer-type starfighters herself."

Task Group Two was completely set in stone. That was easier, in some ways, than Task Group One because no one was trying to hang on to the fusion-drive ships. The UPSF was back up to thirty-five reaction-drive battlecruisers with recommissioned *Jaguar* ships, but there was *one* gravity-drive battlecruiser.

The ratio was similar with destroyers, though less lopsided in carriers. Per the plan Henry had authored, the *Lexington*s were the focus of the refit process right now. *Lexington*-Gs would move out to replace *Crichton*-class ships on most postings, allowing the bigger and newer carriers to return home for their own refits.

And, like the *Corvid*s, the *Crichton*s already in the shipyards were being completed as G-types. Henry had been grateful to realize that while the UPA had frozen the construction of the twenty battlecruisers and five fleet carriers being built when the war ended, they'd kept all of them intact and secured in vacuum for easy completion.

"Our third task group is not a combat formation," he conceded, bringing the convoy to the front. "We will be combining a military-assistance convoy and our own logistics supply train into a single convoy. Currently, I am being promised that all of the ships will be *Tvastar*-class fast fleet auxiliaries: eighteen ships in a mix of tanker, collier, freighter, and fabricator configurations."

And one ship in an ansible configuration, but even in this room, only Sylvia was cleared to know about that until they left UPA space.

"How much time are we going to have to work up the Fleet as a unit?" Hawthorne asked. "Outside of DesRon Twenty, we do not appear to be receiving complete units."

That had been one of Henry's own concerns, which made it a small mental check mark on his list for his operations officer.

"That's correct," he confirmed. "Unfortunately, we are looking at a three-month journey to our destination, and we have *no* idea what the status of the Sovereignty is—or even what happened to Lord of a Million Miles Okavaz.

"Our orders from the Security Council are clear: as soon as we have assembled the Expeditionary Fleet, we are to be on our way."

It was probably a good thing that no one in the room liked that. If anyone had been okay with that kind of rush, he'd be worried about having them on his staff!

"On the other hand," he continued, "we *are* looking at a three-month journey. That will give us significant opportunities for both virtual and real-space exercises to work up the Fleet. It's not optimal, but it will serve our purposes well enough."

"Do we have manifests for the convoy yet?" Cheng Kai, his logistics officer, asked. "My staff will need to review the stores available on each of our ships and what is already planned for the convoy to make certain we have everything we need for extended operations.

"Based off the timelines, I believe we should be preparing to spend at least two years away from the United Planets Alliance."

Lieutenant Colonel Cheng was a giant question mark in Henry's book. His record *looked* good, but he'd never served outside the Solar System, and his family traditionally served in the *Chinese* space forces.

His father, in fact, was currently commanding one of the two Chinese battleship squadrons. The question mark was over Cheng Kai's competence, not what connections had put the officer on his flagship.

"Two years?" Hawthorne asked. "Isn't that excessive?"

"No," Henry conceded with a nod to the Cantonese officer. "If we went directly to the Londu home system, dropped off the convoy's cargo and came right back, we would be away for half a year.

"Given that our mission is to join the Londu in their war and secure the survival of the Londu Sovereignty against an unknown threat, I would expect the combat campaign to last a minimum of six months and more likely a year. While the factory ships should suffice for the majority of our munition needs over the long term and the Londu should be able to backstop our other supplies, two years seems the *minimum* amount of supplies we should be carrying."

The expression on a couple of the faces in the room suggested that not everyone had fully thought through the timeline of the mission they'd signed up for.

It was too late now, in Henry's opinion. Care had been taken that there would be no officers or ratings whose commissions would be up in the next two years, and as an independently deployed flag officer, Henry had blanket authority to extend enlistments and commissions if necessary.

Fortunately, he *also* had authority to disburse bonuses and issue promotions. If he could manage it, he'd make damn sure no one found themselves extended without sufficient benefits to reconcile them to the burden.

"Will *Archon* be fully loaded with Lancers?" Iyotake asked. "That will make up for some of the shortfalls of our reaction-drive ships."

"Yes. As will *Uracca*," Henry confirmed. The SF-130 Lancer was the most modern starfighter in the UPSF's arsenal, the first implementation of the GMS in their forces. Large enough and with powerful-enough engines to carry both a gravity shield and the same missiles as their motherships, the Lancer was unquestionably the most dangerous starfighter that the UPSF knew of, let alone possessed.

Archon had forty-eight deployable starfighters, but each of the two battlecruisers also carried eight of the strike craft. The *Lexington* he'd been promised would carry eighty—and according to the specifications Henry had seen, *Archon* would carry enough boxed fighters and parts to replace the entire hundred-and-forty-four-fighter strength of the Expeditionary Fleet.

What they couldn't keep in storage, of course, was *pilots*. There was no way Henry would be able to recruit local pilots to fly gravity-drive- and gravity-shield-equipped starfighters, which meant that his starfighter pilots were going to be a resource to husband carefully.

As if summoned by his thoughts, a request for admittance to the meeting chimed in his network. He took a moment to confirm that the commandos outside had cleared the individual—and then saw who had arrived.

Summoned by his thoughts, indeed. His command opened the door into the briefing room, and he watched his people turn around to watch the FighterDiv Colonel stride into the room like she owned the place.

The red-haired pilot was still gawky in a way that would make most people underestimate her age, her legs and arms seeming ever so slightly too long for her frame, but Henry knew Colonel Samira O'Flannagain.

There were people who argued he'd saved her career. He figured he'd just been the Captain with the patience to pull her out of her funk and find the damn fine officer underneath her admitted tendencies toward troublemaking.

She snapped to attention as she reached the front of the room and offered him the standard envelope with a datachip.

"Colonel Samira O'Flannagain reporting, ser," she said crisply. "My orders."

"Thank you, Colonel." He blinked as he processed the orders. "My apologies, *Captain* O'Flannagain."

She *visibly* shivered at the courtesy title. Tradition said she wouldn't be addressed that way except on her own command, but for today, the point was critical.

"Colonel O'Flannagain has assumed command of the *Lexington*-G class carrier *Pegasus* and been assigned to our Task Group One," he told his officers. "Welcome to the team, Samira."

"Thank you, Admiral." O'Flannagain looked...concerned. Not surprising, he figured. He knew her well—well enough to know that she'd been concerned about taking on a full-flight-group command.

"And Commodore Soris?" he asked gently. While, with the downgrade of the *Lexington*s to *light* carrier status, he could see them reducing to a Colonel for Captain, but he'd been paying attention to who was in command of the two GMS carriers in the system.

"He had a heart attack last night, ser," she said grimly. "He lived, but MedDiv has ordered him grounded for the foreseeable future. Not sure of the logic that went from there to *me* assuming command of *Pegasus*, but you saw my orders."

"I did," Henry confirmed. Yesterday, she'd been *Pegasus's* Commander, Air Group, and the main reason he'd been hoping to get *Pegasus* over *Wasp*. Now his rapidly updating table of organization said that Lieutenant Colonel Uche Spyros—presumably her former flight group XO—was now CAG aboard *Pegasus*.

"It's a good choice," he told her. "I have high expectations."

That did nothing for her nerves, he noted, but it was true nonetheless.

"If you'll take a seat, Colonel, we'll quickly run through what we've already discussed to catch you up and then resume questions and concerns."

17

LUNCH WAS A SIGNIFICANTLY MORE casual affair, though the same people were present in Henry's dining room as had been in the briefing. Quaid had outdone himself, in the Admiral's opinion, with dishes individualized to each officer's tastes and dietary restrictions.

Iyotake and O'Flannagain were seated closest to Henry and Sylvia. He hadn't thought to tell Quaid to put them there, but the steward had known what he would want.

That was what made for a good steward.

"Is it as strange for you two to be back aboard *Raven* as it is for me?" he asked his old and new subordinates.

"I, at least, am just visiting," Iyotake murmured. "It's been...four years? Close to that now, since I was your XO aboard her." He shook his head. "I'll admit, I didn't expect my first job as a Commodore to be task group commander under you on this kind of mission."

"A month ago, we didn't expect to be *launching* this kind of mission," Henry pointed out. "All of the signs I was aware of pointed to my taking command of the fledgling APOCOM. I was pretty sure I was getting *Raven* as my flagship for that, but moving into the Apophis Sector was going to be a far different type of mission than this."

That would have been a slow and delicate expansion of trade lanes and security agreements, with the UPSF inserting themselves as delicately as possible into local conflicts to bring about peaceful resolutions.

They'd stabilized the Ra Sector, and the cost in blood and treasure had paid dividends in the same coin. Anderon, the second system the Kenmiri Vengeance Fleet had attacked, hadn't been saved by the UPSF alone.

They'd been saved by an alliance of the key systems of the Ra Sector, gathered and *led* by the UPSF. It was a critical difference—and one that made the difference between victory and defeat on that horrendous day.

"I'll admit, *Pegasus* versus *Wasp* was the last real question in the Fleet's makeup," he told O'Flannagain. "I'm glad to have you, Samira, but you'll forgive me if I'm even happier to have *Pegasus*!"

"She's a damn fine ship, ser, though calming superstition takes up more time than I'd like," the Colonel told him. "No one likes changing ship names."

"That's right," Iyotake noted. "She was…*Ark Royal*, right?"

"Right. And then the *Crichton*-class *Ark Royal* was laid down and the *Lexington*-class *Ark Royal* was mothballed. But she was conveniently to hand when Admiral Wong here fired up his plasma cutters and started looking for ships to chop the engines off of."

"And then, as with any ship from the List of Honor, tradition got involved," Henry said drily. "*Ark Royal* was one of the first carriers back in the twentieth century, but time and technology marched onward, and she was obsolete twenty years later.

"So, her *name* was given to the Royal Navy's newest and shiniest carrier—but while she wasn't a major fleet combatant anymore, she was still a useful ship to have around. So, they renamed her *Pegasus*.

"And whenever a ship named *Ark Royal* has needed a new name since, she's taken up the name *Pegasus*. Like the *Ark Royal* name, it has proud traditions and a long legacy."

"And corgis," O'Flannagain said wryly. "Let me tell you, *that* was a surprise. I was vaguely aware of that tradition…but *vaguely aware* doesn't prepare you for fifteen kilograms of dog-with-commission deciding you have a perfectly sized lap!"

Henry chuckled.

"We appear to have become home to *Renown*'s previous corgi Colonels," he warned. "So far, either they or their minders have decided not to test the Admiral's patience with animals."

He'd grown up on a ranch, so his patience with animals was significantly greater than his patience with people. He had no great desire to be surrounded by them or to have pets of his own, but animals rarely had a choice in their circumstances, and people rarely gave allowances for their stress levels.

He'd forgive many things from a dog that he wouldn't accept from a human.

"You still have them? I would have expected them to return to *Renown* when she came back online," Iyotake observed.

"The distribution of corgis in the United Planets Space Force is, as I understand it, guided and decided by our British Chiefs," Henry pointed. "No Admiral is so foolish as to think they can argue with the collective will of the UPSF's Chiefs!"

"Not one that's going to keep their stars, anyway," Sylvia murmured. "You have your moments of wisdom."

O'Flannagain chuckled loudly at Henry's discomfiture. She'd been one of the main people aboard *Raven* playing matchmaker, back before Henry had registered the Ambassador as attractive.

His particular brain wasn't wired to find people romantically or sexually interesting until he'd known them for a long time. Sylvia, he suspected, had decided she was going to claim him before he'd seen her as anything except his professional partner.

"I hear you're going to be carrying a bunch of lost Londu aboard *Raven*?" O'Flannagain asked.

"Lord of Fifty Thousand Miles Kahlmor has seven staffers with him," Henry confirmed. "They'll be in our guest quarters, something *Raven* now *has* with the refit."

Before, the battlecruiser had been equipped with enough space for a division commander with a hundred or less staff—and absolutely no diplomatic or presence spaces. Outside of the *Corvid*-Cs, the standing rule had been that a *Corvid* was either a diplomatic ship *or* a flagship.

"I am learning the limits of the original *Corvid* command spaces," Iyotake said grimly. "I was hoping I'd get a carrier with an actual command center, but it sounds like *Archon* doesn't have that anymore."

"No, it has workshops and fabricators in place of, well, everything," Henry told his subordinate. "You can probably put part of your administrative staff aboard, but most of the command workload will need to be carried by my staff here on *Raven*. We have the space for that now."

"I will spend the trip delicately trying to extract the information Kahlmor hasn't told us from him," Sylvia said brightly. "Some of the missing information might be accidental. Some is almost certainly intentional. By the time we reach the Londu border, I hope to know everything."

"Are they lying to us?" O'Flannagain asked, her voice dangerous.

"No," Henry said quickly, cutting off any potential concerns there. "But we are quite certain that Kahlmor both didn't know everything and isn't telling us everything he *does* know.

"By the time we arrive in Londu space, Kahlmor's information will be nine months old." He shook his head. "Even with the best of intentions—and Kahlmor is *desperate* to get help for his people—that kind of outdated intelligence assessment could cause us real difficulties.

"But we will deal with them," he said firmly, surveying the officers at his table. He wasn't sure of all of them, but the ones he did know were rock-solid. He'd handle whatever weaknesses came up, leaning on the strong officers to make up for the questionable ones.

"Speaking of intelligence," Iyotake said slowly, "I'm noting a lack of intelligence officers on your staff."

"If I can get away without one, I will," Henry said quietly. United Planets Intelligence had stage-managed Golden Lancelot very, *very* carefully, including putting Intelligence officers on all of the ships.

Each distinct operation of the plan had been told they were the only one, a demonstration strike to make a point to the Kenmorad that their expansionism *could* hurt them and not just their Kenmiri children.

Only the UPI handlers had known the truth. Even Broos Van Agteren, Henry's intelligence officer, hadn't known that the creche ship *Panther* had fired on had been the last one left.

While that had been United Planets Intelligence, not IntelDiv, the UPSF's intelligence people had found themselves tarred with the same brush. Henry understood that he *needed* an intel officer.

He just didn't *want* one.

18

RAVEN LED the way from Base Halo, and Henry stood at the main holotank on his flag bridge and watched his fleet shake out.

Twenty-one warships and nineteen auxiliaries. Forty starships. Across the fleet, Henry was responsible for roughly twenty thousand lives. It was a terrifying thought, one that made him determined to meet the duties and responsibilities now placed on him.

"Fleet is accelerating at point-four KPS-squared," one of Hawthorne's people—a Petty Officer named Miles Raymond—reported. "We'll hit the skip line to Procyon in seven hours."

"Thank you, Em Raymond," Henry replied. "Let me know if anything changes."

He was still staring at the illusory ships in the hologram. His Expeditionary Fleet might officially be divided into three "Task Groups," but the reality was that the convoy wasn't going to stray far from Commodore Iyotake's ships.

There was a clear division in the fleet's maneuvers, though, with the eleven GMS ships forming a slightly curved shield in front of the rest of the formation. All twenty-nine reaction-drive ships were moving as a unit, with the destroyers almost looking like they were *herding* the freighters.

Silently, he took a moment to locate *Sanskrit* in the convoy. None of the ships in his Task Group Three were expendable, but *Sanskrit* was the ship he could not afford to lose. They'd skip into Procyon—a long jump, just inside the twenty-four-hour safe limit—and then a second star system with a UPA outpost.

When they left that system in three days, *Sanskrit* would become his primary link home. The chain of skip drones would grow ever longer and more fragile as the distance increased. The drones took less time to cross systems sublight than his fleet would, but without relay stations to send messages ahead, the drones themselves had to cross the entire distance between the UPA and wherever his fleet ended up.

Even with the limitations of the ansible and the need to keep it secret and safe, he was going to have a better connection home than he'd had since the Great Gathering.

It would still be sufficiently fragile that no one was going to try to micromanage him...he hoped. Henry smirked slightly at the hologram, knowing no one could see him through it.

Sanskrit was going to move with Task Group Three at all times. Her main defense was being indistinguishable from the rest of the convoy. *Raven*, on the other hand, would be the tip of the spear.

He suspected he'd be spending enough time in different *star systems* from the ansible to make ignoring a micromanager straightforward enough. He had enough faith in Admiral Saren to suspect that she wouldn't try that—his concern was more political.

"Ser, may I have a moment?"

Speaking of politics, Henry smoothed his features back under control at the sound of his new intelligence officer's voice. He wasn't exactly *avoiding* the man, but he knew he hadn't been making it easy on Lieutenant Colonel Dumuzi Larue.

The French officer hadn't done anything *wrong*—yet—but Henry knew perfectly well that his battle against having an intel officer aboard had been partially lost on the fact that *Dumuzi* Larue was the nephew of *Marie* Larue, the current President of the European Union.

"What do you need, Colonel?" Henry asked. He considered, for a few seconds, the extremely petty option of watching the man through the bridge cameras rather than turning to face him.

Instead, though, he turned around and returned Larue's salute.

"I know I was the last of your staff officers to come aboard," Larue told him. "But I've been reviewing our security and counterintelligence arrangements, and, well…" He looked around the bridge.

"I have some concerns, ser," he admitted. "It might be better to have this conversation in private?"

Henry was generally prepared to assume that everyone on the flag bridge was cleared for ninety-nine-plus percent of the information necessary to run the fleet, but he conceded that Larue *probably* had a point.

And the Admiral didn't need to be on his flag bridge for something as straightforward as the maneuver to the Sol-Procyon skip line.

"My office," he told Larue.

HENRY WAS BEING VERY careful *not* to let himself start ignoring the commandos who accompanied him everywhere now. He knew it would be far too easy to let the bodyguards just become part of the background, but his close detail, especially, he needed to treat as *people*.

"Thank you, Joe, Sarah," he told the two as they gently guided Larue to his office. "I think you can stand guard outside, unless Colonel Larue is a security threat and no one has told me?"

Chief Joe Borgia, the current senior member of the two-person close detail, smiled in a manner that suggested Larue had more to worry about than Henry's joke had suggested.

"So far, his checks are coming back clean," he allowed. "We'll let you know if that changes, ser."

Larue didn't manage to conceal his surprise and discomfort at that, but Henry gestured his office door closed before the intelligence officer could say anything to the commandos.

"Your escort seems…overly familiar," Larue finally said as he followed Henry to the desk.

"My escort lives in my back pocket twenty-four hours a day, either outside the door of whatever room I'm in or walking a hundred and twenty centimeters behind me," Henry told the intelligence officer. "*No man is a hero to his valet,* I believe, is the saying? My bodyguard can either be familiar or furniture, Lieutenant Colonel, and I have an aversion to treating people as things."

"I see, ser."

From Larue's tone, he might even actually understand. That was a bit better than Henry had expected from the man.

"Coffee, Colonel? Tea?" Quaid had materialized from the concealed side door like a ghost stepping through solid bulkheads.

"Just plain hot water, if you please, Chief," Larue addressed the steward respectfully.

"Tea for me, Chief," Henry added.

Quaid nodded and withdrew back through the door. Henry wasn't entirely convinced that he needed to have his steward on hand all day every day, but he'd also learned not to argue with how his Chief Steward managed Henry's life.

The Chief returned a moment later with cups and two small pots, one with green tea for Henry and one with plain hot water for Larue.

Henry was half-expecting the intelligence officer to add his own tea or some similar paranoid gesture, but Larue simply poured the hot water into the cup Quaid provided and held it in his hands for a few moments.

"Thank you for making the time for me," he told Henry. "I have the feeling that I am far from your favorite person amongst your senior staff."

"The last time I had an Intelligence handler, Colonel, we committed genocide," Henry said flatly. "Like most officers from Golden Lancelot, I have an aversion to your entire field and specialty.

"This operation will involve us moving far from any sources of information you will be able to provide value from, which limits your role, in my opinion, to analysis just as well performed by my operations team under Commodore Hawthorne."

Larue nodded and took a sip of his plain water.

"I understand where you're coming from," he conceded. "But I think that fundamentally misrepresents the role of the intelligence team in your staff, ser. Which does, I'll note, tie into what I wanted to speak to you about."

Henry supposed it was to the man's credit that he wasn't intimidated by the Admiral disliking his entire specialty, even if he wasn't willing to *give* Larue much credit.

"Well, who am I to argue with IntelDiv?" he asked wryly. "Unless you do something truly egregious, I'll need you to perform that analysis and do your job. You may as well lay out your problem."

He wasn't planning to make any of this *easy* on the intelligence officer. Larue was starting from a rough place, as far as Henry was concerned, and would need to prove his use and trustworthiness.

"The first thing I did on joining the Fleet was begin a review of our counterintelligence positioning," Larue told him. "That was a very short process, given that it appears we have basically *zero* counterintelligence protocols or structures in place beyond the most basic defaults."

"You are aware, Colonel, that we are proceeding into a region of space where no members of our crews are even of the same *species* as the locals," Henry pointed out. "There are less than thirty people in the entire Expeditionary Fleet who speak Londu without a computer translator."

Interestingly, he was pulling up Larue's file as he spoke, and it turned out that the intelligence officer was one of them. Either the file was exaggerated, or Larue was a spectacular polyglot, speaking eleven Earth languages, Kem, and the languages of the six largest members of the Vesheron alliance.

"The Londu and their unknown enemies represent a risk of electronic intrusion, against which this fleet *should* damn well be secured, but the chances of a more-direct intelligence threat seem extremely low."

"One of my tasks, ser, when we reach Londu space will be to reestablish contact with our sentient assets on the ground in the Sovereignty," Larue said quietly. "Assuming that the Londu have no ability to compromise our personnel is dangerous. Even assuming that no one on our ships has already been compromised is a risk.

"Lord of Fifty Thousand Miles Kahlmor and his people would serve as excellent handlers and recruiters for such an endeavor," he continued. "While the risk of preexisting Londu assets among our people is low, it does exist—and more critically, the risk of Kahlmor's people attempting to acquire such assets is significant.

"Which leads to my primary concern, ser. We have placed minimal restrictions on the Londu aboard *Raven* and basically *no* restrictions on the civilian contingent Ambassador Todorovich has brought aboard.

"This is one of the, if not *the*, most advanced warships in the United Planets Space Force. I understand the logic in having the Ambassador's staff and the Londu aboard her, but Lord Kahlmor and his people have *every* reason and motivation to attempt to acquire information on the new systems on this ship."

"The Londu are our allies, but there is a reason those restrictions exist," Henry admitted slowly. "I am open to a review of them from your perspective, I suppose. On the other hand, are you suggesting, Colonel, that we cannot trust our own Diplomatic Corps personnel?"

Larue might speak eighteen languages, but he had never learned to control his microexpressions to prevent cross-species reading of his emotions. His almost-condescending surprise at Henry's question did him no favors.

"I do not expect the diplomats to provide schematics and specifications of this ship to the Londu, if that is what you mean," he said slowly. "But I must remind you, ser, that the United Planets Space Force maintains its own research-and-development and military-design divisions for a reason.

"The national fleets do not, officially, have access to the UPSF tech base," Larue told him. "As a rule, the national fleets are strongly encouraged to purchase UPSF ships for their allotted nova combatants. The last time the UPSF provided full schematics to the national fleets was the guardship program during the war.

"Any of the member states may have compromised personnel serving in the Diplomatic Corps—or even the crews of our ships—as part of an attempt to secure technical information and technology that the UPSF does not want in wide distribution."

Henry didn't visibly grimace, but he had to mentally concede the intelligence officer's point. He *hadn't* considered that aspect of the counterintelligence needs of his fleet. While the technology in the UPSF's hands would inevitably end up in the hands of the national fleets *eventually*—every shipbuilder and company involved was in a member state somewhere, after all—the UPSF at least tried to maintain a significant edge over the member nations.

Beyond the fact that the member nations were allowed two skip-capable warships each, that was.

"My personal assessment of both Lord of Fifty Thousand Miles Kahlmor and Ambassador Todorovich is that neither is involved in those kinds of matters," Henry noted. "But I can't speak with similar certainty to any of their personnel.

"I am prepared to admit that is a blind spot on my part," he said grimly. "At Base Halo, we were covered by the counterintelligence operations on the Base. Now that we are in space, we must see to our own security.

"I will want to review and authorize any steps you take, Colonel, but we will want to proceed with expanding our counterintelligence security as you have noted. I suggest that you consult with Commander Palmerston, my chief of security, as well as Commodore Zeni, our ground-forces commander."

Henry didn't know Commodore Frieda Zeni as well as he'd like, but Palmerston trusted her. That was, at least for the moment, enough for him. He figured he could count on the two GroundDiv officers to moderate any entirely out-of-line suggestions from Larue—and that Larue understood that an Admiral's *suggestions* were simply politely phrased orders.

"I do have one more key concern, ser," Larue said in a voice that held a visibly forced degree of levelness. "Your relationship with Ambassador Todorovich is common knowledge, but I am obliged to note that she is a senior operative from the former Novaya Imperiya in Epsilon Eridani.

"We cannot assume that everything with Todorovich is as it seems, given Eridani's still not wholly willing membership in the United Planets Alli—"

"Stop, Colonel," Henry told the man. He knew his tone was dangerous, a greater emotional leak than he'd expected. Just when he'd been starting to think that Larue might be entirely useful, the man went and shoved his foot in it.

"Have you read Ambassador Todorovich's record?" he asked. "Before or after she began working with me? I am not aware that Todorovich has even been *back* to Eridani in over fifteen years, Lieutenant Colonel.

"If you want to argue that represents some sort of deep-cover operation on the part of a covert remnant of the Novaya Imperiya, *I* am going to suggest that you see the ship's doctors. They are fully qualified to conduct counseling for paranoia," Henry said drily.

"It is my job to be paranoid, ser, and your relationship may—"

"My personal relationship with Ambassador Todorovich arose *after* our professional partnership stopped the Great Gathering turning into a sixty-way firefight, saved the La-Tar Cluster and laid the groundwork for the success of the original Peacekeeper Initiative," Henry said flatly. "My personal feelings in this matter are irrelevant. My *professional* judgment is that Sylvia Todorovich has more thoroughly proven her loyalty to the United Planets Alliance and her value to this mission *than you have.*

"Do you understand me, Lieutenant Colonel Larue?"

There was a long, chilly silence in Henry's office, but the younger man nodded stiffly.

"I do, ser."

"Good. I want your counterintelligence plan on my desk by eighteen hundred hours tomorrow.

"Dismissed!"

19

ESTABLISHING a new mobile embassy out of the assorted teams that Sylvia's supervisors had sent her took more effort than she'd really expected or wanted. She had *two hundred* people reporting to her aboard *Raven*, plus another fifty aboard *Turquoise* because *Raven* hadn't had enough space. She had xenolinguists, accountants, cooks, civil-service security, economic analysts, xenosociologists...everything she could think of.

But they'd come aboard as individual teams of five to twenty people in their specialties. Getting them to talk to each other and work properly together was going to be the work of weeks. Just setting up the protocol and infrastructure for all of her various new departments had consumed the entire time at Base Halo and most of the trip out to the Sol-Procyon skip line.

She'd be busy again when they were in skip and even busier in Procyon, but she'd broken some time free for a meeting she *should* have had when the Londu had first come aboard. A different crisis had been occupying her time then, however, so there she was.

One of her xenosociologists was almost certainly a United Planets Intelligence operative, and if the little kozyol didn't come clean shortly, she was going to end his career and probably leave him in *Raven*'s brig for the entire trip.

Controlling her emotions, Sylvia stepped up to the entrance to the visitors' section the Londu officers had been given. A pair of GroundDiv troopers stood guard and saluted at her approach—though it took a second for her to be certain they were saluting *her* and not the commando three paces behind her.

"I…was not under the impression that diplomats were supposed to get saluted, Petty Officer," she told the senior trooper.

"Some diplomats do," the man said carefully. "And so do some Admiral's wives, so we show respect as we can."

Sylvia managed not to roll her eyes, but she took the gesture in the spirit it was intended.

"Thank you, PO," she told him. "I'm here to see Kahlmor. I have an appointment, though I'm not sure who that gets passed on through."

"Lieutenant Commander Strickland passed it on, Ser," the PO confirmed. "You're clear to go in."

"Thank you."

She nodded gravely to the two troopers and stepped forward through the smoothly opening door. She was unsurprised to find a matching pair of guards on the other side of the door, *this* pair in the iron collars and white robes of the Blades of the Scion.

Unlike the guards outside, the Blades weren't visibly armed. Sylvia figured that was a minor sop to GroundDiv's sensibilities, since she knew damn well that Kahlmor's people had brought energy weapons aboard with them.

Thanks to trade deals with the Ra Sector and slowly upgrading production facilities of their own, the UPSF would *soon* fully reequip the Ground Division with Kenmiri-style energy weapons. For the moment, though, the GroundDiv troopers in front of the door had been carrying projectile weapons of some sort. Her commando escort, on the other hand, *was* armed with a high-quality energy pistol.

"I am here to see Lord of Fifty Thousand Miles Kahlmor," she told the two Blades in slow-but-steady Londu. She was rusty with the language, more sibilant than the staccato Kem or blunt English she normally found herself speaking.

"He awaits, Great Lady," one of the soldiers told her. "Follow."

⁘V⁘

THE CENTER OF THE VISITORS' section was an observation lounge, with an array of comfortable couches and viewscreens pretending to be windows. Sylvia was sure the fact that the viewscreens allowed *Raven*'s security people to censor what their guests could see had *nothing* to do with the structure of the lounge.

Though it also allowed the guest quarters to be deep inside the ship, in part of the old engineering spaces that had contained fusion engines before. Between expanding the height of the ship and opening up spaces used for engines and fuel before, the refitted *Raven* had a *lot* more space.

The section that had been put aside for the Londu had fifteen suites —each basically a small bedroom and bathroom—arranged around the observation lounge and a small mess and kitchen.

Kahlmor was standing in the middle of the lounge, looking at the screens like they would produce the answer to some great philosophical question, while two of the other Londu officers appeared to be reading on the couches.

"Attrasta, Moreal," Kahlmor addressed his subordinates. "Leave us, please."

His Londu was significantly smoother than Sylvia's, making it straightforward for her to follow his speech. The other two officers— both Lords of Hundred Miles, equivalent to a UPSF Lieutenant Colonel —rose and exited silently, leaving Sylvia alone with Kahlmor.

"Your home system is impressive," Kahlmor told Sylvia, running his fingers absently through the thick black mane running down the back of his head and neck. "I do not understand the logic of your sublight warships. The explanation delves into areas that seem foolish to me."

"The Londu and humanity do not have the same government," Sylvia said, keeping her Londu slow to keep herself from mistakes. "There is strangeness from that, but we value the forms we possess."

"We Londu once valued the voice of the many as you do," he observed. "We learned better."

"Then I hope that is a lesson that humanity never faces."

Kahlmor sank into one of the couches and gestured for Sylvia to sit as well.

"This is far more aid than I dared to hope for," he admitted to her. "It is a shadow of me that asks it, but I must know: what price will we pay for these ships and weapons?"

"You already know the price," she told him. "We wish to lock down our friendship, so that when we call in the future, the Londu will answer." She smiled. "We will also look to create trades that will make our merchants money, but it is the alliance we seek to forge that is the price we will demand."

"You will find fertile soil for those seeds in these hours," Kahlmor conceded. "I, for one, am afraid. I do not know what we return to."

"We have no more idea than you do," she admitted.

"But *I* know that a squadron of the Blades' most modern ships should have delivered Lord of a Million Miles Okavaz to your people long before I arrived," he said. "I ask fate that Admiral Wong intends to find out what happened to Okavaz."

"If we can, we will," Sylvia promised. She knew that was Henry's intent—she was pretty sure it was part of his orders, for that matter.

Kahlmor was silent for a few seconds.

"You and Admiral Wong are...flesh and soul?" he asked.

Sylvia took a few seconds to parse the translation and the metaphor there. Context, as always, helped.

"We are..." She trailed off, then switched to Kem, where she definitely *had* the words for this. "We are in a committed romantic relationship."

"I see," Kahlmor replied, still in Londu. "And you were not when we met in Resta, yes?"

"We were not," she confirmed, wondering what he was poking at. "Why do you ask?"

The black-maned Londu chuckled.

"Once we learned Wong was at Resta, I was briefed on him," Kahlmor observed. "There was a suggestion, certainly, that the

Admiral was romantically available to individuals of any alignment or race. I was encouraged to test that theory, given my own alignment."

Again, it took Sylvia a moment to process the phrasing, then she chuckled herself.

"The Admiral's romantic availability is complex," she told Kahlmor. That was all she really needed to tell *him*. Henry was sufficiently open about his demisexuality that she'd known what she was getting into when she'd started to fall for him.

Fortunately, she could be *very* patient.

"I found Admiral Wong quite fascinating then," Kahlmor told her. "As both an officer and an individual. Now I hope he is as capable an officer as I believe. My people's fate may well depend on it."

"Your Scion asked for aid and the UPA has answered," Sylvia said quietly. "We have sent our best. If the ships and spacers of the United Planets Space Force can save the Sovereignty, trust that Henry Wong will see it done."

20

THE EXPEDITIONARY FLEET traveled the Procyon System at speed, crossing the thirty light-minutes between the two skip lines in just over eighteen hours. At a peak velocity of over five percent of lightspeed, Henry was testing his ships' coordination, engines and radiation shielding while still in safe space.

His ships passed the test with flying colors, as hoped. His Task Group One could push harder, but that would leave the rest of the Fleet behind. In theory, the GMS-equipped ships could cut the journey to Londu space by about a quarter—they'd halve the travel time in systems but have the same transit time in the skip lines.

Of course, given that none of his ships had a seventy-day endurance on their onboard fuel stores, they'd need to refuel more often without the tankers accompanying them. That, in Henry's rough math, would add fourteen days to the journey versus the plan for the Expeditionary Fleet.

TG One could make it ten days earlier, *if* they could sustain two KPS^2 for the entire journey and *if* they could find convenient gas giants at the right intervals.

Even with Kahlmor providing the Londu maps and having all of the data from the first consular mission, Henry wasn't convinced everything would break that neatly his way. So, he was traveling with a logistics train, which required escorts, which meant that his GMS ships were restricted by the acceleration of their reaction-drive counterparts.

"We are approaching the skip line to Groombridge Sixteen-Eighteen," Campbell informed Henry from the bridge. "Any new orders, ser?"

Henry glanced around his flag bridge. His staff was working away at a dozen different tasks, but he silently pinged Hawthorne's network.

"Any concerns about the Fleet, Ops?" he asked her.

"Couple of harmonics and a few flickers that we're passing on to Colonel De Veen," Hawthorne told him immediately.

Colonel Miša De Veen was his Ophiuchian Fleet Engineering Officer. She'd make sure that the engineering crews on the ships in question were asked the appropriate questions and given the appropriate supplies to make sure their problems were fixed.

Or, at least, that was her *job*. He wasn't sure yet whether De Veen would live up to his expectations.

"Anything critical that requires us to hold in Procyon for repairs?" he asked.

Hawthorne paused and glanced over at the Chief seated next to her.

"I don't think so. Your opinion, Chief?"

It was another check mark on the Commodore's ledger in Henry's mind that she was both prepared to get her Chief's opinion *and* to do so openly in front of the Admiral.

"*Soma* is showing a bit more of a misalignment on her fusion drives than I'd *like*," the CPO noted. "It's still technically inside variances and it's probably easily fixed, especially since we have a full fabricator setup and eighteen *other Tvastar*-class ships to raid for parts."

"Is it worth holding the whole fleet for?" Henry asked. "Or leaving *Soma* here, for that matter?"

The Chief shook her head.

"That's your call, sers," she pointed out. "But I'd say the risk of doing more than burning an excessive amount of fuel is basically zero, and her engineers should be able to line things up the first time we stop to fuel."

"All right. Pass the order for the Fleet to skip on arrival at the line," Henry told Hawthorne. He *had* a dedicated communications officer, but Lieutenant Colonel Melany Perrin wasn't on duty, and the young Commander running the department was, quite reasonably, deferring to the operations officer.

"Everyone hold on to your stomachs."

Henry wasn't sure *who* had made the crack and didn't even bother to find out. The jump from Sol to Procyon was a long one, with neither of the stars involved being large enough to change the basic timeline.

On top of that, though, something in *Raven*'s icosaspace impulse generators, the "kickers" of the skip drive, had been noticeably off during the twenty-three-hour jump. The kicks had been even more unpleasant than usual—and skipping was *never* a fun experience.

"Captain Campbell *assures* me the skip drive has been realigned and the cleansing incense burned," Henry told his staff. "I'm sure this will be much less—"

The human brain and body had no sense that could truly handle a twenty-dimensional motion. From what Henry understood, it wasn't even like the impulse generators only created *one* twenty-dimensional motion, either. Over the roughly second-long sequence of the impulse, the generators created over thirty different impulses, all intended to move the ship ever so slightly out of phase with three-dimensional reality and send it bouncing along the line of gravity between two stars.

Between the strange three-dimensional components of those impulses and the human difficulty in comprehending the *other* seventeen dimensions…skipping was just not something humanity could process.

This time, it felt like someone stepped on his groin in stiletto heels while he started falling sideways, forward, backward and up—all at the same time—and then promptly reversed a moment later as his stomach tried to revolt.

It was always over quickly enough, but it *felt* like it endured for hours. Henry finally exhaled as the impulses faded and chuckled wryly.

"Well, that was *better*, I think, but I believe *Raven* still has some minor work of her own to be done!"

THE HOLOPROJECTOR in Henry's office had their full course laid out in the air above him. Once they left Groombridge 1618, they were outside of space claimed by the UPA. If they'd cut through the former Kenmiri Empire, they could make it to Londu space in about eighty days, but both his orders and his own inclinations were against that plan.

That left the Expeditionary Fleet retracing the course of the original consular mission to the Londu. Back then, they'd needed to avoid the Empire to avoid both notice and hostile action.

Now, it was as much to avoid entanglements. They had no idea what was going on in most of the outer provinces that the Kenmiri had abandoned. The UPSF had *some* idea of what was going on in the inner provinces that the Kenmiri still controlled, but not as much as they'd liked.

The Kenmiri's death would be a long and extended decline. Their Kenmorad breeding creches had spawned billions of new Kenmiri every year of all three castes. Without them, after six years of no new births, the Drones that made up the majority of the Kenmiri population were rapidly shrinking in number.

The Warriors and Artisans would live on for decades and might even find a technological solution to the loss of the Kenmorad. The drones only lived ten years on average, burning brightly to try to earn remembrance by their longer-lived siblings and parents.

Some would live longer, but the laws of averages said that over half of the untold trillions of drones in the Kenmiri Empire were no more.

Still, the inner provinces remained Kenmiri-controlled, and the Kenmiri remained too powerful for anyone to make war to free the slave worlds still under their rule. The outer provinces, renamed *sectors* by agreement at the Great Gathering, were more amorphous—

and, in many ways, more *dangerous*—areas to operate in for the UPSF.

Stabilizing Ra had taken years and vast amounts of blood and money. It had swiftly proven more than worth it by any standard the UPA measured by, but it had not been easy. The other eleven outer sectors were still unknowns. Traversing them to reach the Londu risked both threats and entanglements that the UPA was not yet ready to deal with.

Henry knew that they were avoiding people who might ask them for help, and that bothered him—but the UPSF could never have taken control of the wreckage of the Empire. So, instead of dealing with old friends justifiably angry at the UPA's absence, he would skirt those stars and stay focused on his mission.

Not that the stars beyond what had been Kenmiri space were empty. Without Kenmiri forced-colonization plans, though, they were more sparsely populated, with habitable worlds without local sentient life mixed with worlds that had produced both Ashall and other sentients.

The course from the original consular mission would avoid every system they'd known was inhabited then. His people had adjusted it because there *were* systems where they'd found people and he had the contrasting priorities of both needing to avoid contact and wanting to ask if anyone had seen Okavaz's ships.

That meant there were actually *three* courses hanging in the air in his office. A pale blue line connected the stars the first mission had traveled through. A similar pale orange line marked the planned course of Lord of a Million Miles Okavaz's squadron.

And cutting between them was the green line marking his planned course. With Londu intelligence and maps added to clear up their information on that end of the course, he knew that he could make his way all the way to the Sovereignty and avoid any entanglements.

Except that course didn't intersect with Okavaz's course until the very end. If he followed the current plan, they'd have almost *no* chance of finding the missing Londu squadron.

There were options. The easiest was just to take the inverse of Okavaz's course—except that Okavaz had similarly been trying to avoid attention, and the Londu maps of the regions they were traversing were worse than the UPA's.

To avoid potential conflict, Okavaz's course was plotted to avoid any star likely to have habitable worlds or significant traffic. That meant his course had avoided both the giant stars whose mass allowed for longer-range skips and many of the regular sized stars the "normal" skip speed was based on.

Okavaz's course had been a zigzag, bouncing between smaller stars and adding almost twenty days to his journey. It had already been long enough since Kahlmor had separated from Okavaz and the Londu expedition had left their space that Henry couldn't afford to add almost three weeks to his journey.

Not if he figured he was going to help at all. Either the Londu had handled the situation on their own or it had likely degraded drastically. He'd keep his fleet together, add some time to allow his ships to arrive as a unit with the technical aid accompanying his GMS fleet. He *wouldn't* add three weeks just to find Okavaz's ships.

But there had to be a way. That the Scion had sent for the UPA's help would smooth over a lot of rough edges, but having a Lord of a Million Miles, one of the highest-ranked officers the Londu *had*, backing him up could only help.

And having a Lord of a Million Miles owing him a life debt could make a *huge* difference.

A thought brought up the list of Task Group One's ships. A battle-cruiser, a carrier, a cruiser and eight destroyers. All capable of twice the maximum acceleration of his second task group—and *four* times their standard cruising thrust.

"Strickland," he opened a channel to his secretary with a thought. "Can you get a meeting set up with Hawthorne, Kahlmor, and…" He swallowed a sigh that Strickland shouldn't hear. "…Larue, sometime before we exit skip?"

"Of course, ser," his secretary said instantly. "Should I tell them what the meeting is about?"

"We're going to need a plan to find Kahlmor's boss," Henry said calmly. "I want to touch base with our people before I sit down with Colonel Ivanova."

Svetlana Ivanova was the woman who commanded the newly constituted Destroyer Squadron Forty—Task Group One's eight *Cataphract*-B destroyers.

Destroyers that were probably the best ships for mid-range scouting in the galaxy.

21

SYLVIA MADE a point of being in the bay when the shuttle arrived. There was no honor guard for a day-to-day administrative meeting, little of the pomp that a more-senior squadron commander might claim by her right, but Sylvia knew Svetlana Ivanova did not care.

The Colonel emerged from her shuttle like some Russian Valkyrie forged from iron and ash, taller than Sylvia but just as sharp-edged. Her hair was golden blonde where Sylvia's had begun to fade toward silver, but a stranger would have been justified in thinking they were cousins.

Ivanova saluted Sylvia crisply, practically ignoring poor Lieutenant Commander Strickland standing behind the Ambassador. The flag secretary was the Eridanian officer's *official* welcoming party, but allowances had to be made.

Sylvia clucked her tongue at the younger woman and reached out to clasp Ivanova's forearm.

"It's good to see you, Colonel," Sylvia said. "It's been, what, fifteen years?"

"Seventeen," Ivanova corrected in softly Russian-accented English. "Since the *first* time we went to see the Londu. You, a wet-behind-the-ears new-minted diplomat, hanging on Karl Rembrandt's every word.

Me, an overly gawky brand-spanking-new Lieutenant, glad to see *anyone* from home."

Ivanova was *somewhat* overstating how fresh twenty-eight-year-old Sylvia had been, the Ambassador mentally noted. She wasn't, in Sylvia's opinion, overstating *anything* about then-twenty-three-year-old Ivanova, assistant tactical officer on the destroyer *Locksley*.

Karl Rembrandt had been the senior ambassador to the Londu—and, over time, had promoted Sylvia to *co*-ambassador with the Londu, while they'd forged the bilateral agreements that had turned the Vesheron from barely more than a theoretical common allegiance among rebel factions to the alliance that had won the war.

And a long time before that, under a different name, Svetlana Ivanova had been Sylvia's second real boyfriend.

"Lieutenant Commander Cornell Strickland is here to escort you to your meeting with the Admiral," Sylvia told the destroyer squadron commander. "But I wanted to make sure you remembered me and knew you were welcome aboard *Raven*."

"Commander," Ivanova greeted Strickland with a firm nod, finally acknowledging the official welcoming party. "Apologies. The Ambassador and I go back a long way."

"No apologies necessary, ser," the secretary told her. "I actually have a note from the Admiral suggesting that I see if Ambassador Todorovich is free to join the meeting as well. There are potential diplomatic factors to the plan he's discussing."

"Really," Ivanova said. "I suppose I will find out what the Admiral is thinking in a few moments. Will you join us, Ambassador?"

"If Henry thinks there may be diplomatic factors, he's usually right," Sylvia observed. "Lead the way, Commander."

SYLVIA HAD SEEN Quaid's people set up the flag mess for the briefing on her way out, so she was expecting the room in its new configuration. Instead of a dining table, a circular briefing table now held pride of place.

Several officers were already present, and Henry himself entered the room a few seconds after Sylvia and Ivanova arrived.

"We're still waiting on Lord of Fifty Thousand Miles Kahlmor," he observed. "Welcome aboard *Raven*, Colonel Ivanova. You've met myself and Commodore Hawthorne, of course—and it seems you know Ambassador Todorovich as well. This is Lieutenant Colonel Cheng, our logistics officer, and Lieutenant Colonel Larue, our intelligence officer."

"Colonels," Ivanova greeted the two junior officers as she took a seat. "I feel I should have brought more of my people."

"We'll want to bring your captains into this discussion eventually, but right now we're looking at the high level of the plans and options before us," Wong told her.

One of Quaid's junior stewards appeared between Sylvia and Ivanova.

"Drinks, sers?" he asked. "Some snacks will be coming in a few moments."

The stewards connected with everyone, and Quaid himself intercepted Kahlmor as the Londu entered the room.

"Thank you, everyone," Henry told them all, switching to Kem so Kahlmor could follow. "About half of you got pinned to a wall while we were skipping to Groombridge Sixteen-Eighteen to listen to the idea that struck me. Those of you who were not in that meeting are, of course, the people who are going to have to execute the plan."

He smiled and spread his hands with a chuckle.

"Welcome to the military," he warned.

An astrographic map of their course out to Londu space appeared above the center of the circular table. Two lines, one green and one blue, marked connections between the UPA and the Londu Sovereignty.

"The green line here represents our planned course toward Londu space," he explained. "The blue is the course Lord of a Million Miles Okavaz was planning to take toward our space."

One star was suddenly highlighted in white.

"This is K-L-D-R-Seven-Nine-Five," Henry observed. "The Londu call it the Seventh Rising Dawn."

KLDR-795 was a blue giant, the type of massive star that acceler-ated travel toward it and allowed longer-range skips. *That* was a piece of navigation Sylvia had to know, because those stars were both gener-ally uninhabitable and generally strategically vital.

"It was in the Seventh Rising Dawn System that Okavaz's squadron met a fast freighter group from the Purple Stripe Orange Stripe Green Stripe Red Stripe Drifter Convoy," he explained. "It was this Drifter group that gave Lord of Fifty Thousand Miles Kahlmor a ride to join Red Stripe White Stripe.

"That makes Seventh Rising Dawn the last place that we *know* Lord Okavaz and her squadron were."

The blue line prior to Seventh Rising Dawn vanished from the display, and Sylvia could see at least part of the problem. Their course never diverged massively from the inverse of Okavaz, but it also never aligned with the route the Londu had planned on taking.

"Thanks to UPSF standard patrols and civilian survey missions, we know that there is no sign of the Londu in these systems," Henry continued, highlighting the last few systems on the route to human space.

"These stars in between, however, represent thirty-seven star systems where Okavaz's mission could have gone astray. While Okavaz's infor-mation was more limited, we know that four of those systems are inhab-ited. Hence Ambassador Todorovich's presence in this meeting."

Sylvia nodded to Henry and took over as if they'd planned it. They *hadn't*, but this was information she'd been eyeing anyway.

"None of these systems are El-Vesheron," she reminded everyone. "All are Taishall." The Kem word meant *outside race*, a pretty distinct line. All the El-Vesheron—like the Londu or the humans—were Taishall...but not all Taishall were El-Vesheron.

"Three of the four are Ashall, the fourth a more...fluid life form," she continued. "All four have been contacted by the UPA in the past, and all four were aware of the Kenmiri. They specifically declined involvement in the Vesheron and other interstellar politics."

"Would the arrival of Okavaz's squadron have been seen as a threat?" Kahlmor asked.

"Yes," she told him plainly. "But the original arrivals of our consular missions were seen as a threat, Lord of Fifty Thousand Miles. So long as Okavaz did not *act* as a threat upon her arrival, she would have been encouraged to leave but not attacked.

"I believe." Sylvia raised a warning hand. "Remember that all four of these rejected long-term diplomatic contact with the United Planets Alliance. They chose an isolationist path—one I cannot blame them for, given the state of the galaxy at the time.

"Contact with these systems should be handled carefully. If we are planning on meeting with them, I will prepare consular parties."

One of them she would lead herself. Sylvia had made contact with the Lefe System herself during the war and the Lefen were dangerous. Not hostile, not automatically, but dangerous.

"Thank you, Ambassador," Henry told her. "We'll need those parties."

He gestured at the map in front of everyone.

"We cannot significantly adjust our course without losing time we are not certain the Londu can afford," he said. "We have, thanks to a mixture of our maps and the Londu maps, established what we believe is the most efficient possible course to get us to Londu space. But our overlap with Okavaz's course is limited. We cross her path in no more than three systems.

"We need to know what happened to her and her squadron," he concluded. "And while we cannot divert the main body of the Expeditionary Fleet, Task Group One's GMS ships can sustain cruising accelerations of three to four times the safe sustained speed of our reaction-drive vessels."

The fusion-drive warships, at least, *could* run at one KPS^2. But their inertial compensators couldn't counter all of that thrust, and the crew would be subjected to about twenty pseudogravities of thrust—requiring everyone to move into acceleration tanks designed to protect them from the acceleration. That wasn't an environment the crews could stay in for extended periods.

The GMS ships, on the other hand, were only equipped with inertial compensators for emergencies. The GMS kept the ship in a state of free fall, avoiding any bleed-through to the crew and allowing a far higher sustained acceleration.

"Commodore Hawthorne and her Operations team have put together these subordinate courses," Henry told everyone. New, paler green lines appeared on the map, separating from the main green line, looping out to run along a few of the systems of Okavaz's course and then returning to the main body.

"Of course, Colonel Ivanova, you and your people will need to review the courses and timelines Commodore Hawthorne has put together," he assured Sylvia's friend before the squadron CO said a word.

"The basic system is going to be this: we will be detaching two divisions of two destroyers apiece at a time who will proceed out from the main body of the Expeditionary Fleet at cruise acceleration.

"Depending on our distance and the skips available, they will scout between two and four systems on Okavaz's route, then return to the Fleet. None of them will be away from the main body for more than one hundred sixty hours."

From Sylvia's briefings, that was less than half of the *Cataphract*-Bs' endurance between refueling. Not quite a week, it would give the ships plenty of margin for if they *found* Okavaz's ships and to avoid needing to engage in independent fueling from gas giants.

"Will we have any support, ser?" Ivanova asked. "My understanding, after all, is that Okavaz's squadron consisted of equivalents to our Gem cruisers. If we are hunting a threat that eliminated over six million tons of Londu cruisers, less than two million tons of our destroyers feels…vulnerable."

"Agreed," Henry said. "There is a hard limit to how much we can detach from the Expeditionary Fleet, but the plan is that *Turquoise* will be on *this* course."

A darker green line appeared on the map. It never went as far out as the destroyer sweeps, but it split the distance between the two destroyer divisions.

"If you encounter a threat, you are to fall back on *Turquoise* immediately," he continued. "An enemy that thinks they are chasing two destroyers is going to have a rude awakening, colliding with an *Amethyst*-class cruiser."

"I see, ser. I will want to review the plan in detail, as you suggested, but I do not see anything unworkable here," Ivanova told the Admiral. "If Ambassador Todorovich can provide those consular teams to smooth over encounters with the people we know are out here, we should be able to find Lord Okavaz."

"Unfortunately, I do not expect to find her," Henry said bluntly. "But I do want to know what *happened* to her. Someone or something prevented a full cruiser squadron of the Blades of the Scion reaching the UPA. I very much want to know the particulars, Colonel. Who. What. Where. When. How…and *why*."

Sylvia was surprised he'd been that open about that with Kahlmor in the room and the meeting taking place in Kem. Kahlmor had been Okavaz's Voice of the Steel, after all—the Lord of a Million Miles equivalent to Commodore Hawthorne—and he had to be hoping to find his commanding officer alive!

"I suspect that Okavaz's fate is relevant to our mission to the Sovereignty," Henry concluded. "More, however, I am certain that her fate is *either* relevant to the attacks on the Sovereignty *or* represents a clear and present threat to the UPA itself.

"While finding such a threat would not change *our* mission, we can and will warn our superiors about it."

Faster than most in the room expected, too. Sylvia knew about *Sanskrit* and the ansible. She wasn't sure how many *other* people in the room were briefed on the new subspace-tunnel communicators, but she *knew* that Kahlmor wasn't.

"Okavaz's disappearance is a mystery related to our mission," the Admiral said. "And I refuse to believe that a mystery does not represent a *threat* until I know what it hides."

22

ELEVEN DAYS LATER, Sylvia Todorovich waited patiently on the flag bridge of the destroyer *Hussar* as she plunged back into regular space. The Lefe System was the second of the four inhabited systems they'd check in with—and Sylvia had made sure *she* was the one visiting it.

"You didn't tell me, Sylvia, just what made you so concerned about the Lefens," Ivanova asked.

Sylvia had seen Henry's original plan and *knew* that *Hussar* hadn't been intended to be part of this particular scouting run. Ivanova had apparently figured that if Sylvia thought it was important, she'd make sure she was present.

"*Attila* has exited skip and is taking up formation five thousand kilometers to starboard," a Chief reported before Sylvia could reply. "Captains Chaudhary and Slovacek are beginning passive sweeps, waiting on orders to go active."

"I've danced around the topic since we left the fleet, Ambassador, but now is most definitely the time to tell me what you're worried about," Ivanova said bluntly.

"The Lefens are a prickly lot, determined in their pride and their culture. They are also xenophobic, isolationist and obligate carnivores," Sylvia said calmly. "They *ate* the crew of the Kenmiri survey ship that found them, Colonel.

"Your coms team should have the identification sequences I provided," she continued. "Please tell me we're transmitting them."

"The division is dark," Ivanova replied. "We're not transmitting anything."

A chill ran down Sylvia's spine.

"For the love of *fucking* gods," she snapped. "Transmit the damn sequences. We have *not* evaded detection."

"We're not seeing any signs that—"

"Transmit the sequences," Ivanova ordered, cutting off the operations noncom.

"On it," the woman replied.

Sylvia's old friend turned a level gaze at her.

"How much danger are we in, Sylvia?" she asked.

"That depends on how close their nearest ship was," Sylvia said grimly. "Their weapons aren't any better at piercing gravity shields than anyone else's, but—"

"Contact, contact at four light-seconds! Multiple contacts. What the—"

"But quantity has a quality all its own," Sylvia finished the truism as the operations team cut off their curses and updated the flag tactical display.

"Lay it out for me, Commander," Ivanova told her ops officer, Commander Wu Yash.

"We have six contacts at roughly one-point-two million kilometers," the man said. "All appear to be dreadnought size and mass, minimum one kilometer in length. Energy signatures are denser than Kenmiri standard, but I'm not seeing signs of plasma cannon."

"You won't," Sylvia told Wu. "They don't have missiles, either. Not that it will matter. Each of those dreadnoughts has about as many heavy lasers as the entirety of Task Group One."

Dreadnought was a term with a very specific meaning to the UPSF, and Sylvia used it intentionally. A dreadnought was a ship built out of an asteroid, with dozens of meters of natural nickel-iron armor left intact over its technological core.

The Kenmiri version was smoothed to a mirror shine, decorated with murals, and armed with heavy plasma cannon. The *Lefen* version, on the other hand, was intentionally left rough-surfaced to help conceal the firing lenses of the dozens of heavy battle lasers.

"Both captains are asking for orders, ser," Ivanova's coms officer reported.

"We hold position and see if we can open a channel with the codes the Ambassador has provided," Ivanova ordered. She held Sylvia's gaze. "Can they detect our energy and grav-shields?"

"Likely, but given that the gravity shield is also your engine, you can get away with that, I think," Sylvia told her. "And then I understand they shouldn't be able to detect the energy screen."

"True." The Colonel was silent for a second, then finally turned back to her staff. "Division will raise gravity shields and bring the GMS online. We will fall back from the Lefens at matching acceleration."

"Dreadnoughts are accelerating at point-six-five KPS-squared, ser," Wu reported. "They are building velocity toward us."

"We're still over a million kilometers apart, Commander. We can let them close a little bit. We keep the velocity constant and leave the rest to the Ambassador."

At that implied request, Sylvia leaned forward in the observer's seat she'd been given and networked into *Hussar*'s computer systems.

Even including the crew of the ship that had carried her on her last visit, less than four hundred humans had ever visited the Lefe System. None of them had successfully learned the local language, though the linguists from the two species had hashed out a usable translator with surprising speed.

"Translator is online; I'm hailing the lead dreadnought," Sylvia told Ivanova. "Remember that they're near-humans. They may *look* exactly like us, but they aren't us and don't think like us."

And even appearances could be deceiving, from what Sylvia had heard. While *most* Ashall races were physically compatible in terms of sexuality, the Lefens most definitely were *not*.

But the man who appeared in her network seconds after she sent her electronic call into the void wouldn't have looked out of place on

Hussar's own bridge. He was a tanned-looking man with dark brown hair and a neatly trimmed beard, wearing a uniform that resembled Sylvia's own conservatively cut business suit.

Twelve red buttons had been sewn onto his left shoulder in three even rows, marking him as an *extremely* senior military officer.

"United Planets Alliance ships," he said, the computer translation slow and stilted. "Your codes provide safe arrival. No more. Identify and specify your purpose in Lefe."

The translation would render her own words equally stiff, so Sylvia chose them carefully.

"I am Ambassador Sylvia Todorovich," she told the officer. "These are the United Planets Alliance destroyers *Hussar* and *Attila*."

The names wouldn't be translated, just as the system name wasn't.

"We are looking for allied ships that went missing," she continued. "Six ships, vessels of the Londu, were meant to pass through Lefe, traveling to the Alliance.

"We do not need to approach the worlds of Lefe. We do not challenge the Wall of Stone."

There were basically two safe ways to interact with the Lefens: as a superior predator or as a supplicant. While in the grand scheme of things, the degree to which the UPSF outgunned the Lefen Wall of Stone was mind-boggling, the UPA had never had more than two ships in the system.

Supplicant was easier to sell, even if the necessary obsequiousness could easily stick in her teeth. For all her warnings to Ivanova, the only technology the Lefens really had up to UPA standards was sensors. The six dreadnoughts could almost certainly take out the two destroyers with Sylvia today...but *Turquoise* probably wouldn't even need the rest of the Expeditionary Fleet to obliterate the squadron of slow, short-ranged, heavily armored but basically unshielded local warships.

"Reviewing passive scanners and checking against the signatures for these guys and what we have on file," Wu reported. "Those ships are sneakier than anything that big has any right to be."

"The size is part of it," Ivanova replied. "They can bury a lot of heat in a few million tons of rock. What are you picking up? I presume if we'd seen the Londu, you'd have said something."

"We can't be certain on our IDs of any ships except the six right in front of us," the ops officer warned. "But I think we're seeing another nine squadrons of six dreadnoughts each wandering around the system.

"There's a bunch of civilian traffic between two inhabited planets and some infrastructure around a pair of gas giants, but I'm not seeing anything *except* the dreadnoughts for warships."

There was a reason the UPA didn't build dreadnoughts and that the Kenmiri only used them for their heaviest hitters. The infrastructure needed to reforge an entire asteroid into a ship was massive and expensive. For anything more rationally sized, it made more sense to refine asteroids into plates and panels and assemble ships from scratch.

But if you lacked the complex ceramics and energy-management systems that made up modern armor, asteroid-hulled dreadnoughts might feel like all that was worth building.

"The ships we're looking at do appear more advanced than the consular mission reports," Wu added. "Engines are more powerful; energy density overall looks higher. I'd say each of them is generating about thirty percent more power than the ships we saw ten years ago.

"Weapons fit matches the Ambassador's suggestion, though. I'm not seeing plasma cannon or missiles. Pure laser armament."

"We can out-dance them and nuke them from range if we have to," Ivanova said. "They seem...inefficient."

"They are. They're also very big," Sylvia pointed out. "As it was explained to me, a laser's effective range is a matter of hit probabilities as much as focal distances—and the math is significantly different between firing *two* lasers and two *hundred*."

Ivanova had learned self-control rising to her current rank, but Commander Wu wasn't as practiced at the mask of command, and Sylvia could *see* the moment where the truth of that statement sank in.

"Ser, the Lefen ships have increased their acceleration to point-seven-five KPS-squared," a tech reported.

"Division is to continue matching their acceleration," Ivanova said calmly. "Todorovich?"

"We should be hearing from them in response to my request for information," Sylvia told her. The velocity Ivanova was leaving in place was slowly eating away at the distance, but so long as they matched the Lefens' acceleration, that velocity wasn't *increasing*.

"I would argue that their increased acceleration is a form of response," the Colonel replied.

"They're testing us," Sylvia realized aloud. "Hold steady, Colonel."

"Wonderful. Commander Wu, run a simulation for me, please. Assuming they have comparable targeting systems, sensors and heavy lasers to us and are firing *three* hundred lasers per ship, what is the likelihood of us taking damage at this range?"

Sylvia winced as Ivanova laid out the scenario. So far as their closer scans and analysis from the consular mission could tell, the Lefen targeting systems and lasers had been inferior to their UPSF counterparts...ten years earlier.

"They *will* hit us, ser," Wu reported softly after about ten seconds. "Assuming they have their lasers set up for an appropriate scatter pattern, each ship is statistically likely to score between seven and ten lasers hit on the gravity shield of one of our ships.

"Likelihood of any *individual* laser burning through the gravity shield at this range is minimal, though if they sustain fire, they will get lucky sooner or later."

"And that, Commander, is why we have the energy screen now," the squadron commander murmured. "Todorovich? I am uninclined to sit here until they decide to punch me, but it's your call."

"They are testing us," Sylvia repeated. "Frankly, if they *did* wipe out Okavaz, I'd expect them to have already fired. *This*, Colonel Ivanova, is about proving whose cloaca is tougher."

And Sylvia was not using *that* particular organ descriptor randomly.

"Understood. In that case..."

Ivanova straightened and smiled coldly.

"*Hussar, Attila*, go to full active sensors," she barked. "ID the dreadnought that transmitted and lock her in for missile fire. Stand by full salvos of direct-impact nuclear warheads."

"Against their armor and shields, I don't think we'd do more than burn off some metal vapor," Wu warned. "Even if we got past whatever antimissile defenses they have."

"Oh, I know, Commander," Ivanova agreed. "Squadron will turn over on my command and launch attack run—but hold fire until my order."

Sylvia considered the situation for a few more seconds, then mentally shrugged.

"It's your division, Colonel," she told her friend. "If they don't want to talk…"

"I won't shoot first, Ambassador, but I will damn well make them pay attention to me!"

"Target locked in," Wu reported. "We can read their hull numbers, ser. Two hundred fifteen heavy lasers, plus/minus ten percent. Estimate six hundred defensive laser clusters, again, plus/minus ten percent."

"I'm guessing we don't have much chance of successfully putting twenty-four missile salvos through that defensive net," Ivanova said with a chuckle. "But we'll stick to impact nukes for the first round. Let's see what these buggers do. Prepare to turn over."

The destroyer acquired a chill silence around Sylvia, as if all four hundred–odd people aboard were waiting to see what happened.

"Incoming transmission!"

Sylvia already had the channel to the Lefen dreadnoughts feeding to her network, and concealed a cold smile as the named senior officer reappeared in front of her.

"I am High Foundation Adoran of the Wall of Stone," he introduced himself through the translation program, as if Sylvia's ships *hadn't* just dialed his ship in with seven different kinds of active scanner.

"Your name is known. Your ships are different. Analysis confirms your individual identity." Adoran paused, smiling and revealing that his teeth did not look *at all* human.

"Lefe is aware of the Londu. No direct contact has occurred. No Londu vessels have entered Lefe. No unknown vessels have entered systems scouted from the Wall. Trust or do not. You will withdraw."

"Straightforward enough," Ivanova muttered. "So, do we buy it?"

"It's buy it or fight sixty lumbering dreadnoughts with two hundred–plus lasers each," Sylvia pointed out. "I think we can accept that Okavaz didn't make it this far. Let's get out of here before the High Foundation thinks we look like dinner."

She figured that the Londu squadron had gone missing earlier in their journey than this...but she'd *also* figured that if any of the systems had, well, *eaten* Okavaz's and her people, it had been Lefe.

23

OF ALL THE things being sent over a highly classified, limited-use, faster-than-light communications network, the evening news wasn't one of them.

The difference between the evening news and the UPSF daily domestic intelligence update was, on the other hand, somewhat academic at times. Like most officers, Henry figured the daily update was a touch less biased and a touch more in depth, but if he was honest, civilian "evening news" was basically a shorthand for exactly the kind of compressed news update IntelDiv sent out at this point.

"With the General Assembly vote today, the number of star systems sitting as official full members of the General Assembly rises from eight to fifteen," the uniformed officer presenting the update informed him. Less than ten percent of Henry's officers were getting the update, but those who knew about the ansible were senior enough to *need* to know what was going on back home.

"The exact number of new delegates to be added to the Assembly is under discussion, but IntelDiv is expecting it to bring the Assembly's numbers up to about eight hundred, followed by a reallocation of the delegates by population.

"That reallocation will, of course, have to take into account the two-delegate minimum allocated to the new seven 'nations' we're adding. Given that the seven star systems in question represent approximately five hundred million people in total, none are expected to only have the minimum number of delegates.

"This is going to create tension with a number of the smaller Earth nations who hold national status by virtue of legacy memberships," the analyst warned. "Unless the Assembly chooses to fix their delegate numbers, it is inevitable that national members of the UPA with smaller populations—such as Australia or Senegal—may find themselves losing their additional delegates as the minimum for a third seat rises to thirty or even forty million citizens."

Henry was entirely on board with expanding the membership list of the General Assembly. There were close to thirty star systems inhabited by humans that fell under the authority of the UPA. While the eight traditional star systems of the UPA represented ninety percent of the human race, there were still *five billion* people spread across twenty star systems represented by fewer voices in the Assembly than, say, Turkey.

"In public interviews with Avalon-born Faith Smith of the Recognition Alliance, she has suggested that the RA sees this as a waypoint and not as a complete victory," the analyst warned. "IntelDiv continues to keep a careful eye on the Recognition Alliance in case of radicalization. So far, however, both the group's leaders and grassroots movements have remained pleased with their success within our system, and the organization and movement have proven resistant to hostile acto—"

The chime on Henry's office door sounded and he sighed, freezing and dismissing the update.

The existence of the ansible remained a closely held secret in the Expeditionary Fleet. Henry didn't want to risk someone accidentally revealing it to the Londu while they were in the Sovereignty, so it remained a purely administrative connection. Even *he* didn't have access to it for personal communication.

That meant that access to live updates from the UPA was limited to Colonels and above, with the explicit exceptions of Henry's staff officers and warship captains. He didn't *like* it, but the alternative was risking some poor Lieutenant saying the wrong thing once they were in Londu space and starting a war.

"Enter," he ordered, and concealed a different sigh as Lieutenant Colonel Dumuzi Larue stepped into the room. While Larue had *mostly* been more useful than he'd expected over the last month, he still preferred IntelDiv on the other side of a light-century of distance.

"Colonel. How can I help you?" he asked.

"We have a problem, ser," Larue told him, saluting and then taking a seat without asking.

"Which one?" Henry said drily, eyeing the younger man carefully. "Are we talking about the search for a missing squadron of Londu warships that has, over thirty days and eleven star systems, turned up *nothing*? Or are we talking about the fact that a logistics screw-up means we're going to run out of beer before we even reach Londu space, because someone misplaced a decimal point on how much hops to load alongside the breweries?

"Or are we going with the complaint filed by one of *Ultima*'s Chief Petty Officers that two of *Visigoth*'s Chiefs fleeced an Ensign from *Ultima* of her entire life savings in a rigged poker game? Or my latest brand-new discovery that our auxiliary crews aren't held to the same standards as our fully military personnel, and that one of the freighter Captains didn't have a contraceptive implant?"

The last apparently took Larue by surprise, and he paused, thrown off-balance.

"How is a freighter CO not having a contraceptive implant your problem?" he asked.

"Because the idiot slept with one of his crew, who intentionally turned *off* hers in what appears to have been a misguided attempt at romantic entrapment," Henry told the intelligence officer. "So, now we have a pregnancy in a fleet with *zero* fully qualified prenatal experts and a starship captain with a legitimate claim to a sexual assault charge…except that because *he's* the damn captain, *she* has an equally legitimate claim to press an abuse-of-authority charge *back*."

Henry shook his head. He'd read the case studies and seen it in action serving under other officers, but it had never truly sunk just how much the Admiral of a fleet in motion was the final arbiter of *all* authority and grievances.

He was basically running a town of twenty-ish thousand human beings, in space, that was going to have to be able to make war at the end of the trip.

"Last but not least, I suppose," he said grimly, "is the incipient political transformation taking place back home that could have repercussions and impacts on I don't even know how many of our crew—that I can't even *tell* them about, because less than fifty people in the entire fleet have access to the update briefings sent via the ansible. Is your problem any of those, Colonel, or are you going to make my day even more complicated?"

Not that his probably unjustified rant was a particularly complete listing of the issues that had crossed Henry's desk *that day*.

"Unfortunately, ser, it is definitely the latter," Larue told him. "But the ansible is part of the problem."

Henry nodded, the mask of command finally taking over from his irritation at dealing with the intelligence officer.

"How bad?" he asked flatly.

"We have a spy aboard the fleet. Someone is concealing coded dispatches inside the logistics updates that are being sent back to the UPA," Larue explained quickly. "We haven't yet broken the encryption or managed to identify the source, but just the fact that unauthorized messages are being relayed through *Sanskrit* is a serious issue."

Larue was even polite enough *not* to say *I told you so*, which Henry appreciated.

"Okay." He took a moment to consider the situation. "What do you *know*?"

"We've been sending daily updates via the ansible since leaving Groombridge Sixteen-Eighteen," Larue stated as a baseline. "The first few days were clean, but sixteen days ago, the first dispatch was sent.

"My team missed it," he said flatly. "We only found that one when we went back looking for repeated anomalies. Since then, however, a dispatch has been sent after each skip into a new system. Over sixteen days, someone has sent seven messages back to Earth.

"One of my junior people ran a data-breakdown analysis of our transmissions back. It's not something I would have thought to run because it's a rather brute-force, bit-by-bit comparison that doesn't really tell you anything.

"Except whether your transmission bandwidth is regularly off from what you're expecting." Larue shrugged. "There are more sophisticated ways to find a hidden message, but whoever wrote our spy's code knew most of them—and the countermeasures."

"So, you found the message in…the data-package sizes?" Henry asked.

"That's…a gross oversimplification but fundamentally correct," the intelligence officer confirmed. "Once we knew that something was off —and not *consistently* off, in a way that would suggest a reporting issue somewhere—we backtracked the anomalies, nailed down the impacted transmissions and located the dispatches."

Henry was not a computer-systems specialist, but he'd been a starfighter pilot, a tactical officer and a starship captain. All of those were roles that had required a passing or better-than-passing knowledge of electronic warfare, which gave him an idea of just how much work Larue was brushing over.

"Lieutenant Commander Oluwafemi Kikelomo was the analyst who found this, and he has been at the heart of the effort since," Larue observed. His determination to give his junior credit gave him one of Henry's mental check marks.

Henry was self-aware enough to know that Larue wasn't getting as many of those as most of his other staff officers, and it *wasn't* because of any major failings on the IntelDiv officer's part.

"So, we know someone is sending notes home," Henry said. "What else do you *know*? Any idea of the contents?"

"Nothing definitive, ser," Larue admitted. "The packets are encrypted with what appears to be an evolution of a protocol used by the Eridani about twenty-five years ago."

Henry arched a warning eyebrow. He had *suspicions* about his intelligence officer and the man's prejudices around Sylvia's home system.

"Are you suggesting…"

"No, ser," Larue said as Henry trailed off. "It's too obvious, in my opinion. Someone with enough information on our systems and protocols to write the concealment code used here would know we'd recognize the code base.

"Our spy is attempting to deceive us, which leads me to conclude that they are definitely not Eridani," the man continued. "It is possible, of course, that they are smart enough to predict that we would draw that conclusion, but we can only go so far down that hole before I start using words like *inconceivable*."

"And fortunately, a data packet can't be poisoned with iocaine powder," Henry said mildly, catching Larue's reference with a smile.

The IntelDiv officer chuckled in genuine pleasure.

"Not that many fans of that piece of classic cinema around, ser," he observed. "And I hope to avoid going up against *anyone* with death on the line if I can avoid it. For our purposes, France is *far* too close to Sicily!"

"I am fond of the twenty-three-twenty-three holographic remake, but Alexis Goldman's twenty-two-fifty *Princess's Bride* version, where she plays *every* character, has a certain appeal," Henry observed.

From Larue's sudden pained expression, he might be one of the few other people in the fleet who'd *seen* that particular one-woman show. Henry's enjoyment of it was more due to his ex-husband's running commentary than any virtue of the piece itself.

"But that aside, other than *not Eridani*, do we have any idea who the messages are going to?" he asked.

"Not yet," Larue admitted. "Someone in the SICF is involved, though, because I had a friend back on Ganymede check the updates before they were even relayed to Base Mario. By the time anyone in Sol sees our briefings, the rider is already gone."

"I suppose that removes one of our worries, doesn't it?" Henry said. When Larue looked confused, he held up a finger. "We know, Colonel, that whoever is sending these messages is aboard *Raven* and is fully aware of the existence of the subspace quantum tunnel. We also know that they have a contact on the Sol Interstellar Communications Facility.

"That suggests that they are not after technical information on the GMS ships. With that level of access, any technical information they want they almost certainly already *have*."

"I'm not sure that makes me feel any better, ser," Larue said grimly. "We *still* have a spy aboard, and I haven't found them yet."

"That level of access also tells me one more critical thing, Colonel," Henry replied. "*They are human.* Not just the spy themselves but also the organization they are sending information back to.

"That means that while, yes, we *have* been penetrated and we *do* have a mole, the mole is most likely not an active threat to the fleet or going to prove an impediment to our operations in Londu space."

Henry shrugged. "I may be being overly optimistic there," he conceded, "but the timing you've mentioned of the transmissions suggests that they're sending system survey data home."

Larue was silent for a moment, looking thoughtful.

"That… tracks, ser," he agreed. "And gives me some thoughts on where to start poking."

"Good." Henry gestured for the other man to look him in the eyes and held Larue's gaze. "But you need to understand, Lieutenant Colonel Larue, that the combat effectiveness of this formation is worth more to us than preventing someone sending survey information home to give a colonization corp an edge over their rivals.

"Do you understand?"

"No witch hunts," Larue replied immediately. "I'll keep the hunt quiet, and I'll discuss with you before we make any moves."

"I dislike our intelligence being sold for profit," Henry said. "But I would rather deal with that than have the fragile unity we are assembling shattered. Find out who is leaking data, what they're leaking and to whom, Colonel.

"Then we'll talk about how we'll deal with it."

24

"WELL, that's the last of the *people* we could ask if they'd seen Okavaz," Sylvia told Henry as she finished reading the report from one of her junior diplomats. Lotte Theunissen was a sensible young woman, a bit out of her depth being handed an entire delegation to manage, even a minor one like this—but that was why Sylvia had sent her.

Experience only came from pushing boundaries.

Henry nodded grimly, watching the data on the hologram in their living room update.

"Forty-five days," he murmured. "Almost fifty days left, still. Except…"

"Except that the last eleven of those are in Londu space," she replied, following the map. "And, given where Kahlmor separated from the squadron, we're closer to sixty percent of the way through the zone in which Okavaz could have gone missing."

"Fifteen more star systems," Henry confirmed. "And that's *including* the one where Kahlmor left with the Drifters. Truthfully, though…" He fell silent and Sylvia waited for him to finish his thought.

He was quiet for long enough that she rose and poured herself a fresh glass of wine while waiting. *Wine*, at least, they hadn't been expecting to be able to brew en route with ice water, yeasts and hops, so there was enough of it to last the mission out.

She'd been warned about the beer supply and chosen to give it up for the journey. It wasn't much of a sacrifice for her—but the rumblings she was hearing about the breweries in the logistics group running out of hops worried her.

"Well?" she asked, dropping onto the couch and swinging a leg up onto his lap. If Quaid came in, well, the steward had seen them in more compromising positions than this—and no one else should be entering the Admiral's quarters unannounced!

"We're now in the zone where I *actually* expected to find Okavaz," he admitted. "Neither we nor the Londu know that much about this area of space. There are habitable worlds out here, but they don't have autochthonous populations and no one has settled them."

"None of the four species we knew about along his route have secondary colonies," Sylvia murmured. "That we've learned of, anyway."

"That will change, I suspect. Especially now that the Lefens know the Kenmiri are no more," Henry said. "It was fear of the Empire that kept them contained. The UPSF has them on a list, Sylvia. They're not an immediate threat, but there aren't many species we know of that eat other sentients."

"They're the *only* one I know of," Sylvia pointed out with a shiver. "I'm surprised there are others; I thought I was fully briefed on every sentient we knew about."

"There are species the UPSF doesn't *admit* to knowing about," her boyfriend said grimly. "Mostly because we only heard about them through the Vesheron. In one or two cases, because we ran into them as part of Vesheron operations and we're quite sure they don't know we exist."

He sighed.

"The three sentient-eaters I know other than the Lefens are all the former. If humans have ever met them, that's classified enough that *I* don't know about it."

"Because what the UPA needs is more secrets." Sylvia wasn't hypocritical enough to argue about the secrets they *had*, but she could see a lot of ways secrets about the rest of the galaxy could bite them.

"It's not my call. Or yours." He was still staring at the map, though his hands drifted down to start massaging her calf. "So far, Ivanova's ships have got us some useful updates on the region and the local sentient races, but we haven't found what we're looking for."

"They know how to find wreckage, right?" she asked, remembering his comment to Kahlmor about their odds of finding Okavaz herself.

"They do." He fell silent again, his hands working her muscles to draw a half-intentional purr from her.

"You, my love, are working too much, aren't you?" she asked softly, adjusting to put both her legs in his lap.

"Twenty thousand human beings, four thousand of them civilians," he said quietly. "And a dozen Londu, but I'm not so worried about Kahlmor's people. But twenty thousand people and forty starships, all my responsibility."

"That's why you have a staff, Henry."

"Yeah. Nine officers. Of whom I can, without question, trust one. No, I take that back," he corrected himself. "Palmerston would have told me if Commodore Zeni was a problem. So, I can trust *two* officers on my staff without question: Strickland, who I picked, and Zeni, who people I trust tell me is okay.

"I trust Iyotake completely, but my second-in-command is not my staff officer," he continued. "Of my staff officers, I trust the *competence* of four. Hawthorne, Cheng, Perrin and, grumpily, Larue."

Henry was going to have to get over the chip on his shoulder about Intelligence eventually, Sylvia knew, but *she* wasn't going to be the one working on that. That was what an Admiral had therapists for.

"The others…" He shook his head, apparently refusing to actively criticize his staff even to her. "The others are better than I was afraid of. I was warned my staff was picked to buy favors to get me the fleet I needed. Six out of nine—seven out of ten, counting Commodore Iyotake—isn't bad."

"So, that's Legal, Engineering and Personnel you're worried about," Sylvia said softly. "I can see why Legal and Personnel were slots Admiral Blake figured she could give you underperformers for."

"Except that I'm stuck running a mobile government with a chief lawyer and a chief human resources specialist I'm not convinced could find their personal derrieres without a fully staffed flight-control center providing guidance."

He snapped his mouth shut hard enough that Sylvia *heard* his teeth click.

"And De Veen?" Sylvia prodded. "You may as well lay it all out, love. I'm not going to tell anyone, and I can't *help* unless I know everything."

"De Veen, frankly, is the Peter principle in action," Henry finally said, his hands warm on her legs as he stared into space. "Her record and even her performance here suggest that she's a good single-ship engineer and competent at handling the demands of being the chief engineer on a fleet carrier.

"But she lacks the breadth of horizon to see past one ship at a time." He shook his head. "It's supposed to be her job to coordinate engineering repairs, parts and needs across the entire fleet in coordination with Lieutenant Colonel Cheng...except Cheng and his people are doing all of the parts organization and logistics for her."

"So, Cheng is working *around* her to make sure her job gets done?" Sylvia asked. Cheng Kai was probably the member of Henry's staff she'd worked with most after Strickland and Palmerston.

"Yes. Officially, I know nothing," he noted. "Unofficially, I know that Sharma is making the connections and getting Chiefs to talk to each other. I did *not* authorize that, but I know better than to tell a Fleet Master Chief what her job is."

"So, what happens if De Veen comes back and tells you to rein in the Chief?" Sylvia asked.

"We have a discussion about who is more valuable to me," he said drily. "A Fleet Engineer who isn't doing her damn job, or the Fleet Master Chief who acts as my avatar and voice in situations where the Admiral cannot be seen?"

"Sounds like you have that in hand," Sylvia told him.

"The question, I suppose, is how much more rope I give her and which capital ship's chief engineer I poach to replace her," he said grimly. "I don't know any of our chief engineers well enough to make that call, which is part of the problem."

"But you *need* a Fleet Engineer," she observed. "Because it's not like Cheng Kai is doing everything she's supposed to be doing. He's just backstopping the part of her job that's supposed to be coordinated with him anyway."

"I know." He stayed silent and focused on her legs for a minute, working his way over her tense muscles.

"Well, I can't speak to the engineering side of things, I'll admit," she told him. "But personnel and legal issues? I'm a *diplomat*, Henry. I might not be a lawyer or an HR specialist, but I can definitely defuse a crisis or two if you need me to."

He chuckled.

"I may take you up on that," he admitted. "*Most* issues get resolved at the ship level, but as soon as you have an issue between the crew of two different ships, well, somebody is calling the Admiral.

"And with forty ships, that's enough to keep Strickland busy just managing the calls!"

She chuckled.

"I'll talk to him in the morning," she promised. "We'll find a crisis or two I can take off your desk…but I *can't* deal with De Veen and your other officers for you."

He nodded, gesturing the hologram away and smiling at her.

"I know. I'm just sorting the strategy out in my mind," he admitted.

"A suggestion, love?" she asked.

"Shoot."

"Talk to your other officers," she told him. "I'd suggest Campbell and O'Flannagain, especially. It's your senior captains who'll know how big the problem really is—and which of their chief engineers can take over the job if needed.

"And the consequences of relieving her outside the fleet aren't your problem," she continued. "Her being assigned to your staff might have bought favors that Blake and Saren needed to get you people and ships…but you *have* those people and ships. So long as we manage the issues in the Expeditionary Fleet, issues back home are Saren's problem."

She smiled.

"And everything I've seen, Henry, tells me that Admiral Lee Saren can damn well handle that."

"Fair enough," he admitted, his hand resting on her thigh. "Part of my job is to keep the Fleet's secrets, Sylvia. I don't want to talk too much about work."

"I'm an outsider to the Fleet's internal politics with enough security clearance to know everything going on," she reminded him. "I'm the closest thing to a third party that you *can* talk to about this.

"But you're right." She smiled brightly and reached down to guide his hand. "We should probably stop talking about work."

25

NORMALLY, Henry would instruct a pair of officers joining him to "take a seat." Given that Captain Campbell brought his own seat, that would probably have just sounded bad, and he caught the words before they even left his mouth.

"Make yourselves comfortable, Colonels," he instructed O'Flannagain and Campbell, then paused as a *third* Colonel made a happy barking noise, appeared to teleport out of nowhere and promptly lay down under his desk.

"*Not* you," Henry told Colonel Zebedee. "How did Colonel Zeb even get *in* here?"

"I think he followed me in," Campbell said with a chuckle. "I can…"

"I've got him," Quaid replied swiftly, the steward swooping in with some kind of sausage to lure the corgi out from underneath Henry's desk. Zebedee—whose collar *did* have the steel oak leaf of a full Colonel and *was* on the table of organization as that, even if he looked like an oversized furry loaf of bread—allowed himself to be lured and then scooped up by Quaid.

Once *Renown*'s corgi Colonel had been removed from Henry's office, the Rear Admiral turned his gaze back on his two Captains.

O'Flannagain was in an interesting position. As the Captain of a fleet carrier, she was arguably either the senior or second-most-senior Captain in Task Group One. By actual date of rank and experience as a starship captain—versus flight group commander—she was junior to Colonel Sierra Vishnu, *Turquoise*'s commanding officer and the most junior of the full Colonel starship captains.

By virtue of being an old subordinate of the Rear Admiral, she ended up *acting* as the second-senior Captain of the task group, though Henry would probably have included Vishnu in the meeting if she and her ship had been in the same star system as the rest of TG One.

Turquoise was still playing support for the destroyer scouting operation, though, which left him with only two Colonel-level captains. Colonel Ivanova, his fourth non-staff Colonel, was busy *leading* the scouting operation from the front, something Henry wasn't hypocritical enough to argue with.

Too many of his actions as commanding officer of a destroyer squadron had ended up with capital letters after the fact. The Osiris Run. The Stand of the *Cataphract*s. The Rescue of Convoy Blue Green Orange…

"I'm not sure what required me to come all the way over to the flagship, ser," O'Flannagain said bluntly. If the woman *had* a filter, she'd never exercised it around Henry. "But it's you, so I'm figuring it's a big deal."

"It may be," he conceded. "It might not be, but I suspect it's going to be a giant pain in everyone's day."

Henry might be demisexual and blind to people's feelings with regards to *him*, but he was well trained in reading people's mannerisms in general. He did *not* miss the way the redheaded carrier CO was eyeing his flag captain.

"I know it's been a weird trip so far," Henry continued. "Sharma tells me that the two of you have been in quite a bit of communication?"

Until he'd seen the pair in a room together, he had assumed that had been work. Now, however, he was teasing his old CAG *and* temperature-checking the situation.

"Colonel O'Flannagain is in command of her first starship," Campbell said breezily. "While her general command experience is extensive, that does represent quite a change. Given the many demands on your time, ser, I offered my support in both moral and mentorly fashion."

"I appreciate that, Captain Campbell," Henry replied. "There have been a lot of demands on us all, I think. After a month and a half, I think we all know where we're solid…and where we're not."

Both of the Colonels' body language shifted. It was a subtle thing, but the friendly banter of the start of the conversation was gone and both of them were focused on him like hawks.

"I am confident in my crew and my ship," Campbell said quietly. "I have enough self-confidence to feel that I would not be in this meeting if I was *not solid*. And you've worked with O'Flannagain for long enough that I suspect you'd speak to *her* in private if you had concerns."

"I have no concerns with either of you," Henry confirmed. He chuckled at the *visible* relief that O'Flannagain showed at that. "Really, Samira?" he asked. "You, of the overwhelming ego and unstoppable rocket-jock attitude, were *worried*?"

"I have never commanded a starship before, let alone a goddamn carrier that should have a *Commodore* in charge," she pointed out. "So, yes, my ego was having some issues writing transfers for my skills to cash."

Henry pulled up the last set of readiness reports on *Pegasus* and flicked them onto the wall.

"*Pegasus* is currently operating at ninety-eight-point-four percent efficiency by the standard metrics," he observed. "You were down four starfighters that wanted to be hangar queens—a recurring problem with the Lancers—but you replaced those from *Archon*'s spares, correct?"

"This morning, the new birds arrived just before I left for *Raven*," O'Flannagain confirmed. "I…will admit that my discipline problems had me worried."

"There are more people aboard *Pegasus* than any other single ship in this fleet, Colonel O'Flannagain," Henry said gently as he flicked to that part of the report. "Over the last two weeks, *Pegasus* reported twenty-nine issues requiring your personal intervention, including eight Captain's Masts, and *none* requiring flag-staff legal involvement."

"Yes, ser."

"Captain Campbell, how many Captain's Masts and other disciplinary items has *Raven* held in the last fourteen days?" Henry asked.

"We average five Masts a week, give or take," Campbell replied. "Including non-Mast administrative punishment overseen by either myself or my XO...I think we're at thirty for the last two weeks."

"Thirty-one," Henry confirmed, bringing *Raven*'s report up alongside *Pegasus*'s. "Nine Captain's Masts and twenty-two lesser disciplinary actions. Versus eight Masts and twenty-one lesser actions aboard *Pegasus*."

O'Flannagain was doing the math; he could see it. There were *five hundred* more people on *Pegasus* than on *Raven*.

"On average, Colonel, I expect to see a disciplinary action cross the Captain's desk every week for roughly every one hundred and thirty people aboard a ship," Henry told her. "*Raven* is at one per one hundred and sixty. *Pegasus* is at one per *two hundred*.

"You're just used to only being responsible for the FighterDiv half of the crew, who historically operate both more loosely in terms of required discipline and more *informally* in terms of *applied* discipline."

He smiled.

"Of course, that same tendency is part of why *Pegasus*'s reported issue rate is so low, but it's also why you feel you are seeing more than you'd expect. Suffice to say, Colonel O'Flannagain, I have no concerns about your performance aboard *Pegasus*."

"I'm glad to hear that," she admitted. "Especially given how much time Sharma has spent aboard!"

"If Master Chief Sharma had found a problem with your crew, she would have reported it to you," Henry told her. "If she had found a problem with *you*, you and I would have spoken about it.

"As we've already discussed, you are not here because I have any concerns about either of you."

He waved the two sets of reports off the wall and focused on the two officers.

"The rest of this conversation is to remain confidential for the moment," he told them. "I will likely be actioning it, but I need to know and you need to know that everything we say in here right now will be held in confidence."

They both nodded their understanding, and Henry laced his fingers together on the table in front of him as he considered his next words.

"It is an open secret, I suspect, that I did not select the majority of my staff," he finally said. "Their positions are the result of a string of favor- and horse-trading carried out by the Joint Chiefs to pull together the ships for the Expeditionary Fleet. Admiral Blake did her best to make sure we got *competent* politically connected officers, but no one is perfect.

"Obviously, I have my own direct concerns here and, equally obviously, officially I cannot ask you to criticize my staff or your superior officers. I do, however, want to hear your opinion on how the flag staff is supporting your ships."

Both of his subordinates hesitated. Henry figured that was reasonable, given that he was basically asking them to criticize his people in a roundabout fashion.

"Overall," O'Flannagain finally began, "I can live with the support we're getting. No problems with supplies, coordination with the logistics, tactical training, anything like that."

"I've dealt with worse staffs, I have to agree," Campbell said. "But you're asking because you know the problems exist."

"Yes."

There was a moment of silence, then O'Flannagain sighed.

"I haven't commanded a ship in a fleet before," she pointed out. "But I've been a carrier Commander Aerospace Group, a battlecruiser CAG and a carrier flight group XO. In most of those roles, I've been able to rely on the ship's legal and personnel officers to provide support. Explicitly, though, their support is limited, and they have regularly fallen back on the flag staff to meet our needs.

"I...have needed to rely on Colonel Campbell's informal advice repeatedly at times when I feel that I *should* have been able to call on the resources of the flag staff for legal and personnel matters." She grimaced. "That's part of why I feel the disciplinary issues are worse than they might seem, I suppose. I've been dealing with them out of

Pegasus's onboard resources, and even my ship legal officer has admitted to not being able to reliably contact Colonel Marszalek.

"Personnel issues have been fewer, but my officers say that they have had problems reaching Lieutenant Colonel Jacquet."

Anil Jacquet was on Henry's list of potential issues, and he nodded slowly.

"Campbell?" he prodded.

"I have the advantage of being able to send Chiefs to politely knock on people's doors," his flag captain pointed out delicately. "Not a tool or an option I'm supposed to need with your flag staff, but certainly one I've used with both Marszalek and Jacquet. There's been a few conversations with other Captains and assorted bulkheads suggesting similar issues to what O'Flannagain is suggesting."

The entire hoverchair twitched slightly as Campbell touched a control by accident. The Colonel glared down at his hand for a moment, then chuckled grimly.

"The problem *I* have, ser, is that Hong Mi is going to fucking *murder* your Fleet Engineer if she doesn't get the *hell* out of *Raven*'s engineering spaces."

"I hope that Commander Hong is not quite to the point where we need to check her armory access," Henry said drily. "But that…aligns with my suspicions."

"Colonel De Veen is not *Raven*'s chief engineer," Campbell said. "But *she* doesn't appear to realize that."

"That is…about the opposite of Commander Sturm's issue with De Veen," O'Flannagain admitted. "Arnold basically says the same thing about De Veen that my administrative officers are saying about Marszalek and Jacquet. He can't get ahold of her without hitting buttons that should be reserved for *actual* emergencies."

"I see." Henry considered the situation. De Veen, so far as he could tell, was an excellent engineer. But to be a Fleet Engineering Officer, she needed to be more of an organizer than a hands-on engineer. Even the team leadership required of a chief engineer paled against that needed for her current role, and she was clearly having problems making the switch.

Which left Henry with the difficult choice of just what to do about it…and what was more important: salvaging the career of a talented officer in over her head or preserving the combat capability of his fleet.

"Let us start from the assumption that we do not wish Colonel De Veen to be murdered in a dark airlock," he said drily. "So far, if I am being honest, her key shortcomings have been backstopped by the deft handiwork of Master Chief Sharma and Lieutenant Colonel Cheng.

"This isn't sustainable, of course. Both Sharma and Cheng have other jobs they should be doing. I don't, unfortunately, feel that Commander Giovanni Salamon, her senior subordinate, is ready to make the leap to Fleet Engineering Officer."

"I'm afraid I don't have any suggestions, ser," O'Flannagain admitted. "Not for replacing her, though…"

She hesitated and Henry arched an eyebrow at her.

"Samira?"

"Two things, ser," she said slowly. "First, I can't help but remember a certain officer who thought she was out of her depth and definitely *was* screwing up all over the place, until you yanked her upright and got her moving in the right direction."

Henry remembered the same officer, *vividly*. She'd managed to both take a swing and make a pass at him in the same minute, while drunk completely off her gourd.

"And the second?" he asked.

"If the problem is that she can't help but focus on the ship she's on, perhaps the question is *which* ship should she be on," O'Flannagain said. "The largest portion of the Colonel's job is supposed to be being aware of the fleet's engineering needs and coordinating them.

"Some of that is logistics, some of that is personnel, a lot of it is parts and coordination. All of that could be done from, say, *Ribhus*."

Henry considered that. *Ribhus* was one of his three factory ships, a *Tvastar*-class auxiliary stuffed full of fabricators and capable of taking an asteroid apart and turning it into everything from cutlery to nuclear warheads.

And because *Tvastar*s were built to what was still sometimes referred to as the "Kalashnikov standard"—supposedly, the ability to take something apart, dump it in a swamp for twenty years and have it still work when cleaned and reassembled—there wasn't that much work directly aboard *Ribhus* to distract De Veen.

"Both of those points deserve consideration," Henry allowed. "At the end of the day, though, we reach Londu space in forty-three days. Upon arrival in the Sovereignty, this fleet must be fully operational and prepared for battle.

"Thank you for your insight, Colonels." He smiled thinly. "I apologize in advance, Captain Campbell. If my conversation with Colonel De Veen does not go well, the best option I currently see is stealing Commander Hong."

Campbell sighed in a melodramatically Scottish fashion.

"I knew I should have kept my mouth shut."

26

"WELL, MASTER CHIEF?"

With just her and Henry in his office, Anita Sharma was basically *lounging* in the chair opposite him. She gave him a moderate degree of side-eye, then chuckled as Arthur Quaid stepped into the room with a large mug of black coffee for her.

"Well, what, ser?" she asked, taking the steaming beverage.

"Arthur, grab a seat," Henry ordered. "I need both of your brains."

There was a reason that Sharma wasn't acting particularly respectfully at that moment. The two noncommissioned officers in his office were, basically, *his* NCOs. Both of their careers were linked to his—Quaid's had been since at least Henry taking command of DesRon 37, and Sharma had, for all intents and purposes, chosen him as her Admiral at the Iron Ring.

There were people who, regardless of the theoretical rank divide, knew all of an Admiral's secrets and functioned as that Admiral's eyes, ears and conscience.

"I'm, frankly, still drowning in the flow of data and problems coming uphill from the Fleet," Henry told them. "But I'm close enough to the surface now to see where some of the particularly mucky water is coming from.

"And I recognize that *delegation* is only an answer to the problem when I have people I can delegate *to*. On paper, every member of my staff is perfectly competent to do their jobs. The reality, of course, is more complex."

"It always is," Quaid said. "But you already know who the problems are."

Henry nodded. A lot of that was down to Quaid and Sharma. Sharma, as Fleet Master Chief, was *officially* Henry's eyes and ears, though the senior noncom of a formation did more unofficial work than most gave them credit for, too.

Quaid, on the other hand, was "merely" responsible for making sure that Henry's life ran smoothly. The fact that Quaid had several assistants *and* Henry had an O-3 for a secretary should help anyone sensible realize that the steward was doing more than making Henry sandwiches.

"I need the three-sixty on Marszalek, De Veen and Jacquet," he said quietly. "What do their people think of them? What's the Chiefs' network whispering?"

"Marszalek is..." Sharma considered her words carefully, glancing over at Quaid for a moment.

"A pompous git too lost in theory-crafting to recognize a *job* if it bit her," the steward finished for her. "Her personal staff, on the other hand, effing *adores* her, so I can't help but feel there's something everyone else is missing."

"Money." Sharma's single-word answer was surprisingly harsh, even for a private meeting like this, and Henry swallowed hard.

"That's a dangerous thing to imply, Anita," he reminded her.

"I don't mean Marszalek is bribing them. Not...explicitly, anyway," Sharma explained. "But she's from a mind-bogglingly rich family and she is personally generous. So, her Chiefs get high-end auto-adjusting chairs and better coffee and a thousand and one other little perks that only cost her money. Which her trust fund accumulates more of faster than she can spend."

"While she fails to do her actual job," Henry said grimly.

"Marszalek has spent her entire career, with a few exceptions, in base or fleet postings inside the UPA," Quaid pointed out. "Those exceptions earned her some medals that JustDiv officers probably shouldn't *have*, so I can't question her bravery."

Henry nodded as he ran through the legal officer's file on his network.

"So, she is personally brave when faced with danger but under normal circumstances works well when cornered and watched like a rat in a cage," he observed drily. "Add in enough money and political connections, and she's avoided having anything unpleasant show up in her actual *file*, and now she has a plum posting that will solidify her career all the way into flag ranks and a position as one of JustDiv's most senior legal wonks?"

"That would be my read, ser," Sharma said. "You want a suggestion?"

"I'm listening, Anita."

"You *could* come down on her like a thousand tons of bricks, wreck her career and make an example out of her," the Master Chief told him. "But, well...frankly, she's not actively creating trouble, and there's a hell of a brain in there if we can aim her.

"So, get her Chiefs to do the aiming."

"Go on, Anita," Henry instructed.

"Marszalek is surrounded by a group of JustDiv NCOs who know *exactly* what she's doing and are letting it slide because it makes their lives easier, too," his Fleet NCO told him. "If I quietly make it clear to *them* that *you* are considering dropping said thousand tons of bricks on the Colonel, they'll recognize that will put their cushy meal ticket in real long-term trouble.

"There's no way she would have made it as high as she has without being *able* to do the job when properly managed, and she's got three senior JustDiv Chief Petty Officers who wouldn't have made it to *their* ranks if they couldn't manage upward."

"And if she's earned enough loyalty to get the kind of mixed commentary we're seeing, they'll start *using* that skill to keep her working and out of trouble," Henry concluded. "Do it."

Sharma didn't need more than his verbal approval, and she nodded calmly.

"As for De Veen," she said slowly. "From what I can tell, she's a damn fine engineer and a trash administrator. Some of her Chiefs love her. Some don't."

"Her commissioned subordinates seem to be fine with her, but the fleet's chief engineers *aren't* her subordinates," Quaid pointed out. "And they seem to be frustrated with her to a one, because she appears to have no modes between overbearing and just straight-up missing."

"My personal assessment is that she knows how to be a chief engineer and is leaning in to what she knows," Henry said quietly. "Which isn't the worst option, I suppose, but we need a Fleet Engineering Officer. On paper, she can do the job."

"And in reality, she's utterly overwhelmed. That should have been anticipated, and someone should have made sure she had a damn solid set of Chiefs, ser," Sharma said glumly. "If she doesn't have the support, she's swimming uphill."

"She's got good Chiefs...on paper," Quaid added. "She might just not be listening to them."

"If some love her and some hate her, is it possible she's getting contradictory advice?" Henry asked.

"Possible. But even then, *she* should know well enough to pick between options," Sharma admitted. "I just can't help but feel that she isn't *getting* the right kind of advice she needs to get up to speed on the job."

"She's had six weeks, Anita," Henry pointed out. "But then...I suppose *I'm* not as up to speed as I'd like at my part of this mess after six weeks. I guess there's one critical question, isn't there?"

Sharma eyed him like she was being led into a trap. Which, in a manner of speaking, she was.

"Colonel De Veen *has* failed as Fleet Engineering Officer so far," Henry reminded them. "Based on your experience, Anita, can she be salvaged? And if she can...can it be done fast enough to avoid compromising this fleet's ability to complete our mission?"

"If the answer is yes, you're going to put salvaging her on me, aren't you?" Sharma asked.

"Yes," Henry confirmed. "A lot will ride on the conversation I'm scheduled to have with her just after lunch, but if you think she can be salvaged, I will give you the chance to try.

"So long as *she* is willing."

Sharma pursed her lips, then slowly nodded.

"I think she can be salvaged. Potentially, Colonel O'Flannagain's thought of moving her to *Ribhus*, at least temporarily, might help. We probably *need* someone to do a deep dive on the capabilities of our mobile repair facilities, and that would give me a chance to go through her Chiefs with a fine-toothed comb."

"You're already carrying the weight, Anita," Henry warned. "If you think you can spend the same amount of effort *teaching* as you've spent going around her and get a better result, I'd rather salvage officers than burn them."

"I'm prepared to give it a try, ser."

"Thank you," he told her. "And Jacquet?"

The two NCOs shared a long look.

"You might have to burn him, ser."

27

ADELAIDE PALMERSTON ESCORTED Colonel Miša De Veen into Henry's office—and even if the engineer had somehow missed the severity of the meeting prior to that moment, her face made it very clear that she was all too cognizant of the presence of the commando officer.

"Ser," De Veen greeted him tersely, stopping in front of his desk and waiting to be invited to sit.

Henry made no such invitation. He did, at least, meet his body-guard's gaze and give her one of his best capital-L Looks.

"Commander, that will be all," he told her gently. He didn't need anyone looming in the room to help him discipline an officer, and he was a long-standing fan of *praise in public, criticize in private*.

The conversations he'd had with his officers and NCOs about De Veen had been critical, but they'd also been private and behind closed doors. He needed to know the critiques his other people had of De Veen, but he wasn't going to broadcast her issues to the entire Expeditionary Fleet.

He waited in silence as Palmerston left the office, and then gave De Veen a calm smile. The lack of invitation to sit was one of several signs he was intentionally sending the woman. There was no coffee, no snacks, no corgi…

Well, Henry didn't usually allow the corgi Colonels in his office, but they *definitely* lowered the tension level when they were present.

To quote a twenty-first century historian, this wasn't a conversation that was going to strain the biscuit jar.

"Colonel De Veen," he said softly. "You're not an idiot, I don't believe, so why don't *you* tell *me* what this meeting is about?"

"I can't be certain of the details, ser, but I assume that you are dissatisfied with the performance of my department of your staff," she said. "Given the relative experience of my Chiefs and myself, I will even go so far as to guess that your dissatisfaction is with *my* performance in specific…and if it is not, I take full responsibility for any shortcomings of my department."

There were days that Henry was quite convinced that some of his subordinates were passing around a psych profile of *what to say to buy brownie points with the Admiral*.

The Fleet Master Chief had already gone to bat for De Veen, which *probably* would have been enough to save the Colonel's job and career on its own. But if she'd tried to throw her subordinates under the bus, he'd have decided that Sharma had made a rare mistake.

Instead, faced with the full-intimidation setup of an Admiral's office, she'd consciously taken the verbal step to put herself between the Admiral's displeasure and her people.

"Sit down, Colonel," he instructed. "This is going to be a long conversation, I suspect."

She obeyed, her back remaining ramrod straight.

"So, you recognize there is a problem," he told her. "What do *you* think it is?"

Henry would lay it out in small words if he had to, but right now, he was trying to get her to ask for help.

"The primary concern I've been struggling with is our failure to get *Raven*'s icosaspatial impulse generators aligned," De Veen told him. "After seven weeks, we're *still* getting excess turbulence on skip. I've been working closely with Commander Hong's teams to get it fixed, but after seven weeks, it's starting to look like the misalignment may be something we either have to live with or deal with in a shipyard."

"I see." He studied her for a long moment. "And what other concerns do you have with your department?"

"I have...some concerns around communication with the rest of the fleet," she said slowly. "There's an attitude problem that the engineering departments appear to be bringing to the table that I have mostly been ignoring and expecting to blow over. I'm not certain of the source, but it's creating friction that's getting in the way of my people doing their job."

Henry exhaled a long sigh and leaned forward on his desk. A series of reports and metrics appeared on the wall behind him—they were mirrored in his internal network, so he knew what De Veen was seeing.

"There definitely appears to be an attitude problem, Colonel, but I'm not convinced it's in the rest of the fleet," he told her. "Standard operating procedure is for Fleet Engineering to act as a clearinghouse, coordinating personnel and matériel needs across the fleet to make sure ships get what they need to make their repairs and complete their maintenance.

"The unofficial metric that I was aware of as a ship captain was thirty-six hours, Colonel. Any request from my ship to the Fleet Engineering Staff was expected to have a response within thirty-six hours—faster, if urgent or critical. The response might well be *We don't have what you need*, but the response was expected within three standard shifts.

"Your team has not, at any point since we left Sol, met that standard. It's an unofficial metric, but it is what the departments on all of the ships are expecting," Henry told her. "Based off the reports I am receiving, in fact, the *only* requests that are getting responses in that time frame are those labeled urgent or critical, and *your* availability, specifically, has been basically nonexistent."

"As I said, ser, I've been focusing on getting *Raven*'s skip drive aligned," she told him.

"Colonel, you are roughly one bad mood or misstatement from being permanently barred from *Raven*'s engineering spaces," Henry said quietly. "And that's assuming that Commander Hong doesn't attempt to test her fusion reactors' contaminant tolerance with *you*."

De Veen jerked back as if he'd struck her.

"*Raven*'s skip drive is *not your responsibility*," he told her. "No individual *ship*, let alone *system*, in this Fleet is your responsibility. Those requests, calls, messages and coordinating meetings that you have been blowing off as an *attitude problem*, Colonel?

"*Those* are your responsibility. Your *job*. You are not a ship's chief engineer anymore, Colonel De Veen. You are a staff officer, the *Fleet Engineer*. A distinction, I feel, that should have been very clear to you when you were given the role."

She was utterly silent.

"Everything I can see of your record and your skills tells me that you are entirely qualified for and capable of doing your job, Colonel De Veen. But as you say, for seven weeks you've been buried in one engineering section, driving my flagship's chief engineer up one bulkhead and across the ceiling."

Henry smiled. He knew it wasn't a warm or friendly expression.

"Does that explain, Colonel, why you are being called on the carpet?" he asked. "You ran the engineering department of a *Crichton*-class fleet carrier with almost a thousand people reporting to you. You *know* how to delegate.

"So, what the *fuck* has gone wrong?"

His curse echoed in the office in a way that no acoustics could account for, and he waited for De Veen to muster her thoughts and speak in her own defense.

"I...have no defense, ser," she finally said. "Given that perspective...I believe I may have screwed up."

"You *have* screwed up, Colonel. That isn't in question, and I'm not interested in a *defense*, not really," Henry told her. "What I'm asking for, Colonel De Veen, is a reason. I need to know where the orders, briefings and support you received went sufficiently off track that a competent officer failed this badly at her job.

"Do you understand, Miša?"

"You need to make sure my replacement doesn't make the same mistake," she said levelly. "As I said earlier, the responsibility is mine."

"A touch less throwing yourself on your sword, Miša, and a touch more addressing the question, please," he ordered.

"I…" She swallowed. "I was—I *am* overwhelmed by the scope of the role. We dealt with a pretty severe impulse-generator misalignment on *Chiana,* and I thought I could be helpful. Then, I guess, I got down in the weeds and got lost."

"And none of your Chiefs flagged this to you?" Henry asked. "Or did you brush that off as an attitude problem?"

She winced and grimaced.

"A couple of them made comments that I think were intended in that direction, yes," she said. "I don't think I classed them as *attitude problem,* but I also didn't catch what they were saying."

That suggested that more was rotten in the Engineering Department than Henry had hoped. It shouldn't have just been a couple of De Veen's Chief Petty Officers who'd tried to pull her up.

Henry would have expected *all* of her CPOs to stage a group intervention before the situation elevated to *his* attention. For that matter, a lot of the day-to-day requests from the other ships should have been able to be managed at the level of the Chiefs and Commander Salamon.

"Do you understand what the problem was now?" he asked her flatly.

"I think so, ser," she said. "I… am prepared to resign my post and transfer to any position you need me in, Admiral."

"Conveniently, Colonel De Veen, where I need you is as my Fleet Engineering Officer," Henry said. "*If* you think you can do the job. Properly."

The room was silent for longer than he expected.

"In theory, I am entirely confident in my ability to do this job," she finally said, very quietly. "And yet I am finding myself overwhelmed and readily distracted by smaller tasks that I think I can fix.

"I can have a word with the Chiefs who tried to warn me and give them a bigger verbal stick, but I am concerned about my ability to recover from the hole I've dug myself into," she admitted, frankly.

Henry studied her face. She was upset and making no attempt to hide it, but she wasn't angry at him for calling her out. She wasn't *unwilling* to change. She just wasn't sure she *could*.

"Miša, there are roughly twenty thousand people in this fleet," Henry told her. "*No one* needs to do things on their own, and fortunately, we have some very senior Chiefs who have experience helping officers dig themselves out of holes.

"If you promise to listen and learn, both I and the Fleet Master Chief will make time to check in with you and see where things are on a regular basis," he continued. "Those check-ins will require complete frankness, Miša, and I still have concerns about both you and your department.

"But if you are prepared to face the reality of where you are head-on and work to fix things, I am prepared to give you the chance to try."

"Also known as *enough rope to hang myself with*," De Veen observed.

"Yes. The choice is yours."

Her honesty had earned her the kind of relief that wouldn't look *quite* as bad on paper—transfer to the fabricator ships and a new role running the engineering logistics shops there, he figured—but he wasn't going to put the effort into fixing an officer who didn't want to fix herself.

"I..." She nodded sharply. "Thank you, ser. I will do my best both to improve and to listen."

"Good. Because we have a mission, Colonel, and I need the Expeditionary Fleet ready to fight when we reach the Sovereignty. A great deal of ascertaining that readiness falls on your team."

Henry couldn't allow Fleet Engineering to fail. That meant he and Sharma were either going to fix De Veen or break her—but so long as the woman across the desk from him was working with them, he was confident on where they were going to land.

28

THE SET of documents Sylvia was reviewing was missing something. It wasn't *quite* a prosecution and defense, but the people who'd been giving the interviews had definitely had that concept in their heads.

Chief Petty Officer Arthur Hardesty's testimony and initial complaint suffered from the fact that Chief Hardesty not only wasn't the victim but hadn't even *been* there when Ensign Rosa Dumont had been gambling with the two noncoms from *Visigoth*.

As Sylvia understood it, there were a lot of issues with the fact that a junior Engineering officer had ended up in a poker game for cash with noncommissioned officers from another ship on a *third* ship. The poker game had taken place aboard one of the transports in TG Three.

Dumont had clearly confessed everything to her Chief, and her Chief had taken it *all* the way up the chain to Rear Admiral Wong. That alone was a sign of some of the rot in Henry's staff, Sylvia figured, since either his Legal or Personnel officers should have engaged with this before it had reached him.

Henry, however, for all of his skill and sensitivity, was still a man. Dumont had said very little in her interview with the legal officer aboard *Ultima*. There was nothing outright illegal about the poker game, though gambling between officers and enlisted was discouraged

—and gambling at the scale that had clearly taken place was *definitely* discouraged.

But Rose Dumont was young and, well, tiny. There wasn't any sign that the young woman had been *intentionally* intimidated and she definitely hadn't been *threatened*, but given that the two noncoms involved outweighed her around four-to-one, she almost certainly hadn't been willing to argue or walk away when things went sideways.

Sylvia had to agree with Hardesty's report that the game was rigged to hell and back. The transport *Svadilfari*'s crew hadn't been able to prove it, though, and since the game had taken place on their decks, it was a long trail of he-said, she-said, they-said. The two noncoms who'd "won" the money, of course, said that everything was entirely on the up and up.

Without any proof that the game had been rigged, all that was *really* available to Henry's staff were some finger-wagging and warnings. If the warnings were *ignored*, of course, that gave the Admiral options.

Sylvia was considered how best to *create* said options when the admittance chime for her office sounded.

"Enter."

Her new chief of staff, Letitia Lincoln, was a New Orleans–born Black African American diplomat well on her way to getting burdened with her own embassy somewhere. Right now, though, Lincoln was in the unenviable position of filling the spot of a woman Sylvia had been training for three years—and it had taken over a year for *that* chief of staff to get up to the speed Felix Leitz had been running at when Sylvia had given him up to act as Ambassador to the Eerdish-Enteni Alliance in the Ra Sector.

Since Leitz had negotiated the deal that had allowed the UPSF to buy the technology behind their miniaturized screens and made the entire dual-screen defense system the new ships used possible...she could accept that had been a worthy sacrifice.

"Ambassador. Are you busy?" Lincoln asked.

"Beating my head against a brick wall of military people being stubborn on the one hand and potentially corrupt on the other," Sylvia replied. "What do you need?"

"Lord Kahlmor has asked to see you at your next convenience," her chief of staff told her. "And the Rear Admiral, too, but I'm thankfully not responsible for organizing your boyfriend."

"Believe me, Letitia, Henry has *plenty* of people to organize him," Sylvia said. "I'm presuming either Strickland or Quaid has given us a time when Henry will be available?"

"In about twenty-five minutes," Lincoln confirmed. "I can probably push 'em back if you need…"

"No, I'm not going to get any further with this right now." Sylvia grimaced at her files, then packaged it up and flicked it over to Lincoln. "Take a look at this while I'm talking to Kahlmor and Henry," she instructed. "Technically, it's a fleet issue, but Henry asked me to take a look. It's a mess and, honestly, I think the best option might just be to reimburse the losses out of pocket and give the troublemakers a sharp lecture.

"But if you see anything else, I'm down to consider it!"

KAHLMOR WAS ONCE AGAIN ALONE in the observation lounge at the center of the guests' section. The black-maned Londu officer had clearly sent his people away and was waiting, silently staring at the stars on the screens above him, when Sylvia entered the space.

"Lord of Fifty Thousand Miles Kahlmor," she greeted him in Londu. "You have questions?"

"I don't know," he admitted, still staring at the stars. "Is Admiral Wong joining us?"

"He'll be another couple of minutes, but if there is something that you'd find easier to say in Londu than Kem…" She shrugged.

He chuckled.

"'The ashes of night haunt the souls of the mountains and break the minds of the Lon,'" he told her, what sounded like poetry rolling off his tongue with swift ease. "Grief is born in ashes, Ambassador, and fear is born in night.

"I cannot read the poems of my people in Londu, but perhaps the distance between words and soul will serve us all."

"I know that stopping to translate every sentence sometimes causes me to think," Henry told them in Kem. He smiled as Sylvia glanced back at him in surprise. She'd missed him entering the room and he'd clearly followed *some* of the poetry.

"I have not had the time to learn enough Londu to *speak* it," he warned. "But I have spent enough time learning that I can make sense of what the translation program gets wrong."

"We are all fluent enough in Kem for anything but poetry," Kahlmor said, switching to that language. "I am grateful you both made time. You are busy and I feel that I am…not very important right now."

"You are the senior representative of the ally we are rushing across several hundred light-years to assist," Sylvia pointed out.

"And whose superior officer we are still trying to find," Henry added. "What do you need, Lord Kahlmor?"

The Londu picked up a tablet from the table and tapped a command. The device was of Londu manufacture, sturdier than the UPA's civilian equivalent. The UPSF didn't *use* portable computers as a rule, given the omnipresence of the internal networks, so Sylvia could see why *Raven*'s crew had rigged the Londu device to connect to the ship's systems.

She hoped—well, *assumed*, really—that the crew had taken proper security precautions when they'd set up the connections.

Kahlmor's commands opened a familiar astrographic map on the observation lounge's windows and the Londu stared at the overlay of physical positions and white lines marking skip connections.

"We are well over halfway through our journey," he said. "And we are rapidly approaching the system where I parted ways with Lord of a Million Miles Okavaz. I have received no news, though I trust your promise that you are searching for her."

"We are," Henry confirmed, looking at Sylvia and meeting her eyes. "We have had no luck, Lord Kahlmor. I did not, I will confess, expect to find her close to our stars. Between the known inhabited systems on her journey and our own scouting, I believed we would find her in the first half of her journey.

"We are into that space now, Lord Kahlmor, and we still have seen no sign of her or her ships. We must face the unfortunate reality that

Okavaz ran into difficulties, most likely an ambush, and that at the very least her *squadron* is no more."

Sylvia saw Kahlmor sag and wondered if the Londu man's relationship with the Lord of a Million Miles had been as purely professional as it should have been. She doubted they'd had a romantic relationship —that was as taboo for the Blades of the Scion as the UPSF—but Kahlmor's reaction suggested they'd been close.

"Is there anything Lord Kahlmor can do to assist the search?" Sylvia asked them both. She didn't know the tricks and technical details herself, but she *did* know that Kahlmor was likely willing to break more than a few of the usual rules if he thought it would help.

"Six of our most modern ships," Kahlmor said softly. "One of our most extraordinary commanding officers. Over three *thousand* Blades of the Scion. If there is *anything* I can do, tell me!"

Sylvia suspected that Henry's sigh was theatrical, exaggerated to cross species and cultural boundaries.

"Your ships, like ours, have secured data recorders intended to survive the destruction of the ship," Henry reminded Kahlmor. "But my experience is that yours are even more concealed and secretive than ours. I have assisted in the retrieval of Londu recorders, and the devices never appeared on my scanners.

"Those recorders and beacons, Lord Kahlmor, are the only chance we have of finding Okavaz's ships at this point. I need to know how to find them."

Kahlmor was silent for a few moments, still staring at the map.

"There is a low-power communications frequency that the beacons respond to," he finally told them. "Absent the correct sequences sent on the correct frequency, our final-warning cases do not transmit. On receipt of the correct codes, they will reply with their location.

"If your ships sweep the areas they pass with those transmissions, any final-warning case present will reply."

From Henry's nod, Sylvia presumed all of that made sense.

"I need a copy of those codes and the exact frequencies, Lord Kahlmor," he said. "We *might* find Lord Okavaz or her people without them, but the ability to locate their final-warning cases and learn their fates may make all of the difference."

"I will provide this," Kahlmor promised. "Find Lord Okavaz, Rear Admiral Wong, and many things will be made possible that may not have been before."

From everything everyone had said, Sylvia knew that Henry didn't expect to find the Lord of a Million Miles.

All he was hoping for at this point was to find out what had *happened* to her.

29

"SKIP SIGNATURE at the line from Talon-Thirty-Eye."

Henry was only half-paying attention to the flag bridge around him, though something emerging from a skip line in the same star system they were in was important enough to pull more of his focus away from the latest digest of metrics on parts and people movement between his ships.

He'd been looking for—and, thankfully, *finding*—signs that the engineering situation was improving. The announcement from one of Hawthorne's analysts pulled him toward the more-immediate concern, however.

"Anything in Talon-Thirty-Eye that we're expecting to be heading our way?" Henry asked.

Sixty-plus days and over four hundred light-years from the star of humanity's birth, many of the smaller stars around them didn't have catalog numbers in Earth's databases. They did, however, have catalog codes in *Londu* databases.

But to human eyes, the separation between the modern Londu alphabet and the original hieroglyphics was nowhere near as complete as between the Roman alphabet used by the English language and, say, Egyptian hieroglyphs.

So, the catalog numbers had ended up as descriptions of symbols mixed with numbers when entered into human databases. They were currently in the Wing-One-Crown-Five System, a dim but massive star that was one of the few locations where the Expeditionary Fleet crossed Okavaz's planned path.

"*Visigoth* and *Dragoon* are on schedule to scout the system," Hawthorne told him, his operations officer now standing and looking over her tech's shoulder. "We're definitely looking at one of our skip drones, too.

"Lightspeed lag and skip delay alone put its deployment a minimum of twenty-six hours ago," she continued. "The destroyers were only scheduled to enter Talon-Thirty-Eye from Crown-Talon-Six thirty-two hours ago.

"Assuming any kind of flight time for the drone in Talon-Thirty-Eye, they must have launched the drone within four hours of entering the system."

"I assume Perrin's people are already on downloading and decrypting the drone?" Henry asked.

He got a vaguely waved thumbs-up from the coms console. Hardly a formal report, but given that he *very* much wanted to know what was on the drone, he'd give the Chief Petty Officer that much leeway.

The skip drones were still fusion-drive tools, robotic spacecraft pulling three times the acceleration of his GMS ships and with enough fuel for forty-five days of endurance. They were still limited to the same skip-line rules as everything else, though, only giving them about a thirty-percent speed edge over long distances.

But drones, even the extended-range versions Henry's fleet carried to reach all the way back to the UPA, were cheaper than starships. So, the Expeditionary Fleet carried hundreds of the robotic spacecraft—and still tried to retrieve them wherever possible.

As Henry watched, the Chief running his coms desk on this shift passed maneuvering the drone off to *Raven*'s communications department while they focused on downloading and decoding the message.

"Ser, they got a ping on the Londu codes," the Chief snapped —*again* with the lack of a formal report, but for that news, Henry truly did not care.

"Talk to me, Chief," he ordered, rising from his seat and crossing over to the coms desk.

"They were still several light-minutes out when they sent the drone," the noncom told him. "They'd done a system-wide sweep with the codes for those 'final-warning cases' and got a very faint response.

"Lieutenant Colonel Tosi says the signal doesn't match anything we were told to expect, but it *was* a response to the call for the black boxes." The Chief looked up at Henry, apparently suddenly nervous to have the Rear Admiral standing at their console.

"I'll forward you his message, ser," they told him. "But he's not sure they've found the black boxes...and it's sufficiently odd that he doesn't want to take the destroyers in without backup."

"Thank you, Chief," Henry said. "Send the message to my network."

He gave the NCO a firm nod and crossed back to his seat and the newfangled holographic projector system. A dozen commands flickered out as he looked at the display, assembling the answers to most of his queries without even involving his staff.

Hawthorne was standing at his shoulder by the time he'd finished laying out the information in the display.

"Sounding board, ser?" she asked.

"Please." He considered the information he'd laid out on the display. "DesRon Forty has two divisions out scouting. Colonel Ivanova's Charlie Division is the *source* of the message, but we have no means of reaching Delta Division without a forty-eight-hour minimum turnaround.

"So, we can count on DesDiv Forty-Charlie but not DesDiv Forty-Delta," he noted. "That cuts our GMS destroyer strength by a quarter, possibly half, depending on what's happening in Talon-Thirty-Eye as we speak.

"But we don't need GMS destroyers—or the GMS ships at all—to secure the convoy. TG Two and Three have only just entered the Wing-One-Crown-Five System; they're eighty light-minutes behind us.

"*Turquoise* is here." Henry highlighted the cruiser on the display. "She's about halfway between the skip line to Talon-Thirty-Eye and the skip line out to where DesDiv Forty-Delta is supposed to be."

"*Pegasus* and DesDivs Forty-Alpha and Forty-Bravo are here, with us." Henry considered the positions and the current vectors.

"My eyeball estimate says we can hit the Talon-Thirty-Eye skip line in fourteen hours with everything *present* of Task Group One, including *Turquoise*," he concluded. "We can order the drone to turn around immediately. If we do, Tosi will have updated orders within sixteen hours."

And Lieutenant Colonel Ahmed Tosi, *Visigoth*'s Captain, was senior to Lieutenant Colonel Shu Czajka, *Dragoon*'s CO. Destroyer divisions didn't get separate commanding officers, though they were formal enough that Tosi was *also* Commanding Officer, Destroyer Division Forty-Charlie as well as Commanding Officer, *Visigoth*.

"What orders would those be, ser?" Hawthorne asked.

"Hold position and wait for support," Henry told her. "We'll leave TG Two and TG Three here, with orders to wait for an update. We take TG One into Talon-Thirty-Eye and proceed to investigate the signal at full battle stations."

His operations officer was silent for at least ten seconds, but he felt her nod.

"I'd like to say that's paranoid and overkill, ser," she told him. "Except that the Londu exploratory cruisers were as big as, more maneuverable than and as heavily armed as our pre-refit *Corvid* battle-cruisers.

"Six of them, even without gravity shields, were a powerful force. If something happened to them, we need to consider the possibility that whatever did the happening is still there."

"Exactly." Henry considered. "I'll still want to review Colonel Tosi's message, but get Perrin on duty and start the fleet moving, Commodore. Even at *our* cruise acceleration instead of the full Fleet's, a light-hour is going to take us a while to cross."

"I've time to confirm the orders I'm sending Tosi."

"One question, ser," Hawthorne said. "We sent destroyers out scouting. *Cataphract* destroyers. So... when you send your orders, what are the instructions for them if they've already poked a hornets' nest?"

"At that point, there's only one order I can give Colonel Tosi," Henry said quietly. "*Survive.*"

30

IT WAS the first time since Henry had come aboard *Raven* that the battlecruiser had truly been able to stretch her legs. One and half KPS^2 wasn't the peak of the ship's acceleration capabilities, but it was her standard "full thrust."

Sticking with the fusion-powered TG Two, *Raven* and *Pegasus*, at least, had spent the entire journey at either one-third or two-thirds power—point-five and one KPS^2, respectively. Now, with both excuse and reason to truly *push*, the two capital ships surged to their full power with ease.

"Any concerns, Colonel De Veen?" Henry asked. More of his senior officers had almost magically appeared from the woodwork as the task group had begun its run toward Talon-Thirty-Eye.

"I'm watching *Pegasus* and *Raven*'s gravity field alignments," the engineer told him. "But I'm not *concerned*. This is the first time either of the capital ships has gone to full power since their trials, and *Pegasus* looks like she's burning more power to sustain it than I like. I'll pass my notes on to Commander Sturm, but he'll deal with his own ship.

"I would be concerned if we were pushing any of Task Group One to flank acceleration," De Veen admitted. "There's been a few warning signs in the reports back from the scouting destroyers."

"We ran DesRon Thirty-Seven at flank thrust for days at times," Henry said.

"Yes, that's how I know what they *should* look like," she told him. "So far, I think it's an oddity born from the new power plants, but I'm watching and so are the ships' chief engineers."

De Veen had, at least, learned when to butt out. The concern, of course, was whether she would now know when she *did* need to insert herself into an individual ship's problems.

I feel like I should have been aware of that, he sent via private text message.

It's not something we're sure of, she replied, equally silently. *It just doesn't look quite right, so I'm watching it. And I'm glad we're not pushing that hard today. This level of strain will give me and the chief engineers a better idea of whether there* is *a problem.*

Keep me informed, he instructed. If TG One couldn't make their flank acceleration for extended periods, he needed to know that. From the sounds of it, though, *no one* was sure. De Veen was just concerned.

Nothing about the Rear Admiral's star was making Henry find a concerned engineering staff any less stressful.

At that moment, though, everything was green as his six ships accelerated toward *Turquoise* and the skip line out of the system.

"If anything comes up, I'll be in my office," he told Hawthorne. "Once we're close to arriving in Talon-Thirty-Eye, I'll be bringing Lord of Fifty Thousand Miles Kahlmor onto the flag bridge as an observer."

"Make sure the right protocols are in place."

From his operations officer's expression, *her* assessment of the "right protocols" would be *Don't bring the alien military officer onto the fleet flag bridge.*

Clearly, though, Hawthorne also wasn't going to argue. Sometimes, diplomacy required decisions that might be less than optimal from a military perspective.

And even from Henry's *military* perspective, having the senior local officer on his command deck when he started poking where he figured an entire squadron had died seemed damn valuable.

"YOUR LIEUTENANT COLONEL IS CORRECT. This is not right."

Henry grimaced at Kahlmor's words. The Londu officer was seated in Henry's office—Palmerston was outside the door as a show of trust, though Henry knew the commando officer was listening to everything in the room—reviewing the message from Tosi on a UPA-style flimsy tablet.

The Londu seemed a bit taken aback by the delicate nature of the civilian hardware—the "flimsies" were well named, with all of the strength and thickness of a sheet of cardstock—even after *Raven*'s techs had loaded a Londu operating system skin onto it.

No one was giving a *Londu* tablet even read-only access to any of *Raven*'s major systems. They'd given the devices access to the guest quarters' systems, but those were carefully designed to allow for just that.

"Tosi said that they transmitted the challenges you provided on the frequencies you gave and that was the response," Henry observed. "But while it was responding to the right things and on the right channels, it was not just a locator beacon."

"And all that you should have received from a final-warning case was a location beacon," Kahlmor said. "One that should have stayed active for seven hours."

"Instead, we got a data pulse that repeated three times and then shut off," Henry noted. "A data pulse that is completely meaningless to us."

"I am afraid, Rear Admiral, that I cannot translate this at a glance," Kahlmor said levelly. "I would ask for you to provide a copy for my people to review on our systems, except…"

Somehow, Henry wasn't surprised by the fact that it was more complicated than they'd hoped.

"Except what, Lord Kahlmor?" he asked.

"As I presume you have guessed, Admiral Wong, this is someone sending an encrypted data packet on an emergency channel," Kahlmor said. "The triple repeat, the channels used, that it came in response to a scan for final-warning cases…"

"You know what has been sent."

"The details? No. But…this is still a locator beacon, in a way, Admiral," the Londu told him. "It is a *survivors'* beacon, a message providing a location for pickup that a hostile would not be able to identify.

"All it should contain is their coordinates, but the nature of the transmission is its own kind of message."

Henry nodded grimly.

"It means they were shot down and they think that whoever shot them down is still around, does it not?"

"Exactly. Were I able to give suggestions to your Colonel, I would *suggest* that he avoid the area this beacon transmitted from and sweep the rest of the system with the beacon pickup codes. There likely is at least one final-warning case somewhere in the star system."

"How badly would the squadron need to have been mangled for them to return to the Sovereignty?" Henry asked.

There was a long silence.

"Talon-Thirty-Eye is three skips and roughly five days' travel from where Lord of a Million Miles Okavaz and I parted ways," Kahlmor finally said. "From there, a retreat to the Sovereignty would have taken no more than sixteen days."

Limited to the point-five KPS^2 of his logistics fleet, it would take Henry's Expeditionary Fleet over twenty days to make the same journey to Londu space. The Londu cruisers were faster, though, and that let him follow through Kahlmor's thinking.

"If someone had gone home to report in, would a new delegation have been sent?"

"As swiftly as possible, potentially in even greater force," Kahlmor replied. "The Scion..."

"Is afraid," Henry finished for the Londu officer.

"I would not use that word. But the Scion recognizes that your people's assistance is necessary."

"A new delegation would either have already arrived in the UPA or we would have encountered them along the way," Henry estimated, considering the map now burned into his brain.

"But if no one made it back to the Scion, he would have assumed they remained on mission."

"Meaning that Okavaz's entire squadron was wiped out," Henry concluded grimly.

"I...I must hope and speak to fate that that has not occurred," Kahlmor said quietly. "Okavaz was a mentor to me, parent to one of my dearest friends."

"We cannot change what has occurred," Henry told Kahlmor. "We can only find out what happened and save whoever is left—and hope and speak to fate, as you say, that Okavaz is among the survivors."

Kahlmor nodded, his expression shaky.

"The Londu have other enemies," he admitted. "But I fear that this may have been the Enigmas and you may face the wrath of our enemy sooner than we feared."

Henry smiled thinly.

"They will not know what hit them."

31

A SILENT CRASH echoed through *Raven* as the continued slight misalignment of her skip drive's impulse generators left Henry—and the rest of the crew—feeling like they'd returned to reality at the wrong angle.

At least it had faded to *merely* a sense of disorientation on emergence into regular three-dimensional space, but Henry had never experienced *any* feedback on the return to reality. The actual process of entering the skip and the reinforcing pulses along the way were always uncomfortable, but this was unusual.

Still, the feeling that the universe was about thirty degrees off-kilter faded after a few seconds, and while *Raven*'s sensors shared the same disorientation as her organic crew, the *rest* of the task group's sensors did not.

"Task Group One has emerged and is in formation," Hawthorne reported. "Position variances are sub–one hundred meters."

Henry nodded and allowed his people to see a pleased smile. That was *good*. The UPSF's skip transition formations were structured around a full-kilometer error radius for emergence, though Henry had never known a Captain who would be *happy* with anything over five hundred meters.

"Captain O'Flannagain reports CAP is launching," Perrin said from the coms section. "She's putting two squadrons in space for local patrol and has three more on standby for immediate launch."

And unless O'Flannagain had lost some of her paranoia while Henry wasn't looking, the *other* forty starfighters would be ready to go only a minute or two after the *immediate-launch* squadrons.

"Do we have a location on *Visigoth* and *Dragoon*?" he asked.

"Working on it," Hawthorne reported. "Geography is on the display, with the location of the beacon they picked up."

Talon-Thirty-Eye wasn't a system anyone was going to write home about. It was a dim red dwarf of above-average size, with four rocky planets, a sparse asteroid belt and a single gas giant sweeping up anything outside the belt. The beacon *Visigoth* had detected had been in the region of the innermost planet, and Henry studied Alpha for a moment.

"Wait. Commodore Hawthorne, can you have someone double-check those spectrographic readings on Alpha?" he asked.

"Chief Hanson is already on it," she confirmed, glancing over at Senior Chief Petty Officer Alan Hanson, the most senior noncommissioned officer in the Operations Department.

"Confirmed, ser," the Senior Chief said a moment later. "Eighteen percent oxygen, average surface temperature forty-two degrees Celsius. Other signs of life are present but sparse. Alpha is habitable. I'm not aware of many species that would *like* living there, but it's survivable."

"And it's *not* listed as such in the files we have from the Londu, correct?" Henry asked.

"That's right, ser."

"Thank you, Chief Hanson." Henry studied the planet for a few long seconds, considering. Tosi probably hadn't reconciled his scan data against the Londu databases—for a scouting run like the destroyers were doing, that would come *very* late in the process. What the destroyers *could* see was more relevant than what they *should* have seen.

Talon-Thirty-Eye's other planets and asteroid belt were sufficient to support a basic level of infrastructure, but there was nothing unusual there. If Alpha had been hospitable instead of merely habitable, Henry could see someone colonizing the system. If one of the other planets had possessed something worth utilizing, Alpha could have made accessing it far easier.

As it was, though, it was a system that would sit on the bottom of anyone's list of colonization targets. The only thing that had drawn Henry and the Expeditionary Fleet there was that it had been on Okavaz's planned route.

"We've got a ping on our destroyers," Perrin reported. "*Visigoth* and *Dragoon* are orbiting Charlie. With current orbits, it's the closest planet to Alpha."

"Of course it is," Henry said with a chuckle.

Destroyer crews and captains were instilled with a culture of aggression and speed. A gravity-shielded destroyer had a better chance of survival against, say, a Kenmiri dreadnought than a Kenmiri escort with no shields at all.

But their handful of missile launchers wasn't going to threaten that dreadnought. Their only chance of actually *hurting* a dreadnought was to close to point-blank range and punch through its shields and armor with the destroyer's lasers.

That culture had worked handily for Henry when he'd commanded a destroyer squadron, but that only made him *more* aware of the chance that his destroyer division might have done something…precipitous.

Hanging out barely four light-minutes from an unknown potential threat zone was practically *restrained* for destroyers.

"What's our ETA to join them at Charlie?" he asked.

"Roughly five hours, ser," Hawthorne told him. "Then four for the full task group to reach Alpha, assuming zero-zero at each planet."

"Pass the courses," Henry ordered. "Then let Captain Tosi know I want a more-complete update on what they've seen here."

"THERE'S MORE than one reason we're hanging out here at Charlie, ser," Tosi's hologram told Henry. Still almost seven light-minutes away, the message was a recording, but the white-turbaned officer looked disturbingly pleased with himself.

"First, Alpha's got enough moons and assorted miscellany in orbit that we didn't want to get mixed up in it," Tosi noted. "If I was hiding anywhere in this star system, I'd hide in the asteroid belt—but assuming I couldn't do that, I'd be somewhere in Alpha's quartet of little moons."

Henry had seen those in the scan data. Alpha's companions were more like Phobos and Deimos than Earth's moon, captured asteroids a fraction of the planet's mass, but the four of them made for a large *aggregate* mass. The trails of debris woven between the four moonlets confirmed the *captured asteroid* identification as well.

He'd seen planets with busier orbitals, but those were mostly artificial, the organized chaos of inhabited industrial worlds. That much debris in orbit of an uninhabited planet was rare, though not exactly unusual.

"Secondly, since *us* hiding was pretty pointless but I didn't want to walk into an ambush, I wasn't going to check out Alpha regardless. Which brings me to point three: we followed Lord Kahlmor's instructions and swept the rest of the system with the call-and-response codes.

"It's going to be a few days before we've refueled all of our sensor drones, but I can tell you with certainty now that there are no Londu black boxes in the asteroid belt or around Delta and Epsilon."

Tosi smiled, showing sparkling white teeth that contrasted with his tanned skin.

"I am not as certain about Beta," he admitted. "We got some fuzzy ghosts on our probe in the area, but nothing that looked like a response to the Londu codes. On the other hand, well, I am very certain about Charlie's new guest."

The holographic image of Lieutenant Colonel Tosi vanished, replaced by a two-dimensional image: an orbital shot of what looked like a desert plain. The sand was a dark green color, a shade Henry hadn't seen much of in natural terrain, but planets always had their own tricks.

Charlie *had* an atmosphere, too, which might have been distorting the color. If that had been the case, though, the crashed starship wouldn't have stood out *quite* so thoroughly.

Like the Londu battleships Henry was more familiar with, the cruiser had a flattened-teardrop shape, angling from a broad, mostly flat prow to a narrow stern holding some of the most energy-dense fusion engines the UPA had seen in anyone's hands.

The two-dimensional image dissolved into a holographic projection of the crash site, and new data flickered onto the screen. The cruiser had been two hundred meters long and almost that wide at her prow. A good chunk of her starboard side was buried in sand, but large chunks of what was visible had been wrecked by weapons fire. Strange weapons fire that had cut massive gashes through the hull like the marks of a starship-scale axe.

"We traced the one black-box beacon we found here, and I've sent in landing parties," Tosi's voice told Henry over the image of the ship. "You'll find their full report attached but it doesn't make for pretty reading.

"We're not entirely sure what the hell cut up the hull like that. Battle lasers transmit energy basically instantly, but my tac team's best guesses are a lower-wattage, longer-duration, weapons-grade laser," the captain said. "No sign of plasma-cannon fire or missile strikes. Someone seems to have *cut* her to pieces."

And then she'd crashed. Million-ton interstellar starships didn't *crash* very often, which told him that the cruiser had probably been far closer to the planet than was wise when the hostiles had cut into her engine sections.

"Bad news is that we didn't find any survivors," Tosi continued. "The black boxes are intact; we've extracted them and will transfer upon rendezvous with the fleet. We might have been able to crack them open, but I figured there wasn't much point in hacking the boxes when you've got a Londu detachment aboard *Raven*.

"The rest of the news is weird but, I *think*, good," he noted. "Key systems appear to have either been removed or destroyed in place. Some of it was definitely preset demolition charges, but a few spots we think were wrecked manually. Might have been before the crash, but we're thinking after because we found this."

The three-dimensional view zoomed in on a flat area next to the wrecked ship. Two things were immediately obvious to Henry: one, that Londu ships actually designed their shuttle-bay doors to serve as emergency ramps on planetary surfaces, and two, this ship was even more definitely a war grave than before.

Mostly because of the actual *graveyard* someone had installed in the lee of the wreckage. The shuttle bay had been opened, its ramp converted into a bay—presumably to allow extraction of the shuttles themselves—and then the ground next to it had been marked with a series of metal signs.

"We left the graves alone, obviously, but we did confirm that at least one shuttle was removed and launched," Tosi told him. "Someone survived, stuck around at least long enough to bury their dead and secure the classified systems, and then got a shuttle working and left.

"Presuming that Londu shuttles aren't any more capable of skipping than our shuttles, I only see one place they might have gone, ser. Which matches with the presence of the beacon on Alpha.

"Frankly, ser, if I hadn't received your hold order before we realized that, rescue ops would already be underway. I respectfully suggest we move quickly. I don't know what resources the poor bastards landed on Alpha with, but it doesn't look like a comfortable place to be shipwrecked to me!"

Survivors. Henry had hoped—especially when they were looking at a non-default beacon that definitely didn't appear to be attached to a ship!—but a graveyard clearly dug after the starship crashed was proof.

The data from the report downloaded into Henry's network, and he dug for the piece of information he needed, grimacing when he finally found it.

Generous Leaves wasn't Lord of a Million Miles Okavaz's flagship. Some of her crew might have survived, but if *Leaves* was the only ship survivors had escaped from, Okavaz wasn't among the people they could rescue.

There was only one way to be certain—and Henry was with his subordinate. They were the best, if not the only, hope the survivors of Okavaz's delegation had.

There was no time to waste.

32

"SURVIVORS. HOW MANY?"

Kahlmor was nothing if not pessimistic, Henry figured, but the Londu's presence on his flag bridge was welcome. Hopefully, he'd manage to get what he needed out of the Lord of Fifty Thousand Miles without needing to get harsh or speak in private. He and the Londu might be speaking Kem, but *all* of his staff officers and most of his bridge enlisted understood the trade tongue perfectly well.

"We are not sure," Henry warned. They were now close enough to have a live conversation with Tosi—or his GroundDiv landing party leaders, for that matter—but he figured everything they needed was actually in the reports.

They were almost two hours out from Charlie, heading toward Alpha at over three percent of lightspeed and about to flip and begin deceleration. Or, if the conversation with Kahlmor went poorly, adjust course and burn for the skip line at flank acceleration.

"Our landing team counted two hundred and thirty-six grave markers," Henry continued. "I do not know how many crew *Generous Leaves* carried, which makes it difficult for us to estimate the number of survivors."

"The flagship carried four hundred and ninety Blades," Kahlmor said instantly. "The other explorer cruisers had a crew of three hundred and ninety. If that many were gone, that still leaves a hundred and fifty of the Blades of the Scion trapped in this star system."

"And we will rescue them, Lord Kahlmor," Henry said. "But *Generous Leaves* was attacked by weapons I'm not familiar with." He chuckled. "I suppose that tells us it was neither Kenmiri nor Vesheron who attacked them."

For twenty-two years, Henry had been fighting with and against groups equipped with basically the same outfit of weapons and defenses. There were variations in there, of course—the UPA's gravity shields, the Londu's high-density fusion rockets and other similarly unique systems—but by and large, the Vesheron had been equipped with stolen Kenmiri weapons and the *El*-Vesheron had adapted to simplify logistics.

Plus, from what he had seen, both Londu and UPSF missiles had *sucked* compared to their Kenmiri counterparts at their first encounters.

Henry mentally commanded the big holodisplay on the flagship to show the scan of the ship on the surface, highlighting her damage as Kahlmor looked at it again.

"We sent you the report, Kahlmor," he said quietly. "Is this our Enigmas in action? The tech seems...crude for that."

"No," the Londu officer replied slowly. "It is not the Enigmas. What evidence we have of their weapons suggests...an extravagant use of exotic particles, especially antimatter explosives. We have only seen the aftermath of their strikes, though. Anyone who might have provided sensor data is dead and their records, even their final-warning cases, destroyed."

"So, the fact that the final-warning cases survived is also proof that this wasn't the Enigmas," Henry guessed. "Which is something you should have mentioned, Lord Kahlmor."

"Perhaps. But I am bound to keep the Great Scion's secrets except where their reveal is necessary."

"Is this one of those secrets, Kahlmor?" Henry demanded, gesturing at the display.

"Yes. And no. It is..." The alien trailed off in a very human way, staring at the display. "What are they thinking?" he demanded of the air.

Henry waited to let Kahlmor sort through his thoughts and clear confusion.

"These weapons are known to me, as you guessed," Kahlmor finally said. "The lack of any sign of missile strikes or kinetic weapons aligns as well. These strikes are precise and distinctive. They would have known any Londu officer of my generation would recognize them.

"So, *why*?"

"Who, Lord Kahlmor?" Henry prodded. He needed a more basic question answered than the Londu was asking.

"This damage pattern is from Octal attack drones," Kahlmor told him. "They are the reason that we possessed starfighters when we encountered you and the rest of the Vesheron. Their drones are deadly and powerful, as fast as our missiles then and carrying powerful cutting lasers.

"But we are not at war with the Octal. We have not *been* at war with the Octal since before we met the Vesheron," the Londu said. "In the face of first contact with the Kenmiri, the skirmishes involved and our scouts' impression of the scale of our new enemy, the Scion went to them himself to ask for peace."

Henry wasn't as familiar with Londu politics and structures as Sylvia was, but he could take a guess at how big of a concession it was for *any* kind of head of state to personally go negotiate peace, let alone a constitutional autocrat like the Scion of the Londu.

"You were fighting them when you met the Kenmiri?" he asked.

"Yes. The Scion and the Heralds had declared them the next protectorate," Kahlmor told him. "I was a very junior officer then, but I saw some of the fighting. Our advance was...slower than we predicted."

Translation: the Londu had figured they were going to get a short, victorious war and had proceeded to get their asses kicked. Unfortunately for the Octal, the Londu were *also* good at taking a beating, figuring out what they'd done wrong on at least a tactical level, and coming back to return the favor.

It was an endearing trait in an ally. Not so much in an enemy.

"But you made peace successfully?" Henry asked.

"They agreed to an armistice and, later, a supposedly permanent peace so long as we put our fleets between them and the Kenmiri," Kahlmor explained. "There was some token contribution of resources that ended with the Fall of the Kenmiri, but they kept their word to us."

"So…"

"We will keep our word to them," the Londu replied, as if that were obvious. "We had other focuses with the move into the New Protectorates, but we would not have moved against them, regardless.

"We started the last war. We were not planning on starting another one—their integrity when we faced the Kenmiri earned them our friendship."

"But *Generous Leaves* was shot down by Octal attack drones?"

"I…hope and speak to fate that I am wrong," Kahlmor said. "But the damage pattern is consistent. I must see the data from the final-warning case."

"My people applied the codes and protocols you gave us," Henry told him. "The data storage was corrupted. That seems unlikely."

"But the wreck was last in the hands of my people." Kahlmor clearly didn't like Henry's train of thought.

"So we believe, yes," Henry agreed. "We will find out soon, I suppose."

"I will have my staff prepare a summary of what we know of the latest generations of Octal attack drones," Kahlmor promised. "It should not take long."

"I hope not. We don't *have* long."

⋎

TWO AND A HALF million kilometers and thirty minutes still separated Henry's Task Group One from orbit of Talon-Thirty-Eye-Alpha when the summary arrived. Reprocessed by Hawthorne's tactical team, it uploaded into his internal network and filled in his worst-case scenarios.

"Commodore," he called the Ops Officer over. "Your opinion?"

Sharma appeared at the same time as Hawthorne, the Fleet Master Chief not *explicitly* summoned but knowing when she was needed.

He didn't *think* he'd seen psychic powers and precognition on the course schedule for the NCOs at the Iron Ring, but the Master Chiefs and Command Master Chiefs of the UPSF had a reputation—one that Sharma had been proving utterly true in his experience.

"They're a lot less crude than we initially assumed," Hawthorne said bluntly. "They probably *started* as worker drones of some kind, but I'd guess that was at least a century ago."

"Or more," Sharma said. "Something like this being the weapon of choice of an interstellar empire? They must have gone through decades, at least, where their drones could have been rendered obsolete by missiles or shipboard lasers. The engines and lasers on them might have been unavoidably unsafe at one point, but they're most definitely unsafe by *choice* now."

"Chosen focuses and efficiencies," Henry agreed. "Kilo for kilo, the data suggests that the Octal's lasers are a *lot* better than the Londu's, but they're also small and a lot more radioactive than I'd want in a weapon mount."

"What maniac uses an aligned uranium crystal as a lasing medium?" Hawthorne asked. "I'm no engineer, but that can't give them *that* much extra power."

"Probably not," Henry agreed. "But if your primary striking weapon is a wholly automated ranged-attack platform, gaining a couple of percent throughput by making the laser slightly less safe for organics isn't a big concern, is it?"

"The power source is barely shielded. The laser *itself* is radioactive. The engines are fusion *pulse* drives—which means they are triggering sequential thermonuclear explosions, not sustaining a fusion reaction for thrust," Sharma said grimly. "All of these are *intentional* choices, meant to improve the efficiency and danger level of a drone. These are not designs for other purposes thrown together into a weapon."

"No, all of this is intentional and custom." Henry glared at the spherical hologram on his display. "So, how do we kill them?"

"Depending on how accurate the Londu intel is, they're somewhere between four and five KPS-squared for acceleration," Hawthorne told him. "Effective range for those lasers against gravity shields will be five, maybe ten thousand klicks at most."

"Our starfighters will cut them to shreds," Henry concluded. "Forward everything to O'Flannagain and the fighter wings. I want every starfighter we've got up and out in front."

"I'm not seeing any presence, ser," Hawthorne warned.

"Someone went into *Generous Leaves* after the Londu evacuated her and scrambled her black-box data," Sharma pointed out. "I'd bet a week's vacation the black boxes we pulled don't even *belong* to *Leaves*. We wouldn't be able to tell that someone had plugged new ones in, would we?"

"Presuming the survivors took the black boxes with them, you think the Octal planted the ones we have?" Hawthorne said slowly.

"I hadn't thought of that," Henry admitted. "I assumed the Octal had just scrambled the boxes after the Londu had left—but pulling them out with them makes sense. But if that was the case, they'd have ambushed *Visigoth* when she and *Dragoon* pulled into Charlie's orbit."

"There are days, ser, that I wonder if you have a nasty enough mind for your job," Sharma told him drily. "It's not about setting up an ambush for the first people to show up. It's about wiping out the entire rescue fleet—and probably taking out the remaining survivors at the same time.

"This isn't even about covering their tracks," the noncom concluded. "This is just outright *sadistic*. They want the survivors and the people rescuing them to think they've pulled it off and are about to get everyone out…"

"And then the drone fleet they've hidden in the debris trails of Alpha's moons jumps them at point-blank range," Henry finished. He shook his head. "I'd got as far as what they were doing and where the ambush was, but I wasn't thinking about *why*."

"The Londu might *know* that they were going to honor their treaty and feel that the Octal had earned a measure of friendship by not stabbing them in the back during the war," Sharma observed. "But to the *Octal*, the Londu may as well *be* the Kenmiri. They won't trust them to keep their word and…well…"

"They hate them, and probably for a damn good reason," Henry said. "Choices and allegiances, people. We know who our allies are here, even if they're not exactly our favorite people sometimes.

"Plus, if all of this has been set up the way I think it has…" He shook his head. "We have man-in-the-loop treaties and laws for a good reason. I don't care who they belong to or why they were deployed.

"I'm never going to be overly bothered by wiping out a fleet of autonomous weapons!"

33

"EVERYTHING IS CLEAR SO FAR."

Henry figured they were probably taunting fate by even saying that aloud, but it was what the sensor feeds were showing. The natural debris fields in Alpha's orbit appeared to be just that: natural, the rock and stone left from the tails of captured comets and asteroids.

"Do we have a location on that beacon?" he asked.

"No, ser," Perrin replied. "It wasn't designed to be localized from the range *Visigoth* and *Dragoon* picked it up from. We'll need to ping it again if we want to locate it."

"Hold off on that for the moment," Henry ordered. "Campbell, have your people get me more detail on *here.*"

He highlighted a cube of vacuum near Alpha-3, part of the debris trailing the moonlet. Something in the shapes there had caught his eye —and when *Raven* focused her passive scanners on it, it snapped into focus.

It was the front half of another explorer cruiser, and he heard Kahlmor inhale sharply as the Londu recognized it.

"Can we ID her from this range?" Henry asked quietly.

"Working on it," Hawthorne replied. "Spreading the destroyers out to get us a wider view."

Using starfighters for the multiple viewpoints might have made more sense, but Henry wanted every one of his Lancers in position to protect the capital ships from the threats they figured were present.

"Multiple damage points," Campbell's tactical officer reported from the bridge. "Similar cutting patterns to *Generous Leaves*, only… more. *Leaves* was crippled, with key conduits severed. This one was… well, sliced in half."

"Eventually," Henry concluded. "After one of the key fusion reactors had its containment cut open, I'm guessing."

"*Sardonic Dream*, ser," Hawthorne reported. "That was…"

"Okavaz's flagship," Kahlmor interrupted in Kem. The Londu was distressed enough that he wasn't pretending not to understand English anymore. He couldn't *speak* it, but Henry had figured out that the Lord of Fifty Thousand Miles had a translator earbud or something similar a long time before.

"Any chance of survivors?" Henry asked. "Half of the ship lengthwise is still most of her volume and mass."

"No energy signatures. No life signs." Hawthorne shook her head grimly. "One of her shuttle bays was in the missing half. The other, well… Only about a third of it is in the wreck.

"She doesn't have atmosphere and it looks like she didn't have enough integrity to maintain one for long after the killing blow. I suspect most of the crew died when the reactor lost containment, ser— and if there were any survivors, they would have needed someone else to come rescue them."

"Thank you, Commodore," Henry said quietly. He turned to Kahlmor. "We do not believe there were survivors," he told the Londu in Kem. "Lord Okavaz likely died with her flagship."

Kahlmor's eyes were closed, though his eyelids were pale enough that Henry could almost make out the Londu's eyes through them.

"Any sign of the other ships?" the man finally whispered, his eyes still closed.

"Nothing so far, but there is a lot of crap in Alpha's orbit," Hawthorne told him, switching smoothly to Kem to answer the alien's question. "Our best bet to locate survivors is still to ping the beacon."

"I do not see any other options," Henry said in the same language, then switched back to English. "Hawthorne, Perrin. Bring the Task Group to Condition One."

Battle stations. In the flag bridge, there were minimal visible changes, but elsewhere in the ship Henry knew that subtle lighting strips were turning red, emergency lights were coming online—just in case—and anyone who wasn't at their duty station would be getting the orders in their internal networks.

New icons appeared on the displays and projectors around Henry, and information poured into his internal network. He was unsurprised to see most of his ships reporting Condition One in half of the standard time.

Everyone had been expecting the order, after all.

"All ships report Condition One, ser," Perrin reported. "All lasers, plasma cannon and grav-driver capacitors are charged. All ready missile magazines are filled. All launchers are loaded. Dual-screen shields fully online across the Task Group."

Even mentioning the dual-screen shield systems around Kahlmor was probably pushing security protocols, but if things went the way Henry expected, it wasn't going to matter, soon enough.

"Hawthorne?" Henry said. Coms would pass on the initial reports, but it was Operations' job to tell him the fleet was ready.

"Ops confirms," Hawthorne replied. "Expeditionary Fleet Task Group One is at Condition One and standing by for orders."

"Good. Perrin, ping the beacon."

For a moment, nothing changed. Then a pulsing ring appeared on the surface of Alpha, each flicker of the circle narrowing in as *Raven*'s sensors resolved the location of the transmission.

"We have it," Hawthorne reported a second later, the pulsing ring snapping into a stylized antenna icon. "Getting overhead."

The display of the planetary surface zoomed in as they locked telescopes on the target. Henry was unsurprised to see a Londu-style long-range radio transmitter sitting alone in a cleared space on top of a hill.

The clearing was clearly artificial, not least because the impromptu lumberjacks had used the wreckage they'd created to form a rough barricade around the crest of the rise. Except for the area the presumed

Londu survivors had cleared, the hill was just as covered in dark red vegetation as the jungle around it.

Topographic analysis patterns flickered across the display as Henry watched and the holographic display updated with a three-dimensional analysis. The hill with the radio tower was part of a region of rolling rises and valleys cut by rivers, all of it hidden under the jungle.

"No sign of the survi— Wait."

New icons flickered up on the display as Hawthorne cut herself off.

"We've got a crash site about forty kilometers north of the beacon," she said. "Looks like she's in even rougher shape than *Generous Leaves*. Came down hard, and million-ton ships aren't generally designed to land in the first place."

"That's three," Henry murmured. There were three more cruisers out there somewhere, but he was pretty sure all of them were in this star system. Somewhere. Most likely in pieces.

"The survivors won't be anywhere near the beacon or the wreck," he observed. "Kahlmor, where would your people have dug in?" he asked in Kem.

The Londu was standing next to the holographic projection now, studying the map of the jungle around the beacon like it would give up its secrets to his icy glare.

"That depends on whether they thought they had safe air transport or not," he admitted. "If they think they can safely use their shuttles, they will be a minimum of fifty kilometers from the beacon.

"If they have reason to believe air travel is dangerous, they will need to be within one day's travel to be able to reach the beacon for regular maintenance, especially in these temperatures."

"And *nobody* is traveling quickly in jungle with eighteen percent freaking oxygen," Hawthorne said grimly. "They will need water supplies—preferably potable, but they can mix purification and using the water for cooling to conceal whatever technology they have operating."

As the Operations Officer spoke, her Chiefs were adding new details to the projection. Rivers became clearer as they identified what were active waterways versus paths that had been cut in the past.

"They would use water as a path," Kahlmor pointed out. "That would give them a greater distance."

"And *these* rivers meet at the bottom of the hill with the beacon," one of the Chiefs observed. "This one, though, heads back toward the ship. That would make them easier to find, which leaves us with these three."

"If they are well concealed, we will need to get closer to pick them out," Henry said. "Prep a drone," he ordered, switching back to English. "We'll do a low-altitude sweep to loca—"

"Contact! Bogies in the debris field, multiple new contacts!"

The report from the bridge was even less of a surprise than the isolation of the radio beacon.

"Attack drones?" Henry asked.

"Ninety-plus percent. Might be starfighters, but they are *not* looking friendly—and the explorer cruisers didn't *have* starfighters."

"Inform Colonel Spyros his people are to engage at will," Henry said. "Destroyers are to continue sensor sweeps. All ships will defend themselves as necessary, but there are launch platforms out there.

"And *those*, people, are what *Raven* and *Turquoise* are going to kill."

A LARGE PORTION of Henry's job was to appear confident. The first wave of sixty drones didn't overly challenge his ability to do that.

Neither did the second. The *third* started to become a stretch—and by the time the *sixth* wave of sixty drones materialized from the debris fields, the first was hurling themselves at the Task Group's defensive fighters.

The drones had a third again the acceleration of the Lancers, Henry noted absently, but their programming clearly expected a notably *higher* acceleration edge. It also rapidly became clear that the drones weren't designed to handle gravity shields.

Lasers sparkled in space, second-long bursts of coherent light that slashed into the UPSF fighters like the swords of ancient gods. In turn, the Lancers salvoed missiles at point-blank range, demonstrating an ancient truth of warfare: just because you now have something *better* doesn't mean you should get rid of the old weapon.

Lancers, unlike their predecessors, carried the same missiles as capital ships. But the missiles the UPSF had used previously had the virtue of being *smaller*—so where a Lancer normally carried three full-size attack missiles, they *could* carry three pods of three missiles apiece.

The first wave of drones vanished behind the energy signatures of missiles blazing out from the eighty-eight starfighters Lieutenant Colonel Spyros had taken out to defend the capital ships. Three missiles blazed in on each drone, and a cascade of nuclear explosions wiped the first sixty drones out of Alpha's orbit.

The range was short enough that the initial clash was over in seconds—but the drones' lasers connected dozens of times in those seconds.

"No losses so far," Hawthorne reported. "The drones appear to be expecting kills when they actually *hit*."

"Against TIEs like the Londu birds, that makes perfect sense," Henry murmured. "Against *us*..."

He caught himself, remembering that Kahlmor could hear him and the Londu understood English. Hopefully, the alien wasn't sufficiently familiar with human culture to realize just how dismissive "TIE fighter," the nickname for an unshielded starfighter, truly was.

"Well, there's *some* kind of brain back there," Hawthorne said grimly. "Second wave is spreading out to make our people's jobs harder, but the rest of the drones are falling back to clump up. Even our fighters are going to have trouble at four-to-one odds."

Plus, even using the pods, the Lancers had fired off a third of their ammunition in one shot. A second salvo lit up the displays as Henry watched, and *this* group of drones had seen what happened to the first one.

"Their programming is adapting," he said grimly. "It's not good enough yet, but I'm not liking the trend."

The GMS starfighters' greater maneuverability and survivability had clearly been a surprise, but they'd *already* adapted to the maneuverability. The hit ratio was rising, *fast*. So far, though, the grav-shields were holding.

And Henry's *ships* had an entire damn planet between them and the drones so far.

"Horizon in sixty-five seconds," Hawthorne warned. "Second wave down. No losses, but they're *definitely* catching on that they need multiple hits to take down our birds."

"Let's leave them guessing on the fighters, Commodore," Henry told her. "Distribute targets and all ships will open fire with missiles. Starfighters will fall back on the Task Group."

The range was terrifyingly low by space-combat standards—but so were the velocities. Everyone involved was basically operating from rest relative to the planet and each other. Missiles were more vulnerable than usual, and Henry suspected that the drones would shred the munitions his warships were launching.

The fighters had been firing at point-blank range, after all. He was counting on that, though. So far, the drones had been adapting rapidly to everything his people had done—not *instantly*, each lesson costing them an entire group of drones, but rapidly.

Which raised interesting questions, and he turned his attention to Kahlmor.

"Lord Kahlmor, is there going to be anyone living over there?" he asked in Kem.

"No. The Octal do not risk their personnel when they can avoid it," the Londu told him. "There will be superior intelligences on the launch platforms providing command and control."

That was what Henry had hoped for, and he turned his attention back to Hawthorne. His conversations with his people were faster, carrying side channels through their internal networks that minimized what had to be said aloud.

"Find those platforms," he ordered. "Destroyers will screen the capital ships; all ships are released for laser and missile fire."

Which *also* meant they were to hold fire on the gravity drivers and plasma cannon—an order that was only relevant to his two cruisers.

"Good news, bad news," Hawthorne told him a second later. "We are identifying platforms—because they're launching another set of drones!"

New red triangle icons flashed into being on the hologram as his

Operations team pinned down the location of the launch bases. Four. Six. *Ten. Eighteen?!*

And each time his people located a platform, it was accompanied by a new set of ten drones—and as his Operations team located them, the concentrated wave of two hundred and forty drones collided with the UPSF's first missile salvo. There were more drones than missiles in that clash, and their lasers proved as effective in defending them as he had feared.

Less than two dozen drones vanished from the screen—and the launch platforms had added almost two *hundred* to replace them.

"How many drones do they *have*?"

"Ready group of twenty, thirty in reserve," Kahlmor told him in Kem, answering what had been a rhetorical question.

"Right." Eighteen platforms with fifty drones apiece were a much bigger problem than Henry had allowed for, and the first big wave of drones was about to smash over his fleet like a tidal wave.

"Destroyers, screen *Pegasus*," he ordered. "*Turquoise*, form on *Raven*. Campbell, Vishnu…time to clear the damn road. Flank acceleration; we cut over the pole and we kill those platforms before they get their last drones into space!"

The starfighters were interlacing themselves with the destroyers without further orders from him. What Spyros might lack in experience, he clearly made up in being willing to listen to and learn from his Captain, and *Pegasus*'s fighter wing knew their job.

The attack drones knew how to fight destroyers and starfighters. They were maneuvering by attack group now, ten of the robotic ships slicing at a target at once. Even the UPSF's shielded starfighters were finding themselves the focus of ten or more drones at a time.

Raven and *Turquoise* launched away from the main body of the task group at two KPS^2, leaving several groups of drones to slice empty space. Red omega symbols began to flash across the displays as Henry's fighters began to die.

The Lancers had gravity shields and gravity drives, but they'd been designed when energy screens required installations bigger than the fighters themselves. They could survive a *lot* of fire, but it was a probability game.

And unlike the new-generation warships, when a Lancer's number came up, that was all she wrote. They had no interior shields, no armor, no structural reinforcement—fitting everything necessary to *be* a GMS starfighter into a hull had required huge sacrifices. The starfighter itself was astonishingly fragile.

Raven and *Turquoise*, however, were not—and Henry realized that his Captains had taken the urgency of the situation to heart. Neither starship was ever meant to enter atmosphere, but the battlecruiser and her escort cut the angle on Alpha's horizon *far* closer than they should have.

"Energy screens are taking a beating," Hawthorne warned. "Friction heat is doing a number on the stress capacitors."

The gravity shears that made up the exterior shield couldn't do much about an atmosphere. The spike from zero to thousands of gravities and back again was utterly destructive to anything needing to remain intact, but atmosphere had no such requirement.

The energy screens could absorb the heat and the impact of pushing into the air envelope of a planet...to a point. Henry hadn't ordered the two ships to push the cut that hard, but as more of his fighters flashed omega and alerts began to appear on his destroyers, he didn't complain.

"Clear." Henry wasn't even sure who made the one-word report— and it didn't matter. The moment *Raven* broke free of Alpha's atmosphere and had a clear line of sight, the entire battlecruiser shivered as her main weapons spoke in anger for the first time since her refit.

The new gravity driver fired the same round as it had before—the same round *Turquoise* carried for her version of the cannon, in fact— but where *Raven* had been built with a weapon with a muzzle velocity of seven percent of lightspeed, the cannon *now* fired its round at *ten* percent of light's velocity.

At thirty thousand kilometers per second, the first platform targeted likely hadn't even realized *Raven* had fired before the weapon arrived—and Campbell had clearly judged that the launch platforms didn't require anything fancy. There were multiple special munitions available for the gravity cannon, but sometimes, two hundred kilograms of iron at a tenth of lightspeed was *more* than enough.

The lasers fired a moment later, pairs of beams hammering into two more platforms and vaporizing them just as effectively, if somewhat less spectacularly. *Turquoise* joined the fun a moment later, her gravity driver firing at a *mere* seven and a half percent of lightspeed—but her plasma cannon tearing into the platforms even more quickly.

A third of the launch platforms vanished in seconds—and then the hundred and eighty just-launched drones turned on Henry's two ships to protect their home bases.

"Targeting drones with missile defense lasers," Hawthorne reported. "Main weaponry focused on the platforms." Pause. "Second grav-driver salvo away. *Turquoise*'s plasma cannon firing at maximum cycle."

Energy flickered across the icons of Henry's two warships on the displays and sensor feeds, but the truth was that he wasn't worried about his capital ships. He'd risked—he'd *spent*—starfighters to confirm the strengths and weaknesses of his enemy, and their tactics weren't up to overcoming the dual-screen defenses of his warships.

Only five of the eighteen platforms lived long enough to get their second reserve squad off. That left both halves of his split task group facing over two hundred drones—but within moments of the last platform dying, he could *see* the change in the drones.

"They've lost all coordination above the squadron level," he observed. "And they seem to have forgotten what they learned about our fighters."

Henry had just enough time to be certain he'd saved his starfighters from further casualties—the ships and pilots they'd already lost were going to be bad enough—when the drones proved they had a fallback program for just this circumstance.

"Drone courses changing," Hawthorne snapped. "Mother of—"

The range was too short for anything to react when the drones switched to ramming courses. The saving grace, Henry noted absently and with a calm that surprised even him, was that there was *no* coordination or sensible targeting parameters involved. Drone groups lunged toward the closest targets, leading to everything from three drones hurling themselves at *Visigoth* to over thirty hurling themselves at one unlucky Lancer.

The weapons around *Raven* and *Turquoise* ended up almost evenly split between the two ships, and the gravity shears of their defensive shields exerted deadly tidal forces.

The problem was that the drones were both explosive and radioactive. Not one drone made it through the gravity shields intact, but high-velocity cascades of shrapnel and plasma remained to hammer into the energy screens.

Warning icons flickered across the displays for *Raven* and *Turquoise*, but none of his other ships were showing even those minor concerns. Given the same resources as the Octal attack force, he'd have sent every drone in each force at one target—*Raven* and *Pegasus*, respectively.

Instead, the suicide strike had been spread out randomly across his ships, sparing the entire task group from serious damage. Still...he steeled himself as he pulled up the damage list for the starfighters.

They'd lost fourteen ships. Some of those pilots would have ejected and the *fighters* could be replaced from stocks aboard *Pegasus* and *Archon*, but that was still more than painful.

Then Henry blinked as he saw the report from *Pegasus* Delta-Five, the unlucky pilot who'd found themselves the target of thirty-two drones in the final seconds.

Unlucky was perhaps the wrong word. Over half of the drones had collided with *each other*, allowing the not significantly larger GMS fighter to outmaneuver the rest and only take four hits on the gravity shield.

"Not bad, pilot," Henry said aloud, making sure the woman got his words. "Not bad at all."

He blinked again, expanding his attention from his internal networks and the holographic display to the rest of the flag bridge.

"Let's bring the Task Group back together and prepare the probe sweep to find the survivors," he ordered. "We'll spend the time we have to, but we're still running against the clock. Let's find these people so we can bring them home!"

34

SYLVIA WAS REASONABLY sure that Lord of Fifty Thousand Miles Kahlmor, an equal to Henry in rank and theoretically the primary envoy of the Londu to the United Planets Alliance, had about as much business being on the shuttle plunging toward the surface as Henry did.

But Henry had Commander Adelaide Palmerston to sit on him when he felt like being stupid—and the commando officer had the full backing of Commodore Frieda Zeni, the senior Ground Division officer of the Expeditionary Fleet.

No one had actually tried to stop Kahlmor from boarding the shuttle. Not his people and certainly not the humans. Sylvia would admit, where she knew he couldn't hear her, that her four Commando Regiment escorts were as much to watch the Londu as to protect her.

Though she also knew perfectly well that neither Henry nor Palmerston would have let Sylvia go down to the planet with *merely* a shuttle stuffed full of powered-armor Ground Division assault troops for security if she'd left them a choice.

"Drone puts the camp here," Lieutenant Mithra Olmos, the shuttle's pilot, reported as he highlighted the location on everyone's internal network. "Penetrating radar says the river widens and turns into something of a long shallow lake. Local plant life manages a mutually supporting canopy that conceals it—and the same radar says there are some solid-sized caves in the hills next to the lake."

Olmos chuckled.

"And we got a definite signature on a standard Londu transport shuttle, just in case the value of the position wasn't enough of a clue. I *think* they might have flown her under the canopy from the crash site, though, as there's no sign anything has breached the treetops here."

"Is that going to last, Lieutenant?" Petty Officer First Class Hadrian Rothschild, the platoon gunnery chief, asked.

"Oh, hell, no; *I* am only worried about Londu surface-to-air missiles and know that the skies are friendly. We're breaching the canopy about three klicks north of the target and coming in from there. If the Lord of Fifty Thousand Miles's recording serves its purpose, they probably won't even shoot us!"

"So long as you are transmitting, they will not," Kahlmor told the pilot.

Sylvia found it more than a touch amusing that Kahlmor had entirely stopped pretending he didn't understand English. He was still replying in Kem, but enough of the humans understood that to make it useful—if not enough to make it practical for the humans to operate in Kem.

"Good. Hitting the treetops in twenty seconds," Olmos said. "We'll be on the ground in two minutes unless the survivors are feeling twitchy and are better shots than I think they are. Then we'll be on the ground *much* faster!"

NO ONE SHOT their shuttle down as Olmos brought them in to a gentle landing on the surface of the wide river. Pontoons automatically inflated to keep the shuttle on top of the water as the pilot guided them in to the riverbank.

The cave opening that the scanners had picked up was obvious even to Sylvia from there. She wasn't any more sure than Olmos about where the Londu had brought their shuttles down, but the cavern was large enough to allow the transport shuttles to be moved inside.

A single shuttle was visible, partially covered in camouflage netting —a large chunk of which was pulled back to allow a work party to attempt repairs.

The Londu had clearly left those repairs incomplete but hadn't bothered to re-cover the shuttle once they realized they'd been located. Two dozen Blades of the Scion in combat armor with faux-hammered-iron torso plating were in clear overwatch positions, with medium and heavy arms covering the shuttle.

"Wait here," Kahlmor instructed in slow and somewhat mushy English. "I will arrange safety."

The ramp slid open, stretching out to connect the shuttle to the ground. Kahlmor moved forward—and while he left the shuttle on his own, a series of silent commands from Petty Officer Rothschild put a pair of troopers with heavy energy weapons right at the ramp behind him.

"Hail!" Kahlmor shouted in Londu. "It is Lord Kahlmor. Is Okavaz among you?"

There was a long silence.

"No," someone called back. "Lord Okavaz didn't make it to the surface. We do not know her fate. You live, Lord Kahlmor?"

"I live," Kahlmor confirmed. "I reached the humans and they have brought me here, seeking Lord Okavaz's squadron. Are these...all the survivors?"

"I speak to fate that we are not, but I fear the answer it gives," the voice told him.

"Is that you, Chalna?" Kahlmor asked.

"Yes. Come out into the light, my lord. We do not know that shuttle."

Kahlmor stepped away from the shuttle ramp and onto the shore. A Londu officer clad in the black breastplate and robes of regular-duty wear, though her robes were stained with mud to the point of being as dark a reddish brown as the woman's mane, emerged from the cave to meet him.

"Lord of Thousand Miles Chalna," their Londu envoy greeted the woman. "Your ship?"

"*Righteous Claim* is no more," the Lord of Thousand Miles told him. "We were ambushed by Octal attack drones. I was knocked unconscious, and my crew dragged me from the command deck."

Sylvia shivered. She couldn't make out details of the Londu woman, but she doubted Chalna liked those memories.

"*Claim*'s final fate?" Kahlmor asked.

"Obliterated, my lord," a second Londu officer told him, stepping up next to Chalna and gesturing for the soldiers to lower their weapons. "Four of us from the bridge survived, dragging the Lord of Thousand Miles with us to the escape pod. Someone in Engineering triggered the scuttling charges, and only one shuttle escaped."

"Sixty-two survivors from *Righteous Claim*," Chalna said grimly. "One hundred eighty from *Silent Hunt*. Eight from *Sardonic Dream*. Forty-five from *Honest Stride*. None from *Generous Leaves* or *Driven Flight*."

"None from *Leaves*?" Kahlmor asked. "Then there must be others. We know at least one shuttle from *Leaves* escaped her crash and, I presume, headed here."

"They did," Chalna's subordinate said flatly. "The Octal were waiting. Drones ambushed the shuttles in orbit and cut them to pieces."

Sylvia had been afraid of something similar once *Raven* and her compatriots had run into the drones. It hadn't just been *rescuers* that the aliens who'd ambushed Okavaz had laid the trap for.

"We must make them pay, somehow," Kahlmor swore. "Do you have wounded? The humans have sent medics and supplies."

"We have done what we can, but we are running low on almost everything," Chalna said. "We will take whatever aid they can offer, but there is only one thing we truly need."

Sylvia took that as her cue, following Kahlmor off the shuttle. Her commandos fell into formation behind her, and the GroundDiv medical team was only a few steps behind them.

"I am Ambassador Sylvia Todorovich of the United Planets Alliance," she told the Londu officer in their language. "As Lord

Kahlmor has said, we have medics and supplies with us, but I believe your *one thing* is a ride home, yes?"

Chalna was a starship captain and had admirable control of both her features and her microexpressions, but Sylvia's speaking in Londu and recognizing her hopes clearly caught her off guard.

The Londu took a moment to recapture her composure, especially as she recognized at least the equipment the GroundDiv team behind Sylvia was carrying.

"We...will gladly accept your medics," Chalna said. "Master of One Hundred Kasor, show the medics to our wounded. Do they speak Londu?"

"They do not, I am afraid," Sylvia admitted. "Does your Master of One Hundred"—equivalent to a UPSF Commander—"speak Kem?"

"I do," Kasor said calmly. "And I would translate via any machine I could rig for medics to aid our people!"

"Lead on, Master of One Hundred," the senior medic told him.

The medical team surged past Sylvia in a momentary flutter of chaos. It took only a few seconds for Chalna to lead Sylvia and Kahlmor—and Sylvia's bodyguards—off to one side.

Sylvia didn't put much more thought into it until her internal network chimed softly, her bodyguard highlighting the half dozen armored Blades who still had clear lines of sight and fire on their location.

Chalna was desperate but she was not stupid. The remaining crew from the six cruisers was fewer people than she'd commanded when she'd been in charge of *one* cruiser. The less than three hundred Londu under her command were the last survivors of her squadron, and she wasn't going to let *anything* happen to them.

"Can you take us home?" she asked Sylvia flatly once the medics were on their way into the cave.

"Yes." Sylvia's single word cut strings she hadn't seen holding Chalna up, but the Lord of Thousand Miles recovered swiftly. "We are on our way to the Sovereignty with a small fleet, to assist the Scion in dealing with your Enigmas.

"The Octal were not something we anticipated," she continued. Or had been warned about, but that was a different conversation and one

Chalna didn't need to suffer through. "Still, we have enough space aboard the ships we have in orbit to load all your people aboard and move on.

"We will likely transfer you off our warships onto our logistics train once we rendezvous with the rest of the fleet," Sylvia warned. "We only have our forward striking force in this system."

She knew that Colonel Larue and his people would already be working like crazy to design an appropriate set of protocols for having *three hundred* Londu officers and soldiers aboard the most advanced warships in the UPSF. She'd give the intelligence officer enough credit, though, to concede that he hadn't raised the slightest question about doing so—only about the best way *to* do so.

"We will need shuttle support," Chalna admitted. She turned to gesture to the spacecraft half-covered by the camo netting. "That's our last somewhat-functional shuttle, and honestly, we're just using her power plant to run our food-preservation systems. However bad you think this planet's plant life is for machinery, you have underestimated it."

That was fascinating to Sylvia. She'd figured the low oxygen and carbon dioxide levels would have slowed the plant life down and kept it from causing too much difficulty—but she supposed the greater amount of light and heat compared to most habitable planets would have the opposite effect.

Sylvia, for her part, was grateful that her formal suit went over and integrated with a civilian shipsuit—and since the shipsuit was designed to protect her from being accidentally dumped into space, it could keep her safe and moderately comfortable in forty-seven-degree heat.

For a while, at least.

"That bad?" Kahlmor asked.

"It would be manageable," Chalna said slowly, "if the local bacteria hadn't turned out to have a taste for the composite fiber we use for power-conduit casings. We had two shuttles completely inoperable and a third triggering safety warnings on our scanners when bringing the main reactor above five percent before we realized what was happening."

Sylvia was no engineer or technician, but that sounded…bad.

"We will need to be careful of our own shuttles," she said. "But we should be able to bring down more than enough transport to move all your people into orbit and see them cared for. You have my word, Lord of Thousand Miles Chalna, your people will go home."

Chalna slapped her closed fist to her chest in a salute that no Blade of the Scion should ever give an alien.

"And I thank you, Ambassador."

"We need to know what happened here, Lord of Ten Thousand Miles," Sylvia told her gently. "Our Fleet did not know of the Octal at all. My understanding from Lord Kahlmor is that they are no longer enemies of the Londu."

"They *were* no longer enemies of the Londu," Chalna said grimly. "This is not their space. We are over eighty light-years and a minimum of three skips from the territory of the Octal, and they are not known for their recklessness."

"Quite the opposite," Kahlmor observed. He met Sylvia's gaze. "The Octal are not Ashall. They are far longer-lived than any of the Seeded Races and reproduce significantly more slowly. Their aggregate population is comparable in many ways, but their military takes excessive measures to prevent risk to even individual Octal."

Sylvia could follow the logic, at least. If an Octal lived four times as long as a human, say, and would have a quarter as many children on average, then the population growth on a *species* level would likely end up about the same. But the extended life-spans would make the loss of any individual seem that much greater, culturally.

And she could see how that would create military doctrines revolving around risk avoidance, automated combatants and safe, steady operations.

"I am not sure what the Octal fleet was doing in Talon-Thirty-Eye," Chalna said. "But they were here when we entered the system. Twelve command carriers and twenty cruisers.

"I suspect Okavaz would have assumed a smaller force was friendly, but thirty-two control ships are a real fleet. She challenged them. They answered with fire: attack drones and droid corvettes ambushed us immediately.

"We never stood a chance. We were outnumbered five to one, and a single command carrier matched our entire squadron. Okavaz ordered the squadron to scatter, to try and get at least a courier drone back to the Scion.

"But ships with organic crews cannot outrun droid corvettes and attack drones. We scattered, and it only increased the volume of space and time in which we died."

"I am sorry, Lord Chalna," Sylvia told her. "I do not know what the consequences of this attack will be, but we will deliver you and your people to your Scion. *He* will decide what happens then."

"I fear, Ambassador, Lord Kahlmor, that the fleet that engaged us was preparing to move against the Sovereignty," Chalna warned. "The Scion may already know we have been betrayed."

"Do you have sensor data from the battle?" Kahlmor asked. "I would like to make multiple copies and scatter them through the human fleet—both to enable them to plan for what may come and to make certain that the information makes it back to the Sovereignty."

"The shuttle's computers have a full record," Chalna confirmed. "We also inscribed copies to hard crystal as soon as we realized what was happening to the power systems. We needed to be certain that, even in the worst case, the record of the Octal betrayal survived."

"Then we will make certain it makes it home," Kahlmor promised. "And I will make certain that our allies have a copy. If the Octal are between us and the Sovereignty, we still may not make it home without a fight."

35

"FRANKLY, Em Todorovich, the United Planets Alliance knows *nothing* about the Octal."

Kyla Antonella Napoletani looked a lot fresher than Sylvia possibly could. The Head of Archives for the UPA Diplomatic Corps—and unofficial second-in-command of the Corps—had the image of a tiny Italian grandmother down to a fine art.

"I wasn't necessarily hoping for anything *useful*," Sylvia told the other woman. There was a small but noticeable delay in the transmission before the hologram standing on top of her desk chuckled at her.

Raven had reassembled the Expeditionary Fleet and was now heading toward the Sovereignty once more. That, among other things, meant that Sylvia was able to call home. The separation between the components of her boyfriend's fleet, however, meant that *Sanskrit* was about a light-second away from the battlecruiser.

That light-second was adding more of a delay than the hundreds of light-years between Earth and the Expeditionary Fleet. The ansible was useful, a solid step in the direction of once more having galaxy-wide communications.

"We have nothing useful," Napoletani said drily. "We have *nothing*. Some of the records from Karl Rembrandt's embassy with the Londu mention the *name*, but you were there." The diplomat-turned-librarian shrugged.

"I am afraid, Em Todorovich, that the best source we have for what you're looking at is you. All we really have in our records is a mention in the summary reports by one of your analysts on Londar. One of the Lords of a Million Miles mentioned them as a potential threat in a meeting, only to be shut down by the Scion and informed that the Octal were expected to honor the armistice.

"I would love to provide more, but that is all we have."

"I had a copy of that in my own files," Sylvia admitted. "I'll have my people package up everything we got from the Londu recently and send it back. It's almost entirely focused on their military capabilities."

She shook her head.

"About the only thing I can be sure of is that the Londu are convinced that the Octal are not the Enigmas. That would have made things too simple, I suppose."

"You wrote our psych profile on the Londu and the Sovereignty," Napoletani reminded her. "Do I need to tell you how the Scion is going to react to the Octal breaking a peace treaty like this?"

"No. It's going to be war," Sylvia said softly. "And our mission was to preserve the Londu, so that doesn't give us much choice about getting involved."

"That's between you and Rear Admiral Wong," the Head of Archives told her. "You don't need me to remind you that you have plenipotentiary authority, to declare war or make peace by your own word.

"But as head of the Diplomatic Archives, I *will* remind you that I want copies of all paperwork and recordings of all conversations with the Londu—at least the diplomatic ones, though I'm not going to turn down recordings of the military meetings. War, after all, is politics and diplomacy continued by other means."

War is not merely a political act but a real political instrument, a continuation of political intercourse, a carrying out of the same by other means. Sylvia had been a wartime diplomat, tasked with using words and alliances to augment the capacity of the United Planets Alliance to complete its *political* goal of securing their long-term safety—a goal that, against the Kenmiri, could only be accomplished by war.

With the Octal, the Enigmas and the Londu…the political goal laid out by her superiors was both more complicated and vastly easier than that of *Save humanity from conquest.*

"I'll be sure to pass that on to the Admiral," Sylvia promised. "All my diplomatic files should be being sent you in a regular precis whenever we can activate the ansible."

"Good luck, Ambassador. If you're getting dragged into a two-front war, you're going to need it."

IT WAS IMPOSSIBLE—OR, at least, *unwise*—for Sylvia to update Henry with the nonexistent findings from Earth when she saw him next. She was the last person to enter the small breakout conference room attached to the Admiral's day office, and both Kahlmor and Chalna were already there.

So were Commodore Hawthorne and Lieutenant Colonel Larue, sitting with Henry to fill out the UPSF side of the meeting.

"Apologies for the delay," she told them all in Kem, to make sure everyone understood. "You would think that traffic would not be a problem on a starship, but corgis disagree."

And if the delay had been, at least initially, her stopping to *pet* a Colonel, no one could prove that.

"We had not begun," Henry said. "You are less than a minute late, after all. It is just that the rest of us are soldiers."

Sylvia took her seat on his right side and, as a senior diplomat possessed of immense gravitas, did *not* tickle her boyfriend for that quip.

"What does the UPSF require, Admiral Wong?" Kahlmor asked. "Our time is growing short. Your own projections say we will reach the Zal System in sixteen days."

"Yes," Henry confirmed. "And I need to know what I am looking at, Lord Kahlmor. I understand that none of us know *anything* about the Enigmas except that they are possessed of gravity shields and anti-matter weapons.

"The Octal, on the other hand, appear to have added themselves to the threat parameters, and I need a full briefing on what that entails. And at this point, I need to know what the Zal System looks like in detail. Before, I was expecting to barely slow down as we passed through Zal, sending a friendly wave to the nodal defense fleet.

"Now there is a very real chance that the UPSF Expeditionary Fleet will need to fight to relieve Zal from an Octal or Enigma assault. I have to know the lay of the ground."

The two Londu were silent, then Chalna glanced at her superior.

"We did not receive any updates after you departed. Your information is as up-to-date as ours."

"I did not provide Admiral Wong with information on the Octal," Kahlmor said. "They were supposed to be treaty-bound, neutral if not yet a friend."

Given everything Sylvia knew about the history between the Londu and the Octal, she wasn't surprised that the Octal had decided that they couldn't trust the Sovereignty long-term and had attacked during a moment of Londu weakness.

She'd delved deeply into their culture and history while she and Karl Rembrandt had negotiated the relationship between the UPA and the Londu. She understood the pressures and parameters and sense of honor that meant that, yes, the Scion was more likely than not to see the Octal keeping their word during the war against the Kenmiri as grounds to keep the peace forever.

But Sylvia Todorovich was, at her core, a *Russian* diplomat. She understood realpolitik in her bones, and she knew that *she* wouldn't have trusted Scion and Sovereignty not to resume their conquest once the absorption of the Isis Sector was complete.

"We need to know *everything*," Henry insisted. "Start with, well, what they even *look* like!"

Kahlmor produced one of the heavily built Londu tablets and swiftly demonstrated one feature the metal slab had that Terran flimsy pads didn't: it had its own holographic projector.

The image that appeared above the tablet was an odd creature. It resembled nothing so much as a large cockroach with an octopus mounted on its back.

"The Octal are colony organisms," Kahlmor told them. "This is their usual configuration, with a name that translates into Kem as *shell walker*. Other preferred configurations vary…"

The hologram rippled and shrank, adding three other images of the Octal. One was very clearly an aquatic creature, looking almost like a dolphin but with massive armored blades instead of fins. The second new image appeared to be the smallest, a swift-looking creature with four legs and two arms, its centaur-like lines marked by armor plates that resembled the fins on the aquatic version.

The last was the largest and Sylvia recognized several of the component organisms from the other types. The armored plates and even two of the heavily shelled beetles of the shell walker configuration were locked into each other to form an immense behemoth that looked like it could break through walls.

"There are eleven different organisms that can be combined into the forms of the Octal," Kahlmor warned. "While they have preferred configurations, like these, some Octal experiment with different forms.

"At the core, though, every Octal is this."

The example configurations vanished, replaced by what looked like a particularly sturdy jellyfish.

"Their core body is amphibious and carries significant electrical charge that they exert a fine control over," Kahlmor observed. "At what point that control became them puppeteering the other organisms of their configurations is long lost, as six of the ten 'living limbs' predate their known history.

"The other four are artificial creations of a more recent time." The Londu shrugged. "None of the living limbs are sentient in their own right. My understanding is that without an Octal controlling them, most would starve without assistance."

Sylvia wasn't sure she'd call the Octal a *colony organism*, though she suspected some subtlety and detail were lost in the translation to Kem. *Parasitic* or maybe *symbiotic* was a better description in her mind—but she wasn't sure what the technical language would be.

She was a diplomat, not a doctor, after all.

"A fascinating species," she murmured.

"And dangerous. Why invest in powered armor, after all, when you can convert yourself to a behemoth form in about the same time as it takes to put on the armor?"

"Indeed. You said they are long-lived?" Henry asked.

"Average lifespan of an Octal is dependent on the health of the core organism," the Londu told him. "But it is roughly four centuries."

Kahlmor paused, considering his information it seemed, then sighed.

"Even we Londu know almost nothing about their reproductive cycle," he observed. "They protect those secrets *very* closely, but we do know that their overall population grows only slightly slower than that of an equivalent Londu colony. That suggests a reproduction rate proportional to their extended life-spans—which results in their cultural desire to preserve even their soldiers at all costs."

"Which appears to feed into their military designs," Henry said.

"Yes. As does the degree of control they exert over life forms around them. I understand that the UPA has strict rules on the use of high-level synthetic intelligences and the development of self-aware intelligences."

"We do," Sylvia confirmed.

"We ban them," Kahlmor said flatly. "That was part of how we learned to listen to the wise instead of the many. The price of the lesson was high, and we learned that these intelligences are a danger best avoided by not creating them at all.

"The systems used in our military computers are very carefully designed to avoid *any* level of self-awareness. Outside of our military and very specific civilian uses, computers above a certain level of hardware complexity are forbidden.

"The Octal do not feel the same way."

Suddenly, Sylvia felt that calling the UPA's rules around synthetic intelligences "strict" might be more of an overstatement than she had previously realized. By the twenty-second century, humanity had a very good idea of where the distinction between a learning algorithm and a self-aware synthetic intelligence was. It had taken until the early twenty-*third* century for humanity to be able to reliably create the latter, but they'd known how to *prevent* emergent intelligences for over two hundred years.

Creating a true AI was a heavily regulated endeavor because such a creation was functionally a birth, creating a new person—and a new, legally protected citizen. The UPA would no more build a custom AI for a warship than they would draft children from the streets to fly their starfighters.

Yet the entire edifice of modern warfare was, as Sylvia understood it, built upon an immense array of hardware and software that vastly exceeded mere *programs*. The software that operated in the underlayer of a modern internal network was very, very intelligent...and completely and utterly unaware.

"What do the Octal do with AI?" Henry asked, breaking Sylvia's chain of thought.

"We do not use AI because we do not trust it," Kahlmor told them. "The Iron Warriors of our past left nations, continents—in one case, a *world*—devastated. There are plains on Londar that once fed half our civilization that remain tainted by the fire and salt of the Iron Warriors' strikes.

"The Octal, however, *enslave* their AI. We do not understand the details, but their computers are far more intelligent than ours and still utterly obedient and bound. They have tiers of the things, from the most basic systems operating their combat drones to the superior intelligences that manage their droid corvettes and long-endurance deployment platforms.

"They have no attachment to these intelligences they have created. You saw that at Talon-Thirty-Eye. Over a dozen of their superior intelligences, self-aware entities theoretically capable of immortality, sacrificed as a distraction to prevent anyone reporting Okavaz's fate.

"Their entire military apparatus is constructed similarly. For every Octal, there are a dozen superior intelligences running a thousand lower-tier AIs."

A new set of holograms took shape above Kahlmor's tablet. One, even Sylvia recognized from Talon-Thirty-Eye. The other three images were, presumably, other starships.

"You are familiar with their attack drones," Chalna said. "You saw them in isolation in Talon-Thirty-Eye. They are the key weapon system but only part of their operating tactics.

"In a full-fleet combat, the drones will be supported by these droid corvettes," she continued, poking at a hologram that consisted mostly of a single jagged spike. "They carry a superior intelligence and an array of the same lasers the drones are armed with, plus an internal complement of their own drones.

"Their cruisers carry five such corvettes and one hundred drones, plus missiles of a type you would be more familiar with. The command carriers have quadruple the armament and complement of their cruisers.

"Both crewed ships have relatively small crew by Londu standards, with shortcomings made up for with drones and superior intelligences."

It might be her interest in old science fiction, but Sylvia found herself wondering if there were a way they could turn the shackled intelligences against their Octal masters. That was probably more complicated than they could manage with the resources available to them out there, but it was still a tempting thought.

"The cruisers are roughly one million tons and the carriers five million, the size of our battleships," Kahlmor said. "If there were ten command carriers in Talon-Thirty-Eye, that is *already* two more than we believed they possessed. The Octal are not what we sought your aid for, Ambassador, Admiral, but we may be in more trouble than we believed."

36

HENRY LISTENED to the description of the enemy ships and kept his face still and calm. He still had people working on converting and sanitizing the data from the Londu survivors to load it into their systems, but what he was seeing was enough to start from.

"They are not the Enigmas," he observed. "If nothing else, there are no reports of gravity shields in the battle in Talon-Thirty-Eye, and that was not a battle where they would have held anything back."

"For the moment, I am not committing the Expeditionary Fleet to fight the Octal," Henry continued. "Not outside of Sovereignty space, anyway. If we can pass them by in safety as we proceed to the Zal System, then pass on your information to the Blades command there, we are better off."

He was reasonably confident in the ability of the Expeditionary Fleet to run circles around the thirty Octal capital ships that had ambushed Okavaz. His losses against the first Octal fleet had been minimal, with the starfighters and their pilots already replaced from the logistics train.

Not that he had many replacement pilots and not that the six young officers lost in Talon-Thirty-Eye hadn't hurt both him and O'Flannagain deeply, but against hundreds of a brand-new enemy, the Expeditionary Fleet had been blooded.

And his people had risen to the challenge splendidly.

"They have already broken their oaths and attacked us once," Kahlmor warned. "I believe they will judge you a threat and attack as well."

"I expect the same," Henry agreed. "But we will give them the chance to avoid a conflict if we can. Neither we nor your Sovereignty wish to fight a two-front war, Lord Kahlmor."

"Against this treachery, my Scion will see no choice."

"Perhaps. But that is your Scion's decision to make, not mine," Henry told the Londu. "Sylvia and I will attempt to negotiate if we meet them—I see no reason to even tell them we have Okavaz's survivors aboard."

"And if they are already attacking the Zal System?"

"Then your people will make an excellent anvil for my hammer."

The metaphor might not have translated, but Henry's intent did.

"Which brings us to my original questions," he continued. "The Zal System, the guardian of the Sovereignty's spinward flank. I know it is a nodal fleet base and that is all I know. If there is a chance that the Enigmas or the Octal will have attacked it, I need to know *everything*."

"That delves into the secrets of the Scion that we are not supposed to share," Kahlmor pointed out.

"I do not need to know about the secret weapons laboratory on the moon of the fifth world," Henry said drily—and from the way Chalna started, his random snark had actually hit closer to home than he'd have expected.

"What I *do* need to know is the basic layout of the defenses and the fleet base," he continued. "I need to know what the Octal are likely to see as worth attacking and what the local commander will see as worth defending—and what resources they'll have to do that defending.

"I have the sinking feeling that the *Octal* attack may already be resolved one way or the other, but it still feels all too likely that Zal will be where the Expeditionary Fleet fights its first true battle. I need to know the ground I will fight on."

Though he was going to make sure that some of their better sensors were pointing at the moon of the fifth world when they passed through.

"That is fair and honest," Kahlmor told him. "I will review our files, but I will tell you what I can now."

He fiddled with the tablet, and the images of the Octal warships vanished, replaced by a star system anchored on a yellow star.

"Zal has eleven planets and four asteroid belts," the Londu officer told them. "Generally, the innermost and outermost two planets are regarded as too distant from key skip lines and the habitable planet to be of use.

"The two inner asteroid belts flank the fourth planet, Zalta, the heart of the colony. Zalta is an extremely hospitable world, with temperature, atmosphere and life all friendly to Ashall populations."

Which was, of course, why there were enough industrial platforms orbiting it on the hologram to blot out the light if they weren't properly laid out. The space stations *were* properly laid out, but the Londu had quite sensibly refused to put any heavy industry on a planet that hospitable to their colonists.

"The third and fifth worlds, Zalti and Zalok, are not *inhabitable*, per se, but with careful management of temperature and atmosphere, they can be lived on. That enables secondary population centers and resource-extraction facilities. The inner asteroid belts are readily reached from all three inhabited worlds."

Henry guessed, from the iconography, that there was more funny business at Zalok than just whatever weapons lab he'd accidentally mentioned.

"Zalok has been a military reservation for the last fifty years, with no civilian traffic allowed," Kahlmor noted. "Both Zalok and Zalta are heavily protected, with significant orbital fortifications. The majority are old, but their missiles have been updated to modern standards and should suffice against most threats.

"The rest of the system is a mix of gas giants and two more asteroid belts, plus a lot of ice and comets. There are significant presences around the gas giants, but the majority of the population and industry is in the three inhabited worlds and the asteroid belts between them."

Henry had known most of the geography of the system already, but how that broke down in terms of colonization and use was information he'd had only the vaguest notions of.

"What kind of force does the defense fleet possess?" he asked.

The two Londu officers shared a telling look.

"Two battleships and attendant escorts," Kahlmor said bluntly. "It is possible that even those forces have been drawn down."

There were *supposed* to be seven nodal fleets guarding the Sovereignty. One for each cardinal direction and one in the Londar System itself. Prior to them being stripped down to supply the war with the Kenmiri, they'd held six battleships each—and the fleet in Londar had been twice as powerful as the rest, for a total of forty-eight battleships in their defensive formations. An additional twenty-four battleships had formed the Striking Blades, the Londu's offensive fleets.

The war had seen the defensive fleets cut down to four battleships, freeing up sixteen battleships for offensive operations—and UPSF intelligence had said they had a new twelve-ship Striking Blade fleet under construction at the time of the Great Gathering.

A lot of the battleships sent against the Kenmiri had been destroyed, but Henry's information said that the Sovereignty should have rebuilt to at least their original seventy-two battleships.

If a nodal fleet had been drawn down to *two* such capital ships, the Blades had either lost a lot more ships than anyone else had realized, or control of Isis had drawn them farther and farther out.

Henry was betting on both.

"The bases around Zalok are home to significant numbers of fighters," Kahlmor noted. "Those are less likely to have been pulled away to support other borders, but given that this region of space has *no* sentient occupants, the spinward border has always been first to be weakened to provide resources elsewhere."

"We will deal with the situation as it is when we arrive," Henry said, concealing a sigh. "If those ten command carriers attacked Zal, what would the likely result be?"

The two Londu officers were quiet for a few seconds, then Kahlmor growled in the back of his throat—an unpleasant sound Henry was glad wasn't aimed at him.

"Lord of Fifty Thousand Miles Initch would attempt to push them from the system, but unless they coordinated their component forces *perfectly*, it is likely that the Octal would be able to defeat his mobile forces.

"Ten carriers would not suffice against the massed missile batteries of the orbital defenses, however, and both Zalok and Zalta should be impregnable against even larger forces."

That did not, Henry recognized, sound promising for Zalti or any colonies in the asteroids or gas giants. If the Blades lost control of deep space beyond the range of the orbital launchers, a lot of people's safety and survival would be dependent on the mercy of the Octal.

The same people who'd blown apart the evacuation shuttles heading to Talon-Thirty-Eye-Alpha. The people on those shuttles had at least been military, but no laws, morals or even cold necessities of war Henry could see justified killing people abandoning wrecked starships for the nearest remotely habitable planet.

"And the Enigmas?" he asked quietly.

"We left a year ago," Chalna reminded him. "At that time, they had almost *pointedly* not engaged any of our fixed defenses or even fought our mobile ships at a range where station scanners could provide details."

"Our people may have more answers now, but you know all we do about the Enigmas," Kahlmor told Henry. "And you knew that when you agreed to help."

"We are still going to *help*, Lord Kahlmor," Henry replied. "We came to help defend the Londu Sovereignty and we will fight. But the more I know, the more effectively I can fight."

"I…understand. I apologize. The news only grows more stressful as time proceeds," Kahlmor said. "I speak to fate that we are not too late."

37

"WHAT EVEN *IS* THAT?"

Henry chuckled at Campbell's question as the battlecruiser captain's chair floated into his office. A massive holographic image hung in the middle of the space, a single edifice of rock, stone and technology.

"Apparently, *that* is what the Londu mean when they say their defenses are old but have been updated," Henry told his flag captain. "That is the Eye of Zalok, the primary defensive command center for the Blades of the Londu in the Zal System."

Campbell's hoverchair shifted over to let the Scotsman stare up at the fortress.

"I was going to guess I was looking at a dreadnought, but I've got the scale wrong, don't I?" he asked.

"Kenmiri dreadnoughts are about a kilometer long," Henry agreed. "The Eye of Zalok is a *tad* bigger than that. Also a lot less mobile."

The Eye was roughly sixty kilometers long across its major axis. A roughly oval shape, it lacked the smoothing and landscaping the Kenmiri did to their asteroid-hulled dreadnought ships, but it also *wasn't* a ship.

It was arguably an artificial moon, though Zalok's actual moon was a few hundred times its size. It had been towed into orbit when the military reservation had been set up around Zalok, and served as an administrative center, an armored shipyard—though Henry's information was *very* vague on the size of her internal building slips—and one of the single most powerful fortifications he'd ever seen.

"One thousand missile launchers and five hundred starfighters," Henry said. "No heavy lasers or plasma cannon—I think she predated Londu plasma cannon—but that's still a fortress I'd prefer to tackle with a fleet."

"I see that." His flag captain settled his hoverchair down and sighed. "Fortunately, we don't have to fight her at all. If anything, she's going to be the anvil to our hammer, yes?"

"We hope. If nothing else, if the Eye of Zalok is gone when we arrive in the star system, I might write this whole endeavor off as a bad plan," Henry said grimly.

If their enemies had managed to obliterate the primary orbital fortress, he was going to evacuate whatever was left of the civilian population and run for home like a scared rabbit. He was there to help the Londu, not die pointlessly, and a force that could destroy the Eye in direct combat could probably take the Expeditionary Fleet with one eye closed.

"Our Londu friends are as settled as they are going to get until we get them home, I think," Campbell told him. "I'm sure your staff have more stories about how they're doing on the logistics ships, but we've only got Chalna and a few other key officers added to Kahlmor's team aboard *Raven*."

"You've seen the records of the battle at Talon-Thirty-Eye now," Henry noted. "When we run into these people, how would you stack *Raven* up?"

"Put *Raven* and one of those command carriers in a ring, no other factors? We're going to clean their clocks for them," Campbell said. "Her only real advantage over us is at very long range. Their missiles are slow to accelerate and their launchers are *trash*, but they've got fifteen percent more delta-v than the standard missiles we, the Kenmiri and the rest of the Vesheron use—and ten minutes of active thrust versus five covers a lot of sins.

"But while their drones can out-accelerate us, even the droid corvettes only have the same flank acceleration as we do. The cruisers and carriers are limited to one KPS-squared, and I will fly *circles* around them with *Raven*. And while they're trying to work out how to get us into range, I'm going to put armor-piercing kinetics through everything they might need to fight me—at ten percent of light!"

"That was about the logic I was following, yes," Henry agreed with a grin. "But I think you're also seeing the same problem I am."

"A fleet of ten carriers with twenty cruiser escorts is going to give Task Group One a run for their money, ser," Campbell agreed. "Thanks to the dual screens, I think we'd still come out ahead, but we'd be playing chase-the-rat across half a star system along the way.

"But with TG Two and TG Three in tow, it becomes more complicated. TG Two has the firepower to tip the overall balance well into our favor, but they can't out-accelerate Octal capital ships, and they don't have the inner energy screen. Plus, if TG Three is available as a target, they're going to throw drones at it, and we can't afford to lose *anything* in the logistics train."

"I drew the same conclusion, Captain," Henry admitted. "Which leaves me with an interesting conundrum. What do you think will hurt us more—not having TG Two's battlecruiser and starfighters, or having TG Three as a big fat target we can't afford to lose?"

"If we lose even one ship from Task Group Three, we could be in real trouble," his flag captain pointed out. "Hell, if we lose a certain *specific* ship, we're going to be lined up against a wall and shot when we get home."

"Even if *Sanskrit* is destroyed, I don't think we'll get executed for treason," Henry said mildly. "But yes, if we lose the ansible, that's worse than losing any other ship in the convoy.

"We have to leave the convoy behind—the *whole* convoy, which means both TG Two and TG Three. Which means that if there's any trouble, we will need to make sure that any enemy is kept well away from the skip line so Commodore Iyotake can get the convoy the *hell* out before trouble reaches them."

"I'm not overly concerned about that, ser," Campbell admitted with a grin of his own.

"Oh, Captain?"

"I know my inclinations, ser, and I know your record," *Raven*'s Captain told him. "If there's a problem in the Zal System, they aren't going to be looking for our logistics train. They're going to be wondering what bolt from hell just showed up and started steering for the sound of the guns.

"We're not going to be hanging back at the skip line, making them think we're waiting on reinforcements. There are too many civilians in that star system, and if the Blades' mobile forces are gone, every hour —every *minute*—might be being paid for with thousands of lives."

"And if I order *Raven* and the rest of Task Group One into the breach, to stand and die so that Londu civilians can live?" Henry asked softly. "I lost most of my last squadron saving Anderon, Captain Campbell."

"I am the Marquess of Lorne," Campbell told him flatly, the first time in the weeks they'd worked together that Henry's flag captain had mentioned his rank. "I was raised to that line, ser, and the quote may belong to a different Marquess, but it still stands:

"'He either fears his fate too much, or his deserts are small, that puts it not unto the touch…'"

"'To win or lose it all,'" Henry finished the toast—from the Marquess of Montrose, as he remembered.

"I know damn well whose flag I'm carrying, ser. If I'd been with you in Anderon, I'd have been skipping through that planet right beside you. I'd prefer to avoid *that* particular stunt," Campbell said drily, "but if it's a choice between *Raven* and a few million civilians— even someone *else's* civilians—well. I put on the damn uniform this morning."

"Thank you, Captain," Henry said. "I have no illusions of what my own choices might be, not really—you don't make it through the Iron Ring with many illusions, I hope—but knowing how my people feel about that is important."

"Any captain who wasn't willing to repeat the Stand of the *Cataphract*s knew damn well to get a transfer before this Fleet left UPA space. We'll follow, ser, and our crews will fall in line. We'll do what we must."

"I have watched too many planets die, Captain. I won't do it again."

Campbell said nothing, then exhaled a long shaky sigh.

"I get the feeling, ser, even one is one too many."

And Henry had almost seen it happen *twice*.

38

"WE HAVE A CONTACT."

"WE HAVE A CONTACT."

Henry concealed a grimace at the inevitably vague report. They were now only five days out from Zal, and the tension was starting to edge up across the fleet. Every passive sensor aboard the Expeditionary Fleet was peeled to the nth degree, which meant that their first detection reports were closer to ghosts than actual reports.

The Eye-Seven-Crown System wasn't making the sensor reports easy, either. A bloated, barely pre-nova red giant, Eye-Seven-Crown had long ago consumed any planets it had possessed. It didn't have the mass to augment skip pseudovelocities, but it definitely had the scale and radiation output to screw with a lot of their passive scanning.

"The only thing in the area where we're getting the blip is the skip line toward Stone-Sixteen-Eye," Hawthorne told him. "It might be a meteor or comet, but the initial scans are all wrong for that. Looks artificial, but…"

"No power signature," Henry concluded. "Did you look at the information Kahlmor provided on Zal's patrols?"

"We're inside their patrol radius, but this far out, there'd only be a ship every couple of weeks," she told him. "I mean, we're still twelve hours from the skip line—twenty-four for the convoy."

He nodded grimly. TG Two and TG Three were now trailing his forward Task Group by twelve hours' flight. That meant Task Group One was currently pushing over seven percent of lightspeed and was "only" twenty-five light-minutes from their destination.

And the unknown signature.

"Suggestions, Commodore?" Henry asked. There was a logical next step, and he'd give the order without it being suggested, but part of his job was to train his staff—and while Hawthorne was proving perfectly competent, there were times he could tell she'd never served outside the UPA.

"If it's a ship, it's offline," she warned. "And we're not picking up enough energy signatures for it to be...well...*fresh*. We could ping them with Kahlmor's black-box codes—if it's one of their warships, that should get us some confirmation."

"We could also send starfighters ahead to investigate," Henry pointed out. She'd suggested what he was hoping for, but he also wanted her to think about why *not* to take the other option.

"If it's a starship, they're already dead, ser," Hawthorne said grimly. "And if it's a trap, starfighters and search-and-rescue shuttles are a lot more vulnerable than *Cataphract*-Bs, let alone us or *Turquoise*."

"Agreed. Have Perrin's people send the signal, and let's see what happens," he ordered. "I'm going to go grab a sandwich while we wait."

It would, after all, be almost an hour before they got any response.

AT SEVEN PERCENT OF LIGHTSPEED, even with the Task Group decelerating toward the target, the hour timeline for a back-and-forth lightspeed transmission meant that they moved enough closer to change the timeline.

Still, it was a full hour before Henry's people had put together Kahlmor's activation signal, sent it off and the clock estimating when they'd get a response ticked down to zero.

"Nothing," Hawthorne reported, then paused. "I take that back; we've got a ping."

That...wasn't actually good news, Henry knew.

"We're sure?" he asked.

"Matches Kahlmor's information on the 'final-warning cases,' yeah," she told him. "I'm still not getting anything to suggest the ship is operational or has anyone aboard, ser."

The presence of a Blades of the Scion black box meant that their contact was a warship. That wasn't truly a surprise—three skips out from the official border of the Sovereignty, there weren't going to be many Londu civilians.

"If we take TG One to full acceleration, what would our revised zero-zero be?" he asked.

"We'd cut four and a half hours off the trip, ser," Hawthorne replied instantly—quickly enough that he was sure she'd already asked the navigation team the same question.

"Which would put the convoy sixteen and a half hours behind us, in case something goes wrong." Henry eyed the display. "Do it.

"And have someone inform Commodore Zeni that we're going to need her GroundDiv troopers. I'd like to think this is search-and-rescue...but frankly, I suspect it's going to look more like an autopsy."

39

HENRY HAD SUCCESSFULLY GENTLY REMINDED Commodore Zeni that *she* had no more business leading the boarding party than he did. Not that such a sense of responsibility had stopped Henry from inserting one of Palmerston's commandos into the boarding op to give him a set of eyes and ears he felt less guilty riding.

"Someone had a *real* fucking bad day," the lead GroundDiv Petty Officer declared as their squad jumped. A dozen green-highlighted figures appeared on the flag bridge's main display as the power-armored troops left their shuttle, momentum and their suit thrusters combining to deliver them to the hull of their target.

"Be advised, PO Levi, that just about every senior officer in the Task Group is listening in on this," Commodore Zeni said quietly.

"Uh…so, someone had a real *frigating* bad day," the PO said. Accompanying their voice was a highlighted scan of the ship.

Henry had to agree with Levi—and *he* leaned toward their first description. The ship was close kin to the exploratory cruisers of Okavaz's squadron, a flattened teardrop two hundred meters long.

Or, at least, it *had* been before someone put thirty holes clean through her and a gash along one side. Some of the damage patterns were recognizable as the cutting beams of Octal drones, but others had clearly been much heavier beams. When the blows had landed, every soul aboard would have died within moments.

"Octal cruiser beams," Kahlmor said flatly. Henry had summoned the Londu officer up once they'd been sure what they were going to see, and the Lord of Fifty Thousand Miles had arrived in full ceremonial uniform.

He'd known what he was going to see.

"She seems similar to your exploratory cruisers," Henry observed in Kem. He vaguely hoped that Kahlmor's mastery of English wasn't up to following the profanity of the boarding troops, but he was a realist. There was *no way* an alien military officer hadn't learned English profanity *first*.

"The evolution is the opposite," Kahlmor said quietly. "Our exploratory cruisers give up engine power and munitions capacity in exchange for fuel and supplies, but their armament, crew size and overall form are fundamentally that of a patrol cruiser."

Which meant the wreck in front of them was one of the Blades' patrol cruisers, at the far end of its range when it had met the Octal.

"We're going through the hole in the outer hull," PO Levi reported. "I have no signs of energy or life. The only signal we're picking up is the black-box beacon."

"Keep your eyes and sensors peeled for heat signatures of any kind," Henry said. "It's not likely we have survivors, but if there are any..."

"Anybody still alive on that ship is hanging on out of sheer bloody stubbornness," Campbell observed. "We are *not* leaving them."

"Are your scanners seeing anything from the outside, Captain?" Henry asked.

"No," Campbell admitted. "At least some of the hits look to have been intended to breach any remaining atmosphere integrity. Whoever took these people down wasn't taking prisoners."

Or leaving survivors. Even knowing that the Londu had started their first war with the Octal, Henry was running out of sympathy for the new aliens.

AFTER AN HOUR, Levi and the rest of the Ground Division team had located the black boxes and made it clear there were no survivors aboard the cruiser *Silent Rise*. They hadn't located all of the ship's crew, but enough of the three hundred Blades who had been aboard had been tagged for Henry to be confident they knew everyone's fate.

"We may not be able to retrieve the data from the black boxes ourselves, but let's bring them back aboard," Henry ordered. "We'll hand them over the Blades at Zal if nothing else."

He sighed.

"Is there anything else we need from the ship?" he asked. "Kahlmor?"

The Lord of Fifty Thousand Miles hadn't moved from his position next to the holographic display for the entire time Henry's troops had been aboard the ship. Like the humans, he'd clearly held out no real hope for survivors, but the lack had still hurt.

"I watched as your people retrieved the final-warning cases," the Londu said in Kem. "The computer cores are shattered. Our enemy knew well enough to target them once the ship had been disabled.

"The weapons mark this as an Octal attack, but...the determination to deny us intelligence feels more like the Enigmas."

"You are still certain they are not the same?" Henry asked.

"Yes. What I am no longer certain of, Admiral, is that they are working separately. The Octal appear to be learning from them and adjusting their operations to a similar level of secrecy." Kahlmor stared into the display.

"It has been a year, Admiral Wong. I fear what has happened since I left. The final-warning cases will not release even the time of their destruction without authorization codes I only have for Okavaz's fleet."

"But the Zal Blades will have those codes?" Henry asked.

"Yes."

"Then we bring the cases to them." He looked over at Hawthorne and switched to English. "Commodore, do we have any kind of timing on the beam strikes?"

"Six to nine weeks," she told him. "That's a ninety-five percent interval; we could be wrong, but that's our estimate based on the cooling pattern around the damage points and the orbital paths."

Henry saw Kahlmor exhale a long sigh. That was more recent, he figured, than the alien had feared—but still too long past for peace of mind.

"Does that help?" he asked the Londu.

"It is a vague timeline, but it is something," Kahlmor conceded. "We know, then, that the Zal fleet base was likely still intact forty-two to sixty-three days ago."

"It is something," Henry agreed. "Is there anything else you need from us before we pull our people back?"

"It feels...much to ask," the alien said quietly, "but I would request the use of one of your thermonuclear warheads. Safety protocols have almost certainly rendered *Silent Rise*'s weapons inert, but I would send her crew to the fates with a chariot of fire."

"We can do that," Henry said. He switched channels and languages. "Commodore Zeni, can your people shuffle one of our portable charges over to *Silent Rise*? Lord Kahlmor is requesting that we scuttle her as a pyre for her dead."

40

FOUR DAYS, three star systems and nine thermonuclear "chariots of fire" later, Henry watched the numbers count down toward the final entry to the Zal System. When they'd left the UPA, the border system had simply been a waypoint for him, eleven days short of Londar.

Now, as he followed a trail of wrecked starships—and only six of those had been *warships* before the Octal had found them—toward his destination, he knew that whatever they found at Zal, it wasn't going to just be a waypoint.

"Strickland said you needed me?"

Sylvia had unfettered access to his office. She also *had* that access because Henry trusted her, beyond reason, to know when she should and shouldn't take advantage of it.

When he'd told his secretary to call his girlfriend because he was too busy staring at the consequences of his own choices was *definitely* an appropriate time for her to walk into his office unannounced.

"Seal the door," he ordered aloud. "Security Protocol One."

Sylvia arched a sharply groomed eyebrow at him and took the seat across his desk.

"I'm assuming that you aren't using the highest security lockdown we can manage so we can have sex on your desk," she said drily. "So, what's going on?"

"Message for our eyes only from Earth," he told her. "Though now that you mention it, I should keep that idea in mind for another time."

She clucked her tongue reprovingly at him, but he could tell her heart wasn't in it.

"For both of us?" she asked. "Recorded?"

"I'm keeping TG One almost twenty hours' flight ahead of the convoy," Henry pointed out. "That means we're never close enough to *Sanskrit* for a live conversation. I could see something coming up that would make me *get* us close enough, but I'm worried about time."

"Then let's see what Earth has to say, shall we?" she asked.

With a thought and a gesture, Henry unlocked the message. It asked for network IDs from Sylvia as well before it fully decrypted itself and resolved into a three-way holographic recording.

Secretary-President Ji-Yeong Ottosen was on their own, as was Fleet Admiral Lee Saren. The third view held three people, of which Henry only recognized two.

The first was Patience Mbeki, the senior Diplomatic Corps official he'd met on Earth. The second Henry hadn't seen in a long time—since, in fact, *Panther* had pulled Ambassador Karl Rembrandt out of a Kenmiri prison.

His network quickly filled in that the third person was Director Gerda Lindberg, who had been absent from the meeting with Kahlmor and the Security Council—fascinatingly so, given that Lindberg *ran* the Diplomatic Corps.

"Em Todorovich, Rear Admiral Wong," Ottosen greeted them. "I believe that between you, you know everyone here, but I'm going to run through the Diplomatic Corps folks anyway.

"Ambassador Emeritus Rembrandt you both know and have worked with. Director Greta Lindberg, I know Sylvia knows but I don't believe Henry has met." Ottosen smiled thinly. "Patience Mbeki officially has no title, but we can afford no circumlocution today.

"Patience heads the Diplomatic Corps' Intelligence Integration and Analysis team."

"I am not a spy," Mbeki said. "But I have *been* a spy and my task is to make sure our diplomats get the information they need out of UPA Intelligence and the UPSF's IntelDiv.

"Analysis and synthesis are my task, and I have spent the last few days working very closely with our intelligence teams to put together our assessment of the reports we have been receiving."

"I don't think the Admiral needs our assessment of his own intelligence," Saren said wryly. "But Em Mbeki has helped us get everyone aligned here."

"The situation in the Sovereignty appears to be significantly more complex than we feared," Ottosen observed. "That's why, despite his many complaints that he is old, decrepit and possibly senile, we have temporarily pulled Em Rembrandt out of retirement."

Even from the limited view, it was clear to Henry that Rembrandt was still in a hoverchair. The extraction had been…sixty percent successful, in that they'd only got about three-fifths of the diplomat out of the Kenmiri prison. A heavy energy weapon had claimed both of the man's legs—and the lives of three of the GroundDiv troopers escorting him at the time.

"Sylvia, Henry," Rembrandt greeted them. "I told them that Sylvia knew everything I did about the Londu. Then I told them I was a cripple. *Then* I tried the argument that I was too old and senile."

He sighed and chuckled.

"Unfortunately, Gerda has known me for sixty long years, and she has always seen through my bullshit. The concern, which I still think is foolish, is that Sylvia has been too busy handling a dozen other species to remember everything about the Londu."

"At which point Em Rembrandt informed me that his memories of the Londu were in his left leg and sadly somewhere in the Kenmiri Empire," Lindberg said acidly. "And at *this* point, my dear friend should actually do his job."

Rembrandt chuckled again.

"I'm *retired*, Gerda, and I'm here because you needed a Londu expert who wasn't about to enter the Sovereignty." He smiled. "Good translation, that one. We used *Imperium* internally, but I never wanted that in a report. It biases people, and the Londu's government already does them no favors in our people's eyes.

"But I sat down with Mbeki, IntelDiv's Admiral Kosigan, and the UPI's current top black hat, and we went over the data and our psych profiles of the Scion. I've been through a lot of historical data in the last weeks, catching up on what's happened since Henry and his friends managed to pull half of me out of a trap that was supposed to keep all of me."

Karl Rembrandt, Henry reflected, was not at a point where he needed to play nice with anyone. His sense of humor also appeared to have been etched with acid.

"I agree with the assessment that the Londu almost immediately moved to secure the Isis Sector after the Great Gathering and the destruction of the subspace network," Rembrandt continued. "I do not agree, however, with the assessment of how difficult that would have been for the Londu.

"IntelDiv really needed to read my reports more carefully," he told Saren. "Twelve new battleships." He scoffed. "Linguistics and metaphor and context are important, my friends.

"The Londu weren't about to complete twelve new *battleships* at the time of the Great Gathering. They were finishing up twelve new battleship *yards*."

"Bringing their capacity up to thirty battleships under simultaneous construction," Saren said. "I read your report this time, Karl. That kind of expansion in their construction capacity reads like they were preparing for major expansionism to me."

"Well, we did all just agree that they annexed—or tried to, anyway —an entire Kenmiri Province of five hundred star systems and sixty inhabitable worlds," Rembrandt pointed out. "To the Scion's mind, the ability to turn out thirty battleships every three years probably seemed like the minimum necessary to *hold* his new Protectorates."

"This is relevant to you, Admiral, Ambassador, because everything we are hearing suggests that the Londu may well be on the ropes," Ottosen told them. "A year ago, when Kahlmor left, they were seeing convoys raided and remote outposts threatened.

"Now your reports show a hostile fleet was operating near Zal not long after that and appears to have *continued* operating in that region and playing havoc with Londu scouting. We can hope that means the

Londu have heavily reinforced Zal, but that would require them to pull forces away from elsewhere."

"Forces that all evidence, even reassessing their capital-ship production, suggests they simply do not have," Saren told them. "Your Fleet is a relatively small formation versus the power that the Londu Sovereignty commands, but you are a force that isn't already tied down—and one that possesses technologies they do not."

"We sent you out as a show of good faith as much as anything else," Ottosen said grimly. "We did not—and *do* not—expect you to fight the whole damn war for the Londu. But you have the weapons samples and technology databases to enable the Londu to mass-produce anti-gravity-shield weapons.

"We are just facing a reality that suggests that *may not be enough.*"

"You were given, both on the military and civilian side, very strict limitations on what you could and couldn't share with the Londu," Lindberg told them. "We…"

"We still need those limitations to be a consideration," Saren said as the head diplomat trailed off. "We don't want to see a massive prolifer-ation of gravity-shielded and GMS-equipped starships in the hands of allies and enemies.

"But we recognize that the situation may be more dire and more unique than we dared imagine," the UPA's uniformed military commander concluded. "Secretary-President?"

"The guidelines you were given remain," Ottosen said. "The Secu-rity Council has decided that certain securities of our own remain a higher priority than anything except preventing the complete genocide of the Londu."

Henry now found himself wishing that this *was* a live conversation. What he'd seen so far of the Octal's reaction to the ships they'd encountered, military and civilian alike, suggested that risk was higher on the list than anyone wanted to think.

"I have limited authority to override the United Planets Security Council," Ottosen said flatly. "But I do have some. You were given hard and strict orders and limitations, Admiral, Ambassador. Those are now *guidelines* only.

"You have full plenipotentiary authority. Even with a shorter communication loop than the Londu expect, that authority is critical. You are authorized, on the judgment of the two of you alone, to provide the Londu with whatever you feel is necessary to preserve the survival of their citizens."

Ottosen's phrasing was pointed. Their *citizens*. Not the Scion. Not even necessarily the Blades. And *definitely* not the Sovereignty itself.

"If it is at all possible, Admiral Wong, Ambassador Todorovich, we still would prefer that they remain in ignorance of the subspace quantum-tunnel communicators," Saren said quietly. "But we are almost a thousand light-years away.

"We have no choice but to place our faith in your judgment. There is a reason we placed the Expeditionary Fleet and its diplomatic delegation under the charge of you two."

"No pressure," Sylvia murmured.

"If the game was easy, they wouldn't have sent us," Henry reminded her. "I've confidence enough for both of us that we'll make the right call."

He realized the message was still playing and watched as Rembrandt leaned into the pickup.

"Admiral, the main key point that is concealed in the context our other intelligence missed is the location of their new shipyards," the retired Ambassador said grimly. "There is no question: all twelve of the new capital-ship yards were built in one of their nodal fleet bases. Our pre-Gathering intelligence is unclear on which one—except for one thing: it is associated with the main weapons research facility the Londu operate outside their home system.

"One of their nodal defense bases contains both their top-level weapons lab *and* forty percent of their military shipbuilding capacity. And the evidence we've seen of the intelligence capacity of these Enigmas suggests that they will know which one.

"We'd have separated them, but it appears the Londu concentrated their assets. After Londar itself, that base is probably the most critical piece of military infrastructure they have."

"If that base is half of what the Ambassador is implying it is, it could rebuild their fleet with the technology you can provide. Do not let the Londu fool you into thinking that Londar is their only ship-building complex.

"We think they're in trouble, and we want to help them and keep them alive, but let's not trust them completely, shall we?"

Ottosen chuckled grimly.

"If I have read my timing correctly," she noted, "you will have entered the skip line to Londu space by the time we get your response. Good luck, Rear Admiral Wong, Ambassador Todorovich.

"May God speed your way and guide your hand."

The hologram froze and Henry stared at it silently for several long, long seconds.

"Henry?" Sylvia asked.

"Fuck. The maned idiots have fucked themselves and we're going to walk right into it," he told her.

"Henry?" she asked again, her tone sharpening.

"I joked, when asking Kahlmor and Chalna about the Zal System, about a secret weapons laboratory on the moon of the fifth world," he told her. "I got an...*interesting* reaction, but even if such a lab existed, it wasn't a major deal.

"The Eye of Kalok, after all, is a major defensive installation and the entire planet is a military reservation. The one moon around there isn't going to be at the top of anyone's radar, and frankly, where the Londu keep their covert weapons research is irrelevant to me," he continued.

"Except that Rembrandt figures their major new shipyard is next to said lab," Sylvia said.

"Which means that the *updates* to the Eye of Kalok were turning the handful of cruiser slips that they told *me* the station had into a series of concealed battleship yards—a massive covert shipyard hidden inside what's supposedly *merely* an asteroid fortress."

"And the Octal and the Enigma know it," she murmured.

"We're walking into a hornet's nest—and right on the tail of the people poking it with a fucking stick."

41

THE SKIP LINES made interstellar travel possible, but when it came to interstellar *war*, they had some interesting effects. Most importantly, they were *lines*, a connection drawn between stars with the cross-section of the smaller star, and while there were default emergence points, they were questions of *doctrine*, not *physics*.

That meant that Henry knew where a Londu force would have emerged into the Zal System. He knew where a UPSF would normally have emerged—a piece of information the Londu, at least, would have.

So, Task Group One emerged from the skip five full light-minutes, ninety million kilometers, from where doctrine would normally put them. They were a lot farther out than Henry would prefer, but he also needed to not fly his fleet straight into an ambush.

"Get me an update," he ordered Hawthorne. "I'd love to hear that everything is fine and we're being paranoid."

His Operations Officer shook her head grimly as she looked back at him.

"There's no civilian traffic, ser," she said flatly. "There's definitely *some* ships in motion, but this system should have hundreds to possibly *thousands* of civilian ships…and there's nothing."

Henry carefully didn't look at Kahlmor where the Londu sat, staring at the main display. He suspected that the alien officer was wishing that he *didn't* understand English at that moment.

"Understood. Threat assessments, people," he barked. "Find me the threats and lay them out."

"Contact one," Hawthorne said flatly. "Three gravity-shielded ships on the skip line! Moving out from the star, appears to be a patrol. Range is twelve light-minutes."

"Enigmas," Henry replied. "Get me what details you can, Commodore, but keep the scans spreading wide."

He'd suspected that whatever was going on, he'd see both Octal and Enigmas in the Zal System. But they needed to know *everything*.

"Contact two," Hawthorne reported, new icons dropping on the plot. "At least fifteen unshielded fusion-drive warships near Zalta. Initial scans suggest Octal due to the presence of attack drones, minimum three command carriers."

Those ships became Henry's main focus. He'd managed to render the Enigma skip patrol irrelevant by emerging farther out than they expected, but the price he paid for that was the distance from every-thing *else* of interest.

And something wasn't right about Bogey Two.

"Contact three," the report continued. "Three gravity-shield warships along the skip line to the Vo System, the route to Londar. Contact four! Second unshielded fusion-drive group, same strength, in a trailing orbit of Zalok."

Those were the four points Henry had expected enemy forces. Security along the skip lines to manage any incoming ships like his and then heavy forces moving against the main planets.

"Are the Enigmas coordinating with the Octal?" he asked.

"Unclear; but there do *not* appear to be Enigma ships with the Octal battle groups," Hawthorne reported.

"What about...defenses?" Kahlmor asked in halting English.

Hawthorn looked surprised at the Londu officer asking, but she nodded quickly.

"Orbital forts and platform constellations appear intact above both

Zalta and Zalok," she told him. "But…I have no signatures suggesting Londu warships *anywhere* in the system. There may be—there likely are—both civilian and military ships hiding under the defensive constellations, but no major capital ships."

"Lord of Fifty Thousand Miles Initch followed their honor and not their duty," Kahlmor said, slipping back into Kem. "I speak to fate that they have not doomed others."

"What about civilian shipping and stations outside the two constellations?" Henry asked. He suspected the answer. He didn't want to know the answer, but he *had* to.

From the long silence, his suspicions were correct.

"There are no significant energy signatures outside the defensive perimeters other than our bogeys," Hawthorne reported. "No ships. No stations. They've purged the system, ser."

Such mild words for an act even the Kenmiri had regarded as the ultimate sanction. The insectoids hadn't wanted to lose the populations of their slave worlds or the conquered homeworlds. So, if one of those worlds had betrayed the Empire sufficiently, the Kenmiri would destroy all of the space infrastructure. The core population of their slaves would survive, but the deaths of millions and the economic and industrial devastation were more than painful.

"Hawthorne, get *Raven*'s tactical team analyzing the Enigmas," Henry ordered, pushing down his disgust and still keeping himself from looking at Kahlmor. The Londu's silence told him everything he needed to know.

"I want *our* people on Bogey Two and Bogey Four," he continued. "Their acceleration is too low, and their vectors don't make sense to me. Even combined, the Octal ships aren't enough to threaten the forts over either world—so why are they divided?"

"On it," Hawthorne replied.

"Got eyes on the gravity cruisers," Campbell said in his ear. "It'll be fifteen minutes before we see how they react to *us*, but my team are drawing conclusions."

"Lay them on me, Captain," Henry ordered. Every minute they were in the system gave them more information—but also more time for the enemy to realize what was going on and react. Bogey One, for example, would see them twelve minutes after emergence. *Henry* wouldn't see Bogey One's reaction for another twenty minutes or so, but the time until they *did* see his ships was passing quickly.

"They're not just using gravity *shields,* ser," his flag captain told him. "We're definitely picking up the gravity-well patterns of a gravity maneuvering system. My tac team thinks their shields are weaker than ours, probably on par with an end-of-war *Jaguar*-class battlecruiser, but we think they can match us gee for gee in acceleration."

Time gave them more details flickering onto the display for all four contacts. Bogey Three, the Enigma ships on the route to Londar, was where he had the least information—but as more information updated on Two and Four, it seemed like Hawthorne was only producing *more* questions.

Bogey Two was sixteen big ships—four command carriers, twelve cruisers—heading toward the garden world of Zalta. But while there were at least five hundred attack drones buzzing around the formation, none of the droid corvettes the Octal used for relayed control were visible.

And *something* next to the Bogey was diffusing heat signatures in a way that didn't quite make sense to Henry. It was *familiar,* but it wasn't a ship…

"Danger close! Multiple contacts, two hundred thousand kilometers inward along the skip line!"

The report tore through *Raven's* flag bridge like a bomb. It took even Henry a few seconds to realize that what the computers initially labeled Bogey Five was actually Bogey *One.* The Enigma cruisers had skipped along the line toward Eye-Ninety-Two-Crown, the system *Henry* had come from—but instead of traveling toward the distant star system, they'd skipped a mere twelve light-minutes.

No UPSF ship had sufficient fine control over their icosaspatial impulse generators to manage that—and while Henry would have said it was a pointless trick, he now very clearly *did* see the point.

The moment the Enigmas had seen his fleet, they'd prepped their skip drives and closed. While the Expeditionary Fleet had figured they had twelve more minutes before they even saw the Enigmas' response, they instead had *no* time.

The enemy was there.

Fortunately for Task Group One, it appeared that the short skip was just as disorienting as a longer one—and the Enigmas had emerged back into reality before the initial kick in the metaphorical guts had passed.

That bought Henry's people the time to react—and half of his starfighters were already in space.

"Formation Gamma-Five," he ordered. "Starfighters will focus on defense. Cruisers, hit the leader with everything we've got!"

The disorientation of the emergence lost the Enigmas the advantage of surprise. If Henry's people had, say, *not* been at battle stations, it would still have been enough to turn the tide.

Instead, it just gave the unknown aliens the first shot—and what a first shot it was.

"Missile launches detected! Unknown energy detected! *What the fuck?!*"

It wasn't a particularly *useful* report, but given what Henry had just seen happen to UPSV *Dragoon*, he couldn't argue with it. Seven strange energy pulses had blazed out from each Enigma ship, traveling at easily sixty percent of lightspeed.

Like any other weapon thrown at gravity-shielded starships, most of the energy had been broken apart and scattered uselessly across the entire fleet. *Dragoon*, however, had been the closest of the destroyers to the enemy and had taken over half of the incoming shots.

Whatever had survived being shredded by the gravity shield had still hit the destroyer's inner energy screen with enough power to trigger a full-system collapse. The inner shield had gone down, leaving the destroyer to suffer dozens of thankfully smallish explosions across her forward sections.

"Antimatter, ser," Hawthorne finally reported flatly. "They're firing antimatter pulses at us."

"Pull *Dragoon* back behind the other destroyers," Henry ordered.

That was when *their* response finally activated. The lasers hit first, the lightspeed weapons faster than anything the enemy had deployed so far, but the Enigmas' gravity shields scattered photons as readily as the UPSF's had scattered antihydrogen.

Turquoise's plasma cannon were only slightly more effective. There was a reason, after all, that the UPSF had never given the Kenmiri's main weapon system a great deal of respect—it needed heat, mass and velocity to cause damage, and the gravity shield tended to rob the plasma blasts of *all* of that.

The gravity-driver rounds were a different story. Henry hadn't even bothered to order his Captains to load skip-penetrator warheads. They'd already known he expected to face Enigmas.

At ten percent of light or seven and a half, the armor-piercing slugs would have been ripped apart by tidal forces. *These* warheads activated miniaturized skip drives designed for courier drones. Without the endurance to cross between stars and only aligned with a skip line by fluke, they didn't gain any pseudovelocity from the skip drive.

Instead, they slipped into a different part of the twenty-dimensional space the skip drive used to cross the stars and bypassed the real-space zone containing the Enigma's gravity shield.

Raven's shot hit first, the slug's cee-fractional kinetic energy a threat on its own, but in this case, it was backed by a five-hundred-megaton thermonuclear warhead as an exclamation point.

The Enigma cruiser survived *Raven*'s shot, but *Turquoise*'s arrived two seconds later with the same argument. Reiteration of the UPSF's point was apparently sufficient, and the enemy starship vanished in the second ball of fire.

Then it was the Enigma *missiles*' turn, alongside a second salvo of antimatter torpedoes. *Dragoon* had pulled back, sparing her the direct fire of the antimatter weapons—but the missiles followed her into the destroyer formation.

Still, pulse after pulse of superheated antihydrogen plasma crashed into Henry's ships. Spread across three destroyers instead of one this time, the inner energy screens stayed up—but Henry could read the warning signs their engineering teams were sending up the chain.

"Ashes of fate and harrow!"

Henry didn't know *much* Londu, but he knew *that* much Londu—

and he felt *Raven* lurch impossibly underneath his feet as Kahlmor swore.

Each of the cruisers had fired fourteen missiles. Thirty-two of the weapons all lunged toward *Dragoon*, the wounded destroyer's retreat buying her sisters time to protect her.

Henry's worst fears were wrong. There were no penetrator or resonance warheads in the Enigma salvos.

Henry's worst fears had failed to even *begin* to consider what the enemy had brought, and he stared in horror as the surviving missiles dissolved into six short-lived black holes. Gravity shields and energy screens alike could do nothing against the gravity vortices as they tore into his fleet and tidal forces hammered into *Dragoon*.

One moment, the destroyer was wounded, retreating to take cover behind the rest of the fleet.

The next, her back was broken as tidal forces tore into different pieces of her at different strengths. The entire Task Group lurched to the sudden gravity shear—but it was *Dragoon* that two of the gravity implosion warheads *hit*.

And for the first time since his promotion, Henry Wong saw a starship under his command die. The gravity wells, a more-focused version of the shears that made up their own gravity shields, ripped *Dragoon* in multiple directions and scattered pieces of the million-ton destroyer across the stars.

"Spyros, Bedrosian, you saw that," Henry growled at Task Group One's pair of CAGs. "Priority one for your fighters: *none of their missiles get through!*"

Whatever the Enigmas might be using for ranged weaponry, their antimissile defenses were familiar. They'd likely guessed that the hundred-plus missiles headed their way had the same penetrator systems and fusion warheads that the gravity-driver slugs carried, and threw everything they could at them.

But two ships clearly designed to rely on their gravity shields didn't have the lasers to stop seventy missiles each. It didn't matter, in the end, how many missiles got close enough to activate their skip penetrators.

It was *enough*, and both Enigma cruisers vanished in fire.

"Get SAR shuttles up," Henry barked. "That kind of damage should have survivors."

"On it," Campbell promised.

"We may have a bigger problem, ser," Hawthorne said grimly. "We just worked out what the hell is going on with the Octal battle groups."

42

HAWTHORNE'S TONE warned Henry that he wasn't going to like it.

"Given that we have four hundred people dead or floating in space, you *know* what the standard of *bigger problem* is, Commodore," Henry told her. "Tell me."

The main holographic display zoomed in on Bogey Two, finally with enough resolution for a clear optical view of the formation. Energy and heat signatures had just said something was odd, with part of the flotilla eclipsed and their vectors off for their established acceleration of the Octal capital ships.

The computer-interlaced imagery from two dozen telescopes across ten starships allowed them to *see* the enemy—and that made the problem very clear.

A smallish asteroid, still at least five kilometers long, trailed the Octal formation. Dozens of droid corvettes were embedded in the surface, their engine heat lost against the immensity of their cargo, and their thrust barely managing to accelerate the rock at all.

"The asteroid is closing on Zalta at just over two percent of light-speed," Hawthorne told him, her voice clipped in a mix of anger and fear. "Final impact velocity will be at roughly four percent."

The estimated mass of the asteroid—a billion metric tons, give or take—popped up on the hologram as she spoke, and Henry's internal network ran the numbers for it.

It was giving him *megatons* of impact energy using scientific notation. He readjusted the units and swallowed hard as the final conclusion came out.

"Over twenty-five petatons of impact energy," Hawthorne concluded. "That won't just end civilization on Zalta's surface. That might just shatter Zalta like a fucking rotten egg."

"Time to impact?"

"Just over six hours. The defenders have to have realized what's happening, but…"

"The Octal will cover the impactor with drones and corvettes all the way in," Henry said quietly. "Zalta's only chance is a massive sequence of hits on one side of the rock, but once they've *picked* a side, they're going to be trying to put their missiles through almost three thousand drones and over a hundred corvettes. The constellation could take those out, eventually, but not quickly enough to still let them divert the rock."

"No, ser."

The silence on the bridge was frozen ice. The Octal had set up their attack knowing the defenses. It would take hundreds—possibly *thousands*—of missiles to push the asteroid far enough aside to spare Zalta. With Bogey Two's drones and corvettes to protect the rock and potentially restore its course, there was no way Zalta's defenders could save the planet.

"Zalta has three and a half billion people on it," Kahlmor said in Kem, his tone as frozen as the air in the bridge. "It's a garden world; there are few like it. Zalta is one of our largest colonies and critical to the Sovereignty."

"Our time to intercept?" Henry asked Hawthorne, putting Kahlmor's words aside for the moment. The Lord of Fifty Thousand Miles wasn't giving him information that was going to *change* his assessment.

Task Group One could fight Bogey Two or Bogey Four. He even figured he'd have a decent chance at them combined, which raised the question…

Hawthorne's expression told him the answer before he even asked it.

"Bogey Four has the same thing, don't they?" he asked.

"Timeline to impact is the same, within ten minutes," his Operations Officer confirmed. "Asteroid is slightly bigger and appears to be aimed directly at the Eye of Zalok. Our math suggests the asteroid is enough bigger than the Eye to just…push the fortress ahead of it."

"Into the planetary surface," Henry concluded.

"Yes, ser."

"Our intercept times," he growled.

"At flank acceleration, risking the engines and not slowing for a zero-vee intercept, we can intercept Bogey Two in four and a half hours, less than two hours before impact. We'll pass at a tenth of light-speed, which will augment our missiles and gravity-driver hits but limit our engagement window."

"And Bogey Four?" Henry asked.

"Four hours, fifteen minutes, passing at eleven percent of light-speed," she told him. "And no, the planets aren't lined up for us."

Zalok was closer, only thirteen light-minutes away. Zalta was fifteen light-minutes away—but they were in entirely different directions. Whichever planet they went to, they'd need to shed almost all of their velocity before heading toward the other. Four and a quarter hours to Zalok, four and a half to Zalta.

"There has to be a way we can stop both," he told her.

"Split the Task Group or invent an in-system faster-than-light engine, ser," Hawthorne said bitterly. "But we need the entire Task Group to engage either bogey, ser."

And Task Group Two was sixteen hours behind them now. By the time Commodore Iyotake arrived, both impactors would have hit. Just shedding the remaining velocity of their first intercept would take more time than they would have.

The default solution would be detaching his starfighters, but eighty-eight starfighters into the teeth of thousands of attack drones was suicide. He needed the entire Task Group.

Which meant that Henry Wong not only was going to be forced to watch his enemies destroy a world…but he was going to have to *choose* which one he couldn't save.

"ADMIRAL, there are aspects you don't know," Kahlmor said slowly. Even across the language and culture barrier, Henry could hear the self-loathing coming through the Londu officer's voice.

Still, he turned to face the alien and met Kahlmor's gaze.

"Your people have concealed weapons-development facilities spread across the Eye of Zalok, the planet's surface and the moon," Henry told the other man bluntly. "That, I presume, is where you're working on both gravity shields and anti-gravity-shield weapons, along with other systems I don't have enough information to guess at.

"Plus, your expanded shipyard capacity since the war is mostly there too, isn't it?" he demanded. "How many new battleship yards are in the Eye of Zalok, Lord Kahlmor?"

There was a long silence. Too long, for the timing they had.

"Fourteen, when we left," Kahlmor said quietly. "And they had just laid the keels of battleships to be equipped with our first experimental gravity shields and new-generation beam weaponry. Those ships won't be ready yet, but they may be the only hope the Sovereignty has against this enemy."

"*May*," Henry repeated. "We cannot sacrifice three billion lives for a dozen warships, however powerful."

"Against this foe, our current generation of ships are clearly helpless," Kahlmor told him. "I hate the words as fate demands them of me, but we *must* save the fleet. Without those battleships, the Sovereignty will fall."

Henry was silent, then gave the Lord of Fifty Thousand Miles an understanding nod. Not an accepting nod. Not an *agreeing* nod.

An understanding one. He knew what the Londu was saying, what the other officer meant and where he was coming from.

"Commodore Hawthorne, our course is for Zalta," he ordered in English. "Lord Kahlmor, do I need to have you removed from the flag bridge?"

The decision was not Kahlmor's. The argument the Londu had made had its value, but even if Henry was *convinced*, he couldn't do it.

"No," Kahlmor whispered. "I just…"

"The worlds may be yours, but this fleet and therefore this decision is mine," Henry told the Londu as *Raven* shivered around him. Even at flank acceleration, the gravity well itself didn't have any perceptible impact on the ship. The shiver was the *projectors* straining to put that much power out into the universe.

"Two hundred seventy minutes to contact," Hawthorne reported. "Two hundred sixty-four to estimated Octal missile range, assuming they don't maneuver to meet us. Five minutes after that to *our* missile range."

"We will have a limited window before we blast past the rock and are no longer able to hit it with missiles," Henry said grimly. "Get the Tactical Officers and Captains on a conference and run the scenarios. We need that thing to pass at least a light-second away from Zalta to be sure we protect the orbital infrastructure.

"Run the numbers and run them as conservatively as you can. Whatever it takes, Commodore, to deflect that rock. If we have to take the entire firepower of that fleet on our gravity shields to put enough delta-*v* into the impactor, I need to know that *now*."

"You'll have that answer in…thirty minutes," Hawthorne told him.

"Do it."

Henry spent half a second or so considering Kahlmor, wondering if he should say something to explain his thinking—but the Londu had his attention locked on the display, and for all that he'd *argued* for saving the under-construction battleships at Zalok, his eyes were on Zalta.

"Ser, we have an incoming coms pulse from Zalok," Perrin reported. "Tightbeam, directed at the fleet. Time lag would have seen it sent before the Enigmas jumped us."

Henry nodded grimly. His main attention turned to the local region, where *Raven* and *Pegasus* were still deploying SAR shuttles to search for survivors from *Dragoon*.

He was torn. He didn't want to leave his people behind—but three billion lives versus three hundred wasn't a choice at all. On the other hand, TG Two and TG Three were only sixteen hours behind him. The shuttles could operate for that long, easily.

The question was whether they could keep all of the *survivors* intact that long and avoid attacks. One of those questions was answered even as he considered it, though, as two *much* larger small craft cleared *Pegasus*'s decks.

The tenders were designed to expand the carrier's ability to refuel and rearm her starfighters, but if they had been loaded with, say, oxygen tanks and emergency rations instead of missiles, the two support shuttles would be more than enough to keep the small fleet of shuttles operating until Commodore Iyotake arrived.

"I think I owe O'Flannagain a beer," he told Sharma on a private channel with his Fleet Master Chief. "Especially knowing she'll *tell* me if that wasn't her idea."

"I live in the back brain of every Chief in the Expeditionary Fleet, ser," Sharma replied. "From their commentary, no, that wasn't someone else's idea—and you're going to have to arm-wrestle Chiefs if you want to buy Colonel O'Flannagain a beer for it anytime this *decade*."

Henry considered the situation and found a small positive to work with. Given that his starfighters were the most vulnerable part of his fleet to the attack drones, he could justify giving up some of them to salve his conscience.

"Commander Bedrosian." By the time he spoke, a mental command had opened the channel to *Raven*'s Commander, Air Group. The battle-cruiser only carried eight fighters, a single squadron, to *Pegasus*'s eighty—which worked for *this* purpose.

"Admiral. What do you need?"

"*Raven*'s flight squadron is going to stick with the search-and-rescue flotilla," Henry ordered. "You'll do more good for the efficiency of the fleet securing our survivors and our morale here than you will adding eight more planes to our anti-drone defenses at Zalta.

"Keep our people safe, Commander, so that we can bring them home."

"Understood, ser. We'll watch the rescue birds and lost chicks till you or Iyotake come collect us."

"Thank you, Commander," Henry said with a pale shadow of chuckle.

With that handled and the division of his task group for the necessary maneuvers decided, he turned his attention back to Perrin.

"Send me the message from Zalok," he ordered. "Let's see who's still alive and in charge of this place."

43

HENRY WAS SUFFICIENTLY CONCERNED about the possible content of the message that he directed it to his internal network. *He* would see it, but no one else would. After a second's thought, he pinged Sylvia and looped her into a very private channel to play the message for them both.

The ambassador was in her own office in the diplomatic section of the ship, a space that would allow her to run all kinds of communication and analysis with her own people rather than needing to impose on his staff.

She entered the channel with the silent electronic equivalent of a shoulder-squeeze, and he started the message.

The recording showed a space that Henry guessed was a command center of some kind—presumably aboard the Eye of Zalok—with dozens of Londu officers in white robes and black breastplates working away in the background.

The focus of the image was a Londu woman in a more-formal version of the white-robed uniform. The gold markings on her armored breastplate declared her a Lord of Hundred Thousand Miles, senior to Kahlmor and equivalent to a UPSF Vice Admiral.

"Human ships, I am Lord of Hundred Thousand Miles Tallah," she introduced herself in slow but understandable Kem. "I presume that you are here in response to Lord of a Million Miles Okavaz's delegation.

"Connect me with her," Tallah ordered peremptorily. "I have instructions for your fleet's involvement in this system's defense."

The rest of the message was locked behind an encrypted code and Henry sighed.

"Does she think that Okavaz is in command over here?" he asked Sylvia. "Because this seems...arrogant, even for a Londu. Especially, I suppose, for a Londu in the straits she's in."

"I would guess that Lord Tallah has difficulty conceiving of a situation where a Lord of a Million Miles would surrender command authority," Sylvia told him. The electronic message carried her disdain for the thought.

"Even among the Londu, that may well hold her back from earning that rank herself."

"Well, diplomatic question I suppose," Henry murmured. "Do I have Larue crack the encryption on this and respond as if she'd sent me her request, or do I let her know Okavaz is dead and carry on my current course for twenty-six minutes while she sorts out her own feelings on that?"

"Are you likely to change your plans based on anything she says?" Sylvia asked. "Because from a *diplomatic* perspective, letting her decide how much to tell us—and quietly cracking the message without telling her—is the best option.

"But the military situation is a fucking disaster, so I can see not wanting to lose the time."

Henry grimaced.

"Unless she wants to tell me that there is a miracle gun in orbit of Zalta that means the garden world is invulnerable, no," he admitted. "I have to fight the Octal battle groups in detail. TG One can take down either of their forces on their own, but we can't split our forces to deal with them both.

"And I can't think of anything Tallah can add to the parameters that will change the need to save the civilians over the military base."

"Then let her sort it out and use the time lag to take away her choices," Sylvia said quietly.

"That's the problem, Sylvia," Henry told her. "I don't think Lord Tallah *has* any choices except whether or not to die with dignity."

He left that hanging and brought up the recording software. He supposed he *could* ask Kahlmor his opinion, but at this point, he didn't want any of whatever consequences came out of this to splash on the Londu officer.

"Lord of Hundred Thousand Miles Tallah, I am Rear Admiral Henry Wong of the United Planets Space Expeditionary Fleet," he told her. "Lord Okavaz is not with us. Her squadron was ambushed and destroyed by an Octal fleet. Likely, units of that fleet are present in this system as we speak.

"I need to know what happened here. My current assessment is that I can intercept the kinetic impactor headed toward Zalta, but I will not be able to engage the second Octal battle group until almost ten hours afterward.

"I must leave the defense of Zalok in your hands. I require all of your information and scan data of the battle and events in this system —and I must also know how much has been relayed to the Scion at Londar."

He reconsidered the message for a few moments. It was potentially harsher than Tallah deserved, but he couldn't really soften the blow. Whatever happened over the next six hours, Zalok was almost certainly doomed. Unless the Lord of Hundred Thousand Miles had something tucked away on her fortress that Kahlmor hadn't told him about, the Zalok impactor was going to get through.

BY NOW, the Octal flotillas had to know that the Expeditionary Fleet was in the system. Even more than Henry, though, they could have no idea how their ships and drones would stack up against his.

He'd half-expected to see them sortie out to intercept him, trying to combine their fleets to smash Task Group One between two forces. Of course, without the guardian battle groups, the Londu defenders would probably be able to deflect the impactors.

"Attack-drone formations are adjusting, but we're mostly seeing cruiser movement in Bogey Two so far," Hawthorne reported. "Bogey Four appears to have recognized that we're heading for Zalta. They've moved more of their cruisers around to the side facing us, but their focus is still Zalok.

"Bogey Two, on the other hand, knows we're coming for them. All twelve cruisers have fallen back to position themselves between us and the impactor. The command carriers are remaining between the impactor and Zalta, though, and they've only detached a thousand drones to support the cruisers."

The droid corvettes continued to serve as tugs, Henry observed, hundreds of the small robotic ships pinned to the asteroid as much by their own engines as anything else. Many of them would never be able to extract themselves from the impactor.

"Acceleration and time to impact remain the same," his Operations Officer continued. "Our analysis suggests that, assuming their droid corvettes attempt to counter any vector change, we need to hit one quadrant of the asteroid surface with approximately fifty gigatons a minimum of two hours prior to impact."

"And how does that scale up as it gets closer?" Henry asked.

"It will basically double every twenty minutes," Hawthorne said grimly. "By the time the impactor is only an hour out, if we're somehow still in range, we're going to blast the damn rock to pieces before we can deflect it—and those pieces will still hit the planet at four to five percent of lightspeed."

"That's not without value, though," Henry said. "The orbital defenses *do* exist, and they can deal with smaller pieces. If we can break it up far enough, they can finish the job and Zalta just gets one hell of a light show."

He was understating how dangerous that would be, he knew, but the planet getting hit with enough dust to add a few degrees of temperature change was a *lot* better option than million-ton meteors hitting the ground at twelve thousand klicks a second.

"We will have laser range for about twenty-five seconds after we pass the impactor," Hawthorne pointed out. "If we *haven't* hit it with enough force to deflect it by the time we pass, we're not going to be in position to shatter it.

"We *might* do enough to the vector that the locals can finish it. But their missiles will be in ballistic mode. At those closing speeds, they won't get many salvos that will have fuel left when they reach the asteroid."

"But what they do have is ammunition and plenty of it," he observed. Kahlmor hadn't given them definitive numbers, but Zalta was an industrialized world that *produced* missiles. If her orbital defenses didn't have a few hundred thousand missiles to hand, he'd be shocked.

The problem was that they only had a few hundred *launchers*, and to divert or destroy the asteroid would require hundreds of precisely targeted hits. Those hundreds of missile launchers were more than the Octal fleets could deal with in an actual fight, but the drones could defend the impactors sufficiently to avoid them being deflected.

Maybe. Henry could *hope* they would fail—especially at Zalok, where he was leaving the fate of the planet to the orbital forts—but he couldn't count on it, and he suspected the Octal had run their own analysis.

"Ser, we have a new transmission from the Eye of Zalok," Perrin warned him. "Same channel as before?"

"Yes, please, Colonel," Henry ordered.

It was time to find out how reasonable Tallah was going to be.

The Lord of Hundred Thousand Miles was in the same place as before, her translucent skin gleaming almost blue in the harsh light of her command center and her eyes almost black as she glared at the pickup.

"Lord Okavaz's fate is unfortunate," she told Henry. "She was an old friend and an officer I trusted. I do not know you, Henry Wong, but it seems I have little choice but to entrust you with some of our greatest secrets.

"The Eye of Zalok has been retrofitted into a major shipyard complex. This has two consequences, I am afraid. The first is that we have sacrificed a significant portion of the Eye's magazine capacity and starfighter strength. We are not as able to defend ourselves or the rest of the fleet base as we should be.

"The second is that this complex has been the anchor of the Scion's new-ship-development program. While the designs have been relayed elsewhere, this station contains the only modern battleships under construction in the Sovereignty.

"Losses across our territory have been severe. The loss of these new ships *will* cost us any chance at victory. Potentially at *survival*. The Octal are attacking Zalta as a diversion. It is Zalok whose fate will decide the course of this war.

"As the senior officer of the Blades of the Scion, I am ordering you to bring your fleet to Zalok, Admiral Wong. Any other course would be a betrayal of our alliance."

The message ended, and Henry noted that there wasn't even any additional information. None of the scan data or records of the battle were attached. *All* he'd received from the Lord of Hundred Thousand Miles was orders.

Orders he would not obey. Orders he *could* not obey.

"Henry?" Sylvia's voice asked in his network. "You..."

"I am not obliged to obey her orders," Henry replied. "We are not operating a combined command structure, and frankly, even if we were, I'd reject these orders."

"But I *need* that information."

He could, *barely*, still intercept the second impactor before it hit Zalok. If he abandoned three billion civilians to save a few million and a shipyard, he could probably do it. He'd committed worse and more direct sins in his life, but...

"Saving those ships isn't the right decision," he told Sylvia. "If they were going to make a difference in the short term, they'd be complete enough to be evacuated. In the long run, an industrialized planet with billions of people is a far greater asset than one shipyard, however technologically sophisticated."

"It sounds like Tallah thinks the Sovereignty will be lost before that long of a run," Sylvia said. "Except... preserving the Sovereignty isn't our mission."

"It is," he argued. "But it falls behind preserving the *Londu*. No. We save Zalta and let the chips fall as they may at Zalok."

"So, what do you tell Tallah?" Sylvia asked.

"The truth."

He knew she could sense his grim smile through the channel, and turned his focus back to the recorder.

"Lord of Hundred Thousand Miles Tallah, I will not do you the dishonor of acknowledging those orders," he told her flatly. "We both know what the correct moral and military decision is here.

"The UPSF will not abandon civilians to protect your warships. If you can move them—send them off into deep space—I will be able to act to retrieve them. Whether or not we can salvage the *ships*, I strongly recommend you evacuate as much of the fleet base personnel as you can.

"I repeat, however, that I need to know what happened here. I need that information, Lord of Hundred Thousand Miles Tallah, because my orders are to help protect the Londu. The more data I have, the better I can do that.

"But I am not under your command, and I will not abandon Zalta's civilians. Fight for Zalok, Lord Tallah.

"We will save Zalta."

WITH A CONVERSATION LOOP NOW past thirty minutes, there was no way that Lord Tallah's response could arrive in time for Henry to reverse course. He presumed *she* would realize that, which would avoid any further arguing.

Certainly, it helped delay her response.

Task Group One was only three hours from entering Bogey Two's missile range when he finally received Tallah's response. Strangely, the first thing he noticed was that the venue had changed. The Lord of Hundred Thousand Miles was seated behind a desk that appeared to be made of stone, with a screen behind her showing the view onto Zalok's chilly surface.

Out of the view of her staff, whatever mental mask she'd

commanded was gone and he could *see* the exhaustion in the lines of her face.

"The ships are incapable of movement," she said flatly. "There was enough discussion and experimentation around how the new ships would be propelled that the engines were held up.

"Fourteen battleships and twenty cruisers, Admiral Wong. An entire battle fleet, forged with gravity shields and ion beams; the arms and armor to save our Sovereignty from the trap we have walked into.

"We will attempt to evacuate, but we know the Octal. They have no concept of the clemency of fates. Their drones and missiles will pursue anyone we send away. They know, too, what the fleet building here is capable of."

She stared blankly into space.

"Four of the cruisers were complete enough to deploy with Lord of Fifty Thousand Miles Initch," Tallah said softly. "They died alongside the rest of the fleet. Scan data will be attached. I break oaths and laws alike, but regardless of how I regard your choice, it is made.

"And this information must reach my Scion. We have been under attack for fifty-two days. First small raids, then larger strikes. All Octal. The war has resumed, despite our Scion's efforts.

"Eight days ago, a major Octal battle fleet penetrated the system. They underestimated our orbital defenses, and Lord Initch managed to lure them into a misstep. Ten command carriers and their escorts were obliterated, a crushing victory we hoped the Scion could use to bring peace.

"Our last courier ship left the system to bear that news to Londar seven days ago. Civilian shipping fled ahead of the Octal fleet, but we had held the line. We had time for things to normalize.

"Then five days ago, the Octal returned, and they brought the Enigmas' gravity-shielded warships with them, armed with weaponry from our worst nightmares. Key skip lines were blockaded faster than we believed possible, by ships with an acceleration I have only seen matched...well, today. By your fleet.

"The new cruisers joined Initch's fleet but were not enough. They inflicted losses, but the enemy fleet held everything outside range of our fortifications. They made one attack with Enigma ships against Zalok, but we had the firepower to drive them off.

"But what you see here, Admiral Wong, is but a fraction of their strength. They took most of the Enigma ships and half of the Octal fleet with them, leaving these ships behind to purge the system.

"Three days ago, the rest of their fleet left for Londar. Whatever happens here, Admiral Wong—and my fate, it seems, is sealed—you *must* go to my Scion. The fate of my people and my nation depends on it."

Notes flickered across Henry's network, and he swallowed harshly. An initial skim of the sensor records confirmed her reports on the strength of the Enigma Fleet: just as many command carriers and cruisers as remained in Zal, but those served as a reserve force to a core fleet of Enigma cruisers and a dozen mighty ships he had to assume were battleships.

"I don't know who these Enigmas are," Sylvia said in his network, "but this feels...genocidal."

"I know. And that, my love, is why we're going to stop them," Henry said grimly. "But we're *starting* with the bastards headed for Zalta. One problem at a time."

He'd start with the three billion lives he could save today. Only after that could he begin to plan how to save an entire *empire*.

44

EIGHTY STARFIGHTERS. Seven destroyers. One cruiser. One battlecruiser. One carrier. Ten starships against an enemy fleet of sixteen, plus dozens of droid corvettes and hundreds—*thousands*—of attack drones.

By any measure of mass, numbers or firepower, the Expeditionary Fleet's Task Group One was out of its depth. The four command carriers alone outmassed Henry's entire force by a slim but real margin.

The reality was that none of those numbers mattered. Two things mattered: whether the Octal could breach the dual-screen gravity and energy shields of the UPSF ships, and whether Henry's people could divert the billion-ton impactor far enough from Zalta to save the planet.

"Estimate we'll enter *their* missile range in fifteen minutes," Hawthorne reported.

There was a familiar chill stillness across the flag bridge. Henry had felt it before—the calm before the storm. Unlike most of the other such calms, though, he was confident in how this was going to end.

"Do we have a target point?" he asked Hawthorne.

"Yes, ser. We've marked a fifty-kilometer-by-fifty-kilometer square on the out-system side of the impactor. All of our ships have it loaded in."

"Thank you, Commodore."

Henry focused on the holographic display and his internal network feeds. He was *aware* that Kahlmor remained standing by the display, unmoving as the Londu watched the fate of his people's star system play out.

"Remember that *this* group doesn't know the lessons the launch platforms in Talon-Thirty-Eye learned," he reminded his people. "I don't plan on giving them a chance to work them out, either."

That meant that the first pass between the attack drones and the starfighters would go entirely his people's way. They'd seen it before: the Octal drones were set up to attack TIE fighters, not the UPSF's grav-shielded Lancers.

Until either their masters or the superior intelligences on the control ships intervened, the drones would assume that one hit would kill a fighter. They'd learned quickly last time, and Henry expected them to learn just as quickly this time.

But that gave him options.

"First strike will target the impactor," Henry ordered. "The starfighters will remain in defensive formation and add their missiles to the salvo. You said we need a hundred direct hits to throw the impactor off course."

"At this point in her approach, yeah," Hawthorne confirmed.

"Well, let's hope two hundred and fifty missiles get us those hits," he said grimly. "That's a hundred and twenty-eight from us and another hundred and twenty from the fighters."

He *saw* the Operations Officer do the math in her head and swallow her question. She could find the answer quickly enough, but Henry had learned that the trio of Murphy, Sod and Finagle required respect.

And if they weren't given respect, they *took* blood sacrifice.

"Do we hold fire until just before they hit us, ser?" Hawthorne half-asked, half-suggested. "I mean, we'll be in range three hundred–ish seconds after they fire, but they have a *six*-hundred-second flight time according to Londu intelligence.

"If we hold fire until thirty seconds before impact, our alpha strike will have a sixty-second flight time instead of a five-minute one and our accuracy will be improved."

"There's a value to that, Commodore," Henry agreed. "But what's our launcher cycle time?"

"If we're keeping our salvos combined, we're limited to *Pegasus*'s launchers. Forty-eight seconds."

Henry was occasionally reminded that, despite all of her upgrades, *Pegasus* had been built as the *Lexington*-class carrier *Ark Royal* and was the oldest ship in Task Group One by almost a decade. *Raven*'s launchers were faster—and *Turquoise* and the *Cataphract*-Bs were faster still.

Not quite fast enough to get two salvos to the carrier's one, though, and *Pegasus*'s sixteen launchers weren't anything Henry could give up.

"So, every forty-eight seconds we hold fire costs us a full salvo of missiles from the capital ships," Henry said softly. "How much accuracy, Commodore, are a hundred and thirty missiles in space worth?"

He wasn't shutting her down. But he needed her to think through the situation and run the numbers. Henry had a decent idea of how they broke down, but *she* was the one with the numbers in front of her —and if she was going to become as good of an officer as she was trying to be, she needed to be able to answer that question.

Because unless she surprised him by ceasing to improve, it wouldn't be that long before Emilia Hawthorne was making those decisions under fire, overprotective Admiral relatives be damned.

"We gain the largest benefit by not firing at the most extreme range," she told him. "At twenty million kilometers' launch range, their missiles will suffer severely degraded accuracy. At the ten million kilometers of our extreme launch range at these velocities, our accuracy will also suck.

"By nine million kilometers, our targeting solutions will improve by roughly twenty-five percent, in terms of estimated hits," she continued. "That would cost us our sixth salvo to add several dozen hits to our alpha strike.

"Holding longer than that costs us too much. But I would recommend holding our first salvo to a maximum range of nine million kilometers—roughly forty seconds after they launch."

The alpha strike wasn't everything, since there would *definitely* be an aggregate effect of further hits. But the Octal missiles would arrive just before *Turquoise* and *Raven* could fire their gravity drivers, and easily forty seconds before anyone was in range for lasers or plasma cannon.

"I'm not running the full numbers, but the back of my envelope here agrees with you," Henry told Hawthorne. It took her a moment to realize he was being metaphorical—the *back of the envelope* in this case was basically an algorithm-assisted spreadsheet scratchpad that lived in his internal network.

But compared to the full-model calculations that Hawthorne was running with the flag deck's computers, it might as well have been scrawled on a conveniently available envelope.

"Fire as per that projection," he continued. "Focus everything on your target zone on the impactor. Every missile we have, Commodore Hawthorne, hits that thing until it isn't aimed at Zalta anymore."

"Am I clear to release drivers, cannon and lasers to the control of the individual Captains?" she asked. "We might see some benefit from concentrated fire, but we're not going to be able to do enough damage to reduce their overall firepower in the time period we've got.

"Not without the missiles, anyway."

"We're better served keeping our ships intact through this mess," Henry said. "And for that, I need our Captains focused on keeping their commands alive by focusing their fire on the most immediate threats. We'll control the missiles. Release the guns to the Captains."

"Yes, ser."

"Ten minutes to Octal missile range!"

"If anyone needs a drink, a ration bar or a bathroom break, now is the time, people," Henry announced in response to the Chief's report. "Because once we go back to battle stations, it's *catheters in* time."

"VAMPIRE. MISSILE LAUNCHES DETECTED."

There was something about the flag bridge, even more than the command bridge of a warship, that isolated the people in it from the immediacy of what they were facing. Even on *Raven*'s bridge, behind just as much armor and just as deep a gravity shear, Henry would have never been quite so calm at the announcement that missiles were heading his way.

That was the *point*, of course. He and his staff *cultivated* that. They *needed* to be separate from the chaos and violence, to be the ones taking the step back and making the decisions above the moment-to-moment tactics of survival.

"Three hundred twenty missiles inbound," the Ops Chief continued their report. "Initial velocity relative to them... One hundred KPS. Initial velocity relative to *us* is over ten percent lightspeed.

"Acceleration marks seven-point-five kilometers per second-squared. Estimated time to impact, six hundred seconds and counting."

One hundred KPS was a joke. Part of what had made the Enigma missiles so dangerous in their close-range engagement had been their higher initial velocity.

On the other hand, their intelligence from the Londu was pretty clear: six hundred seconds *was* the active flight time for the Octal's missiles. What the enemy lost in acceleration and initial velocity, they more than made up in endurance.

The next UPSF battle group might have a surprise for everyone on that point—Henry *had*, after all, helped write the guidelines and direction for the current round of weapons development—but the Expeditionary Fleet had the same standardized thousand-KPS launchers and ten-KPS² missiles that the Vesheron and El-Vesheron had stolen from the Kenmiri.

"Six minutes to our launch window," Hawthorne noted.

Henry nodded silently, more reports flickering across his feeds. He was so focused on the upcoming exchange of fire that he almost missed Kahlmor finally moving from his ironclad focus on the hologram and walking over to stand next to the human Admiral.

"You are confident," Kahlmor said quietly in Kem.

"I am. The question was never whether I could stop the impactor and escorts I went after, Kahlmor," Henry told the Londu. "It was which impactor I stopped."

He very carefully had *not* run the numbers on whether Task Group Two might have been able to intercept the impactor headed for Zalok. He'd left Commodore Iyotake's ships behind with the logistics train for damn good reasons. TG Two's *job* was to protect the auxiliaries— but if they'd gone to the tanks, they could have managed a full KPS^2 to try to intercept the Zalok impactor.

They might not have made it. At one KPS^2, the thirteen light-minutes would have taken longer to cross, and whether Iyotake got there in time would have been a toss of a coin—but they could have at least *tried* to intercept both if Henry had brought all of his warships.

"They are evacuating the station and the fleet base," Kahlmor told him. "It is unclear whether they will be able to move any of the hulls out of the construction bays. The disadvantage of building inside an asteroid is that the same armor that protects the ship makes it slow to remove."

"And they don't have engines," Henry said grimly.

"The ships were meant to be wholly new, and there was a design for a new reactionless drive system," the Londu said. "It failed late in testing, proving to have sufficiently low energy efficiency as to require *more* fuel for the same thrust and delta-*v* as a fusion rocket.

"According to the files Tallah sent, the decision to give up on the reactionless engine and install the same fusion engines as our current-generation ships was made only a few months ago. Every ship that was far enough along to be able to generate thrust also had weapons and gravity shields, so…"

"So, they went out with Initch's battleships," Henry finished. "I am sorry, Kahlmor. I know even Lord Tallah thought those ships would be necessary, but there are other ways to turn the tide of a war."

"I know. And you brought a fleet, I suppose, so we end with the same number of fleets when it is over."

"Just tell me Tallah is getting all of the people out she can," Henry told the Lord of Fifty Thousand Miles. "Zalok is not a habitable world —and orbital industry, science labs and shipyards can be replaced. But trainers and weapons researchers and yard workers cannot."

The personnel of the military base and the secret research lab that they both knew existed were worth far more than the infrastructure.

"The Octal may try to intercept our evacuation flotilla."

"They *will* try, if they are half as genocidal as they have shown themselves so far," Henry said grimly. "I lay no blame on your people for the Octal's actions today, but…" He shook his head. "What the *fuck* did the Londu *do* to them?"

"I do not know," Kahlmor told Henry—and tone and microexpressions alike suggested he was telling the truth. "We invaded them, yes, and I will accept the honor of their grudge. But we did not destroy their worlds or slaughter their civilians. That is not our way. The greatest true value of an annexed world is its people."

The Octal appeared to believe that the greatest value of a Londu was as a corpse. Regardless of said Londu's job…or, given what Henry understood about much of the Blades' support structure, actual *species*.

Kahlmor glanced back at the display, where a second salvo of three hundred missiles had joined the first—and thousands of drones were now maneuvering behind them.

"I would like to believe that we did not do such things as would deserve this fate," he said grimly. "The Octal are ruthless in war, we knew this, but this… This is beyond all that we have seen of them."

"Drones are coming our way," Hawthorne warned in English, seeing what Henry had seen and providing the details. "Coming out behind the missiles at three KPS-squared, estimate…"

She trailed off, exhaling sharply.

"Estimate twenty-five hundred, two-five-zero-zero, Octal attack drones outbound toward us."

"Still no droid corvettes," Henry murmured. "They're all pushing the impactor, I suppose."

"Sensors are picking up at least a hundred of them on the surface of the asteroid," Sharma's voice said in his head. His Fleet Master Chief wasn't even *on* the flag bridge—she was in one of the work centers that filled the rest of the flag deck, working with De Veen to make sure the essential engineering reports made it to Henry.

"De Veen's also being cagey, but she thinks there's something more down there," the Chief continued. "Not clear on what, though, so she's not telling you yet."

Henry concealed a sigh from the crew on the flag bridge. He hadn't assigned Sharma to back up De Veen to allow the noncom to spy on the other woman, but he would definitely prefer it if De Veen told him what was on her mind!

"Prod her on the concept that many minds make simple questions," Henry told Sharma. "Because we are launching missiles—and we are rapidly approaching *way too late* for new discoveries!"

"I'll poke, ser."

Launch alerts cascaded across Henry's network feeds and holographic display as ten warships and forty starfighters salvoed every missile they could. Two hundred and forty-eight thousand-gravity attack missiles with the best electronic-warfare systems the UPSF could build.

There were no fancy warheads or penetrator systems on these missiles. They didn't carry the short-lived skip drives of grav-shield penetrators, or the specially sequenced and intentionally flawed gravity projectors of anti-shield resonance warheads, or the shaped "shotgun blast" fusion charges of so-called conversion warheads.

They were "just" carrying five-hundred-megaton thermonuclear weapons set for contact detonation.

"The die is cast," Henry murmured. "Four minutes to incoming fire. Four minutes to grav-driver range of the enemy fleet."

The Octal warships were moving out toward TG One. Three hundred drones and two cruisers remained between the impactor and Zalta, scanners pulsing space for the missiles the defensive fortresses had just started firing. It would be a while before any of those weapons were close enough to threaten the impactor, but the Octal were taking no chances.

Henry had to wonder what was going through their minds. A lot of Octal were going to die in the next few hours, no matter what happened. He was going to risk TG One to take out the impactor, but they had to know that failure would only drive him to vengeance.

There was no way in heaven or hell that the Octal could rejoin their fleets in time to prevent the Expeditionary Fleet pinning them down and wiping them out in detail. He couldn't save Zalok or the fleet base there—but Henry would be *damned* if he didn't avenge them.

"Drones will be in laser range of us as the missiles arrive and we open fire with the drivers," Hawthorne said quietly. "Do you have orders for the fighter wings, ser?"

"Spyros knows his orders," Henry told her. "They're to remain in defensive formation and engage with their antimissile lasers. We don't have time to rearm them."

The clock ticked. Seconds passed by with a crescendo of silent bells ringing through Henry's nerves. Nine thousand spacers, pilots and soldiers on ten ships...it wasn't much to hang the fate of an entire planet on.

But it was what he had, and it would be enough.

45

AT A CLOSING VELOCITY of twelve percent of lightspeed, the Octal missile salvo strained the ability of Henry's ships to track and engage the weapons. *Strained*, however, did not mean *exceeded*.

And as the missiles closed, Henry was "eavesdropping" on the tactical network shared between his Operations team and the Tactical departments of his individual ships. They had the basic parameters of the weapons from the Londu, but there was so much they'd never be certain of until they saw the weapons in action themselves.

The conversation between the tactical teams was entirely mental, a link between the internal networks and ship's computers of ten star-ships and several hundred humans. Data flickered around at the speed of thought as the profile took shape, the results of the first laser salvos feeding into the profile that aimed the later volleys.

The first thing Henry noted about the profile was that the difference between the people who had fought the Kenmiri and a species that *hadn't* was very clear. Between stealing from the best, borrowing from each other and the harsh selection criteria of war, Vesheron and Kenmiri alike had reached a very high base level of competence and technological prowess.

That had been shifting since the war, but he'd spent all of his time in Ra dealing with people who'd either been Vesheron or were working entirely with stolen Kenmiri systems. The Octal lacked the template and baseline that all of those factions, ally and enemy alike, had been working from.

Octal electronic-warfare *hardware* was good. Possibly better than that of the Londu, though UPSF missiles had a small but noticeable edge. Their *software*, on the other hand, was only slightly better than what, say, the Londu had entered the war against the Kenmiri with.

The jammers and decoys of Henry's ships had a far larger impact than their calculations expected—and the software and computers aboard the Expeditionary Fleet sliced through the jamming and ECM of the incoming missiles with disturbing ease.

His active defenses were at least a third more effective than he'd expected—but ten ships couldn't really stop three hundred missiles. Not without being *much* larger ships than he had, anyway.

What they *could* do was gut the salvo, breaking up any focused concentrations and leaving no individual ship facing more than a dozen remaining missiles. As those missiles cascaded down on his command, Henry only barely managed not to hold his breath. If the Enigmas had given the Octal the hellish gravity warheads they'd used themselves, this was going to be a very bad few minutes.

"What the..." Hawthorne's exclamation was smothered into silence —but at least it wasn't a *horrified* exclamation.

"Report, Commodore," Henry asked. None of the missiles had connected with his ships. No damage reports at all. It was like the missiles had just hit the gravity shields and vanished.

"Contact nukes, ser," Hawthorne told him. "Every one of their missiles was carrying contact nukes. Tidal forces of the gravity shields ripped them apart; we took minor kinetic hits on the inner screens."

"They had to know that wouldn't work," he said grimly. "Their allies have gravity shields. Hell, according to Tallah, they've faced *Londu* gravity shields."

Before Hawthorne could say anything, two things happened. First, *Raven*'s main gun fired, the ship shivering around them as the gravity driver pulsed an unimaginable amount of energy along the core of the battlecruiser.

Second, the attack drones arrived, and things got very, *very* busy.

Henry didn't know what Campbell had fired his ship's primary weapon at. It would take a few seconds to see the result, even with the closing velocity providing a *twenty*-percent-of-lightspeed effective velocity to the projectile.

The attack drones were far more obvious and far more focused. A few dozen drones swarmed over each of the destroyers and cruisers, but the lion's share of the robotic spacecraft went for the largest ship in Task Group One: *Pegasus*.

Two *thousand* attack drones swarmed the carrier, lasers flashing out in half-second pulses that would have torn her bare hull to shreds, armor or not.

Except that *Pegasus* was the first of the refitted *Lexington*-G type ships and she had far more than her relatively light armor wrapped around her. The gravity shield was a probability game against energy weapons. Every shot had a small chance of getting through with enough momentum left toward the original target to connect.

Against two thousand beams, the law of averages said that beams were getting through—especially as the drones closed to point-blank range. Dozens of strikes burned through the gravity shield. Some would never have connected with the hull, passing through the gravity shear with enough force to hit but diverted sufficiently that they would still miss.

The rest hit the energy screen. The energy screens, based on a design provided by the Enteni of the Ra Sector and refined for the UPSF use case, were a straight numbers game—they could absorb so much energy in any given time frame.

The screen could never have stopped two thousand cutting lasers. As Henry watched, *Pegasus*'s defenses proved that they very much *could* handle two dozen.

And the drones were now within reach of the *other* defenses of O'Flannagain's command. Henry didn't need to say a word, simply watch as the antimissile lasers of his fleet ripped the attack drones apart in job lots.

Their enemy would learn. They *knew* that—they'd seen the so-called "superior intelligences" on the drone platforms in Talon-Thirty-

Eye sort it out in a single engagement. But *this* time, the enemy had sent almost their entire force of drones in the first wave.

His people didn't need specific orders to make sure that the Octal didn't get a chance to give *these* drones a new set of orders. Spyros's fighters tore into the robots. Antimissile lasers tore into the robots. Even the heavy battle lasers every ship but *Pegasus* herself carried got into the fight, beams designed to breach the armor and shields of kilometer-long Kenmiri dreadnoughts absolute overkill against ten-meter-long unshielded drones.

"Ser! The impactor!"

Henry didn't even need to move his head. His attention shifted—and both his network data feeds and the main holographic display shifted with it, focusing in on their alpha strike as it closed with the asteroid.

The droid corvettes were almost entirely there to move the asteroid toward its target, but their lasers made for an effective antimissile screen. The main Octal fleet had taken their own toll on the Expeditionary Fleet's missiles too, but over a hundred missiles descended on the target zone Hawthorne had flagged.

And hit the energy screen that snapped into existence around the asteroid. Even the *Kenmiri* couldn't shield something that large, and Henry hadn't even *considered* the possibility that there would be a screen around the impactor.

Enough missiles had survived to provide the delta-*v* they needed... and it didn't matter. The energy-shield projectors that De Veen had likely seen but been unable to definitively identify overloaded and exploded, the sparks of light tiny on his display.

The shield only lasted a few seconds, but those were seconds Henry hadn't expected. The entire alpha strike, the only salvo that had been likely to put the hundred missiles they needed on target, vanished with the shield itself.

And then the Octal demonstrated that *their* first salvo had either been a test, a bluff or just a straight-up troll as their *second* salvo reached its own effective range. Almost five hundred kilometers short of the Terran fleet, the surviving eighty or so missiles all detonated as one—each turning into at least half a dozen bomb-pumped X-ray lasers.

The lasers stabbed out in multiple directions, but *most* were aimed at their target—again, *Pegasus*—sending over two hundred deadly powerful short-range beams into Samira O'Flannagain's carrier.

The gravity shield still deflected most of them, but many struck home against the inner screen—a screen already weakened by the attack drones' cutting lasers. It flickered and overloaded, and Henry's breath caught in his throat for a moment.

"*Pegasus* reporting multiple hits," Perrin said. "Passing everything on to De Veen."

Henry nodded grimly and connected directly to his engineering officer.

"Colonel, what are we looking at?" he asked flatly.

"Which part?" she snapped, then audibly swallowed. "We picked up what I now know are the shield generators just before we launched the alpha strike. Even if we'd IDed them, I don't think we could have done anything different.

"As for the missiles, I think the Octal were testing to see how close they could get their missiles with the first volley. Then they set the laser warheads for a conservative range allowance to attack our shields.

"*Pegasus*'s damage is minor so far. She's lost about four percent of her heat radiators and has three hull breaches. None are in critical areas and they have no casualties. Energy screen is already back online, and they're holding off the drone hits."

"Thank you, Colonel," Henry said, ignoring her initial outburst. "Keep me informed." He paused, considering the battlespace as the first gravity-driver rounds hit home. The Octal didn't have gravity shields, and though their cruisers were big enough for old-style energy screens, that wasn't enough to save the ship Campbell had targeted from the force of tungsten-capped armor-penetrating slugs.

The ship came apart, but she had eleven sisters and TG One would be practically *among* the enemy before *Turquoise*'s rounds hit.

There was no time. They were almost in laser range of the enemy fleet. It was down to the next thirty seconds, and only the network gave him any ability to formulate their responses at all.

"Do they have a second shield layer?" he asked.

De Veen paused, a quarter-second feeling like an eternity as they rode the currents of the ship's network.

"Almost certainly, ser," she told him. "It might be weaker, but I'm still picking up an entire second set of what I think are shield generators."

"Damn. Thank you, Colonel."

"I don't have any suggestions, ser," she admitted. "Just…keep hitting the rock with every missile we've got."

Henry dropped the channel and looked at the holographic plot again. More missiles were descending on his fleet, but they *knew* what kind of warhead the enemy had now. Plus, the attack drones had been effectively wiped out, the survivors well past his ships and out of their own laser range.

His people could manage a few hundred laser warheads on those terms.

The problem remained what the problem had always been: the billion-ton rock that they had *not* managed to move as far as he'd like. The Octal were holding their second energy screen in reserve, letting his smaller salvos crash down on the target zone and relying on the droid corvettes to push the impactor back onto line.

They'd added more side vector than the corvettes could recover from, but they hadn't added *enough*. A billion tons of asteroid didn't move easily or quickly—that was *why* the Octal were using a hundred and forty robotic starships, ships that might have changed the balance of the battle in space, to maneuver the damn thing.

"O'Flannagain. Spyros." His network connected him as he spoke the two officers' names.

"We're still here," O'Flannagain said flatly. "Even as a pilot, I have to admit it never quite sunk in *why* we kept carriers out of the battle line."

"Needed your missile launchers today, I'm sorry," Henry told her. "Spyros?"

"Still here," the CAG replied. "We're killing missiles as fast as we can, ser."

"GOTH plan, Colonels," Henry said. "How paranoid were you when you put that together?"

Both of them knew which *Go to Hell* plan he meant—the reason why only half of their starfighters had contributed to the alpha strike.

"If you are asking do I have penetrator warheads in my missile pods... Oh, hell, yes," Spyros told him. "O'Flannagain insisted."

"That's what I was hoping, Lieutenant Colonel. GOTH is go. They're going to pop a shield when they see the mass launch.

"Make that shield a wasted effort, Colonel Spyros. You know how many people are counting on it."

MORE X-RAY LASERS stabbed through Henry's fleet. The Octal were still focusing on *Pegasus*—while Henry's people were following the opposite logic. The Octal command carriers had more missiles each than the cruisers did, but the cruisers were a *fifth* of the mass.

By the time they hit battle-laser range, the grav-drivers had smashed three of the Octal cruisers, and it turned out that the Octal carriers, like *Pegasus*, didn't have lasers. Nobody actually built their carriers for the clash of battle lines.

But Henry's focus wasn't on that clash. It was on Flight Group Zulu, the second of the two five-squadron sub-groups of *Pegasus*'s starfighter wing. As the lasers began to slash through space between the two fleets, forty of the starfighters lunged forward at their full acceleration.

His fleet had been accelerating fast enough and the starfighters had stuck so closely to his capital ships that the Octal didn't seem to have realized that his fighters *could* go faster. They didn't adjust their targeting parameters quickly enough to stop Flight Group Zulu from emptying their missile pods.

The missile pods didn't have the range of the full-size missiles Flight Group Alpha had launched with the fleet. They *did* have the same warhead suite, and when Spyros had put together the armament for the Everything Goes to Hell plan, he'd ordered every one of the three hundred and sixty missiles in those pods equipped with penetrator warheads.

At the range and distance Flight Group Zulu fired, the missiles were in space for less than ten seconds—long enough, still, for the Octal to bring up their second energy screen.

An energy screen the missiles bypassed, adding a vector in the *other* seventeen dimensions of icosaspatial reality for a critical half-second.

They needed fifty gigatons of impact force to deflect the impactor too far for the droid corvettes to put it back on target.

Spyros's Go to Hell plan put over a *hundred* and fifty gigatons on target at the last possible moment.

46

"WE'RE CLEAR."

New vector cones and spheres were propagating across the main holographic display as Henry's ships broke past the asteroid impactor and its escorts. Lasers continued to flicker back and forth for a few seconds more, but once they were about two seconds past the Octal fleet, even that ended.

"Damage report," Henry ordered.

"*Pegasus* got worked over," De Veen told him, the Engineering Officer clearly having spent the last few seconds aggregating what Henry would need. "Two of her missile launchers are offline and she's lost *all* of her reserve heat radiation ability. But she only has twenty-two casualties and no fatalities.

"*Raven* and *Turquoise* both took a few solid hits, but nothing was taken offline. Eight casualties between them; again, no fatalities."

"We were damn lucky," Henry murmured.

"No, Admiral. *Zalta* was lucky," Kahlmor told him in Kem. "Lucky that you were here at all."

Henry nodded to the Londu.

"Hawthorne, likelihood that the impactor can get back on course?" he asked.

"Zero. Their current vector will take them almost a million klicks clear of the planet, no matter what their corvettes do," Hawthorne told him. "And what's left of Bogey Two is running for the hills. Just staying out of the range of Zalta's orbital defenses is going to take every scrap of delta-v they can generate over the next hour."

"And what *is* left of Bogey Two?" Henry asked. "I know we hit them, but how bad?"

"We left the carriers alone," she reported. "But between the gravity drivers, *Turquoise*'s plasma cannon and the lasers aboard everything except *Pegasus*, we wrecked their cruisers. They've got two left that appear to have working lasers and two that are barely managing to keep their engines running.

"Everything else is debs and bad dreams."

Henry rose from his command chair and took the two steps to stand next to the holographic display, exchanging a firm nod with Kahlmor.

"Orders to the Task Group, then," he said. "We let Bogey Two run. Our course is for Bogey Four—we might not be able to stop the impactor, but we can damn sure make them think about whether it's worth chasing the evac flotilla."

Hawthorne highlighted those ships on the display without him giving the order. There were no Londu *warships* left in the system, but there were, it turned out, still a *lot* of starfighters.

Four hundred of the Londu's unshielded attack craft now formed a frail-seeming bubble around the dozens of civilian and military support ships fleeing Zalok. Many of those ships, Henry judged, didn't even have skip drives. Their only hope for safety was reaching Zalta ahead of the enemy.

Task Group One had kicked the crap out of Bogey Two, though, so he suspected that the surviving Octal warships from the failed Zalta attack weren't going to threaten the evac ships.

And while it would take Henry almost three and a half hours to bring his velocity to zero relative to Zalok and start heading for the planet, Bogey Four couldn't leave the impactor to start *pursuing* the evac fleet for another two hours.

The Eye of Zalok and the rest of the defensive constellation might be down to a skeleton crew now, but they were already spitting missiles out in absolutely mind-boggling numbers. Bogey Four couldn't breach Zalok's defenses.

But they *could* shoot down those missiles after they ran out of active engine time and were relying on just their velocity to reach the impactor. Over two thousand drones were spread out in front of the asteroid to do just that, and Henry didn't even need Hawthorne's modeling group to know there was no chance of enough missiles getting through to change Zalok's fate.

"We'll rendezvous to get between the Octal and the evacuation ships as soon as we can," he said quietly. "Our fighters are rearming and we'll get them in position a bit faster, but we also need to keep our eyes on Bogey Three."

There were still three Enigma cruisers in the system. They hadn't twitched from their position on the skip line deeper into Londu space, but he couldn't rely on that remaining the case forever.

If they came for Henry, Task Group One could handle them. If they came for the evacuation fleet, things could still go very wrong.

EVERYONE in the entire star system, it seemed, was waiting with bated breath for the hammer to fall. Over the final hour, the Eye of Zalok and her accompanying fortifications fired over a *million* missiles at the incoming asteroid and its escort.

The space between the planet and its oncoming killer was absolutely filled with fire. The Octal lost drones by the hundred—lost warships, too, with even one of the command carriers dying in the cascade of nuclear fire.

But despite firing off the entire annual production of a dozen missile-fabrication lines, the Blades of the Scion couldn't change Zalok's fate. Still over fifteen light-minutes away, Henry's view of the impactor's arrival was badly delayed—but it wasn't like he could have changed it if he'd been any closer.

The Octal had measured their angles and velocities perfectly. The asteroid stolen from the belt between Zalta and Zalok descended on the defensive fortress like the fist of an angry god, the collision of the two massive asteroids an apocalyptic event all on its own.

Debris scattered from the impact point, but the core pieces of both asteroids continued the impactor's course toward the planet. What the strike lost in velocity hitting the orbital fort, it more than gained in mass.

Zalok had no liquid water on its surface, but the ground itself *rippled* as the rocks fell from the sky. Henry couldn't see details at this range. He didn't *need* to.

At this point, Zalok's fate was most readily described by geological terms as anything else. What fragile biosphere the frozen military reservation had possessed would be dead within hours. There was a decent chance that the planet might even break in two, spitting up a new moon much as Earth's moon had been born.

Anyone on the surface was dead. Anyone still on the orbital fortress was dead. As debris tore through the rest of the orbitals, followed by Octal missiles, Henry knew that anyone who was even still *in the planetary system* was probably dead.

But they did not die alone. One last vindictive gasp of one-shot plasma mines, laser satellites and missile launchers unleashed themselves as Bogey Four guarded the impactor all the way in. None of those weapons could have stopped the asteroid—but it turned out they could definitely *avenge* the planet they'd been supposed to defend.

Bogey Four entered the orbital space of Zalok, half-hidden behind their impactor, with three carriers and eight cruisers left.

Not one of those ships *left* Zalok orbit.

47

"BOGEY THREE JUST SKIPPED."

That wasn't entirely a surprise, but Henry hadn't *dared* hope for it. His task group had come through the battle relatively unscathed, all things considered, though the morale damage of having to let one impactor hit wasn't anything he was going to dismiss.

"And Two?" he asked.

The destruction of Bogey Four at the posthumous hands of Zalok's defenders had reduced his problems significantly.

The system's fifth planet was…*burning* wasn't technically accurate, but as metaphors went, it worked well enough. But saving Zalok—or even trying to extract anyone *left* on Zalok—was a lost cause.

Zalta's defenses were still intact and formidable, and they'd taken a slice out of Bogey Two as the remaining Octal ships had passed by. The loss of the Octal's damaged ships probably helped them more than it hurt, though Henry knew *he* wouldn't have felt that way in their position.

His problems now boiled down to two immediate issues, one medium-term problem and a long-term disaster.

"Virtual conference," he ordered his network softly, sending mental pings out to his staff officers, Master Chief Sharma and Sylvia. A moment later, he added Campbell.

When Admirals called, lesser beings made it happen, and he had his conference in place around him. A good half of the people on the conference were on the flag bridge around him, and he wondered for a moment if he could rope Kahlmor in.

The Lord of Fifty Thousand Miles would have input on several of the problems. But Henry wasn't giving the Londu's limited cybernetics access to *Raven's* computer systems—and, unless Kahlmor had taken leave of his senses in the last few minutes, *he* wasn't giving an alien computer access to his implants!

"We've done okay, people," Henry said calmly as he "stepped" into a virtual briefing room. "Better than I hoped, to be honest, even if things are still...bad."

"I'm in discussions with the commander of the evacuation convoy," Sylvia told him. "It might not be as bad as you'd fear, but...well, there were three million people on Zalok, and there are about sixteen hundred thousand on the convoy. They don't have enough food, water or life support to do more than run for Zalta on the most direct course possible."

"Which is our first and most critical problem," Henry agreed. "Bogey Two, so far, doesn't appear to be willing to launch a suicide run at the convoy. My biggest fear there just skipped out toward Londar."

"But protecting and bringing that flotilla into Zalta as quickly as possible remains our highest priority." He chuckled. "That would be why we currently don't have fighter cover of our own."

Every starfighter from *Pegasus* was well ahead of the fleet now, blazing across space like particularly clever missiles as they headed for rendezvous with the convoy and *their* fighters.

At low accelerations, gravity maneuvering systems were significantly less detectable than traditional fusion rockets. At *high* accelerations, they were dramatically *more* visible, radiating heat like tiny white holes.

"So far, they appear to be clear," Hawthorne noted. "I think we can call that winning."

"Except for one tiny little problem of time and space," Henry told them. "Bogey Two is trying to run back the way they came. Which means *they* are heading for the same skip line *we* emerged from...the skip line, people, where TG Two and TG Three are going to emerge in about eight hours.

"And right now, Bogey Two is going to be at *just* the right distance to be able to adjust course on top of them once they see them. Commodore Iyotake will rip them to pieces...but the attack drones will do the same to our logistics train."

"We need to make them change their course. Even if they're just going somewhere closer in to Zal, that will take them from the rest of the Fleet," De Veen observed. "I'm...not tac track, but it sounds like we need to spook them."

"For that matter, are they likely to pick a fight with TG Two when they see them?" Anil Jacquet asked. "Sounds like we're worrying about nothing."

Sooner or later, Henry knew he was going to have to do *something* about his Personnel Officer. The problem was that there always seemed to be something more pressing, and he couldn't justify excluding one of his key staff officers from these meetings.

"They're not even going to *notice* the fucking battlecruiser," Cheng Kai said flatly. "They're going to take one look at the massive fat convoy of freighters and hurl everything at them. And while they're at least *Tvastars* with gravity shields...we've already seen that the drones get close enough to get about one-in-one-hundred burnthrough on average.

"And Bogey Two still has about five hundred attack drones left," Henry agreed. "And five of those cutting lasers *will* wreck one of our auxiliaries. And we *need* those auxiliaries."

If nothing else, Henry was pretty sure the Londu had got at least one battleship hull out of the Eye, and if the factory ships and fabricators of his Task Group Three couldn't rig up the yards to finish her quickly, he'd eat *Raven*.

"The answer is right in front of us," Colonel Larue said politely. "If I may?"

"I'll admit tunnel vision toward the politics and the enemy fleet,

Lieutenant Colonel," Henry conceded. "If you have an idea, I'm listening."

"You're thinking in terms of matériel, hardware and firepower," the Intelligence Officer pointed out. "Which I guess means my idea might not be as obvious as I think it is, because *I* think in terms of information, deception and who-knows-what-I-know.

"*We* know that TG Two and TG Three are due in eight hours," Larue said. "Everyone in this system knows that Bogey Two will hit the skip in about nine and a half hours. The Octal, though, don't know what's coming through the other way. They're not actively *trying* to intercept our logistics line—and they are, at this point, probably scared shitless of us.

"My math says that twelve megatons of UPSF ships just bloody *shattered* thirty-odd million tons of theirs. And again... *we* know that TG One is the most powerful formation the UPSF has."

"They don't."

"You think they'll run when they see TG Two?" Henry asked. That was the same point Jacquet was making, but Larue was at least *arguing* it instead of *assuming* it.

"No." The Intelligence Officer shook his head grimly. "Like you said, they're barely going to notice TG Two because all they're going to see is TG Three. We need them to see a threat *before* our people arrive.

"Which we can do."

Henry didn't follow for a few seconds, then Larue gestured and brought the icons of thirty-odd small craft up in the middle of the virtual conference.

"Eight starfighters. Two depot shuttles. Twenty-four search-and-rescue ships. We left them behind for a reason, and so far as I can tell, Commander Bedrosian has been keeping everyone very, very quiet back there."

"So, the Octal don't know they're there," Henry murmured. "And those depot ships carry ECM transmitters. Hell, unless they offloaded their normal supplies, they've got spare fighter-scale gravity projectors aboard."

"I need to sit down with Colonel De Veen and get Colonel O'Flannagain and her people on a conference call," Larue admitted. "But I think there has to be a way we can use the gear they have out there to fake the arrival of at least a couple of cruisers. It's pretty far away; it doesn't have to be perfect.

"It just has to make them blink."

"Get on it," Henry ordered. "De Veen?"

"I believe Colonel Larue is correct. If we can drop off the conference?"

"Go."

The two officers vanished, leaving Henry with the rest of his staff and the Ambassador.

"Our next problem is as much for Ambassador Todorovich as us," he noted. "My initial read is that civil authority in Zal is currently quite pleased that we saved their lives…but the *military* authority on the convoy is pissed.

"We *think*"—he gestured to Hawthorne—"that they got at least one battleship clear of the Eye of Zalok, but they're not telling us about it."

"Military answers to civil authority, doesn't it?" Marszalek asked, the Legal Officer looking concerned. "Doesn't the civilian government being on side cover any issues with the troops?"

"Not in the Sovereignty," Henry said grimly. Something that his Legal Officer should have already known. "They are significantly less definitive on the concept of civilian control of the military."

"Civil and military authority among the Londu run in parallel, always," Sylvia told them. "Both, ultimately, answer to the Scion. Both…don't truly answer to each other at any level."

"Which is part of our problem. I can manage the Governor, I'm quite sure. I am not so convinced about Lord of Fifty Thousand Miles Okath."

"Leave him to Kahlmor," Sharma said bluntly. "Internal politics of the Londu aren't *our* problem, are they?"

Henry turned to the Fleet Master Chief and considered her for a long, long, moment.

"Point," he conceded. "Especially when we consider our last and ugliest problem."

"The main Enigma Fleet," Hawthorne said grimly. "Five days ago now, a fleet anchored on what the Londu data suggests was sixteen *battleship*-sized, gravity-shielded warships left this system on a direct course for Londar.

"No Londu ship could catch them. They had no couriers left to send, since they'd used them all up, reporting on the Octal attacks."

"They did take an Octal fleet the size of the one left here with them," Henry noted. "On the one hand, that means they've got eight command carriers and twenty cruisers to support the Enigma's own fleet.

"On the other, that means they're moving at more normal acceleration rates and will take eleven days to reach Londar.

"Task Group One can make that journey in seven."

"But we can't leave this system as things currently stand, can we?" Cheng asked slowly. "We need time to rearm and refuel from the logistics train and to see off the last Octal ships…"

"We do," Henry agreed. "But every hour we spend in Zal is an hour the Enigmas get unopposed in Londar. We must spend our time here wisely.

"Because we may be buying that time in the only currency that truly matters: innocent lives."

48

"WHAT DO YOU NEED, ADMIRAL WONG?"

Kahlmor's precise Kem sounded as exhausted as everyone else on *Raven*'s flag bridge felt.

"I need to know if you are senior to Lord of Fifty Thousand Miles Okath," Henry said bluntly. His last attempt to communicate with the new senior Londu officer in the Zal System had been met with a resounding silence.

"Okath is not known to me at that rank," Kahlmor said slowly. "If the Lord is now in command of the system, he may have the authority to command *me* regardless of rank. Why?"

"I do not know if he's in command of the system, but he sure as hell is in command of the evacuation flotilla and is senior to the officer in command of Zalta's defenses," Henry said. "And he has ordered that latter to stop listening to my suggestions."

Since, as an allied-but-foreign flag officer, Henry couldn't *technically* give Lord of Ten Thousand Miles Tyrol *orders*—but the woman had been cooperative right up until Okath had started sending orders.

"We are utterly dependent on your fleet for the security of this system," Kahlmor noted. "Whether I can override him or not depends on the exact nature of his orders from Lord Tallah, but I can make contact."

"I need you to do so," Henry said. "Potentially from a shuttle, unfortunately."

"A shuttle?"

Henry gestured and the holograms in his office came alive. The positions of TG One, the evacuation flotilla, Bogey Two and the estimated arrival point of the Expeditionary Fleet were marked in highlighted icons on the model of the Zal System.

"If Lord Okath had been cooperating, I would have more time," he said quietly. "There appear to be munition colliers and tankers in his flotilla. They've mostly been co-opted as personnel transports, but I would hope there would still be enough fuel and missiles to fill the dent in Task Group One's stock.

"But since Okath is no longer even *talking* to us, I have no choice but to rendezvous with my logistics train. An awkward, time-consuming endeavor—especially since we are also trying to make certain that the Octal don't ambush them when they arrive."

"After all you have done, I am certain I can organize whatever supplies you need from Zalta," Kahlmor said. "Give me some time."

"We have no time, my friend," Henry said quietly. "Task Group One is currently on our way to where I expect Task Groups Two and Three to emerge from the skip line. Assuming the trick that is about to fire off diverts the Octal, they'll exit this system harmlessly back toward the frontier.

"But the problem remains the Enigmas. Londar itself is in danger, and I am here to preserve the Londu and the Sovereignty."

And while he might be willing to sacrifice the Sovereignty to preserve the people, both the Enigma and the Octal appeared to be planning on genocide.

"We cannot ask you to pursue an enemy into the heart of our space," Kahlmor said stiffly. "The First Guard…"

"Has eight battleships?" Henry asked. "Ten? Or were they even *more* gutted for forces to support the Isis Protectorates than the Zal nodal fleet? Even with the fortifications around your home system, Kahlmor, do you truly believe that sixteen *battleships* equipped as we have seen the Enigmas to be equipped can be stopped by the First Guard?"

Henry shook his head.

"You do not need to ask, Lord of Fifty Thousand Miles Kahlmor. We are allies, and no ally can stand by while worlds are burned. Task Group One can, once refueled and rearmed, make it to Londu in seven days."

Kahlmor clearly hadn't done the math. He had, Henry suspected, given up on his home world and been focusing on preserving what he could reach. That focus would have *broken* the man, sooner or later, but at that moment, it had been letting him function.

And now Henry had torn the scab off his fear and offered him hope. Fragile hope.

"I will speak to Lord Okath," Kahlmor said slowly. "But will your logistics convoy be safe? I have seen the—"

"Look."

Henry's holograms zoomed in on Bedrosian's starfighter squadron as Larue's plan kicked off. Even *knowing* what the starfighters and depot ships were doing, *Raven*'s scanners were fooled for a moment as the heat and gravity signatures of four *Amethyst*-class cruisers flickered into existence.

"*How*? You do not have...a trick, as you said," Kahlmor concluded, swiftly regaining control.

"If the Octal are paying close attention, our detached ships could not produce the energy signature of an emergence," Henry said. "But I suspect our genocidal friends are feeling *far* too skittish to stand and fight anymore today."

And there they went. Everything they were seeing was delayed by lightspeed, and the angles were wonky. Bogey Two had seen the deception long before Henry had, but Henry was seeing *their* reaction with almost as much delay as he'd seen Bedrosian's trick.

And their reaction was everything he could have hoped for. They weren't just diverting away from the squadron on the skip line. They were diverting away from the *entire skip line*, pushing their acceleration up another twentieth of a kilometer per second squared as they ran for the Wing-Twelve-Crown System.

"They do not have to run for long to make the difference we need," Henry observed. "Give it ten minutes, and it will be very clear whether we have won this battle completely or if there is still a risk to my logistics fleet."

"And then?" Kahlmor asked softly.

"Then I will be collecting those starfighters and the people they pulled from the wreckage of *Dragoon*," Henry told the alien. "I will refill Task Group One's fuel tanks and magazines, and stuff spare parts in every corner of my ships they will fit.

"And then, Lord of Fifty Thousand Miles Kahlmor, I am going to go save your homeworld, your people, and your Scion.

"You do not have to ask. Thirty billion lives are at stake. I do not have it in me to not try."

JOIN THE MAILING LIST

Love Glynn Stewart's books? Join the mailing list at

GLYNNSTEWART.COM/MAILING-LIST/

Be the first to find out when new books are released!

ABOUT THE AUTHOR

Glynn Stewart is the author of *Starship's Mage*, a bestselling science fiction and fantasy series where faster-than-light travel is possible–but only because of magic. His other works include science fiction series *Duchy of Terra, Castle Federation* and *Exile,* as well as the urban fantasy series *ONSET* and *Changeling Blood*.

Writing managed to liberate Glynn from a bleak future as an accountant. With his personality and hope for a high-tech future intact, he lives in Canada with his partner, their cats, and an unstoppable writing habit.

VISIT GLYNNSTEWART.COM FOR NEW RELEASE UPDATES

CREDITS

The following people were involved in making this book:
    Copyeditor: Richard Shealy
    Proofreader: M Parker Editing
    Cover art: Sam Leung
    Typo Hunter Team
    Faolan's Pen Publishing team: Jack and Robin.

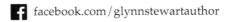 facebook.com/glynnstewartauthor

OTHER BOOKS
BY GLYNN STEWART

For release announcements join the
mailing list or visit **GlynnStewart.com**

STARSHIP'S MAGE
Starship's Mage
Hand of Mars
Voice of Mars
Alien Arcana
Judgment of Mars
UnArcana Stars
Sword of Mars
Mountain of Mars
The Service of Mars
A Darker Magic
Mage-Commander
Beyond the Eyes of Mars
Nemesis of Mars
Chimera's Star *(upcoming)*

Starship's Mage: Red Falcon
Interstellar Mage
Mage-Provocateur
Agents of Mars

Starship's Mage Novellas
Pulsar Race
Mage-Queen's Thief

DUCHY OF TERRA
The Terran Privateer
Duchess of Terra
Terra and Imperium
Darkness Beyond
Shield of Terra
Imperium Defiant
Relics of Eternity
Shadows of the Fall
Eyes of Tomorrow

SCATTERED STARS

Scattered Stars: Conviction

Conviction
Deception
Equilibrium
Fortitude
Huntress
Prodigal

Scattered Stars: Evasion

Evasion
Discretion
Absolution

PEACEKEEPERS OF SOL

Raven's Peace
The Peacekeeper Initiative
Raven's Course
Drifter's Folly
Remnant Faction
Raven's Flag
Wartorn Stars *(upcoming)*
Honor & Renown: A Peacekeepers of Sol Novella *(upcoming)*

EXILE

Exile
Refuge
Crusade
Ashen Stars: An Exile Novella

CASTLE FEDERATION

Space Carrier Avalon
Stellar Fox
Battle Group Avalon
Q-Ship Chameleon
Rimward Stars
Operation Medusa
A Question of Faith: A Castle Federation Novella

Dakotan Confederacy

Admiral's Oath
To Stand Defiant
Unbroken Faith *(upcoming)*

AETHER SPHERES
Nine Sailed Star
Void Spheres *(upcoming)*

VIGILANTE
(WITH TERRY MIXON)
Heart of Vengeance
Oath of Vengeance

Bound By Stars: A Vigilante Series
(With Terry Mixon)
Bound By Law
Bound by Honor
Bound by Blood

TEER AND KARD
Wardtown
Blood Ward
Blood Adept

CHANGELING BLOOD
Changeling's Fealty
Hunter's Oath
Noble's Honor
Fae, Flames & Fedoras: A Changeling Blood Novella

ONSET
ONSET: To Serve and Protect
ONSET: My Enemy's Enemy
ONSET: Blood of the Innocent
ONSET: Stay of Execution
Murder by Magic: An ONSET Novella

STANDALONE NOVELS & NOVELLAS
Children of Prophecy
City in the Sky
Excalibur Lost: A Space Opera Novella
Balefire: A Dark Fantasy Novella
Icebreaker: A Fantasy Naval Thriller

Made in the USA
Middletown, DE
22 October 2023

41231057R00205